P1

Jenny Hale

"Jenny Hale writes touching, beautiful stories."

—RaeAnne Thayne, *New York Times* bestselling author

The Beach House

"A charming and intriguing love story." —Shelf Awareness

Christmas at Fireside Cabins

"[Read] for the grumpy-with-a-heart-made-of-ice coffee shop owner… This book will bring Christmas joy and festive magic to your life!"

—Buzzfeed

Christmas at Silver Falls

"Hale brings the beauty of the Great Smoky Mountains alive in this heartwarming Christmas romance… Authentic, dimensional characters enhance the emotionally charged love story. Fast-paced and brimming with holiday spirit, this is sure to please."

—*Publishers Weekly*

Summer at Firefly Beach

"A great summer beach read." —*PopSugar*

It Started with Christmas

"This sweet small-town romance will leave readers feeling warm all the way through." —*Publishers Weekly*

The Summer House

"Hale's rich and slow-building romance is enhanced by the allure of the North Carolina coast…North Carolina's beautiful Outer Banks are the perfect setting for this sweet, poignant romance, and authentic characters and a riveting story make it a keeper worth savoring."

—*Publishers Weekly* (Starred Review)

"Like a paper-and-ink version of a chick flick…gives you the butterflies and leaves you happy and hopeful." —*Due South*

Christmas Wishes and Mistletoe Kisses

"[A] tender treat that can be savored in any season."

—*Publishers Weekly* (Starred Review)

"[Jenny] Hale's impeccably executed contemporary romance is the perfect gift for readers who love sweetly romantic love stories imbued with all the warmth and joy of the holiday season." —*Booklist*

we'll always have Christmas

ALSO BY JENNY HALE

Christmas Wishes and Mistletoe Kisses
The Summer House
It Started with Christmas
Summer at Firefly Beach
A Christmas to Remember
Summer by the Sea
Christmas at Silver Falls
The House on Firefly Beach
The Beach House
A Lighthouse Christmas
An Island Summer

we'll always have Christmas

JENNY HALE

FOREVER

New York Boston

Forever
Hachette Book Group
1290 Avenue of the Americas, New York, NY 10104
read-forever.com
@readforeverpub

Originally published in 2017 by Bookouture, an imprint of StoryFire Ltd.
First Forever Edition: October 2024

Forever is an imprint of Grand Central Publishing. The Forever name and logo are registered trademarks of Hachette Book Group, Inc.

LCCN: 2024935719

ISBN: 9781538756072 (trade paperback)

Printed in the United States of America

CW

10 9 8 7 6 5 4 3 2 1

we'll always have Christmas

Prologue

Noelle Parker breathed in and let the aroma of Christmas overtake her. The fragrances of peppermint and hot chocolate mixed with the smell of spruce trees filled the air. Christmas shoppers, bundled in hats and winter coats, were chatting as they gathered around the edges of shops, pointing to the display windows full of sparkly packages and Christmas trees, while others bustled by with smiling faces, despite the cumbersome bags they carried. The sky above was a blanket of white, the clouds promising the possibility of snow. A choir farther down the street was singing "We Wish You a Merry Christmas" in the background.

Noelle pulled her coat tighter, the cold slithering down her collar, despite her scarf, making her shiver. She felt like a block of ice from the freezing temperatures during all the window-shopping she'd done with her best friend, Jo Phillips. As she walked by market stalls overflowing with impulse gift items, Noelle noticed the absolute joy on everyone's faces, their relaxed chatter and festive spirits.

Even though she was trying her best to embrace the holiday mood, Noelle could feel the tension in her back and, while she hadn't brought up the big reason she'd asked her friend to meet her today, she'd have to sooner or later. She couldn't put it out of her mind forever. While she hated to admit yet another setback to Jo, who seemed to have her life in perfect order all the time, Noelle knew that Jo was the one person who could make her feel better. Because everything was changing this year, and Noelle was hoping for some Christmas magic to make things right again…

Chapter One

Noelle made her way gingerly across the icy cobblestones and entered the coffee shop, feeling the shock of warmth on her skin.

"Will you get me a latte? No extras," Jo asked. Her caramel-brown hair fell in shiny waves onto her belted wool coat as she turned to scan the crowd, the coffee shop door swinging to a close behind them, shutting out the Christmas music. "I'll find us a table." She handed Noelle a ten-dollar bill and disappeared behind a group of women who were alternating between chattering and bursting into rounds of laughter, their table full of cakes and cookies, a pile of Christmas novels in the center.

Usually the holiday crowds warmed Noelle, but this year was different. The small counter was teeming with customers, all holding shopping bags in various shades of red and green, their joviality jarring with her feelings, only serving as a reminder of her changed circumstances. When Jo had mentioned she was spending the day shopping, Noelle knew it would be the perfect opportunity to see her friend and clear her head. She'd made the twenty-minute drive into the city to talk to Jo, who could always keep a level head and give the best advice.

She unwound the chocolate-colored chunky-knit scarf her colleagues had gotten her for Christmas, before they'd all gone their separate ways, their jobs taken from them. A company in New York had acquired the firm Noelle had worked for, and they had laid off nearly everyone to replace them with the new company's chosen employees. Her life was uncertain once more. This hadn't been the way she'd expected to finish off her year at all.

She stepped into the line at the counter. Finally, left alone with her thoughts, the fear that had made her call her friend to meet her in the first place crept in again, so she peered over at the pastry window to try and take her mind off it.

An insignificant pedestal held a few mass-produced cookies, their icing drawn on like one giant color-by-number pattern. Scattered around it was an assortment of cupcakes, the choices unoriginal—vanilla with white icing and a plastic Christmas tree jabbed into the center, and chocolate with matching sprinkles. The selection didn't hold a candle to the offerings back home at Hope and Sugar, the bakery her family owned.

Hope and Sugar Bakery was a tiny stone historic house, nestled in a miniature yard full of buttercups, creating a golden two-foot plot between the street and the cobbled entrance every summer. It was the epitome of charm: built in the seventeen hundreds, it had a modest glass-paned door and original slightly wavy-glassed double bay windows that they used for display. Inside, around the fire, her gram had made a small sitting area years ago with a comfortable sofa and a few padded chairs where folks could get a cup of coffee and a specialty pastry, and warm up as the snow fell outside. The bakery had a special place in Noelle's heart.

She took a step behind the person now ordering, her attention on the coffee choices. Once she'd settled on something, Noelle dug around in her purse for a few bills, Jo's ten still wadded in her fist, trying not to think about how she shouldn't be spending money on frivolous coffees. It was all going to be okay, though, because she had a plan. Gram had told her once that dreams become reality the minute one has a plan. Whenever anyone was in crisis, Gram had a strategy to help them, and Noelle, having such a similar personality to Gram, had learned that skill very well.

Noelle ordered the coffees, handed the barista a wad of bills, giving her name for the order, and took the change over to Jo, dumping it onto the table along with the receipt, a dime rolling away and finally stopping with a clatter, coming to a rest next to Jo's phone. Her friend ignored it, her face crumpled in concern. Noelle had avoided opening up while they'd been shopping, waiting for the right moment to share her worries, but there was a part of her that just wanted to close her eyes and sink down into the chair with her coffee and her best friend first.

"Noelle?" the barista called, waving two paper cups, decorated with little dancing Christmas trees, with red plastic lids and cardboard rings around them.

Jo stood up. "I'll get them," she said, leaving her chair, her coat draped on the back of it.

Noelle looked around at the white lights in the windows, the Christmas tree in the corner, the plastic holly on every table, before the whole terrible situation finally felt real. She remembered Gram saying, "Cheer up, darling. When things get tough, we always have Christmas to make them better." Then she'd wink at her and toss her a gumdrop from the glass dish on the bakery's counter.

Noelle shrugged her own coat off and twisted to put it on her chair, smiling her apologies for nudging the person beside her. What had she been thinking, agreeing to meet Jo on a Friday during the start of the Christmas season? Normally she'd have been at work today, but as Noelle had neglected to tell her friend when she'd said she needed to have coffee, she didn't have a job to go to anymore. Jo had immediately agreed to meet her, obviously sensing something was wrong—she could always tell. They'd known each other forever. Jo, short for Joanne, had never gone by her full name. They'd first met when Noelle's parents had moved into their new home when Noelle was eight. Jo had come over with her mother to bring a freshly baked loaf of bread as a housewarming gift. Noelle and Jo had crawled under Noelle's bed that day and shared all their secrets as if they had been friends for years. Jo told her about the tree in her back yard where her friend Phoebe Nichols swore that whenever she wished, the wishes always came true. Noelle had met Phoebe the very next day. From then on, the three of them had become inseparable, walking to and from school together every day, having sleepovers, and taking care of each other into adulthood. When she needed optimism, Noelle called Phoebe, but when she had to hear it straight, she called Jo.

Jo returned, setting one of the cups in front of Noelle and plopping down dramatically. "How's Lucas?" she asked, sliding her bag under their table with her foot, out of the way of other patrons.

"He's great," Noelle said with a smile at the mention of her son.

"Good," Jo said, blowing a lock of hair off her forehead. She tucked it behind her ear and it still looked like she'd spent hours on it. But then again, she had the money to buy the most expensive products; her haircut probably cost a fortune. How different their lives had turned out to be.

Ready to conquer the world, Jo and Noelle had applied to the University of Virginia, both of them getting acceptance letters, but when Noelle found out she was pregnant, she knew that she wouldn't be able to juggle classes and still make enough money to support herself and a child. She and her boyfriend, Rich, hadn't dated terribly long when she'd found out she was pregnant. She'd met him at a bar one weekend and she'd been taken by his quick wit and warm smile, and the way he'd treated her like a lady.

At the end of the night, she'd given him her number and he'd called her to go out for a date. That date turned into two and then three and, before they knew it, they were an item. But, while she felt herself falling for him and she could tell her feelings were returned, their relationship just hadn't grown deep enough to support the emotional weight of having a baby. What completely blindsided her was that he'd seemed almost spooked about the baby from the beginning and, when they'd finally called it quits, he hadn't wanted anything to do with his child.

Noelle was devastated and heartbroken, but not for the loss of her relationship—she could get over that. She was heartbroken for the loss of a father for her child. Rich moved away, and, while she could've hunted him down for money to help with Lucas, she didn't want anyone in her son's life who didn't completely adore him, so she'd let him go. She had raised Lucas with the help of her parents, Gus and Nora, working her way through temp jobs and supporting them both.

Meanwhile, Jo had gone on to law school. She now worked at a firm in Richmond and was married to a doctor. But despite all her success, Jo had remained the same over the years, and she was always there to pull Noelle through the hard times.

"Okay. You've been very quiet and in your head all morning. Spill," Jo commanded, her full attention on Noelle as she looked at her over her cup, the steam from the coffee dancing in front of her face.

"They just let us go," Noelle said, still in disbelief. She'd told Jo about the takeover as soon as it had happened, but she hadn't wanted to worry her friend about the possible consequences of it until it was final. "The executives all got severance packages, but I was hourly, so

I only got this month's pay in full." Noelle had worked her way up at the property management firm where she'd been employed for over the last three years. She'd had her own accounts, and she was managing a small staff. She'd heard rumblings that layoffs were coming, but she'd been in denial, never believing they would actually do something like that during the holidays.

"Heartless." Jo shook her head. "You know if you need anything..." she began, but Noelle stopped her with a look.

It was the same look she'd given her when Jo had offered to help with Lucas's hospital bills when he was born. While her friend was very sweet to offer, Jo knew better. Noelle would never take handouts.

"What's your next move, then?"

It all seemed silly now, but Noelle had imagined biding her time until she took over Hope and Sugar Bakery.

When the time came, and Pop-pop was ready to retire, she'd leave her job to run the bakery, hopefully having enough saved to put her own stamp on it. After Gram died, Pop-pop threw himself into work at Hope and Sugar, and Noelle often thought he channeled his grief into running the bakery. She wondered if by keeping it alive, he felt he could keep Gram alive in a way. Her mother and father were helping Pop-pop until he could retire, because he just wasn't financially able to yet, despite the fact that he was seventy.

"I've moved back in with my parents." Just saying it out loud made Noelle want the floor to open up and swallow her. Everyone she knew had created their perfect lives: they had their own apartments and houses; they'd gotten married; they had babies. And in two days, Noelle had been able to pack up everything she and Lucas owned, sublet her apartment, and move back with her parents. The idea of her son not having a permanent home made her more uncomfortable than anything ever had. She'd always told him, "This is just a stop on the way to where we belong," but every time she said it, she worried that she wouldn't deliver. She suppressed the urge to shake her head in disbelief, her pride not allowing her.

"Minor setback," Jo said, offering her a napkin. Jo could always make her feel better. Of the three of them—Noelle, Phoebe, and Jo—Jo was the one with the no-nonsense answers, Phoebe was the dreamer, and Noelle was always making plans. Jo fluttered the napkin in the air.

Noelle only realized just then that the lid on her coffee hadn't been placed on tightly and she'd dribbled some down her sweater. *If they'd served it in a mug like Gram*, she thought angrily, but stopped herself. It wasn't the coffee shop's fault that she was in a foul mood. With a huff of irritation, she blotted the spot.

"Tell me your plan. You always have one."

Noelle slid her scarf back onto her shoulders and, repositioning it to cover the coffee stain, she said, "I asked my dad if I could work at the bakery, maybe pick up an extra Christmas shift or something. He said he's wanted to talk to me about it. I'm going by to see him and Pop-pop after this. But in the meantime, Heidi found me a full-time job, until we sort things out at the bakery."

Jo's eyebrows raised. She wrapped both hands around the paper cup, revealing her new manicure and David Yurman ring. "Heidi saves the day!" she said with an upbeat smile. "Your sister is the best!"

Heidi was five years older than Noelle, and she had been a kind big sister to her growing up. She'd always included Noelle and her friends, painting their nails, doing their hair, and all the great things big sisters could do, she did. She looked out for them, and it was Heidi whom Noelle looked up to. Heidi had been the first to learn about Noelle's pregnancy and about her decision to forego college. She was just old enough to have more wisdom than Noelle, but young enough not to give her a judging eye. So when she'd lost her job, Noelle had turned to Heidi first.

"What's the job?"

"Well, Heidi saw an inquiry on the bulletin board in the staffroom at the country club where she works: someone looking for a caretaker for an elderly man. Apparently, calls had been made to the club to see if any of their on-staff physical therapists were available. When no one showed interest, the notice was put up and it was mentioned that discretion should be used, as this was a lucrative client, but to pass the word along. I called the woman on the notice and nailed the phone interview."

"So what will you be doing?"

"The woman I spoke with was named Melinda Burnett. She's the house manager. Have you heard of her at all? She's local." It wasn't at all what Noelle had imagined doing for a living, but Heidi had said she'd heard the pay range was good, and Noelle couldn't afford to be picky.

Jo frowned, shaking her head.

"I hadn't either. When she called back to say I had the job, I asked for details, and she said she'd email them all to me, and then I could decide if it sounded like something I'd be interested in pursuing. I know the elderly man's name is William but that's it. I don't know anything else yet. But to be honest, it doesn't really matter. I need the job. I still want to make Christmas special for Lucas and I'd like to be able to move out of my parents' house sooner rather than later." Noelle didn't want to divulge her finances too much, but the truth was, she was broke. She'd scraped together the last bit of her paycheck to pay rent before the sublet took over, and she was hoping to use the remainder of her earnings before Christmas to buy presents for Lucas.

All she had was a savings account with a small amount of money that she was keeping in case of emergencies.

"It will be nice to be back home, though," Jo said, focusing on the positive. "You'll live even closer to Phoebe." She laughed before she'd even said anything funny, and Noelle knew why: Phoebe was a hoot to be around.

"It will be good to see her," Noelle said, laughing right alongside her.

Chapter Two

After she'd left Jo, going their separate ways following lunch, Noelle dropped her shopping bags off at her parents' house in a slightly better mood. Just as she'd thought, Jo had made her take stock of what mattered. She had the opportunity to make a living, and that was a good thing. Maybe things would turn around. The house was oddly empty, so she headed straight to see her dad and Pop-pop at the bakery, wondering where everyone else was.

When Noelle arrived, she opened the glass front door of Hope and Sugar bakery, and, even a year after her grandmother's death, it was a shock not to see her behind the counter, her white hair pinned up, away from her remarkably youthful face, those blue eyes sparkling like sapphires as they reflected the happiness in her smile.

Noelle's attention was drawn toward her favorite spot as a child: the bookshelves Pop-pop had built. He'd covered one entire wall with mahogany shelving. Noelle was nine when he'd built it—she could still remember. The radio had been on, and a good song played, causing Gram to come around the other side of the counter, that smile on her face. She pulled Pop-pop's tools from his hands and danced with him. As the song played, he spun her around, and she twirled as if she were young again, her giggles like wind chimes until Pop-pop silenced her with a kiss. That was the first time Noelle had been old enough to really understand the affection between them. They were perfect together.

From the floor to the ceiling the shelves were full of books that people placed there when they'd finished reading. The policy was that if a person left a book, they could take one, but the donations over the years had been so plentiful that the books were pressed into any available space, some sitting sideways or stacked on others. Regulars were known to leave bookmarks with their names in them, coming back to pick up where they'd left off. Noelle couldn't imagine a time when there wasn't someone reading in one of the chairs.

Surfacing from her memories, she looked at her family sitting in the small dining area by those bookshelves, their attention on her. Her mother and father, Pop-pop, and her older sister Heidi were all there. So this was where everyone was.

"I came right away, but there was traffic," Noelle said, out of breath.

She had run up the street, her heart pounding from more than just the effort it had taken. When she'd called her father after having coffee to tell him she was on her way to the bakery, there'd been an awkward silence before he'd said, "We need to talk, Noelle." That was the second time he'd said that. His voice had been unreadable and he'd refused to go into detail until they could meet face to face. She couldn't imagine what in the world he had to tell her that was so serious that her family was all there. Was it good news? Was she finally going to be able to run Gram's bakery and begin the new chapter of her life that she'd been waiting for?

But now Noelle stepped in to a silence that enveloped her. Immediately she realized it was an eerie silence—not like the kind that bounced around just before happy surprises. It was the heavy sort, as if some type of energy had settled upon them like a fog and was about to lash out at them all when they weren't expecting it.

She searched Heidi's eyes for any indication of what was to come, but there wasn't the slightest hint of a suggestion. Her mother was too still, a wad of balled tissue hidden in her fist as her eyes darted over to Noelle's father. Pop-pop was looking down at his shoes while fiddling with the cuticle of his nail. He looked up as she passed him but didn't meet her eye. Slowly, Noelle lowered herself into one of the chairs that had been pulled away from its table to make a circle for them all. Her heart still slamming in her chest, she didn't bother to take off her coat for fear she might need to run out into the street to catch her breath after seeing everyone like this.

"Noelle, we're closing the bakery," her father said, getting right to the point.

She felt the icy sensation from the paleness that must have washed over her, only her breath coming through her lips, words absent. It felt as though a freight train were speeding through her head. Gram had promised her the bakery. She'd told her that Pop-pop would run it until he had enough to retire and then it would be hers. Her sister hadn't been interested in taking on the responsibility of running it completely, but she'd been thrilled at the idea of keeping it in the family, and she'd said she wanted to still be a part of it. Her parents had retired, so they were ready to spend their days leisurely. All of that was just fine for Noelle because running the bakery was in her blood.

A planner by nature, she'd been dreaming about how she'd manage it her whole life. Even as a child, she had a notebook full of ideas that she carried with her every time she went to the bakery with Gram. While her grandmother kneaded the dough for her pastries, flour up her arms, she'd nod and offer her opinions as Noelle read her ideas out. Over the years, Gram's sweet smiles at Noelle's thoughts became concentrated focus, and it was clear that Noelle was the right person to take on Hope and Sugar. She and her gram were alike; they always had been, which was why they were so close. Noelle learned the business from Gram and she'd been ready for years, just waiting for the moment that Pop-pop decided it was time to rest.

She remembered that second week in November when her grandmother would open up the giant jukebox in the corner—its gleaming silver and pearly white bright against the ruby-red piping—and replace the usual records with Christmas classics. For a quarter—she'd never bothered to raise the price—people chose their favorite carols. They played softly in the background beneath the chatter and local gossip. It had stopped working shortly after her death, and, as far as Noelle knew, it hadn't been repaired. No one in the family could bear to take the Christmas records out or ship it anywhere for service. Now it would be packed away, collecting dust, God knows where.

Just thinking about it all gave Noelle an acidic punch in the gut. She'd never allowed the thought to come through, but she, too, had felt like Pop-pop: letting the bakery go would be letting a piece of Gram go, and she didn't know if she could handle it. All those memories, all that wonderful time there—it would be carried out of that building piece by piece, crushing her.

Noelle's dreams to inherit the business and run it one day slipped away like ice down her body. But worse than that, she knew that her father had planned to keep the bakery open to fund Pop-pop's retirement. Without the money from the bakery, she had no idea what he would do. Noelle found herself frantically searching the bakery with her eyes; for what, she didn't know herself. Her gaze settled on the empty chair by the fire just as a sob rose in her throat.

If she closed her eyes, she could still see Gram, holding two mugs—they were cream-colored ceramics speckled with toffee brown—the thick, bittersweet coffee steaming to the brim in her delicate hands. With her head tilted just so and that look that said she'd make it all better, she'd hand one to Noelle and then wrap her fingers around her own as she sank down into that chair by the fire, ready to listen.

Noelle couldn't say she'd taken those moments for granted, but she certainly didn't realize how much the absence of those conversations would hit her when Gram was gone. She missed Gram so much that just the smell of pastries and coffee would make her tear up on the right day. If only she could be here now. Noelle needed her. What was she supposed to do?

"It isn't turning a profit anymore," her father said, once she'd turned toward him again, her vision glazing over like she was peering at him underwater, the way she had at the public pool when she was a girl. This time the sting came from tears instead of chlorine. She blinked them away and tried to steady herself, trying to refocus and think of ways to salvage this.

"Maybe there's something I can do," she said, her mind going into overdrive. "Certainly, there must be some way that we can bring in more income. It turned a profit before. We might just need to rethink our offerings."

Her father shook his head. "It won't matter what we offer. We're not turning a profit because the rent on this place is so high now."

"Can't we—"

"No." He cut Noelle off gently before she could offer any more ideas as to how to keep it afloat. "The new rental rate is incredible—too big for a small family company like ours. Believe me, we've tried to think of every possible scenario, and it just isn't going to work.

We've already let the owner know and they've extended the lease to someone else."

Pop-pop finally looked at her. "I'm sorry, honey. We'll be open through Christmas, but then we're closing the doors for good. There's nothing we can do."

Pop-pop's words pinged around in her head, sounding tinny and hollow, as she sat there, trying to keep herself from falling apart. What kind of Christmas would it be if she knew that the bakery was closing? It wouldn't be a Christmas at all. She felt like she'd had the rug ripped out from under her. All she'd worked for was gone just like that. And she was letting Gram down.

Gram had trusted her to carry on her dream. It had taken all of her meager savings and even some of Pop-pop's—he'd given her the money to start it before they'd even gotten married. Gram had told Noelle that Pop-pop had teased her, telling her that they were starting with nothing but a hope and a prayer. Gram had corrected him, saying, "No, dear. I've had more than just one prayer over this. We're starting with a hope and some sugar." That was how they'd named the bakery.

She felt like the walls were closing in on her, and she wasn't getting enough oxygen, her chest not allowing her to catch her breath. She glanced around at everyone—their sad faces only making it worse. She had to get out of there. Everything around her reminded her of Gram and how she wasn't there to help Noelle through such awful news. She didn't know how to deal with this without Gram. Noelle ran out of the bakery and into the icy chill without saying anything. She stopped at the end of the street, putting her hands on her knees, still unable to breathe and feeling lightheaded. No one tried to stop her, but she didn't expect them to. They all knew how much the bakery meant to her.

Chapter Three

Noelle had driven around for hours. She'd texted her mother and told her she wasn't ready to come home yet, and her mom had said she'd get Lucas from school. So many thoughts had gone through Noelle's head. She remembered how great Gram had been whenever things had gone wrong in Noelle's life, and how valuable her support had been. Noelle knew that she, too, could be that strength for her family. But, while she had come to terms with the fact that the rent was high, she wasn't quite ready to let the bakery go, and she wasn't going to give up without a fight.

She pulled into the driveway of her parents' house and turned the car off. The large brick colonial was aglow with Christmas lights, the tree twinkling in the front window. The light outside had greenery spiraling up the pole, exploding in a bright red Christmas bow, cascading scarlet ribbon falling down toward the ground. She and her mother had spent all yesterday decorating for Christmas and continued after breakfast this morning. Noelle had only stopped helping her so she could meet Jo, and it was no surprise that her mother had finished while she was gone.

Muffy, her parents' cocker spaniel, was at the glass front door as Noelle climbed the steps. The dog's tail was wagging furiously, so much so that her whole hind end was swinging back and forth on the entry rug. Her parents had brought home the puppy seven years ago, when Noelle had gotten into college, claiming that they weren't ready to be empty nesters yet. Her mother had told her that she couldn't imagine her house without her babies in it. Little did she know they'd have a baby to dote on sooner than they thought.

As Noelle made her way to the porch, treading lightly on the icy steps, Lucas, now standing behind Muffy on the other side of the storm door, pressed his forehead against the glass. He was a quiet boy, keeping to himself a lot, but he always stopped what he was doing to greet his mother. He stepped back when she let herself in.

"Hi, baby!" she said to Lucas, bending down to give him a kiss. She'd always called him "baby" when she came home to him, just like her mother had called her. Noelle couldn't break it, even though he was six years old. She'd probably call him that all his life. It was her term of affection for him.

Even so, she tried very hard not to baby him. He was small for his age and always seemed a little uncertain whenever they were out together, and she wanted him to feel strong and comfortable in his surroundings. She knew that it was her job to build the man within him and help him to see his strengths, but she wanted him to know that, in the end, she was still his doting mother. If he had his way, he'd spend the whole day in his room, reading.

Noelle used to check the books that he chose at the library before he read them to make sure they were age-appropriate, but he'd started reading before he'd even gotten to kindergarten and he'd gotten so fast in the last year that she couldn't keep up, so she had to scan the blurb and ask the librarians for their opinions. It was the only place she saw that light in his face, that twinkle in his eye. He nearly ran to his section, having learned almost the whole place by heart.

With meticulous speed, he'd drag his finger down the shelves, looking for that one book he hadn't been able to get last time because he'd hit the check-out limit. She took him as much as she possibly could, because that was the time when he'd talk to her the most. She just adored seeing his happiness. While his voracious reading didn't bother her, his self-seclusion did, and she tried very hard to make sure he spent time with people.

She'd signed him up for baseball with the other kids in his class, but every practice, as they'd load the car with balls, bats, and water jugs, his bag full of equipment, the excitement that she saw in his eyes when he was in the library was completely absent. He never threw a tantrum, but it was clear that he was doing it for her. One day, she peeked into the dugout to take a photo of him and his friends as they sat in a long row on the bench in their uniforms, laughing with each other, the excitement of the game buzzing all around them. Lucas was at the very end, a good foot or so away from his team, alone, his feet swinging above the dirt. Her heart broke. At the end of the season, she didn't sign him up again, and he never mentioned it, so she figured she'd done the right thing.

Heading toward the kitchen, Noelle reached down and greeted Muffy, who'd been pawing her leg before she'd even gotten the front door shut, letting the normalcy of the atmosphere settle in. It was clear that her mother was making an effort to enjoy the evening, so Noelle put on a smile and decided to make the best of it too.

"Did you and Grandma make cookies for the neighbors?" she asked Lucas, the buttery, sugary aroma wafting out from the kitchen. Every year, her family made enough cookies to supply their close neighbors with a hefty assortment, and still they had tins of them left over to nibble during the holiday.

Lucas nodded with a quick smile.

Noelle kissed the top of his head, and then admired the twinkling Christmas tree through the door separating the kitchen and living room. Muffy, who had followed dutifully behind her through the room, had stopped to sniff one of the presents that was positioned on the edge of the tree skirt.

"I never got to ask you, how was coffee with Jo, dear?" her mother called over her shoulder. The water was running, drowning out the Christmas music that played.

Noelle and Lucas both took a seat on two barstools at the island counter. Her mom had candles burning—the peppermint ones in the large jars—Nat King Cole on the small CD player by the microwave, and plates and plates of cookies covering the counter. She turned around. "Jo doing well?"

"Yep." Noelle snagged a gingerbread cookie, stopping briefly to admire the white-and-red piping her mother had so meticulously drawn on it just like Gram had taught her. Gram had insisted that whether by birth or marriage, every woman in the family should know how to ice a cookie. Noelle could still remember the lesson: "Hold the piping bag in your fist or your hand will shake too much," Gram had said. Then she'd winked at her.

Noelle admired her mother's cookie again and then took a bite.

Lucas had climbed down and sat in the middle of the kitchen floor with the dog. Muffy was kissing his cheek, nuzzling his face, and licking the cookie crumbs off him. Watching them lightened her mood—she was so thankful for Lucas. Without him, she probably wouldn't be in the Christmas spirit at all this year with the loss of the bakery, but she was determined to give him one. He brought out the best in her, and gave her strength she didn't even know she had.

"How many cookies has Grandma let you have?"

"Not too many," her mom said when Lucas didn't answer. "But it's after Thanksgiving. That's close enough to Christmas to start celebrating, I say! It's just one long party after Thanksgiving, isn't it?"

Lucas allowed a little amusement at his grandma's answer to show, his gaze bouncing back and forth between Noelle and her mother. Muffy had maneuvered through Lucas's legs and started to walk away. Noelle reached down and pet her as she walked past, and she turned around, coming back for more.

"Where's Dad?" She knew how hard he was probably taking this. Gram was his mother, and he had spent many nights listening to Gram's big plans for when Noelle took over the bakery. Gram had always offered it to Heidi as well, but it was Noelle who'd shown interest, talking until the wee hours of the morning with her dad and Gram, and her dad had told her that Noelle's interest was because she and Gram were so alike. He'd also told her that he couldn't imagine Noelle doing anything else with her life; she was such a natural like her gram.

"He took the truck to get more wood for the fire. The temperature's dropping tonight and it's gonna get cold."

"It's already cold!" Noelle brushed the gingerbread crumbs off her hands over the sink, which was full of dirty bowls and spoons from all the baking. Now everything was making sense. Her father had been quiet at dinner last night, and she could tell he was keeping to himself. She knew him well enough to understand that it was because he blamed himself for the bakery failing—she just didn't know why the rent had gone up so high.

Her mom sank a cake stirrer into the batter of yet another bowl. "Does Lucas have warm pajamas to wear?"

The question had only been intended to keep the mood light, but Noelle had heard questions like these since they'd arrived yesterday morning. Her mother had showered her with them the moment she'd arrived. While she was just concerned, Noelle took the inquiries harder than she probably should because her mom's worry meant that she didn't trust Noelle to have it all together for her son.

The truth of the matter was that Lucas *didn't* have winter pajamas—he'd grown out of them. Instead, he had a sweatshirt and a pair of long johns. Those were perfectly fine and warm, but Noelle remembered how her mother would always buy the whole family matching Christmas pajamas growing up, and Noelle put pressure on herself to create those kinds of memories with Lucas. But right now, what he had would have to do because they were nice and comfortable. "He has warm pajamas, Mom," she said.

Noelle's phone pinged with an email notification. It was Melinda Burnett. Suddenly, this job offer that Heidi had found for her took on new importance without the possibility of her working at the bakery. It was now her only potential source of income. "Do you mind if I just pop into Dad's study to check this message? It's about my new job."

"Not at all. Lucas and I were getting ready to stuff gift bags with cookies for everyone." She dropped a special dog cookie that she made each year into Muffy's bowl. "Lucas, wash your hands, sweet pea, and you can help me fill them."

"Thanks." Noelle turned to Lucas. "I'll be right back." With a renewed air of excitement at the idea of something going according to plan, she gave him a quick peck on the cheek and left the room, feeling relieved about the fact that soon she'd be able to pay her bills without worrying about every penny. While this job wasn't what she'd intended to do originally, she reminded herself that it was just a stop on her journey, and the fact that she'd gotten a job this quickly was a Christmas miracle.

I hope this email finds you well, she read, skimming along quickly to get to the meat of it. Melinda Burnett had been asked to manage William's affairs in the interim until Noelle could take over. She read on and then her eyes nearly popped out of their sockets when she saw the salary. She double-checked the top of the message to be sure this was the real Melinda Burnett and not someone playing a cruel joke on her. The pay was more than she'd ever made at the property management firm, and she was being given an apartment-sized suite at the house for her and Lucas. Noelle looked up, her vision not registering anything; her thoughts were racing. A prickle of elation spread along every inch of her skin as she resumed reading.

Then, she stopped when she saw the man's whole name: William *Harrington*. She scanned further for the address, locating it and immediately recognizing it. The elderly man she'd be caring for was the grandfather of Alexander Harrington, who lived at the old Harrington mansion up on the hill by the school she'd gone to as a girl. As they'd walked past it, Phoebe had swooned over Alexander Harrington, blabbing on to her and Jo about her dreams to marry a prince like that. He *was* like some sort of prince, having gone to the most elite schools while they all attended the one in the neighborhood.

So Noelle would be making a ton of money *and* working in a mansion? It took but a moment for her to consider the position. Immediately, she fired off an email, accepting. Then, she clapped a hand over her mouth to stifle her squeals of joy. Things were looking up!

"Hey," her mom said, peeking her head around the doorframe. Her brows furrowed. "You okay?"

"Yes!" Noelle said. "Totally fine." She was more than fine. She was overjoyed!

"Just wanted to tell you that Pop-pop and Heidi are coming over for dinner tonight. Has Jo finished her shopping yet? You could see if you could catch her before she heads home. Maybe she'd come out for a good made-from-scratch meal. And maybe Phoebe? I've got a huge roast to go in the oven. We need people to help us eat it." She winked at Noelle, and her heart swelled with love for her mother. She was really trying to take Noelle's mind off the bakery and she knew that having her friends and family around would be just what Noelle needed.

"Okay," she said, still trying to straighten out her grin.

"What is it, dear?" her mother said, smiling herself at Noelle's reaction.

"I'll tell you at dinner."

"The suspense is killing me." Her mother rolled her eyes playfully, annoyed that she had to wait. But she was a good sport about it.

Chapter Four

As soon as Noelle mentioned the bakery was closing its doors, Jo was more than ready to come back out to see her friend. And all Noelle had to do was say Phoebe's name, and Jo had already sent their friend a text.

"I love that you're close now! We haven't all gotten together in ages!" Jo said, her voice bouncy on the other end of the line, making Noelle smile. She knew that Jo could sense her emotions when she'd brought up Hope and Sugar, and that was what had made Jo immediately agree to come out, but Jo was obviously trying to lighten her mood. Little did Jo know that, despite the heartbreaking news about the bakery, Noelle also had something wonderful to tell everyone, and she was so glad her friends were close enough to be there to share in her excitement. While it wouldn't make the loss of the bakery any better, it would at least bring a little joy to the season.

"I know." Noelle couldn't wipe the smile off her face. And she couldn't wait to share the news with her friends. They'd never believe she was actually going to work in the Harrington mansion. The grounds were so big that, as children, the house on the hill had seemed like miles away from the street below, along which they walked home from school every day. Brick walls ran around the large expanse of the property, securing it, and there was a locked iron gate at the front. Sometimes, they'd play hopscotch on the squares of sidewalk alongside the grounds, parting ways at the end of the street.

"I'll bring wine!" Jo said, her voice sing-songy with excitement.

Noelle reminisced about all the times the three of them had spent late nights together before they'd settled far enough from each other that their regular meetings had dwindled. In the days when Noelle had worked as many hours as she could and then run after a toddler until she was ready to drop, one of her friends would show up at her apartment with a bottle of cheap wine and they'd pop popcorn, turn on a movie, and fill up their glasses until it was gone, giggling and ruminating about the good ol' days before their lives had gotten so crazy.

"Only if it's the fizzy kind with the screw cap," Noelle teased with a laugh.

"Oh, Gaawwd."

Noelle laughed out loud, feeling the smile on the other end of the line, knowing Jo remembered those nights just as well as she did.

"Oh!" Jo said, her voice trailing away from the phone. She came back and said, "Phoebe just texted. What time?"

"Mom's dinner will be ready at six."

"Give me twenty minutes. I'll beat her there! With the wine."

❄ ❄ ❄

Heidi had arrived at the same time as Jo, the two of them chattering away as they both greeted Noelle. Noelle had been buzzing around, turning on lamps, lighting candles, and setting out pre-dinner nibbles. The air radiated Christmas: the sound of carols through the speakers in the living room, the smells of sausage, stuffing, and gingerbread wafting around, the lights, and the warm, cozy fire glowing.

Jo swung the bottle of wine into Noelle's view. "Screw cap," she said with a wink, and thrust it into her hands. "Where's that darling boy of yours?" Before Noelle could reply, she let herself in and headed to the kitchen, leaving Noelle with her sister.

"Is Pop-pop here?" Heidi asked, tugging on the wine bottle to inspect the label. She shook her head, amused at Jo's choice, her almond curls bouncing, as she shrugged off her coat and draped it on a chair. Their mother had been puttering around the house behind Noelle for the last few minutes, straightening things and lighting more candles, alight with the joy of having everyone over. She loved this kind of thing, and she was in her element. She swooped in and scooped up the coat, kissing Heidi on the cheek with a loving hello.

Noelle grinned at her mom as she swished away from the door, the coat under her arm. "Pop-pop's not here yet," Noelle said, feeling lighter than she had in days. It felt nice to have a little normalcy finally, and the prospect of a new job didn't hurt her mood either. Her sister scrutinized her curiously, and Noelle knew her constant smiling was giving her away, but Noelle wasn't going to budge on her good news until she had everyone together.

"Gus, the fire is wonderful," their mother nearly sang, Heidi's coat still tucked under her arm as she stopped briefly to warm her hands. He smiled at her compliment, but Noelle thought he still looked tired.

Perhaps her announcement would lighten the mood for him, even if just for the night. Her father had worried about her terribly—he'd told her so when she'd first called them after losing her job. Then she could tell after he'd given her the news about the bakery closing that he'd felt so guilty about it all. Her being let go wasn't his fault, but he'd seemed to take it as if it were. She knew he'd do anything he could to give her the bakery, so whatever had happened with the rent must have been pretty hard to overcome.

Noelle focused on the firebox in the large stone hearth; it was blazing, the flames licking their way up the chimney. The warmth of it was a perfect accompaniment to the six red-velvet stockings that hung from the mantel, all embroidered with their respective names: Gus, Nora, Heidi, Noelle, Lucas, and, of course, Muffy.

After receiving a hello from Jo, Lucas came in and settled on the sofa, a book in his hands. As he got comfortable, he smiled shyly at his aunt Heidi.

"How's my sweet nephew?" she said, plopping down beside him. She tucked a curl behind her ear and leaned toward him.

"Fine," he said quietly, with a happy look on his face.

"Look at you, reading that big book all by yourself," she said, before turning wide-eyed toward Noelle. Noelle knew that the average six-year-old didn't read chapter books, let alone ones as large as that. Even before he'd entered school, he devoured the little storybooks himself whenever Noelle hadn't been able to read them to him. That was when they'd first gone to the library. She'd had to get him a library card at the age of four just to keep up with his reading habit.

Lucas acknowledged her comment brightly, his eyes already on the page.

Heidi left him to it. She was always good at being around Lucas. Strangers would look at Noelle questioningly when his responses weren't like most kids'. He didn't say much to them, but it wasn't because he didn't like people. That was just how he was. Noelle had met with his teachers, worried that he might have trouble making friends, being so quiet. His teachers had told her that, while his relationships were limited, they appeared fine, he didn't seem overly bothered, and his scores at school were exemplary—he didn't show any signs of anxiety over his shyness. When required to answer things, his replies were reasonably relaxed, nothing to cause any concern.

The doorbell rang and Noelle's father answered it. "Oh, no. Not you," he teased, the first spark of amusement Noelle had seen since she'd arrived showing in his face.

Phoebe was at the door. She held up her bustled white gown and stepped inside, the hoop skirt barely squeezing through the doorway. She was holding a cookie tin and wine, her tiara a bit lopsided. Wobbling the bottle of wine upward as she tried to keep the headpiece from completely falling off her head, she said, "You didn't think I'd let you escape from me for an entire holiday, did you, Gus?" Phoebe wedged the wine between her body and elbow now as she leaned in for a hug, wrapping her thin arm around Gus's large frame. She moved her enormous dress before the lace got caught in the door and kissed his cheek.

Phoebe had a shock of red hair and freckles, and it worked for her—she could be on the cover of a fashion magazine, which was perfect, given her choice of profession, as she was an actress. Never quite able to break into the scene, she'd done bit parts in commercials here and there and she kept a string of steady day jobs, always holding out for her big break. She'd just started dating a chiropractor named Paul, and he was always buying her gifts, the latest, a pair of silver earrings. Phoebe had told Noelle that he couldn't wait for Christmas and she'd opened the little box over a gluten-free pizza and two glasses of champagne. While her career was at a standstill, Phoebe was happy and it looked like she might have found her perfect guy.

"Just promise me you won't blow anything up," Gus said with a smirk, ignoring the fact that she was dressed like a wedding-colored

Cinderella—probably nothing Phoebe did surprised him anymore. It was good to see him back to his normal, teasing self.

"That wasn't me! It was *your* daughter! Set him straight, Noelle," she said, walking into the room and kissing both Noelle and Jo on the cheek before swishing her way toward the kitchen, to make herself at home like she always did, puffy layers of satin and lace trailing behind her. She wrinkled her nose with a cutesy smile and a little wave at Lucas, who giggled and looked back down at his book as she left the room.

"She's going into the kitchen!" Gus called out in mock warning, and they all laughed.

When they were nine, Noelle and Phoebe had decided to make a cooking show using her parents' old movie recorder. They weren't allowed to use the gas stove, so they decided to fill the microwave to the brim with the marshmallow-chocolate sandwiches. The sugar in the marshmallows began to caramelize and burn, sending the spongy cubes bursting and splattering. The loud pops and burning smells caused Noelle's parents to come racing into the kitchen where they found the chocolate-marshmallow explosion, dripping and oozing from the microwave while the girls smeared it around on the cabinets, the floor, each other, trying to wipe it up. It had been the running joke that neither of them was ever allowed to cook again, and that joke had followed them into adulthood.

"What in the world are you up to now, wearing that get-up?" Jo asked, her eyes dancing with hilarity already, as they joined her in the kitchen.

"I'm still in character," Phoebe said with seriousness before breaking into an enormous grin. "It's my latest acting gig—good for the résumé. I brought clothes to change into, by the way. They're in my bag," she said over her shoulder as she stood by the large island.

Muffy barked, alerting everyone that Pop-pop was letting himself into the kitchen through the side door. Noelle greeted him as he wiped his boots on the mat, wobbling a little and missing it. He shrugged off his coat and Noelle's mother took it from him after a quick hug. "Hi, Dad," she said. While he was Gus's father, Noelle's mother had called him Dad since they were young. He'd asked her to the minute Gus had told him they were engaged. "I've opened some wine. Want a glass?"

"You know you can assume that every time," he said with a wink. Then he saw Phoebe in her gown and shook his head. "I'm underdressed." Pop-pop knew all too well how playful Phoebe was. She and Noelle would visit the bakery together when they were kids. Phoebe, only in elementary school, would offer a sugary smile to customers and convince them to get an extra pastry, and it worked every time. They'd leave chuckling at her candor, bags of cookies and cakes in their hands. Pop-pop had told her that if she ever needed an extra buck, he'd put her to work as soon as she could legally be behind the counter.

"Yes, you are," she said with a grin, dropping the tin and wine onto the island and pulling off her tiara. "You know the legendary Santa—the one who sits in the bookshop downtown? He needed a Snow Queen. He told me at church last Sunday."

"Mr. Santori? I love him," Noelle whispered, so Lucas wouldn't hear his real name. "He's so sweet." Mr. Santori dressed up as Santa Claus every year. His wife was a seamstress and had made the most gorgeous red-velvet suit with white cuffs and satin buttons. He had even had the local shoemaker design a wide black leather belt to match his boots. Every Christmas, Mr. Santori would sit in the old bookshop, reading books. He started in October, well before the Christmas season, telling the kids that he wasn't working yet. People who lived in town knew that their kids could write early Christmas lists and give them to Santa before the Christmas craze started. The tradition got bigger, and Hope and Sugar Bakery had even supplied milk and cookies free of charge the whole months of October and November. That was before Gram had passed away. Noelle wondered if anyone had provided cookies since.

"My agent sent in my demo for a TV show in LA," Phoebe said, excitedly. "Maybe it'll be The One. Noelle, you in?"

Noelle gave her an excited nod.

Growing up, Phoebe didn't have much support from her family. Her parents were always at odds, and her mother would often spend many days isolated from her due to depression over her marital problems, leaving little Phoebe alone. Because of that, Phoebe spent a lot of time with Noelle, and she'd confided in her once that she needed Noelle because she was the only real family Phoebe had known.

The two of them had made a pact in high school: Phoebe had said if she ever got a big acting part out in LA, she could never make a move like that alone. So Noelle had promised to go with her. They'd decided that if something big came Phoebe's way, it was meant to be and they'd throw all their plans to the wind just to see what happened. Noelle had even mentioned it to Lucas, although she did tell him there was a chance it would never happen.

Pop-pop turned to Noelle. "Hey, pretty lady. How are ya?"

"Great!" Noelle said, wondering, despite the upbeat atmosphere, how soon would be too soon to find out what Pop-pop really thought about closing the bakery. The idea of losing that beautiful property and all her gram's hard work was eating at her. It wasn't like him at all to just get rid of it without a fight, and, now that she'd calmed down, she was dying to know what was going on.

"I've got the table set in the dining room so we can accommodate everyone," her mother said, as she handed Pop-pop his glass of wine.

"Dinner will be ready in about five minutes. Phoebe, I do hope you wear that dress," she said with a laugh.

❄ ❄ ❄

"So what is your news?" her mother said to Noelle, as they all sat around the table after their meal. She was leaning back in her chair, her eyes glassy from the wine, her face calm and relaxed. "I've been waiting the whole dinner for you to tell us." Gus, who was passing out plates of cinnamon-crumble apple pie, stopped to listen, a plate poised in each hand. He hadn't been very talkative all evening, but even so, Noelle could tell that having everyone home had lifted his mood just a bit, and she was glad for that.

Noelle felt that zinging elation again that things were going to be just fine. Her news had come like some kind of Christmas miracle just waiting to be unwrapped for everyone to see. "I got a job!" she said, smiling over at her sister. "Heidi found it for me—but that's not all the news." Lucas sat up on his knees as he listened. Even Muffy stopped chewing her bone in the corner of the room. "You know Alexander Harrington up on the hill?"

Pop-pop looked up from his plate, suddenly interested.

Phoebe was leaning on her elbow, her glass of wine swinging from her fingertips, her eyes round with curiosity and obvious surprise at hearing that name. She'd changed into a cable-knit sweater and a pair of jeans, her Snow Queen dress lumped in a corner of the kitchen. "Oh, yes!" Phoebe said. "We used to walk by his house on the way home from school just hoping we'd get to see him." She tipped her head toward Jo. "Don't you wonder what that mansion looks like inside? I'll bet he eats on gold plates."

Jo chuckled.

"I'll be taking care of Alexander Harrington's grandfather full-time," Noelle said, the idea of walking the hallways of that mansion still surreal even as the words came off her lips.

There was a collective gasp.

Pop-pop dropped his fork, making a clatter against the plate. He picked it up.

"That's who posted the job—the Harringtons?" Heidi said. She shook her head. "I should have applied..."

"You're working in the mansion?" her mother asked. "Are you going to live there?"

"Yep." She could hardly stand the excitement. She'd make a great living, work in a fantastic location, and still live close to her family and friends. "They've got a suite in one of the wings set up for me and Lucas!"

Lucas's eyes danced from person to person, clearly excited at the mention of living in a mansion. Noelle followed his lead, taking stock of every one of their expressions. She wanted to remember giving this news forever. It might be the most exciting thing that had ever happened to her and Lucas. Heidi's eyes were wide, her lips sucked in as if she couldn't believe what she was hearing. Noelle felt the same way, the thrill of it rising up every time she let it. She tossed an enthusiastic grin toward Phoebe and Jo, who both laughed with happiness for her, their heads shaking. But as her gaze shifted to her mother, whose face wasn't joyous like the others'—it was more apprehensive—she looked away, settling on her father and Pop-pop, and they caused her to stop in her tracks.

Gus set the last piece of pie in front of his place and took a seat slowly, his wary eyes on Pop-pop. The two of them exchanged loaded glances, and their expressions showed just enough trepidation to cause Noelle concern, the initial excitement she'd had now floating out of her like runaway helium balloons.

"What's the matter?" she asked down the table toward them.

Pop-pop signaled for her father to explain.

"I'm not too happy with Mr. Harrington at the moment," he said, the gentle smile he'd had earlier now gone. Though it seemed like he didn't want to elaborate, Noelle urged him to with her gaze. Her immediate future was on the line here, and she needed to know what was going on. If he was worried about divulging his thoughts around Phoebe and Jo, he didn't need to. They knew everything about her family, so what was the use in hovering around in mere pleasantries? She didn't need to say anything, though, because Gus continued, "Alexander Harrington is the reason I'm having to close the bakery."

With that statement any remaining thrill drained right out of her with the speed of water through an open floodgate. "What?"

"Hope and Sugar Bakery is closing?" Phoebe said, concern sliding across her face. She set her wine down, the shock causing her to straighten up and shift all her focus toward Pop-pop.

Pop-pop nodded, his features falling in defeat. Noelle could still remember that day in the hospital when Gram's health had slipped so far that they worried about leaving her for even five minutes. With IVs in her hand, her skin translucent from her body's fight to keep going, she'd reached out for Pop-pop's arm, fear on her sweet face. "Don't let the bakery go," she'd said. "I know it won't matter to me in a short time, but I want you to keep it for the girls." Noelle's father had been helping Pop-pop run it ever since.

"Alexander Harrington put us out of business," Gus said, shooting a protective glance over to Pop-pop and ripping Noelle from her memory. "He owns the building and he's the one who hiked the rent up so high that we can't afford to stay." Gus took in a breath before adding,

"Mr. Harrington's even got an interested renter poking around, taking measurements of the space already for some women's clothing shop."

There wasn't a sound in the room as they all looked at each other for help, no one having answers, and Noelle's stomach turning like a stormy sea.

So many memories with Gram were made at Hope and Sugar Bakery. She'd meticulously learned every single recipe, promising her grandmother that she'd pass them along to the next generation. Pop-pop's bookshelves would be torn down, surely, the furniture discarded, the fireplace boarded up with some sort of faux-fire scene or covered over entirely. There'd be no more stockings on the mantel to be filled for the needy, no more cases of cookies, with a basket of broken ones for free, no more visits by the patrons Noelle had grown to love, like the Palmer twins or Richard and Beverly Anderson—those people were just names to everyone else, but they were like family to Noelle.

As all of this settled in her mind, what crept in with certainty was the fact that there was no way, now, that she would feel comfortable working for the Harrington family. At the very least, it was a conflict of interest.

Everyone at the table had fallen into a quiet chatter, nervously asking if Pop-pop would be okay, as Noelle digested everything. She heard her father reassure them that he would, but she didn't know how that was possible. Pop-pop needed the earnings from the bakery—what would he live on?

"I'll email Melinda Burnett and let her know that I won't be able to take the job." Noelle's chest felt like it would explode. What was wrong with the world these days? Laying off people at the holidays, closing family businesses without even a thought about how to save them? As she looked around the table, at all the worry and unease that surrounded her, she remembered Gram's words: *No matter what happens, we'll* always *have Christmas.* But even Christmas wouldn't make this situation any better. Gram would be so sad to see this.

Her mother spoke up. "Noelle, honey, you should take it. It'll get you back on your feet again. We're all grown-ups here; we can understand your need to work, over the issues we have with Mr. Harrington." Her mother seemed to show solidarity with her father by the look she gave him, but Noelle wasn't so sure he agreed.

Noelle took stock of everyone: her friends seemed genuinely worried for her, her mother, encouraging, Pop-pop was misty-eyed, giving her a lump in her throat, but it was her father who gave her pause. He had a look of warning in his eyes, and she knew that it was because he just wouldn't work for someone who went against the family. That was the kind of guy he was.

But Noelle had Lucas to think about, and herself. If she was going to be a good mother, she couldn't be troubled by where the next meal came from. Lucas needed a Christmas. He needed to feel just as special as all his friends at school. He was already starting in a new class since their move back home, and he didn't know a soul. Given how extremely quiet he was, and how he was working above the rest of the class's academic level, fitting in would certainly be hard for him. The very last thing she wanted him to feel was inferior in any way.

Noelle tore her eyes away from her father's disapproving glare and nodded at her mother. "I'll figure it out," she said. Then she looked back at her father. "Maybe I can convince him to bring the rent down or something." She knew it was probably a long shot and by the look on his face, her father thought so too.

Chapter Five

Noelle pulled the car around the perfectly manicured hedges that flanked the water feature in front of the mansion, the little hauling trailer full of her things coming to an abrupt stop behind the car as she braked. Lucas puffed his cheeks out, his eyes the size of saucers, at the sight. Noelle was glad Melinda had allowed them to move in on the weekend so Lucas could come with her and get settled in before starting at his new school.

With a nervous breath, Noelle beheld the brick home, all seventy thousand square feet of it, the windows adorned with green wreaths and silver bows, the fresh garland made of berries and magnolia leaves cascading down the railings, a spruce tree covered in white lights stretching into the heavens.

They got out, shut the doors, and headed toward the four-column portico, its crown an ornamental half-circle the size of her bedroom back home. Glad to be meeting Melinda Burnett, Noelle was hoping to just be able to avoid Alexander Harrington for the moment. Perhaps she'd be so busy with Mr. Harrington Senior that she'd get lucky, and she and Alexander would never meet in this enormous house. Maybe he wasn't even there. They climbed the mass of stairs and rang the bell.

The black double door towered in front of them. Lucas tipped his head back, his chest filling with air as he gasped at the size of it, and

Noelle wondered if the reality of living here was setting in. She looked down at him, amused. There were very few times in his young life she'd seen him this interested, and she knew that, for years to come, they would talk about living in this mansion. She heard a click and then the door creaked open, its heaviness apparent with the slow way in which it swung on its hinges. Noelle let out a sigh of relief, her breath puffing in front of her in the cold air, when she saw a woman on the other side.

The woman, dressed meticulously in a navy skirt suit and heels, her hair combed into an up-do that wouldn't allow a single strand to misbehave, held out a manicured hand. "Hi, Noelle, Melinda Burnett," she said. "It's lovely to meet you."

Noelle shook her hand and Melinda greeted Lucas with a friendly nod.

"Come in. I'll show you two where you'll be staying, and I'm sure you're excited to get the ball rolling with Mr. Harrington. Once I've given you the tour of your suite, I'll take you through to meet him."

They entered the foyer. The floor was covered in glossy white square tiles, each one so big that, even if he'd wanted to, Lucas couldn't play the game he liked where he jumped from tile to tile. Her view moved from the floor to the curving staircases on either side of the room, the railings, wrought iron and ornately delicate, peeking out from under the mounds of greenery and ribbon. They walked past the circular entry table, positioned under a spectacular glass chandelier, and Noelle wondered, by the way it shone, if the beads in it were actually crystals. She could imagine Phoebe, always enamored with this place, saying that given all the Harringtons' money, they were probably diamonds, and Noelle had to stifle a grin.

Phoebe had been infatuated with this house her entire life, and while Noelle wasn't sure if she'd ever seen him, Phoebe swore that she'd had a glimpse of Alexander Harrington when he'd gotten out of his car once, and she'd said he looked like a model. One time, when Noelle had walked home from school alone, she believed she'd seen him too, and she'd thought he was, in fact, gorgeous, but she'd never admit it to Phoebe because she'd have gone on and on about it. She wasn't even sure it had been Alexander, but she had always wondered. Noelle decided it was most likely just wishful thinking on her part. He was probably short and fat with terrible fashion sense. It was highly unlikely they'd meet anyway, since her dealings would be with William Harrington.

"Oh!" Noelle said, her voice echoing as she slammed into the broad, starched chest of a man. She looked up: he had a hint of stubble, green eyes that were like emeralds with little gold flecks in them, and light hair with strands of gold. As that square jaw twitched ever so subtly into a smile, every inch of her was tingling with embarrassment.

"I was looking at the chandelier," she said, realizing just then that she'd been craning her neck backwards to see it as she and Lucas followed Melinda. If she were alone, she'd have slapped herself. *Stupid comment*, she thought.

Melinda cleared her throat. She was standing almost at attention, her hands behind her back, a cordial expression on her face. "This is Alexander Harrington."

When she'd said she'd take them to meet Mr. Harrington, Noelle had assumed Melinda had meant the grandfather William, not his grandson Alexander.

"Call me Alex," he said, looking at Lucas and raising his eyebrows with a smile, before offering Noelle a handshake.

"I'm sorry," Noelle said, holding out her hand as she noticed her lipgloss on his shirt. She smothered a cringe with a weak smile, trying not to stare and draw his attention to it. "I'm Noelle Parker and this is my son, Lucas. I'll be taking care of your grandfather." Lucas waved and then peered up at his mother to see what he was supposed to do.

"Yes," Alex said, as if she'd just stated the obvious, which she probably had.

She bit her lip.

"I've come to see if you need any help with your bags. Melinda, I'll show them where they're staying. You can go now. I know you've got a million things going on before you head off to England for the holidays."

"Yes, Mr. Harrington," she said, and then with a quick smile in Noelle's direction, Melinda shuffled across the large entryway, leaving them alone with Alex. Was that how they were supposed to behave around him? As if they were trained puppies, their every movement dictated by him? Noelle wasn't used to that. She raised her chin and straightened her spine to hide her feelings of inadequacy.

"How many bags do you have?" he asked, turning toward the hallway ahead of them and pausing to allow Noelle and Lucas to follow. His words were direct, not even a suggestion of emotion, but it was as if he were hiding it. She could almost feel a hint of kindness behind them—just enough to make her wonder about it. She looked at him with a skeptical eye.

"A trailer full," she said.

"No problem. I'll have the staff bring it all in once I show you around." He started walking and she noticed the perfectly smooth leather of his shoes, how the bottom of his trousers fell so seamlessly onto his laces that she knew he'd have had a tailor hem them professionally. Everything about him seemed controlled, perfect, unruffled, and she couldn't imagine how that must feel because even though she liked to have things in order, she wasn't sure she could ever achieve the aura that he had.

While they walked, a surge of worry shot through Noelle as she thought about a stranger handling some of the boxes in the trailer. She'd already made such a scene with bumping into him that she didn't want to be difficult on top of it, but she couldn't help herself. "There are a few boxes I'd like to get myself," she said.

The skin between Alex's eyes wrinkled in a shockingly adorable way, causing all the saliva to drain right out of her mouth. Phoebe would die… But there was no way he was going to sway her into thinking he was anything but heartless. She'd heard enough from her dad and Pop-pop to know better.

"Why?" he asked, taking a moment to stop and address her.

"It's my antique teacup collection. I guard it with my life."

He cocked his head to the side. "Oh. Are you a big tea drinker?"

"No. I like coffee, actually. And I prefer mugs for that."

He stood still, clearly processing this. "You collect teacups but don't drink tea?" While it was a question, he said it in the form of a statement, a twinge of confusion showing before he ironed it out. He took in a deep breath, and she wondered if the conversation were frustrating him in some way. Was she using up his valuable time? What did a multi-millionaire do, actually? He must be really busy making all that money—or hiking up rents… She really didn't need his pleasantries regarding her choice of collectibles, even if they did seem a little odd. This small talk wasn't going to make her like him any more than she already did, which wasn't very much, given his complete lack of regard for her family and the shop they'd poured their hearts into. She didn't want to engage in this conversation—it wouldn't change anything—so she stayed quiet. He could think whatever he wanted about her. It had nothing to do with how well she'd take care of his grandfather, so why did it matter why she collected the things she did?

She finally nodded, expecting a huff of disbelief or some other outward expression of disdain for her precious teacup collection, but he didn't make a move. Instead, he said softly, "I'll show you around first and then we can go out together and get them." His voice sounded almost caring, surprising her, her opinion of him wobbling just a bit. Maybe she'd misread him just then; his response wasn't at all what she'd expected.

Lucas hadn't said a thing as he stood beside them both, and Noelle noticed that he was looking at Alex in the same way she'd been looking at the chandelier. With his pressed shirt, tailored trousers, and leather belt and shoes that matched, he looked smart as well as incredibly fashionable; he was probably very different from any other man Lucas had ever encountered. Alex seemed to notice too, a smile showing more in his eyes than on his lips as he observed Lucas.

"Follow me," he said, resuming their walking.

They made their way down a long, open corridor, the entire second floor suspended above them on a balcony with more chandeliers and enormous windows. A woman wearing a housekeeper's uniform was in one of the rooms, fluffing pillows on a sofa. She didn't look up. The only sound was the clicking of their shoes on the wooden floor until they rapidly came to a halt and Noelle saw why. Lucas had stopped in the doorway of a colossal room, filled with wood paneling and bookshelves, a domed ceiling of stained glass at the top and a single piece of furniture—a desk—centered on the circular rug beneath it.

"My office," Alex stated.

Lucas didn't react. He was still gazing into the room.

"Do you like this room?" Alex asked. His tone reminded her a bit of the way he'd asked about her teacups, but it seemed even softer for Lucas's benefit and she was grateful for his kindness, although she wasn't sure if it was entirely genuine. But nonetheless, she was glad for it, as it seemed to put Lucas at ease. He turned his attention to Alex, wonderstruck.

"We should follow Mr. Harrington," Noelle said, trying to hurry Lucas along.

"No, it's fine," he said. "And please, call me Alex."

She was wary of him, wondering why he'd asked her to call him by his first name when Melinda certainly hadn't. He'd hit the volume button on friendly ever since they'd arrived, but she had his number—he couldn't fool her.

He bent down next to Lucas. "What is it that you like about this room?"

Lucas's stare fell down to his feet without a reply. Feeling protective, Noelle wanted to explain his shyness so Alex wouldn't think he was rude in not looking directly at him. But Alex didn't seem fazed by it. He stood up, walked into the office, and beckoned for Lucas to join him.

Hesitantly, her son followed, uncertainty on his face. Noelle wondered if he was worried he'd break something. He walked over to the desk where there was a small glass case with a dinosaur skeleton replica inside.

"Know what that is?" Alex asked.

Lucas finally met his eyes. "Coelophysis," he said, without even a pause.

"Ha!" Alex was clearly surprised and delighted by his response. "You're right," he said, with a chuckle and an astonished glance at Noelle.

She was floored that Lucas had known the name of the dinosaur. She certainly didn't. How had he known? She peered over to see if the name was written on the case, but there wasn't anything there.

"We were breaking ground for a property I was building in New Mexico and we stumbled upon some rock in a quarry. Little did we know, we'd unearthed fossils. The paleontology department at the University of New Mexico, who studied the findings, presented this to me just recently as a thank-you for my cooperation. I haven't found a place for it yet."

"I like dinosaurs," Lucas said, and the biggest smile spread across his face, both the look and his comment surprising Noelle. Lucas turned his gaze upward to view the towering bookshelves. "Do you have any dinosaur books in here?"

"Ah, probably not. I'm sorry. These books are original to the house. They were the private library of my sixth great-grandfather, Henry, who built this house in seventeen eighty-eight."

Noelle was transfixed as she considered the affluence of this family. Alex knew the line of his family, seven generations before his father. That was impressive. Walking along that brick wall outside every day as a child, she'd never imagined the history of the property, or the amount of money it took to build something like this house, that many years ago. It was clear the structure had been upgraded over the years, but to think that someone would have that kind of wealth for generations was astounding.

"That's only five years after the American Revolution ended in seventeen eighty-three," Lucas said, a glimmer of excitement in his eye, another comment catching Noelle off guard.

Alex laughed, an affection showing on his face that took Noelle aback. He was clearly enjoying this. "Yes, that's right. How old are you?"

"Six."

Alex shook his head. His shoulders had relaxed, his expression more open, and for an instant Noelle got a glimpse of what it would be like to know him, to see him talking as though he were with his friends.

She took in the two of them. She hadn't seen Lucas respond this way with other people before: Lucas was in his element. Noelle had never witnessed him being this talkative with a stranger, nor was she aware that he had this wealth of knowledge. Certainly, they'd read together and had talks about things, but he had never divulged little factoids like he was now.

"His name was Henry, and his son was Edward?" Lucas asked.

Alex squatted down again, putting himself at eye level. "Yep. And Edward's son was Alexander, like me."

"And his son?"

"Charles, then Phillip, then Thomas."

"And Thomas's son is the William we're taking care of?"

"That's right." He stood up, acknowledging Noelle, a kind look in his eyes, before tipping his head downward toward Lucas again. "You're a very smart boy, you know that?"

Lucas shrugged, his eyes going back to the books.

Noticing his returned interest, Alex walked over to a large brass-and-wood ladder that moved along a track on the bookshelves, and pulled it, on its rollers, down the wall toward them. "Shall we have your mom climb this and read some of the titles of those books to us?" Alex spun around and for just an instant, the sight took her breath away: both Alex and Lucas were smiling, their eyes dancing in the moment, their eyebrows raised, their faces inquisitive. There was something so perfect about it that she looked toward the books to avoid her cheeks flushing and giving away her feeling. What on earth was going on here? She wanted to keep her poker face with Alex until she could feel out his motives a bit more.

Noelle felt the emotion coming through in her features anyway. She blinked to return her face to a more normal expression. The scene with

Alex and Lucas had made her all jittery. She took a mental step back, keeping herself in check. What could possibly be his reason for charming her son like he was? Suddenly, she felt protective of Lucas again, praying that Alex didn't have some sort of ulterior motive, some sort of business strategy regarding the bakery. Did he know it was her family's?

He scooted the ladder toward them a little more.

The last thing she needed was to climb a ladder that shot straight up nearly three floors when she was this jumpy. She'd probably fall off. "You want me to climb that?"

"Yes," Alex said, with a discreet look of challenge. "It's an old ladder, but it's been well maintained."

"If it's old then I shouldn't climb it. It might break."

"Not under your weight. You're light enough."

"Do it, Mom!" Lucas said with a loud giggle, and she was so stunned by his laughter that she couldn't say no. There was no way she'd let Alex look like the good guy in this scenario. She would show Lucas that she was able to have fun too.

Amazed Alex would even want her on the ladder, she gingerly placed her foot on the bottom rung and hoisted herself up, grabbing the sides to keep herself secure. With steady hands, she climbed.

Carefully, she slid one of the books out a little, not discounting for a moment the value of what she had between her fingers. She could only imagine what one of these books would cost at an estate auction. "*Kirby's Perspective of Architecture*," she said, tilting her head so she could read the spine. "Sound interesting?" she called down to Lucas, twisting just slightly to view his reaction as she slid it back onto the shelf.

He wrinkled his nose and looked at Alex, the two of them speaking some secret silent language as they both grinned. *Oh, now they're best friends?*

"Probably not your subject," Alex said. "Hold tight," he called up before pushing Noelle down the shelves. With a start, she took hold of the ladder, her heart pounding. By the amusement on his lips, he must have noticed her surprise, and when he moved her again, he did it more slowly.

She pulled out another book. "*Manuel du Muséum Français*," she read.

"I don't speak French yet," Lucas said, causing another chuckle from Alex.

"Yet," he repeated quietly. Alex paused this time, to let Noelle know he was moving her again, pushing her along to the next set of books.

"Locke's *Essay Concerning Human Understanding*."

"See, I have a whole library of 'nothing much,'" he said lightly to Lucas, and then winked up at Noelle.

Those books together were probably worth thousands, and Noelle knew that Alex was being kind again to her son, which gave her a little flutter, despite her misgivings about him. She came down the ladder to join them.

"What kind of books do you like to read?" He was crouched down again, always at eye level. Noelle liked how he did that. She bit her lip, forcing her focus to move from Alex to Lucas.

"Chapter books about mysteries, mostly," Lucas said. "And books about science."

"Did you bring any with you?"

"I brought the one I have. The rest I get at the library."

The sting of embarrassment rose from her neck, down her limbs, and up to her face. She wished Lucas hadn't disclosed that he only owned one book. His whole life, she'd brought him up to believe that success wasn't about possessions, and she knew that was the right thing to do, but in this instance, it made her feel ashamed that she couldn't give him more. She wondered if Alex, who had an entire room of books, would understand, or if he'd pity her.

Alex stood up. "You'll have to show it to me."

Why was this happening? Lucas was more relaxed than he'd ever been with a stranger before today—she couldn't get this idea out of her head. He was smiling, happy, laughing. Fear pelted her with the force of a thousand needles as she suddenly wondered if he'd been so quiet because no one had been able to reach him before, but Alex was, somehow. Memories started to filter into her mind: baking with Lucas, making snowmen, filling up coloring books. He'd politely done all those things with her and many more, but he'd never shown the kind of excitement she saw right now. This was even better than their trips to the library.

"Let me take you to your suite," Alex said, disrupting her thoughts.

After a short walk from the office, they entered the guest quarters where Noelle and Lucas would be living for the foreseeable future. It consisted of two bedrooms, a sitting room, and a bathroom—in all cases the use of "room" was a colossal understatement. If she knocked all the walls out downstairs in her mother's house, it still might not be as big as the space she was standing in.

In the corner of the sitting room, next to a picture window with at least forty rectangular panes of glass separated by wooden slats, was a real Christmas tree that had to be at least eight feet tall. It had an angel at the top, and from under the angel ribbons cascaded down the tree almost to the bottom in large waves. The tree itself was full of ornaments—all silver and snowy—icicles, snowflakes, baubles, and glass ornaments that shimmered in the white lights. Noelle had never seen anything so breathtaking.

The wall opposite had a curling marble fireplace, the mantel big enough to dwarf the four-tiered candelabra and vases that were the size of potting urns. They were also silver, with white accents—candles and simple flowers. Cream-colored, beaded stockings hung from gleaming, weighted hooks. The grate in front of the fireplace was thick iron with ornamental points on the top of each section.

"If you get cold, the staff will start a fire for you," Alex said, following her line of sight. "Just let them know what you need." He went over to a stack of hinged silver boxes next to the fireplace and lifted the lid on the largest one. "There's wood in here if you don't want to wait for them to do it for you." He lifted the lid on the next box. "And in here, I've put a few blankets for you." Then, he beckoned Lucas over to the smallest box. It was full of bags of marshmallows. "You've got skewers just inside the closet," he whispered with a grin.

Lucas's eyes looked like they were ready to pop right out of his head, he was so surprised. "Thank you," he said, breathlessly.

Noelle was a little breathless as well, but she forced herself to remain in reality. Alex Harrington certainly was a smooth talker, but he was not as charming as he seemed. Given his performance today, Noelle thought he could give Phoebe a run for her money in the acting department.

Chapter Six

Alex had spent a few hours with Noelle and Lucas, helping them to unpack after bringing their belongings from the trailer. He'd been kind and helpful the entire time, opening boxes for them, helping them to lift heavy objects, and he'd even unwrapped her teacups, removing the small knickknacks that were on a glass shelf in the living room and arranging the teacups in their places. Lucas was chattier than ever with him, telling him all about the real science lab he'd seen on TV and how one day he'd like to be a scientist. Finally, Alex had said he needed to head out for a quick meeting, leaving them to finish the last bit of unpacking.

Once their things were all put away, Noelle had texted Phoebe and Jo to tell them all about her new residence and the housemate she'd unexpectedly encountered. She was dying to talk to them about it, but neither of them had responded, annoyingly. It was normal, though—Jo was busy getting her house ready for the big family Christmas she hosted every year, most likely, and Phoebe was waitressing, so she probably hadn't gotten off work yet—but it made Noelle restless.

She felt like she was swept up in a fairy tale in this house with Prince Charming just down the hall. She wanted to enjoy that fantasy with Phoebe, laughing, and then afterward talk to Jo so she could bring her back into reality.

Melinda had returned to tell them that William would be flying in tomorrow from New York, giving them this evening to settle in. She also told Noelle that dinner would be served tonight at six o'clock, and to go down to the main dining room.

Noelle wondered if all the staff ate together and if they did, why the main dining room? Wouldn't that be for the Harringtons' use? Unless they weren't eating with the staff. Would Alex be there? Noelle scolded herself for even thinking about it. Her dad would probably never speak to her again if he could read her thoughts right now. Not to mention, she needed to get her mind on the fact that this was a job and she needed to treat it as such.

At work, there were people who rushed up to the boss the minute he entered the room, smiling, showing off what they'd done, talking a big game—all in the name of a promotion. But Noelle would hang back and let her work speak for her instead. She'd been promoted above the others, getting her full-time job and eventually a small step-up in duties. When she looked at the collective actions of Alex Harrington, she had to tell herself that no matter what front he put on, he was still the man responsible for taking her family's bakery away, the man who'd hiked up the rent for his own personal gain, the man who didn't care one bit about how that might affect Pop-pop or the rest of them.

She'd showered and given Lucas a bath, and they'd put on the best clothes they had to go down to dinner. Lucas didn't protest, but she could see his puzzlement as she held out the little red vest he wore over his Oxford shirt when they went to church. Once he had it over his head, and had poked his arms through, she used her fingers to straighten his hair again. Then she tugged on the bottom of his trousers, the legs looking a little short, Lucas having grown since she'd bought them a few months ago.

"Where are we going?" Lucas asked.

She fiddled with her earring to make sure it was clasped tightly. "To dinner."

Lucas was quiet as he tried to tuck his shirt in, the tails coming out when he moved, making Noelle feel guilty that she didn't have an outfit to really fit him. "Will we always have to get dressed up to eat?"

"I'm not sure," she said. "But I figured, after seeing what Alex wears around the house, that maybe we should get our formal clothes on."

He nodded in agreement.

When they got to the dining room, no one was there yet, and Noelle wasn't sure if she should sit or stand. She looked around in awe. She'd never been anywhere like this. The walls were plastered in ornate panels of the Corinthian style, stark white all the way to the ceilings that were probably twenty feet in the air; the only things bringing them down into view were the two heirloom gold chandeliers draped in greenery, hanging over the classic dining table that seated twenty-two, judging by the number of chairs. It had a wine-colored runner shooting down the center.

"Hello," Alex said, coming up from behind.

Noelle turned around, surprised to find just Alex. She peered over his shoulder to see if any other staff was behind him.

"Hi," he said to Lucas with a smile, showing off his perfectly white teeth. "That is a sharp vest you're wearing."

Lucas pulled on his collar and grinned timidly.

Alex had on designer jeans, a sweater, and a pair of loafers, making her self-conscious of her dress and heels. "I wasn't sure of the attire," she admitted.

His face softened. "Just dress how you'd normally dress."

"I don't know… A casual outfit would make me feel out of place in here." She looked around again.

Understanding dawned and he said, "Well, yes. I agree. That's why we aren't eating in here." Then, he leaned over toward Lucas and whispered loudly, "It's a little bit fancy in here, isn't it?"

Lucas nodded.

"I just asked you to meet me here since it's easier to find from your suite. Dinner's being served in another room. Follow me." He held out his hand, allowing Noelle and Lucas to exit first. Then he came up beside them in the hallway. "I can keep everything warm for you if you'd like to change into something more comfortable?"

"Oh, it's fine," she said, not wanting to make a fuss. So it was just them?

"May I take my vest off and untuck my shirt?" Lucas asked.

"Of course," Alex said, before seeking approval from Noelle.

The vest covered the fact that his shirt was a little short, but Lucas didn't know that. Shaking off the stress of making a good first impression at dinner, Noelle helped Lucas to remove his vest, and folded it over her arm.

They entered a much smaller room; it was almost intimate compared to all the others. It was simpler, with only a little ornamental work on the ceiling, the walls a calming and more current gray, and a craftsman-style table, also understated. On the wall opposite them was a long sideboard matching the style of the table.

"When Henry built this house, he wanted a grand dining room for entertaining." Alex pulled out a chair for Noelle and then one for Lucas. "But he also wanted a small space where he could kick back, smoke cigars, and drink brandy. He had this room built, and our family has used it as our personal dining room for generations." Alex helped Lucas scoot his chair closer to the table. "Enough history though—let's eat."

The staff descended upon them from all angles, setting dishes in front of them, and, even though the setting was more intimate in this dining room, the formality of being served was still quite intimidating.

"Hi, Jim," Alex said, greeting one of the servers.

"Hello, sir," he said. "First course: roasted lobster and artichoke soup with black truffle." He smiled warmly at Alex, placing a soup plate in front of Noelle and Lucas, then Alex. He was tall, and had a kind face.

"Jim, this is Noelle and her son Lucas." Alex turned to Noelle. "Jim has been with the family since my grandmother lived here and he will be of great help if you ever need him."

"It's nice to meet you, Jim," she said.

He nodded and backed away, leaving them to their dinner.

Lucas got a large, heavy goblet of milk with a candy-cane-colored straw. He had to use both hands to pick it up. Noelle was a little nervous until a gleaming plate with chicken nuggets and French fries appeared in front of Lucas.

"I did a search for the most popular kids' dishes," Alex said. "I'm not used to entertaining children."

"You've done very well," she said, unable to hide her surprise at his welcoming behavior. But she was still wondering why he'd invited them to dinner in the first place. Melinda certainly wasn't there eating with him, so why were they? "You really didn't need to do this. We could find something to eat on our own."

"On your first night? I wouldn't dream of it." Consideration slid across his face. "Unless you'd prefer to eat alone?" She could've sworn she'd seen a flicker of insecurity just then, but he'd returned to his commanding presence so quickly that she wasn't sure. Did he spend every night eating alone? Was that why he'd asked them to dinner tonight, because he actually enjoyed talking with them? Probably not.

As handsome as he was, he most likely spent every evening out on dates with high-powered women or having business dinners or something. Just the thought made her uneasy.

"I'm glad you're eating with us," she said, immediately wanting to swallow her words. She'd meant that his invitation had made things simpler because she wasn't sure what to do yet, but it had come out as more personal than she'd meant it to, making her want to kick herself. She'd better get these ridiculous feelings in check.

He broke eye contact a moment, acting as though he were inspecting his dish, but it was clear by the way his features lifted just slightly, his eyes creasing at the edges, that he was happy with her response.

He poured her a glass of white wine.

"I hope you enjoy the dinner. I put in the request before you arrived, but it occurred to me that I didn't know what you'd like."

"It looks delicious," she said, her hands in her lap until she could see which utensil he'd choose so she didn't have some kind of etiquette blunder. She subtly eyed Lucas's fork, hoping he wouldn't use his fingers. He picked it up and stabbed a French fry, to her relief.

There was a knock at the door, Melinda Burnett announcing her presence. She glanced down at Alex's jeans before looking at his face. Her expression was enough to make Noelle wonder if he had dressed down for them.

"I'm terribly sorry to interrupt your dinner," she said, "but I'm about to leave for the day and I received the property agreement you've been waiting for. I thought I'd just let you know it's on your desk."

"Perfect. Thank you, Melinda," he said. "Want any chicken nuggets?" he asked with a slight grin, obviously teasing.

"No, thank you, sir." She laughed quietly. "I'll just be on my way. Have a lovely evening."

"See you tomorrow."

"I'm sorry about that," he said, after Melinda had gone. "I'm waiting for that agreement so I can finish up a sale."

She didn't even want to think about what sale. Was it something to do with the bakery? Just the idea of it made her blood boil. Here he was, drinking his wine, enjoying his dinner, when who knows what kind of turmoil he could be causing another person or a family! He didn't know that after her dad had told her about the bakery closing, even with everyone trying to look on the bright side, Noelle had cried herself to sleep, her dreams dashed, her entire future now uncertain. He didn't know that she'd gotten up an extra hour early to cover up her lack of sleep, putting eye drops in her eyes to reduce the redness, adding cover-up over her dark circles, and plastering a smile on her face so her son wouldn't worry, as she was doing, about what would become of them. He didn't know that if she even thought about the bakery, she had to work to get the lump out of her throat, just like she was right now.

"I'm dying to know," he said, picking up his spoon and dipping it into his soup, the steam rising off the surface. "Why do you collect teacups if you don't drink tea?"

She took in a breath to get herself together before answering. "It's my gram's collection." She nearly snapped, but reined herself in for Lucas's sake. Sitting across from Alex now, seeing how little the bakery's closing affected him, she found herself getting tense. Lucas peered over at her, and she fretted he'd noticed her tone anyway. "When she passed away, my sister got all her cookbooks and I got her teacups. She traveled all over the world in her twenties, and she collected them from different countries. I also got her costume jewelry and one of her dresses that I used to love to put on when I was a girl."

Alex nodded, showing interest. Apparently, Alex didn't know Noelle well enough to sense her agitation like Lucas had, but she'd managed to defuse Lucas's unease with a smile because he'd gone back to drinking his milk.

"Did she get the jewelry in other countries as well?"

"No, I don't think so. I used to just play with it all as a kid." Noelle felt herself relaxing a little again as the memories flooded in. "She had these amethyst-colored earrings that were clip-ons. I would wear them along with enormous faux-diamond rings, a costume dress I had, and her high heels. I'd pretend I was a princess. I don't think any of it has a lot of significance other than my own personal memories. That's probably why she left it all to me. She knew I'd appreciate being reminded of those times. My sister Heidi never took any interest in that kind of thing."

"Have you added to the teacup collection at all?"

Noelle had friends who'd traveled but she was too busy raising Lucas, and they didn't have the kind of income to have those types of vacations. He was her whole world and she felt guilty even thinking about the things she might have missed out on. But if she had to live her life over, she wouldn't change a thing.

She shook her head. "I'd like to," she said. "My gram—her name was Sophia, which means wisdom. It was a perfect name for her; she was so wise. She told me all about the places she'd visited. She was my favorite person in all the world, apart from Lucas." The mention of Gram was making her nostalgic. "I spent all my time with her…" She trailed off, Gram's smile in her mind, the memory of her making Noelle's chest ache. When she looked up, there were thoughts behind Alex's eyes and he was nodding.

"I miss my grandmother terribly," he admitted suddenly, his face sobering so much that it derailed her line of conversation. There was a sadness in his eyes that was undeniable. He cleared his throat and took in a breath. "How are the nuggets?" he asked Lucas, the moment passing as quickly as it came.

Lucas smiled and reached for his milk again, accidentally missing the mark and sending the giant goblet tumbling over. The milk spread across the table, soaking into the cloth and sliding to the edge of the table where it began to drip onto the hardwoods, the milk seeping down between the boards. Lucas searched his mother's face, mortified, and she wanted to lift him up into her arms and tell him it was okay, like she had done when he was a toddler, yet at the same time she was concerned about the mess. She jumped out of her chair but Alex was already beside Lucas, blotting the spot with his cloth napkin.

"Please," he said kindly, "you two eat. I've got this." He looked down at Lucas. "Sorry I gave you such a big glass. I don't have any small ones," he said, his voice unbothered. "What kind of cups do you usually use?"

The staff came in and began lifting plates and removing them from the room. In mere seconds they had the table cleared, the cloth pulled off, and with a flourish a new cloth was on the table, the floor wiped, and brand-new dishes brought out.

"Mom gives me little plastic ones with animals on them."

"I'll bring some for him," Noelle offered.

"It's fine," Alex said. "I'll make sure we have something for him to use."

Another glass of milk was brought out, this one only half full.

"So tell me, Lucas, did you unpack that book you'd mentioned?" Alex was clearly trying to lighten the air.

"Yes, sir."

"Does your mom read it to you before bed?"

"No. I like to read by myself, but she reads her book beside me."

"He's a very quick reader," Noelle said. "He reads faster than I do. He learned before he'd even gotten to kindergarten."

"Could we all read together tonight? Would you read with us?" Lucas asked.

"Certainly," Alex said, clearly surprised by Lucas's offer.

"Oh, you don't have to," Noelle said quickly. It was a kind gesture, but Noelle was there to do a job. It wasn't Alex's responsibility to entertain her son.

But before she could think any more about it, he'd already started talking with Lucas about the book he was reading at the moment.

❄ ❄ ❄

The three of them sat on the sofa in the sitting area of Noelle and Lucas's suite, holding their books. Noelle had tried to tell Alex that he didn't have to spend the rest of his evening with them, but he'd insisted, even suggesting that Noelle finish getting Lucas's bed ready while he and Lucas read their books. She still hadn't unpacked Lucas's favorite blanket and the stuffed rabbit that Gram had given him. It was missing an eye and she'd stitched his ear together more times than she could count. Lucas couldn't sleep without it.

Alex and Lucas had been reading for quite a while before Noelle had picked her book up from beside her phone and car keys, which were still on the table. She hadn't found a good spot to keep them yet, afraid she'd forget where she'd put them in this giant suite. After finally finishing unpacking the bedding, she joined the others.

Noelle sat down next to Alex but then scooted a little too close to Lucas, to give Alex enough space. Alex glanced up from his book and smiled but then resumed reading. She opened her own novel and scanned the words on the page, but their meaning wasn't registering.

She was too busy contemplating the fact that Alex Harrington was sitting beside her, with a science fiction novel in his hands. He was on page thirty-two—she'd looked.

Everything about him made her curious. Out of the corner of her eye, she could see the rise and fall of his chest as his head was turned down toward his book. She let her hair fall in front of her face so she could get a better look at him. His shirt collar was open one button, a slight stubble from the day showing on his chin and cheeks, his jaw set in a relaxed way that could almost be mistaken for a smile.

Suddenly, there was a familiar buzz and a pulsing light from the table, and before she was able to get it, Alex had leaned forward and picked up her phone to give it to her, moving quickly at first and then slowly, his arm still outstretched so she could view the text that had floated onto her screen—the text he could also read. It was Phoebe: *So Alex Harrington IS hot? And nice? I knew it! You're so lucky! I can't believe…*

He handed her the phone, a very subtle look of amusement on his face, curiosity swimming around with it.

"Who is it, Mama?" Lucas asked.

"It's Phoebe," she said, feeling her dinner settling like a rock in her stomach. She stuffed the phone under one of the throw pillows.

"Who's Phoebe?" Alex asked, chewing on a grin.

Noelle tried to look at him, but the fire in her cheeks made her self-conscious and her gaze could only reach his smiling lips before she lost all ability to think clearly. "She's…"

"A friend," Lucas said. "Mom said she used to walk by your house a lot and look for you."

Oh God, she sounds like a stalker! "I think it's probably about bedtime." Noelle smiled, nervous energy making sitting nearly impossible. She couldn't look Alex in the eye at all now. "We've had a big day."

Lucas didn't argue, but he never did. He got up and followed her into the bathroom to brush his teeth, both of them leaving Alex on the sofa. In her peripheral vision, she saw him watching them, but all she could do was offer, "Be right back," without turning around. She gritted her teeth, remembering that her phone was still under the pillow. Oh well, he'd seen the message already. Why did she even care what Alex thought, anyway? She didn't… did she? But either way, she couldn't conceal the embarrassment she felt at the situation.

Chapter Seven

Noelle woke with a start. She'd talked a little about the day with Lucas, and said a prayer. Then she'd lain next to him, but she'd dozed off by accident, and she had no idea how much time had passed. Carefully, so as not to wake him, she crawled out of his bed, wondering if Alex was still sitting on her sofa; he was probably scrolling through all the texts from Phoebe about gold plates and how hot is he and where was she… There was no telling what she might have texted by now—after all, Phoebe did have a flair for the dramatic. Noelle rolled her head on her shoulders to alleviate the pinch.

Cautiously, she walked out into the sitting room.

"Hi," Alex said, looking up from his book. A bottle of wine in a silver bucket had appeared on the coffee table next to her keys, along with two glasses. Why had he gone and gotten them wine?

She'd told him she'd be right back. Did he think he had to stay? "I've kept you long enough," she said, feeling so guilty that Lucas had invited him to read and then she'd left him on the sofa for ages. She'd probably used up his whole evening, and, surely, he had better things to do.

"It's fine. And clearly you're exhausted—you've had a busy day." He set his book down next to hers. "Have some wine."

She noted the fact that he didn't ask—was he used to just telling people what he wanted? She sat down next to him.

"Your pillow's been buzzing," he said, pointing to the spot where she'd hidden her phone.

With a prickle of awkwardness, she took her phone out from its hiding spot, the screen full of texts and a missed call. She silenced it and put it face down on the table. Then she took an enormous gulp of the wine Alex had just poured.

Alex had a smirk on his face, and she knew he was thinking about what he'd seen on her phone, but his playful expression gave her a burst of courage. "Oh fine, go on, let's just get it out into the open."

Alex raised an eyebrow.

"Yes. I sent my friend Phoebe a text…"

Alex took a drink of his wine, not saying a word.

"And I might have said something about initial impressions…"

He threw his head back and laughed, then immediately looked toward the short hallway beyond which Lucas was sleeping. "Sorry," he said in a lowered voice. "I'm flattered. Thank you."

She suppressed an eye roll at herself. How was she supposed to be taken seriously now when she'd just pretty much told him she thought he was attractive? His ease with Lucas and his kindness had made her a little too comfortable and now she felt the need to bring herself back to reality, but the damage was done.

"I apologize," she said. "That was very unprofessional of me. I won't let it happen again."

"Yes," he said. "'Smokin' hot' isn't usually allowed in the workplace…" He broke out into a smile.

She felt her eyes bulge and a streak of heat shoot across her face like a flame to gasoline. *Smokin' hot?* How did he know she'd said "Smokin' hot"? Noelle gasped. "You opened my texts?" She had to close her gaping mouth.

"No," he laughed. "But your friend Phoebe kept texting you and her messages were pinging one after another. I thought there was some kind of emergency. Does she always do that?"

There was a slight fondness in his amusement, giving her pulse a workout. "Yes, she does," she said, shaking her head in disbelief. She grabbed her phone and hit the button, finally looking at the texts that had pushed through to her screen. Sure enough, Phoebe had continued:

Where are you? Is he really smokin' hot like you say?
Can you get him to take his shirt off?
Maybe do laundry for him.
Go spill something on him!

Trying to keep her composure, Noelle cleared the texts and set it face down again on the table. "This is not how I imagined my first night on the job," she admitted, still slightly stunned at the whole thing.

He laughed again. "Drink some more wine. It'll help." Then with a devious glint in his eye, he said, "Just don't spill any on me."

"How do you know I wasn't winding her up?" She cut her eyes at him playfully, but held onto her wine with both hands before they started to shake.

"By the color of your cheeks, and the splotches going down your neck, I assumed you weren't, but then again, maybe you were."

Grasping for anything to eliminate the humiliation, she said, "She's seen you from a distance and thinks you're attractive so I was only teasing her."

"Of course." He topped their glasses off. "I understand."

Oh no. "Only teasing her" might sound like she was saying he *wasn't* attractive. Now she'd told him he was ugly. "I meant..." She let a nervous breath out, scrambling for a better response.

"It's fine." He smiled again, the gesture reaching his eyes and making her pounding heart want to completely stop dead at the gorgeousness.

She pulled her eyes away from him, still struggling for some way to save this moment, and noticed the hearth where flames were dancing their way up the chimney.

He followed her line of sight. "I started a fire. This house gets a little drafty in the winter." The playfulness had dropped from his expression—he was letting her off the hook and moving on to a different conversation.

"That's very thoughtful," she said. "Thank you for your kindness with Lucas today. He doesn't open up to many people and you made him feel welcome, which is a big thing, since he's had to move schools and change houses."

"You're welcome. He's a great kid."

Noelle liked the soft look on his face when he said that. It made her want to talk to him all night about everything and nothing at the same time. But she could feel the exhaustion setting in and she knew that she was caving to Alex's kindness because she was tired. In the morning, her mind would be clearer, and she'd remember all those things she'd told herself about him. The warm glow of the fire and the sweet taste of the wine weren't helping matters.

"So what's your grandfather like?" she said, sticking to business as she swirled the liquid in her glass. She sat a little straighter, trying to push herself to stay alert. She couldn't wait to meet William Harrington, especially since Alex had been such a surprise.

Alex cleared his throat before answering. "Difficult."

His answer shocked her. *Oh, great.* No wonder she'd been chosen for the job. It wasn't her credentials or the fact that she'd had a great interview; it was because no one else wanted it. William Harrington was probably known to be a nightmare or something. Other than the Phoebe-texts debacle, on the whole, things had gone well for her since she'd arrived; there was bound to have been a catch.

"Sorry," he said, forcing a smile. It looked like he was well practiced at doing that. "I just find him hard to get along with." He gazed into the fire as if the thoughts were right there on the surface just waiting to get out. Then, snapping out of it, he turned back to her. "Enough about my grandfather—you'll meet him tomorrow. Tell me," he said with mock importance, "your friend Phoebe…"

She didn't know which was worse: the fact that he wouldn't elaborate about William or that he was bringing up Phoebe again. She thought she'd escaped that line of discussion.

"She's seen me from a distance? Where?"

"Here. Well, outside at the wall surrounding the property," she added quickly, so as not to make Phoebe out to be a crazy person peeking into his windows. "We used to walk past this house after school."

"We?"

"Phoebe and I both went to Winston High School down the road. She and I, along with my friend Jo, walked by this house on our way home, every day, freshman to senior year. We'd balance on the wide brick top of it until it got too high and then jump down onto the sidewalk."

"Ah," he said with a nod. "So you walked past my house every day for… four years? And now you're living here. What a small world."

"Yes, it is." Something in his eyes drove her to say what was on her mind. She'd never told anyone this—she never really had a reason to. "You know, I thought I saw you once too," she said. "You were walking toward an elderly woman. She was carrying a white box and she seemed to be losing her grip on it. You tried to get to her just as she lost hold of it, and she dropped it. I thought I heard her say, 'Oh no! The cake…' I've always thought about that. I wondered if some beautiful cake had been ruined."

Alex searched the air, probably for the memory, until it evidently dawned on him. "I remember," he said slowly. "That was my grandmother." His words came out huskily. He took in a breath. "It was my birthday cake—in the box. I was turning nineteen. She dropped it. She was so upset. She was adamant that she'd make another one, so I helped her."

"How sweet of you," she said. This soft side of him was such a contrast to the articles she'd seen in the local paper about his lacrosse games and the weekend polo matches he played in for charity. He was clearly driven and competitive, even now in adulthood—the way he'd pushed out all those small businesses, making way for larger chains to take over for financial gain.

"Well…" He trailed off, lost in his own thoughts as well. Then he came out of it, but his face was unreadable. "I had a lovely night tonight—thank you." He moved toward the edge of the sofa as if he were going to stand up.

He was cutting things off, just like that? "Thank *you* for taking the time to get to know me and Lucas and making us feel at home."

He smiled. It was weird how relaxed she felt right now in this enormous house, but Alex had a way of shrinking her focus to just the tiny space around them and nothing else mattered in that moment.

"And sorry about the texts." She eyed her phone.

The comment hung between them and it was as if neither of them knew what to do next. She took in the starch of his shirt, the curve of his lips, the shadow of stubble on his neck, the way his hand fell on his knee.

He leaned forward to get his book from the table just as she went for her phone, which was buzzing again, their faces inches from each other. He was so close to her that she could feel his breath and smell the wine on it. That curiosity in his eyes returned, and she wondered if he felt what she felt in that moment. Then, clearly acting on an impulse, he leaned in further, his lips meeting hers for just an instant, barely brushing her mouth, causing the whole world to stop. There was nothing in that moment but him and her. There was a kind of perfection in that space just between them where she wanted to know more, to feel more, the emotion hanging right there. He pulled away, blinking, his face clouded with astonishment.

He opened his mouth to say something but thought otherwise and stood up. She knew just by looking at him that he was horrified at having put her in that position. The strange thing was that she wasn't offended or put off at all, despite the fact this was Alexander Harrington, her boss. She pressed her lips together, unable to avoid speculating about what it would've felt like to really have him kiss her.

"It's okay," she said, standing up and taking a step in front of him.

"I shouldn't have done that. I've overstepped the boundaries."

"Well, now I don't feel so bad about calling you 'smokin' hot'," she teased.

He laughed. "So you meant it?" He flashed that smile, and her stomach lurched in somersaults.

She bit her lip, trying not to beam at him, the excitement whirling around in her head, making her dizzy.

"I knew it," he said with a chuckle. "You're a terrible liar."

She rolled her eyes. "Don't let it go to your head."

He shifted his face to drop his smile dramatically. "No," he agreed. Then he softened into a genuine look of affection. "I'll let you relax. Enjoy the rest of the wine."

She wanted to ask him to stay, but she knew she shouldn't, so she let him go. She was a little panicked by the way her pulse roared like a plane at takeoff as she thought about what had just happened. It was all so wrong and it didn't make any sense at all, given the situation with the bakery. But she found herself fixating on the almost-kiss that was playing over and over in her head like a movie on a loop. She couldn't get it out of her mind.

Chapter Eight

"Are we going to see Alex again?" Lucas asked, as they sat down in the informal dining area the following morning.

Just his question sent a tingle of emotion down Noelle's spine. She felt elation at the thought of seeing him again, mixed with both guilt about spending time with the man ruining everything and the fear of how she was supposed to be around him now.

Melinda Burnett had knocked on the door of the suite that morning and told her she'd let the chef know Noelle and Lucas would be coming down for breakfast. On Sundays the kitchen was booming, she'd said, because they always provided a full breakfast for all the staff. She also told Noelle that she and Lucas could eat before the others, since William would be coming in, and to arrive with an empty stomach; the spread was impressive.

Afterward, Noelle was meeting her mother down the street to take Lucas for the day. He was going to help her deliver Christmas cookies to the neighbors. William was due in from New York around nine in the morning. This would give Noelle time to get acquainted with him before she had Lucas in tow.

"I'm not sure," she finally answered his question.

There were silver covered dishes on the sideboard, plates of fruit, a big basket of southern biscuits, steaming oatmeal topped with granola and dried cherries, and more muffins than she'd ever had in the old bakery window. A crystal flute of orange juice sat at her place and a small plastic cup with a giraffe on it had been set down in front of Lucas. Noelle had to stifle her surprise. She couldn't imagine how Alex had managed to get Lucas a cup between dinner last night and breakfast this morning, but he had, and she couldn't wait to thank him. She looked over at the door, pushing all the other thoughts from her mind, hoping he'd come through it and join them.

As plates of eggs and bacon, stone-ground grits, and mini breakfast quiches were uncovered and adorned with serving spoons, Noelle caught Jim's attention and asked, "Will Mr. Harrington be joining us?"

"No, ma'am," he said. "He flew out this morning."

"Oh," she said, taken aback. He'd just up and left without even letting her know? Well, he didn't have to let her know, certainly, but she would've thought—

Another idea filtered into her mind before she could finish the last: perhaps she'd read into their evening more than he had. Perhaps she'd been only something to pass the time before his trip today. He was probably just being polite and welcoming. Her conversation with her father surfaced and she remembered about Alex's business dealings with her dad and Pop-pop, and she scolded herself for not listening to her inner voice of doubt. What if that almost-kiss had been truly an accident? And even if it hadn't, it would be just like the person she initially thought he was to leave without saying a thing. She'd let herself get drawn in, despite her attempts to ignore the impulse, and she'd gotten exactly what she'd expected to get. Well, she wouldn't let herself be derailed again.

Suddenly, Noelle was glad that he'd gone so she couldn't get swept up in her feelings before having a chance to listen to her brain for a second. She was out of her comfort zone, without her friends and family to weigh in on things, and she worried that her own personal insecurities about not having a family for Lucas or a partner to come home to were playing with her mind. Maybe she was making Alex out to be a better person than he was. And perhaps, if she thought back over it all, he was just playing games with her. She sucked in a breath as she thought, what if he'd been trying to get something from her last night? What if he'd hoped she'd ask him to stay? He'd told her to finish the wine… Had he been expecting something more to happen between them? Anger swept through her. She resolved right then and there not to fall for such a man.

❄ ❄ ❄

"I don't need anyone to babysit me," William Harrington said under his breath, as he trembled on his cane, unsuccessfully attempting to keep himself steady. With an unstable hand, he grabbed onto the ornate railing of the sweeping staircase that led upstairs and planted a foot on the bottom step.

"Mr. Harrington," Melinda said, offering a look of solidarity to Noelle. At least they were in this together. "We've moved your room downstairs. You're at the end of the hall now, remember?"

With his mouth set in a straight line and his brows pulling together in annoyance, he shifted around and leaned on his cane again for support, his head turned toward Noelle, but his eyes distant, his gaze slightly off-target, revealing his loss of eyesight.

"I'll show you where your room is," Noelle said as gently as she could, stepping forward, trying to put the man at ease. But his irritation was clear.

He said quietly, "I remember." And then he started to walk toward the hallway. Noelle shuffled up beside him, nodding to Melinda that she had this under control.

"Call me if you need anything," Melinda said. "I'll be in England for my Christmas vacation, but you have my phone number if you have any questions."

Noelle nodded, wondering how today would go.

"What's your name again, young lady?" William asked, his tone still short, as they walked slowly down the wide, shiny hallway, their steps echoing under the high ceilings. He seemed as though he was looking where they were walking, but every now and again, he'd put out his hand or swing his cane to ensure nothing was in his way.

"Noelle Parker," she said.

He tipped his head up briefly to show his interest, but then the bothered look returned. "Miss Parker," he said, as if trying out the name to see if it fit on his lips. "Well, Miss Parker, you are very kind to walk me to my room, but I can manage just fine. I haven't been gone so long that I can't remember the way, even if I can't see."

How was she supposed to take care of him if he wouldn't let her? Clearly, he must need some help or she and Lucas wouldn't be living there. "If you don't want any assistance right now, that's fine—you can just call on me when you need something. But I'm new to the house. I was sort of hoping you'd show me around since I don't have anything else to do."

He looked up from the floor again, and in that split second, there was a moment of contemplation. He seemed miles away. His eyebrows rose as he surfaced from whatever had stunned him, and smiled at Noelle. "Miss Parker?" he said, his off-center gaze not hiding his curiosity. It was as if he was going to say something but whatever the memory was had slipped back in again and stolen the rest of his words.

"What is it?" she asked. There was so much wisdom in his face, so many years of knowledge, that she was intrigued to learn more about this millionaire old man.

He shook his head, his lips still set in a smile. "You just reminded me of an old story," he said, right before his face sobered. He cleared his throat. "All right," he said, the moment gone. "If you'd like to follow me around like a puppy all day while my grandson pays you to do so, then so be it. But I won't need any help."

"Understood," she said, not wanting to rock the boat on the first day and also wondering how she'd ever get him to take his heart medicine at noon.

They walked the rest of the hallway in silence as William tottered, leaning on his cane with every step. It was whittled in a pattern with a shiny bulb on the top, the wood so smooth it looked like rock. His weathered hands wrapped over the top of it, his grip firm. She wondered about who he'd been as a young man. Had he grown up here? The way Alex had spoken about the line of men who'd owned this home, it seemed that he would have lived here. If so, what had taken him to New York? How long had he been away? He must have sensed one of her glances in his direction, tilting his head toward her, and she quickly looked straight ahead.

"What are you thinking about?" he asked her point blank, her suspicions confirmed.

"I was just wondering if you grew up here," she said honestly.

"I did."

He didn't say anything more, so she asked, "What took you to New York?"

"Business." He stopped walking and swiveled toward her, his cane making a clack on the floor. "What else would you like to know?"

She ignored his brusque tone. "Were you sad to leave here? It's so beautiful."

"It is a very nice house. And yes, I was a little sad to leave." He started walking again.

"So it feels good to be back?" she asked, stepping up beside him.

His response was a sort of grunt that she couldn't define. Was he agreeing or disagreeing? Either way, she didn't have a whole lot of answers, so she just stayed quiet and looked at the surroundings, reminding herself to stick to business.

The walls were empty, stark white, the elaborate woodwork giving them the only life they had, their surfaces starving for more. If William had lived here, why didn't they have anything resembling personal memorabilia in this house? There was nothing anywhere to tell about the people in this family, apart from the enormous antique portrait paintings that hung from gold frames in the entryway. Sure, there were old books in the library, but what did William like to do with his time? What was the Harrington family legacy? Who had lived in this house before Alex, exactly—his whole family? His parents? His grandmother? She had so many questions, but she didn't know how to ask them. She looked down at the hardwoods before she caught William's body language assessing her.

"You're quiet again," he said.

"I just..." She didn't know how to respond for fear that she might offend him. But the one thing she always prided herself on was her honesty. "I feel like these walls could be so beautiful if they were full of pictures. Maybe family photos or something," she said with a cautious smile. "But I'm not a decorator."

He seemed to be staring into the distance above her head thoughtfully and then, with a smile, he said, "They probably could do with a few pictures." He tapped his cane on the floor as he pondered something. Then, he said, "Come with me. I'll show you a great wall."

After a short walk, they arrived at the most magnificent spot in the house. Noelle stood, unable to speak. It seemed as though they'd had a professional photographer to take photos of the family. One had a scene of all kinds of people around a large dining table, smiles on their faces; another recent one showed William leaning against a tree. There were so many! This was exactly what she'd wanted to see—candid, beautiful shots revealing the real people in this family.

"This is amazing," she said.

"Alex put all of them up."

She looked back at them in awe. One of the photos was a close-up black and white of an old woman with white hair in puffy curls, holding a coffee cup, laughing. Her spirit was captured perfectly, her happiness forever retained. "Who is that?" she asked, then wondered if he could see it. "The woman with the coffee cup."

With a moment of introspection, William said, "My wife." He said the words softly as if he were speaking to her, so much emotion behind them that Noelle turned around. "She loved coffee. I hated it. I'd find her sitting by the window, reading and drinking her coffee every morning. As soon as she saw me, she'd stand up and set her book down, greeting me. 'Don't get near me with that coffee,' I'd tease her—I still remember the smell of her favorite kind on her breath: it had a smoky aroma to it; it was so dark it was jet black in her cup. She would ignore me, setting it down and wrapping her arms around my neck and kissing me anyway." William closed his eyes as happiness took over his features, the creases in his forehead and around his cheeks immediately softening, making him look younger. "While I hated the smell of that coffee, when it was mixed with her scent of citrus and flowers, it was uniquely her, and now I'd give anything to fill my lungs with it..."

Of course that picture was William's wife, and probably the same grandmother that had caused the sadness she'd seen in Alex's eyes. Noelle scolded herself for not being more careful in her questions.

She got ready to apologize but he'd moved on, obviously wanting to change the subject.

"They're good photos, aren't they?" he said, looking back up at them. There seemed to always be something behind his expression—this time a judgment of sorts? She couldn't place it. With a straightening of his shoulders the way someone does just before changing the subject to shake off their thoughts, he said, "Where's that boy of yours? I was told there would be a youngster running around."

"He's at my mother's. He'll be with her while I'm at work."

"But you aren't working. We've established that I'm just fine."

She smiled. "Yes, well, Alex might disagree."

"Don't worry about him. I'm still the head of this house."

There was a harshness to his tone, but he was trying to lighten it, she could tell. She thought again about her conversation with Alex. It seemed that whenever the topic of Alex came up, William was abrupt and irritable.

"But he'll be returning," she said, hoping to get confirmation on that. "And after all, he's paying me to be here, so I should at least look after you."

William's lips were pursed.

"So you aren't married?" he asked, his question taking her off guard.

"You don't like to beat around the bush, do you?" She laughed nervously.

"Not at my age. I don't have time for that nonsense. I might die before I get an answer."

After Gram's death, she didn't find that comment amusing.

"Anyway," he said, unfazed by her lack of response, "you're on your own?"

Noelle nodded, the words clouded by her thoughts. But then she remembered that he might not be able to see her so she said, "Yes."

There was an understanding in the air between them, and she wasn't sure how he could possibly relate to the woes of being a single mother, but she saw compassion on his face. "I know what being alone is like," he said.

"I'm sorry you lost your wife," she said.

He blinked a little too rapidly, the subject obviously difficult. "I haven't lost her entirely. There's just enough of her left to haunt me."

Noelle waited for an explanation, and William led her into his suite, where, as in hers, there was a small sitting area by a fireplace. He carefully lowered himself down, clearly working hard to keep his emotions hidden. "She has Alzheimer's," he said evenly. "She's in a home where she can be taken care of."

Noelle noticed the rise and fall of his chest, and how his hand had started shaking again like when she'd first met him, as he rested it on the arm of the sofa.

"Is she close by? Do you get to visit her?"

"Yes, she's less than an hour away. But no, I don't visit her."

"Why not?" she asked.

He licked his lips, buying time while he worked for an answer. Noelle couldn't imagine not visiting a loved one, no matter what state they were in. If Pop-pop were in a hospital, she'd go every day to see him. Didn't he realize how lucky he was to still have his wife there with him? Why in the world wouldn't he see her?

William's hand was visibly trembling now, unable to stop, as if the emotion he'd pushed down was working its way through his body and building up in his fingertips. "She doesn't know who I am, so there's no point."

Noelle saw the pain on his face. He didn't try to hide it this time. She hadn't considered the agony he must feel to have his wife—the woman he loved—not recognize him. How awful. The gray cloud cover outside was giving the room a silvery hue, despite the large windows, so the air in there felt sad just like him. But, while she understood the emotions he was feeling, there was something she worried he hadn't considered in this: what his wife might want. What if she became lucid at times and she was scared? What if she felt abandoned?

"If it were me, I'd want my husband to visit, even if I didn't remember him," she said, her honesty coming out before she could pull it back in.

William didn't seem offended at all. But his eyes became glassy, and he shook his head. "It doesn't change anything. It just hurts *me*, rips out my heart." His voice cracked and he coughed to cover it up. "It's difficult to face all alone."

"But Alex is here. Can't you two go together?"

His hand balled into a fist and he stretched out his fingers as if his joints were giving him trouble. "Alex doesn't speak to me," he said, in a way that made her feel like he cared more than he was letting on. "He's never gone with me to see Elizabeth—not once. He always goes by himself. And he's planning to move to New York anyway, so there's no need to start now."

"He is?" she asked, shock pelting her.

"He's so much like I was at that age: just dying to be in the center of all that madness—always chasing something bigger. He won't listen when I tell him that I was there and it isn't all that it's cracked up to be. But I think he's running. From his family, from this house..."

She considered this. The person she'd met last night, who'd shown Lucas his books and teased her about Phoebe, didn't seem like someone who was running from family only to be in the hub of big business, but the person her father had described sure did. The more she had a chance to process it all, the more she realized that she didn't know him at all, and she'd been caught up in the excitement of this big house and how attractive he was. Instead, what she needed to do was to tell herself that Alex Harrington was *not* Prince Charming and this was no fairy tale. It was real life, where things were complicated and difficult.

They'd both fallen silent until she noticed something. "You don't have a Christmas tree," she said, comparing her own suite and all its glittering decorations to his.

"I told the staff not to bother," he said.

"Why?"

"It's all just for appearances, isn't it? I've been ripped from my apartment in New York, made to come to a house full of memories of my wife who has become a stranger, and I have to live with my grandson who hates me. Not very Christmassy."

"How long did you and your wife live here?"

"We didn't. I left for New York as soon as we married, and we spent our whole marriage there. Well, until the Alzheimer's set in so badly that we worried Elizabeth would hurt herself. That was around six months ago." He pulled the sofa's throw pillow from behind him, fluffed it, and then used it for support again. Even still, he looked uncomfortable.

"It seems a shame that she didn't get to live in this amazing home."

"She spent some time here. She adored this house, but our lives were in New York, so this was her summer home, although she'd come to visit during the winters as well. She was always coming in to see Alex."

"You say 'she' came. You didn't come?"

"No." He twisted uneasily on the sofa.

"Why?"

"I was busy." He nearly spat the words, as if the busyness he'd spoken of had been at fault. "When her memory started failing, she wanted to come back here, hoping the gardens and sunshine would somehow mend her broken brain. We just didn't want to put that burden on the staff and Alex, so I found her a nursing home close by. I was hoping that she could visit here sometimes but I'm too afraid to find out about her prognosis. I suppose I secretly don't want to know if she's gotten worse."

"You have to see her," Noelle said. She felt terrible for Elizabeth, that she hadn't had a chance to return to the home she'd wanted to live in. It must be so difficult to see a loved one in that state, but she just couldn't get over the fact that Elizabeth was alone as well. "Don't you think she'll want to see you again?"

"The Elizabeth I know is no longer there." He tipped his head back. "You know," he said with a deep breath, "she used to write the most beautiful letters." He smiled, shaking his head, his thick eyebrows knitting together in grief. "When I was working late, she left them on my pillow and I'd find them when I got home. Her handwriting rivaled calligraphy and the words she wrote were like an unsung melody in my head as I read them. They weren't long, but sweet and perfect, and they made my night. I'd look over at her sleeping and sometimes I'd get such a thrill from them that I'd jump in the bed and kiss her, waking her up. She never got upset. She just batted me away, half asleep. But I always caught her smile."

"What a wonderful relationship you two seemed to have." She liked it when William opened up about his wife. "Thank you for sharing it with me."

"Thank you for listening."

Noelle wasn't sure how, but with a story like that, she was going to get William to go see Elizabeth for Christmas. She had to.

Chapter Nine

By the end of the day, Noelle had managed to get William to take his heart medicine and she'd gotten him comfortable and offered her phone number in case he needed her while she went to pick up Lucas from the bakery. Her mother had texted that she was taking him there to help her father and Pop-pop organize a list of some of the things he was planning to save once the bakery closed.

The air was icy cold as she walked the familiar cobblestone street, thinking of how she wouldn't have much longer to do that. Noelle had always parked at the end of the road, on the corner, just so she could walk the beautiful cobbles with the little stone bakery in the distance ahead, and admire the quaint shops all around it. As her boots wobbled on the stones under her feet, she looked up at the holiday banners the city had hung from every wrought-iron streetlight. The store windows were glowing with Christmas lights and festive trees inside.

The wooden Hope and Sugar Bakery sign swung from two hinges on a rod just to the side of the door. The sign had been hand painted by a local artist years ago and looked like it could use a touching up, the words having weathered over time. She stepped past the patch of grass that would be peppered with buttercups in the spring, knowing she wouldn't get to see them next year, once the bakery had closed.

As she walked, her thoughts again returned to the wonderful evening she had shared with Alex. He was charming, but nothing more. There were too many other things telling her he was different from the man he'd shown her. So why did the mere thought of him make her pulse run rampant?

With her head starting to throb, she pulled open the door and headed inside.

"There she is!" Pop-pop said with a grin.

His cheeks were rosy and his white hair was combed to the side. He and Lucas were behind the counter, the glass case full of gorgeous Christmas cookies—bells, trees, and little red stockings with white piping. The lights around the display window were on and the Christmas tree was decorated. There was a small fire going on the grate beneath the stockings, which had been hung in just the way Gram had always arranged them. The buttery scent of scones and pastries filled her lungs, making her smile.

"Get your apron on, wash your hands," he said, hopping off his stool. "Lucas and I were going to attempt to make the peppermint cake with Heidi for the window, but now that you're here, we'll leave it to the experts."

Every year, Gram made the most gorgeous cake to display in the window at Christmas time. It was an enormous cube of vanilla sponge with white frosting, homemade peppermint sprinkles, and a red-and-white fondant ribbon tied into a bow to make it look like a present. They displayed it on a bright snowy satin with their signature peppermint candies scattered around. After Gram passed, Noelle and Heidi were the only ones who knew the recipe, so they'd planned to take turns each year making it. This year they'd decided it was Noelle's turn.

Noelle grabbed a cookie for herself and one for Lucas, giving him a kiss, and then went to wash her hands, already feeling the loss of the bakery.

Heidi was in the kitchen stirring a saucepan with a wooden spoon to make the peppermint. "Glad you're here. I'll help you. We can do it together this year," Heidi said with a sad smile.

"Let's make it the very best one we've ever done," Noelle said, producing a smile for Heidi's benefit. She leaned through the open door and gave Lucas a wink. He and Pop-pop were doing a crossword puzzle together. Growing up, she'd always imagined having a bunch of kids. She'd teach them all the family recipes and they'd run around the bakery after school, playing and giggling. She'd even considered having a new corner of the small shop filled with toys so the parents could come and relax with a cup of coffee while their kids played together. But none of that would happen now.

After her hands were clean, and her cookie eaten, Noelle grabbed a few lemons—Gram's secret ingredient—ran them under the tap, and then began squeezing them over Gram's juicer. As she pressed down on the rind, the juice dribbling down into the saucer, she looked at her hand, remembering Gram's weathered fingers in the same position when she'd done it, chattering away about this and that. Right then, it felt like Gram was with her, as though she had some purpose for her in all this mess. She was glad for the feeling because she didn't know how to be hopeful in a situation like this.

Heidi checked the candy thermometer and grabbed the peppermint extract just as Noelle slid the bowl of lemon juice toward her.

"It's like clockwork, isn't it?" Noelle noted. "We don't even have to think about this recipe. We just do it."

"Yeah," Heidi said, pouring in the lemon juice and stirring as the concoction bubbled slightly. "I feel close to Gram here," she admitted, looking at Noelle with glistening eyes, her bottom lip wobbling.

Noelle felt it too. "Please don't get sad—I can't..." she said, knowing that if her sister started to cry, she would too. This was Gram's special place, the place where they'd always been together, where they'd had the best times of their lives, and where they could come and forget their troubles when things were hard.

Noelle remembered when she'd broken up with her boyfriend in high school. She'd been so upset. Gram had brought her here and sat her down with a heavy mug of hot chocolate and two ginger snaps. "You know, before I met your Pop-pop," she'd said, "I had fallen in love just like you. It was a whirlwind—I fell fast and hard—and when we broke up, I felt like I'd been pushed under water, unable to catch my breath."

Gram had sat down next to Noelle, her apron still full of flour with a smear of chocolate at the waist. She'd put her hand on Noelle's shoulder and said, "But if it hadn't happened, and I hadn't met your Pop-pop, you wouldn't be here right now. Things are meant to happen to us. Sometimes, while we're trying to find our own way, God has something else in mind." With concern in her eyes and love on her lips in the form of a smile, she said, "I know it hurts, but if you can just hold on, and open yourself up to it, your destiny will find you."

Noelle was still holding on just like Gram had said to do, waiting. She'd thought her purpose in life was to run the bakery, to have a big family, siblings for Lucas, and a loving partner to share her years. But with every month that passed, she felt more worried about her future, wondering if the big universe had forgotten her somehow.

She and her sister worked in comfortable silence as they rolled the peppermint mixture into little balls and set them on a tray to cool. Lost in her thoughts, Noelle dusted them with the candied sugar that made them sparkle under the lights.

Usually, at this time of year, the bells on the door would continue to interrupt them, as busy shoppers stopped in for a treat, but with so many of the shops having changed hands and been commercialized, the street didn't bring the same clientele in anymore and the bells had been quiet since she'd arrived. The old candle shop next door was now a private postal service, the fabric shop an interior design firm, and the local hairdresser had changed to a computer repair shop. There was one common theme there: they were all high-rent-paying customers of Alex Harrington's. The slow business, the bakery closing—tears came to her eyes as she tried not to think about it. Heidi clicked the radio on to the Christmas station, and Noelle knew she, too, was feeling the tug on her heartstrings.

Once the candy had cooled, Noelle went and got Lucas—helping with this part of the process, which involved shattering peppermint, was the thing he liked to do most. "Ready?" she said, slipping a pair of safety glasses on him and handing him a hammer.

He nodded with a smile.

"Okay. Go!"

Lucas lifted the hammer and banged it down onto the thick pastry bag full of peppermint. It had been Noelle's job as a kid and now it was her son's: smash the peppermint to smithereens so they could add it to the vanilla cake batter. The rest of the candy had been hand wrapped in clear cellophane and twisted at each end, then tied with tiny red-and-white striped bows for display around the cake.

It didn't matter if there weren't many customers this year; she was going to make the very best display to honor Gram and to celebrate the history of this bakery.

❄ ❄ ❄

Maybe they both had it in the back of their minds to outdo all of their Christmas displays with this one, but Noelle and Heidi had made way more cake batter and cookies than they'd needed for the window. They'd started making smaller peppermint present cakes the size of cupcakes and they'd been arranging them around the large one in the window, sprinkling cookies in the empty spots, but they still had an entire counter full.

"Has anyone taken treats to the bookshop this year?" Noelle asked Pop-pop.

He shook his head, his face dropping in thought, and she wondered if he felt like he should've. The problem was that they were all trying to keep up with the pace Gram had set, and it was quite a pace. Noelle didn't hold it against Pop-pop at all that he hadn't delivered any cookies.

Heidi smiled. "We should take them some."

"Is Santa there?" Lucas asked.

"I'm nearly certain," Noelle said. "Phoebe's helping him this year, remember?"

"Let's go then!" Heidi grabbed the delivery basket that they'd always used and began to fill it with the leftover cakes.

"Grab your coat, Lucas," Noelle said, as she helped Heidi put the last of the items into the basket. They'd placed the remaining cakes in individual boxes and the cookies were in small plastic bags. She sprinkled a few of the peppermint candies in as well.

"I'll get Lucas a hot chocolate for the walk," Pop-pop said. "It's cold out there. Supposed to snow soon."

When the basket was packed, Noelle zipped up Lucas's coat and wrapped his blue scarf around his neck while Pop-pop handed him the paper cup of hot chocolate. Then, they all headed down to the bookshop together.

The air smelled like snow and the woodstoves that were in the row homes on the next street over. The sky was an inky black, the stars hidden by cloud cover. Lucas paced along beside the adults, his little legs going as fast as they could, keeping up well, considering that he was holding his cup. His breath puffed out in front of him, the steam from the hot chocolate swirling up into the air in front of his little pink nose.

They entered, and Phoebe greeted them from across the shop in her Snow Queen get-up. "Hey!" she said, clacking down the hardwoods on her pearly heels. "What are you all doing here?"

Mr. Santori waved a white-gloved hand from his throne behind her. He'd combed his long silver hair straight like his beard, his velvet hat hanging on the back corner of his chair as if it was the most ordinary thing to be wearing that suit. He was so natural at playing Santa Claus that it made her almost believe Saint Nick could be real. Noelle smiled at his red-and-green striped socks peeking out from the white furry hems of his suit.

"We brought cookies for Christmas, and Lucas wanted to see Santa." She winked discreetly at Mr. Santori. "I'm surprised that it isn't busier on a weekend night." She looked around, a little worried—surely people would still make their way over to see Mr. Santori. He was a legend. But they were the only ones there.

The owner of the bookshop, Francis Evans, one of Gram's long-time friends, came out from behind one of the bookshelves. She was an older lady, her white hair pinned back in a jeweled clip, a silk scarf draped around her shoulders, always smiling. "Oh!" she said, shuffling over and wrapping her arms around Noelle. "It's so lovely to see you!" She pulled back to focus on her face.

She hugged Heidi next, the basket swinging at Heidi's side before she could pull it into view. "We brought cookies," she said with a grin.

Francis paused, her hand now on her chest and that familiar smile on her face. "Thank you," she said as she looked down at the basket. "Your gram would've been so happy." She fluttered her fingers in the air. "Wine! Let's have a toast. I have paper cups and a bottle in the fridge in the back—someone dropped it off as a gift. I'll just get us all some." Before anyone could say anything, she walked off toward the small cabinet visible through the door of the back room, with the mini fridge and the coffee maker, and pulled down the cups.

Mr. Santori had set down the book he was reading and called Lucas over onto his lap. Lucas crawled up and sat with him politely.

"What would you like for Christmas, young man?" Mr. Santori asked.

Lucas sat quietly, not answering, and all Noelle's insecurities came rushing in as she worried about what he was thinking. Lucas looked down at his cup, his little brows pulling together, his lips pursed.

When it was clear he wasn't going to answer, Mr. Santori leaned in gently, and offered to set the cup on the table for him. "There must be something," he said with a careful smile. Every year, Noelle braced herself for the Christmas list of all the expensive things his friends in school were getting, things she couldn't afford, but they never came. Lucas was very difficult to buy for at holidays because he never asked for anything. Noelle's family often teased that Lucas was just like her. It was difficult to buy for Noelle as well—she just couldn't fathom spending all that hard-earned money on herself—but she worried that it wasn't a genetic similarity at all and it was the fact that Lucas knew how she struggled financially. Growing up, her mother had been such a force of strength for her; Noelle had never worried about a thing because her mother could always provide for her. She feared that Lucas didn't have that same security.

Lucas shook his head. "I want..." He looked over at his mom.

"You can tell him," she encouraged her son. Even if it was something big, she'd charge it on her credit card if she had to. She'd do anything to give him the reassurance he needed that she had things under control.

Shyly, he said, "I want a house with my own room and a big family."

Noelle's heart sank. Francis stepped up beside her and handed her a cup of wine, concern on her face.

"But I'm not worried about it," Lucas added, his honesty commanding everyone's attention.

"You're not?" Mr. Santori said.

"No," Lucas said quietly, looking up at him. "My mom tells me that we'll always get what we need. But we have to make *all* the stops on the way to where we belong. That's how we get there. I don't want to ask for that stuff for Christmas because if I ask too soon, before we've made all our stops, I might not get it. So I'm just gonna wait."

Tears pricked Noelle's eyes and she took a sip of her wine to hide it.

"Your mom's a great mother, and you're a good boy, you know that?" Mr. Santori said, as Lucas hopped off his lap. "The most important thing is to have fun on all those stops." He looked up and winked at Noelle. "Thank you for coming to see me tonight. You made my evening."

"You're welcome, Santa."

"To family and great friends." Francis raised her cup. The others joined in, and despite the thoughts on Noelle's mind, the Christmas spirit was abuzz in the air.

❄ ❄ ❄

"How smokin' hot is he, actually?" Phoebe whispered, sitting cross-legged on the counter of the bookshop, her long Snow Queen dress cascading over her knees and floating above the floor. She held her half-empty paper cup in her lap.

"Pretty hot," Noelle said reluctantly. She didn't want to think about Alex.

Heidi had insisted on taking Lucas back to the bakery so Noelle could catch up with her friends, claiming she needed someone to taste-test her cookie recipe. Noelle wondered if her sister could sense the weight on her chest at Lucas's admission tonight. Heidi was always there to take care of her, and it would be good for Lucas to spend as much time in the bakery as he could. She wanted him to have those memories to draw from later, to tell him everything she could about Gram and his family, and for him to have a vivid picture in his mind of all that his grandparents had built.

Phoebe had called Jo after Francis and Mr. Santori had gone home for the night. Francis, having known Phoebe for years, asked Phoebe to lock up after them. Before she left, Francis had confided in Noelle that the bookshop wasn't doing well. Just like the bakery, there wasn't the same footfall of shoppers on the street anymore, and Alex had increased her rent too. Francis had said she was only trying to make it through the Christmas season and then, she'd consider closing, after forty-five years.

Phoebe leaned down the counter and grabbed the wine bottle, emptying the last bit into her cup before Jo opened the next one—she'd stopped to get some more on the way into town. "Does he eat on gold plates?"

Noelle rolled her eyes. "No. They're white and the utensils are silver. The food's pretty fancy, though."

"Did you have to wear a ball gown to dinner?" Jo teased.

Noelle laughed, tipping up her wine for another sip. "No, but I did dress up! I didn't know what to do. I made Lucas wear his vest. And when we got to dinner, Alex was in jeans."

"How did his butt look in those jeans?" Phoebe asked suggestively.

"I didn't look!" Noelle giggled. "But it doesn't matter. When it comes to Alex Harrington, I'm not worried about anything other than saving the bakery and making it profitable again."

Jo and Phoebe both became serious. "And how are you going to do that?" Jo asked.

"I have no idea."

"I can't believe him," Phoebe said. "You might have to move the bakery to LA like you promised." Phoebe raised her eyebrows up so high they caused creases on her forehead. Noelle knew that Phoebe always struggled if the conversation got too heavy. She never wanted to spend a lot of time on stressful situations, but she was always there for her friends.

"Let's not talk about it anymore," Noelle said. "I need cheering up."

"Okay. Guess what?" Phoebe waited dramatically until both Noelle and Jo were urging her to divulge whatever she had to say. "Do we all still have wine?" she asked, taking stock of each of the cups. "I got a call for an audition in person for the show! It's a primetime TV series. They want to see my chemistry with the lead." Phoebe balled her dress into her fists and squealed.

Noelle's mouth dropped open. This was huge. Phoebe had never been called back on something this substantial. It might just be her big break. Noelle grabbed her friend and pulled her into an enormous bear hug, Jo throwing her arms around them both. All three of them squeezed each other with excitement, and Noelle couldn't help but think of the last time they'd embraced like this before they'd all gone their separate ways after high school. They'd had their graduation caps and gowns on, diplomas in their hands, their whole lives ahead of them.

Noelle was the first to pull back. "Oh my gosh, Pheebs! That's amazing! Are you nervous?"

"I'm trying not to be. There's no sense in getting all worked up until something actually happens. The part isn't mine yet. Let me get it and then I'll be nervous. I'll be totally-freaking-out nervous!"

Jo poured herself more wine. "What did Paul say?"

There was an air of silence, bringing the level of excitement down to a steady buzz.

"I haven't told him."

Both Noelle and Jo froze in confusion. Why wouldn't she tell the guy she'd said she thought might be The One?

"What? Why?" Noelle asked.

"There's no sense worrying him until I get the part."

Noelle scrutinized her friend's comment. There was more to it than that. She knew Phoebe too well. "Wouldn't he want to take this journey with you? Even if you don't get the part, this is big, Phoebe. Don't you want him to be included?"

Phoebe fluffed out her dress, smoothing the creases, and shifted her weight on the counter. "If I get this, I'll have a huge decision to make." The elation had dropped from her face and a muted sort of panic replaced it. "He's built a life here. He has a chiropractic office that is doing amazingly well. His family is just down the street."

"Let him decide that," Jo said, turning her head to the side like she always did when she was listening.

Phoebe looked down at her cup. "I guess I'm afraid that if I get this, I'm going to lose him. We can't stay together when we're living on opposite sides of the country. I just don't want to face that until I have to."

"It's really great that you got the audition," Noelle said. "I think we should celebrate that tonight." She raised her cup. "To my talented friend. We all knew she was a star before anyone else."

Chapter Ten

Noelle sat in the sitting room of her suite, holding a coffee cup and saucer. She had struggled to go to sleep last night, and her eyes were aching.

She'd lain awake, thinking about what Lucas had said to Mr. Santori, and it was eating away at her. What if she couldn't ever give him what he wanted? Would he believe that he wasn't worthy of a good life in some way?

Noelle had thought about keeping Lucas with her, and taking him to school herself, but she was working and she didn't know if he'd get bored while he waited for her. So she'd taken him to her mother's early this morning. Now she just sat, thinking and having her coffee, wondering what to do with her life and feeling like she'd been lying to Lucas all along. Were these all stops on some big journey or just her floundering? If Phoebe seriously went to Los Angeles, maybe she should follow her. If she did, the loss of the bakery would leave a scar on her heart. But then, had she already lost it—was she fighting for something she'd never have anyway? Could she have a better life somehow if she just let go?

She finished her coffee and set out to check on William.

"Good morning," she said, letting herself into his suite.

"Morning." He sat on the sofa with his fingers wrapped around his cane as if he were waiting for a reason to get up. The fire was already lit, the lamps glowing in the early light. She went over to a small table at the side of the room and set down his pills and a glass of water.

"How did you sleep?" she asked, entering the bedroom and fluffing his pillows, leaning them against the headboard, and pulling his sheet and blankets up, smoothing them.

"I had a good night of sleep, thanks. How about you?" he called in to her. The rooms were close enough that she could hear him with no problem.

"I slept okay," she lied, pulling the drapes open. In the muted light coming through the window, she noticed something, stopping to take a look at it. Etched in the glass of the bedroom window were names: Phyllis, Georgia, Annabelle, Maxine, Victoria, Anne. "What is this?" she asked, running her fingers along the names, the glass bumpy under her touch.

She could hear William's movements and the tapping of his cane as he neared her, but she didn't take her eyes off the windowpane.

"I can't see what you're looking at," he said. He lowered himself onto the edge of the bed and placed both hands on his cane. "What is it you see?"

"There are names on this window."

"Ah." He took a moment before he explained, his thoughts seeming to get the better of him. She'd seen him do that before, and she wondered if there were more memories from this house affecting him than he let on. "The first owner of this property, Henry, proposed to a woman by the name of Anne. She was the daughter of a man well known for his tobacco fortune. Her father wouldn't allow Anne to marry Henry unless he could produce a ring worthy of marriage to his only daughter, so

Henry bought a four-carat diamond. The size was unheard of in those times. It was a square cut with smaller diamonds embedded in silver surrounding it, and the band was silver as well, with very distinctive hand-detailed leaves curling up toward the diamond. Engraved on the band was their married monogram: Harrington in the center, Henry's name on the left, and Anne's on the right—HHA. To prove to her father that it was, in fact, a real diamond, she wrote her name in the glass of this window while her father was staying in this room upon his visit to introduce his daughter. Marriages were still arranged at that time, you see. That ring was passed down through generations, and every woman who received it as her engagement ring etched her name in the glass. It became a tradition."

Noelle stared at the names carved into the wavy pane in front of her, amazed by the significance of them. They'd been there for so many years and yet they looked as though they'd just been written. "Wait," she said, pulling her eyes from them to focus on William. "Where's Elizabeth's name?"

He stood unsteadily. "Elizabeth wore a different ring," he said, almost sharply, as if she'd said something wrong. "The original engagement ring was lost, so the tradition ended with my mother Phyllis." He started toward the door.

"Oh, how awful." How could anyone lose a four-carat ring? "You don't think it was stolen, do you?" she called after him, and he turned around.

"No, it wasn't stolen," he huffed. "I know that for sure. But it's gone now, so that's the end of the story." He turned around and hobbled out of the room, but she noticed his hand was trembling on his cane again. "When you finish in there, I'd like you to help me bid on a few antiques," he said as he left. She could only imagine how disappointing it must have been for William not to have that ring to offer Elizabeth. His irritation was clear, but she wondered if it was also sadness. She could hardly imagine losing something valuable of Gram's; how must it feel to lose a family heirloom that special?

He didn't talk about the ring again, so Noelle didn't bring it up. It was clearly a sore subject. It was crazy that no one in the house had found it, which was why she'd wondered if it had been stolen. Perhaps it was lost outside the house? But then she supposed that enough time had gone by that it was gone forever, so best not to speak of it again, even though the thought of the ring had captured her imagination.

They returned to the sitting room. With a few clicks, she opened the Internet on William's laptop.

"I enjoy bidding on antiques," he said finally, settling in beside her. "It's a pastime I have. I try to fill the house with as much period furniture as possible. Elizabeth got me started by finding the first pieces and it became a hobby for us. I have to admit that my original delight wasn't finding good pieces; it was seeing the smile on her face when we had. I suppose I still look for pieces as a way to preserve that happiness Elizabeth had when we would shop for them together. It makes me feel whole." He cleared his throat. "While most of the interior is decorated with original pieces, some things got lost or damaged over the years so I like to try to keep the house as close to how Henry had imagined it for his bride."

"But you didn't live here..." she said, as more of a question for him. He seemed awfully interested in a house that he'd refused to live in.

"No, but this house is important to me. I adore it." With a deep breath, he said, "Elizabeth wanted me to live here. She begged me. But I told her that it was easier to work out of New York than it was Richmond, Virginia. There was nothing for me here."

"What about Alex? Where did he grow up?"

"He grew up here with his parents, and when they died suddenly—he was eleven—he stayed here with Elizabeth. When she was in New York, he had nannies."

Noelle would never allow Lucas to be raised by strangers half the year. The idea of this made her think back to Alex's expressions and how serious he sometimes was, and she felt like she could almost see that little boy he'd been. Had he been scared all by himself in this big house with no parents?

"What are you thinking about?" William asked.

She was taken off guard by his perceptive question. He seemed to know whenever something made her ponder.

"You need your medicine," she said, setting the laptop on the end table and standing up to change the subject. She didn't like having empathy for Alex because it made her want to put her arms around him and tell him it was all okay. His parents had been taken from him at a young age. Did he still ache for them?

She handed William his pills in a little paper cup along with a glass of water. "Can I ask you something?"

William swallowed the pills and held the water out for her to take it, the act of sitting seeming to be a chore in itself. "Sure," he said, the lines in his forehead pulling down with the furrowing of his brows.

"Why don't you and Alex get along?" She wanted a real answer to who Alex really was if she was ever going to understand him and change his mind about the bakery. William had shared a few things with her. Perhaps he'd share this.

William's gaze dropped down to his lap, and he didn't answer at first. Then, clearly after great thought, he said, "Some of it is my fault, but some of it is also his."

"Do you ever talk about things with him, tell him what bothers you?" She moved his cane from the sofa cushion where it rested, leaning it against the coffee table, and sat back down beside him.

William shook his head, annoyance showing in the way he pursed his lips. He didn't add anything further.

"I just hate to see trouble within a family. Family is all we have. My family is the great love of my life, and I wouldn't want anyone to miss out on that."

He smiled, his irritation dissipating. "You are so young," he said. "I've lived a long life and what I've found is that family isn't always picture perfect. Sometimes people get along famously and sometimes they don't. When I think of the great loves of my life, I can pull a handful of experiences out of my pocket, and few of them involve my family."

Noelle didn't have a clue how it would feel to not be close with her parents, to Pop-pop and Gram, to Heidi. The idea of being without everyone was terrifying. "Well, I'd consider Elizabeth to be your family since you married her, and she seems to be the love of your life."

"She is one of them, yes."

"Who are the others?"

"It isn't important," he said, leaning forward uncomfortably. "But here's what I'll tell you: you'll know the love of your life because you won't be able to get him out of your mind—family or not."

When he said it, Noelle's face flushed because she'd been thinking a whole lot about Lucas, but she'd also been thinking about Alex as well, so there was no way that statement could be true.

"Who do you think about?" she asked instead.

"I don't allow myself to think about anyone anymore." He coughed in that way of his that told her the emotion was welling up. "Now, could you please help me get to my feet? I'm tired and I'd like to lie down."

"I'll just sit out here once you're asleep, if that's okay—in case you need anything."

He nodded but it seemed as though he were just appeasing her.

While he slept, Noelle unpacked the rest of his suitcase, which was still sitting on the floor, as best she could and put it all into drawers, piled up the laundry she could find in the bathroom for housekeeping, cleared his dishes from his breakfast, and tidied up his suite.

❄ ❄ ❄

By lunchtime, William was still napping and Noelle was lost in her thoughts. She walked the long corridors toward the kitchen, barely noticing anything until she came to Alex's office, where what she saw on his desk from the doorway caused her to stop.

There was a shopping bag that hadn't been there, and two very expensive-looking cameras. Then, she noticed something brightly colored, nestled in the bookshelves among all the brown and black books. It looked out of place and she didn't remember seeing it before. Upon walking in, she saw a few more, so she went up to one and pulled it off the shelf. It was a children's novel about dinosaurs. She ran her fingers along the bright green lettering, remembering the delight Alex had when he'd said those bookcases were shelves of "nothing much." She slid the book back into its spot.

"Hi," Noelle heard from behind her.

She spun around, facing Alex.

"You're back?" she said, surprised to see him. He was looking at her the way he had the other night and she got a glimpse in her mind's eye of his lips as they came so close to hers. It clouded her judgment for a second.

He walked in and picked up one of the cameras, fiddling with it. "I found these at a shop when I was in New York yesterday," he said, looking as though he'd just told her a secret. He lifted one up, turning the focus on it, pointing it toward the large half-circle of windows at the back of the office. They were enormous, spanning two floors and overlooking the grounds that were a lush green despite the winter cold and the overcast sky. In front of the glass sat an exquisite telescope—its brass and wood had to be as old as the home.

He took a picture, the contraption looking comfortable in his hands, and held it out to show her the digital screen on the back. The shot he'd just taken with hardly a thought was gorgeous—the bookshelves framing the window with the shadow of the telescope slightly off center to reveal a magnificent tree just past it. She hadn't noticed it before. She looked over his shoulder to see if she could view it from where she was, and sure enough, it was there. "That's amazing," she said.

"It's a good camera, isn't it?"

"I was talking about the shot, not the quality of the camera."

He looked up from the screen and smiled tenderly. "Thank you."

She remembered the photos that William had shown her, suddenly speculating… "Those photos in the hallway—the black and whites—did you take them?"

"Yes."

"Oh my God, Alex. They're amazing. You're so talented. The one of your grandmother is beautiful."

Unexpectedly, a different emotion washed over his face. The mention of his grandmother obviously took him off guard. He looked vulnerable.

Noelle knew what that kind of love and loss was like. She felt it every day for Gram. She missed her so much that she could hardly stand it. She used to have difficulty even going into the bakery, but after the initial grief had gone, she realized that staying away from it was the wrong thing to do. Being there made Noelle feel closer to her. Alex should be with his grandmother. "You love her."

"Yes," he said, setting the camera down as if the weight of it was too much all of a sudden.

She came closer and looked up into his eyes. "I'm sorry," she said, feeling heartbroken for him, and for just a second it seemed like he might put his arms around her. Then, shaking his head as if to release the ache in his heart, he walked to a bookshelf and took one of the brightly colored books from it. She wished that he'd confided in her, but he'd cut the conversation off right away, and closed up. It made her feel like any spark they may have had was more one-sided and she wanted to kick herself for letting her guard down again.

"I thought Lucas would like this," he said, his eyes on her, but that affection he'd had was now more neutral. "I bought a few genres." He pointed way up the ladder and she spotted yet another, catching a rare glimpse of the winter sun through the stained-glass dome in the ceiling.

"Why?" she asked defensively, his thoughtfulness confusing her. He couldn't do this with Lucas: just turn his emotion on and off like he was doing with her. Lucas's happiness wasn't a game or something Alex could be involved in when he got bored. Lucas was one of the loves of her life, as she'd tried to explain to William, and she didn't want him to get his little spirit broken.

"Why *not*? He told me he only owns one book. I wanted him to have more. He's a bright boy, Noelle. He deserves to have all the books he can get his hands on."

"Well, it's just that you've known him for a matter of minutes; I've known him his whole life. I know what he needs." She said the words but there was a little prick of fear in her stomach that, after seeing how Lucas had reacted to Alex, she might not know what he needed and that she hadn't picked up on it before. She squared her shoulders to hide her insecurity.

Alex regarded her curiously. "Something else is going on. You seem… preoccupied. Upset," he said slowly. "What is it?"

"Nothing." She wanted to leave before she made a fool of herself by saying something she shouldn't, but she'd have to walk past him to get to the door, so she stayed put.

"Is this about…?"

His gaze flickered down to her lips and then back up to her eyes. He took a step toward her and she froze, unable to process her thoughts. He was so difficult to figure out.

"Have you had lunch?" he asked.

She shook her head.

"Follow me."

As if pulled by some sort of force that was stronger than her will, she followed him.

They walked to the family dining area and he offered her a seat. Then he left the room quickly, returning right away. "I'm having the chef make us a quick bite to eat," he said. "How's lentil soup and grilled cheese-and-tomato sandwiches?"

"That actually sounds delicious," she said, glad she could recognize the fare.

"I don't have a lot of time. I've got a meeting, but you look different today. Something is bothering you. Has my grandfather said anything to upset you?" He pulled out a chair for her.

"No," she said, sitting down, leaning on the table and then remembering her manners and sitting back up. "Why don't you get along with him? He seems like a very nice man."

He pulled his chair up beside her and blew air through his lips. "Well, he isn't."

"He told me about your grandmother," she said.

Alex sat up. "What about her?"

"That she has Alzheimer's and she's in a home."

"Yeah..." His words trailed off and he broke eye contact.

She decided to press him. Normally, she wouldn't dare put her boss in such a position, but he'd nearly kissed her, he was buying gifts for Lucas... "He said he can't go see her because it's too painful."

"No," he snapped, his gaze back on her. "He *won't* go see her. Because he doesn't care. He never has."

"Is this why you don't like him? Because it seems to me like it's just a misunderstanding and it can be worked out. He said he's heartbroken over it."

"Just like you told me with Lucas: you've known him minutes, Noelle. You don't have the whole story."

"Then tell me." Why had she just said that? He'd told her he was busy and he didn't have a lot of time. Not to mention that she didn't need to get any more buried in this family's issues because the more she did, the more she started to care, and she shouldn't allow herself to care about Alex Harrington. By his reaction the situation might be even more complicated than she'd thought. And after the way he'd been in his office when his grandmother had come up, she doubted he'd open up anyway. But there was a pull, an energy beyond her that made her want to know. She couldn't define it, but she could feel it.

Alex rubbed his temples in frustration and then looked at her, and the honesty in his eyes took her by surprise. She couldn't wait to hear what he was going to say. "My grandmother was the only person in the world that I loved."

Their lunches were set down in front of them, Alex thanking the servers before they exited quietly.

"He never loved her," Alex blurted angrily, noticeably surprising himself. It was as if his resentment had gotten the better of him and years of pushing it down came bubbling up the moment someone gave him permission to say what he felt. But, despite his initial hesitation, he continued, "She should be loved. She's the best person I've ever known. He doesn't deserve her."

Noelle was so confused. Neither Alex nor William was being made out to be the person she witnessed. She didn't know what to believe. "How do you know he didn't love her?" she asked.

His eyes grew dark, intense. "Because he loved someone else. She told me. It haunted my grandmother her entire adult life."

His statement was so matter-of-fact that Noelle believed him right away. Her pulse in her ears, she stared at her steaming soup, heat crawling up her body. She'd nearly forced him to tell her this terribly personal information, and now she remembered William saying that he had other loves of his life. Never before had she willingly dug up old family baggage, and she hadn't meant to now. She'd just been trying to get William and Alex to understand each other.

"Don't let him convince you that he's some kind of saint just because he's hobbling around, sorry for himself. He doesn't love anybody in this family," Alex said, placing his spoon in his soup. "He never loved his wife; he never had time for my father either and my father, in turn, didn't have a lot of time for me because that's how he was raised. And I felt it. Every day I felt that void. My parents died in a plane crash when I was eleven. That's a tough age to deal with that kind of loss all alone. All I wanted was for my grandfather to tell me he understood, but that conversation never came. In fact, he was absent, refusing to come back from New York. He's always hated this house. Perhaps it was because we were all here. Even before my parents died, my grandmother listened to my fears, to my confusion, to everything I felt. The rest of the time, I was alone."

Noelle saw the raw honesty in his face and she completely trusted that he was being truthful. He wasn't trying to charm her; he was letting her in. She felt an ache for the idea of Alex, at such a young age, growing up by himself. What a sad and lonely existence. Without even a thought, she moved into his space and he turned to face her. The attraction she felt toward him was stronger than her will, and she put her hands on his face and looked into his eyes.

There it was—that look that she saw glimpses of, that look that could melt her heart: it was the look of the vulnerable little boy that he once was, and the tenderness in his heart swelling up. Before she could process anything else, his lips were on hers, and it was as if they were meant to be there, as if she'd been waiting her whole life to feel this. They were a perfect fit, their movements effortless and exhilarating, his breath mixing with hers, the warmth of his mouth, the taste of his lips...

He pulled back, clearly as shocked by it all as she was.

She scrambled to get the moment back. "Do you have to go to your meeting? Stay."

The corners of his mouth turned up. "Yes, I have to go." It was clear to her that he wasn't thinking about his meeting, yet he'd said he had to leave.

Noelle tried not to let her disappointment show.

"But I'll find you right after."

Chapter Eleven

Noelle opened the door to her suite to find Jim standing in her doorway.

"Mr. Harrington would like you to meet him in his office. He said to bring your coat and scarf," Jim told her.

"Did he give a reason? Should I take anything else with me?"

"He didn't say, ma'am."

"Okay, thank you."

She'd just finished helping William get to the dining area to have a snack. She'd assisted him with a crossword puzzle while he ate, but then William had told her that he planned to have a cup of tea and he'd be happy to find his way back to his room on his own. The slow walk would do him some good, he'd said. And if he needed help, Jim was there to take him back. She'd tried to explain to him that she was here for this particular reason, but he'd shooed her off, telling her he wanted to be alone while he had his tea. She was torn between needing to do her job—the nature of which she still wasn't entirely clear on, as she'd never received a formal job description—and treating him like anyone else she knew, allowing him space when he politely asked for it.

With a quick check of her makeup, she ran a comb through her hair, grabbed her coat, scarf, and gloves, and headed toward the office. When she got there, Alex was in jeans again, wearing a coat, and smiling that smile of his.

"Busy?" he asked.

Unsure how to answer, she said, "I'm working today, but I'm not busy at the moment. William wanted to be alone."

"I told Jim to take care of my grandfather for the next few hours. He likes Jim. You and I have a working date."

"We do?"

"Yep. Follow me."

He led her to the front door and opened it to reveal the most gorgeous charcoal-gray Audi S8 that she'd ever seen. Even in this winter weather, it was sleek and shiny like he'd just driven it off the lot. When they got to it, he opened her door and she slid into the leather interior, the surface so soft that it felt like she was sitting on a bed of satin. The console rivaled NASA's mission control, a navigation screen set for a destination she didn't recognize. Alex got in and started the engine, the car barely making a sound as he put it in gear and sailed off like he was floating instead of rolling on four tires.

"Where are we going?" she asked, noticing how the car must be temperature controlled because she wasn't the least bit chilly, despite the fact that snow was looming in the forecast.

"I want to show you something. I hope you like champagne."

"I do," she said curiously, "but I don't usually drink while I'm working."

"Well, we haven't done anything quite like we usually would, have we?"

She thought back to that kiss and smiled as she looked out the window, trying to hide her elation at his comment. She didn't want to feel like she was feeling; it didn't make things easy, given her situation, but she couldn't deny her emotions. She wouldn't admit to herself that she hadn't asked him about the bakery or let herself think of how he'd ruined it, because then the magic between them would be gone. It was selfish of her, but she just wanted to enjoy herself and this man for a little while. When she was with him, she had fun, and it had been a long time since she'd had feelings like these.

They were quiet as they headed toward their destination, the anticipation nearly killing her. Alex had turned on some music that hummed low in the background as the car swooshed around corners and slid down the road effortlessly. Finally, Alex pulled up outside the city's arena, where Noelle had watched football games and concerts, and put the car in park. It was an enormous indoor facility; it could easily hold twenty thousand people. The parking lot was empty.

Alex walked around to Noelle's side of the car, opening her door. Then he led her to the entrance, where a man greeted him by name and let them in. They were ushered up to one of the VIP press boxes. Inside, a single table was positioned near the window, overlooking the center of the arena. It was empty, a white circle of nothing surrounded by a sea of empty seats below them. She lowered herself down into one of the chairs, Alex sitting across from her. Positioned in front of them were two flutes of champagne and in between, a small platter of cheeses and crackers. His eyes were on her, almost delighting in her confusion.

Suddenly, Christmas music played through the speakers in the room and the lights dimmed. The arena was completely dark with the exception of a single white beam of light at the edge of that empty circle. Then, appearing as if by magic, there was a flash of sparkling red, the scraping of ice skates, and Noelle realized that she was watching a skater on ice.

"That's Melissa Simone, the Olympic ice skater," he explained. "We have exclusive seats to watch her dress rehearsal for tonight's performance of *Winter on Ice*. They prepared a table just for us—we're the only two in the city who get to see it." The woman stopped and waved in their direction before turning and spinning away, gliding gloriously across the ice. Suddenly, she was twirling so fast that she was a blur of sparkles, the music rising to a crescendo and then subsiding. Their press box was close enough that Noelle could see the shavings of ice shooting out from the woman's skates. "How did you manage to organize this?"

"I own the building."

Noelle let that sink in. This wasn't some little bakery or coffee shop. This was a state-of-the-art, multi-million-dollar facility. And he had ownership of it. The words had rolled off his tongue as if it were nothing at all. The scope of this gave her pause and she looked back at the skater. He'd probably made one call and this whole thing was put together immediately. "Do people always entertain you at your whim like this?" she asked. She was willing to bet that they did.

He looked amused, unconcerned by her question. "If I ask, those who work for me do, yes."

"Is that what *I'm* doing now—entertaining you?"

He sobered, and she worried she'd been a little too direct with her line of questioning, but that was the only way she knew to be. It was important he understand that she wasn't going to play around. If he was interested in knowing her better, then fine, but he wasn't going to take her out just to pass the time.

"I wanted to do something nice for you," he said, making her feel like the worst person in the world. "I don't know about your other employers, but I don't usually go around kissing my staff." He rested his forearm on the table casually, as if they were talking about the weather.

Noelle looked out at the skater again as she did a triple turn on one skate, her right leg bent at the knee, her arms in the air above her like a ballerina. When Noelle turned back toward Alex, he was watching her.

"This is amazing. Thank you," she said, feeling uneasy in this new and unusual territory. "I'm just not used to this sort of thing."

The corners of his mouth turned upward in that way of his, fondness in his stare. "What, people being nice to you?"

"No, people arranging previews of sold-out shows for me."

He put his chin in his hand, leaning in with a look as if he couldn't get enough of her, making her feel lightheaded, all the thoughts whooshing out as if they'd been blown by a mental windstorm.

"It's how I show you that you're important to me," he said.

Was she important to him, or was he playing games with her? She didn't want to think that way, but his relationship with his grandfather came to mind, and she had no other explanation. She hadn't said anything, but she could tell he was reading her thoughts.

Alex rolled his eyes playfully. "For whatever reason, you believe that you shouldn't receive attention when you're pretty fantastic. I wanted you to feel that today, so I planned this for you." He took her hands, the music making this all seem like some sort of dream.

"That's very sweet of you to say, but I feel like I don't know you at all," she said.

"What do you want to know?" He leaned across the table toward her, those lips just inches from hers.

"Tell me what you loved about your grandmother," she said, almost breathlessly. She didn't want to turn the conversation to William and sour what was there between them, but perhaps knowing more of Alex's side of things would help her understand if she was making incorrect judgments about him. Maybe she was just wishfully hoping that she and her family were wrong about him, that he was some sort of wonderful person who cared.

His hands moved around to her wrist and then back to her palms where their fingers intertwined. He invaded the last bit of space they had, only the table between them, the spicy smell of him overwhelming her as their movements flowed like wine, perfectly in sync, like coming home.

"She used to sing to me at bedtime," he said. "When I was eleven and far too old for it. I'd roll my eyes, trying not to smile at her, but what I refused to admit was that I loved it. She made me feel cared for, and when she sang to me, it was her way of showing affection, so I soaked it in."

The Christmas song that had been coming through the speakers died down and then there was silence. Alex looked down at her almost giddily. She felt it too, tingling down her spine, making her limbs feel like they couldn't work, causing her to question everything she'd ever done that she thought had made her happy before. Nothing, apart from having Lucas, had felt like this.

"She had so much love to give. Now I think back on those times and wish I'd told her how great she was instead of brushing her singing off like it was a little joke. I should've told her that I'd never forget it. She was alone like I was, and she understood. That was why we were so close, I think."

"But she had William."

"No, she didn't. She spent almost her whole life here raising my father and then me, while my grandfather stayed in New York, only coming back on the odd day. She confided in me once when I was about eighteen that she always felt like she'd done something wrong, and she warned me to make sure that when I found the person I loved, I should let her know how special she was every single day. She was wracked with insecurity about it. She said that she should've known when my grandfather proposed. He couldn't even find the family ring. It had been passed down for generations to the women in the family, and left for him, and he couldn't even keep up with it. He lost it before the proposal."

"*He* lost it?"

"Yes. Once the next-generation Harrington is of marrying age, the ring is passed to him, and a new ring is given to the current ring-holder as a gift, always on the wedding anniversary. My grandfather was given the ring for safekeeping. It's never surfaced. He bought my grandmother a ring, and it was beautiful, but she always wondered if his decision to marry her had been because of pressure from the family instead of love, otherwise he would've guarded the family ring with his life. She worried that he might actually have it and had been saving that ring for someone else. She was a little superstitious about it. It was known that all of the marriages in this house were happy ones. My grandparents never lived together here, nor did they share the ring that the others did. If he was saving it for someone else, or if someone else has it, I'd never forgive either of them."

"Maybe he actually lost it. And maybe it really had been an accident. He didn't seem like he was hiding anything. He really loved her, from what I can tell."

"Well, actions speak louder than words, and he wasn't here very much to prove her wrong." He lifted his champagne, clearly halting the conversation. "We always get caught up in my family when we're together. Let's not do that," he said with a smile. "Let's just talk about us."

She lifted her flute from the table.

"To Christmas," he said with a smile. "And all the surprises it brings. You are a surprise that I'd never expected. I'm so glad you're here. Cheers."

They touched glasses and she turned her attention back to the skater, who'd begun the next routine, trying to keep her excitement at bay. The way his gaze had landed on her made her hands begin to tremble, and if she hadn't turned away, she knew that she'd have rattled her glass onto the table, so she put it in her lap and focused on the performance.

"Are you enjoying the show?"

She nodded, daring to look back at him. With an inhale of breath, she'd steadied herself enough to make eye contact.

"What kinds of things do you like to do?"

She nibbled a cracker before responding, assessing the things she did for fun and wondering what he'd think. But then again, what did it matter what he thought? If he really liked being with her, he'd like doing the things she did, right? "Well, my favorite thing to do is karaoke with my friends Phoebe and Jo. I bring down the house with my impression of Beyoncé singing 'All the Single Ladies.'"

That curiosity that made her stomach do a jig bubbled up. From the way his eyes creased at the edges she could tell he liked her answer.

"I've never done karaoke," he admitted.

"You haven't? Why not?"

He laughed. "I suppose I just haven't had the right person ask me."

"Is that a dare?" His laughter always put her at ease.

"Are you inviting me?" He uttered the question with a challenging undertone.

"It sounds like you'd like to be invited. You must really want to unleash your inner rock star. Go on, you can admit it."

He chuckled, obviously delighting in her banter. "Let me know the next time you go and I'll be there. I wouldn't miss your Beyoncé routine for anything in the world."

The rest of the afternoon went just like that: they shared a few laughs and were able to be completely honest with each other, and she couldn't have had a better time.

Chapter Twelve

"What did you think?" Noelle asked Lucas as he wiggled in the auditorium chair, the seat bottom popping up behind him. Phoebe had given them two tickets to her children's theater production of *The Princess and the Pea*. Phoebe was the princess.

Lucas smiled, the half-empty bucket of popcorn still in his lap.

"Phoebe said we could go backstage if you want to. Once everyone's cleared out, the crew will show you how the stage lighting works. How does that sound?"

Lucas nodded, getting up, the seat springing to a close, and gave her the popcorn bucket. Noelle grabbed their coats and handed Lucas his. Then she snagged a piece of popcorn as she led the way backstage.

Phoebe was still in her princess dress, this one green with a cream-lace trim and matching stockings. She was sitting on a stool, her back to the lighted makeup mirror, a smile on her face. "Hi!" she said, pushing her ringlets away from her face. Noelle offered her the bucket of popcorn and Phoebe plunged her hand in, grabbing a few pieces. "Lucas, how was the show?" She popped the pieces into her mouth, chewing with a smile.

"Good," he said, raising his eyebrows.

"Want to meet the stage crew?"

Lucas nodded, following Phoebe as she took him by the hand. She introduced him to a few of the guys, who led him over to a large panel of switches and levers.

"How's the new job?" she asked after returning to Noelle, pulling the clip out of her hair and running her fingers through her red curls. She then pulled it all up into her fist and wrapped a band round it, her usual after-show bun.

Noelle hoped Phoebe didn't see her flush. She wasn't ready to tell her that she'd kissed Alex Harrington. "Weird," Noelle said instead, and made a face. *Focus on the job.* "I don't know what to do with William Harrington. It's a little like being a babysitter." She remembered William's own words when she'd met him. "I told him I'd run his errands, I clean up after him, I make sure he has his meals and his medicine, and I help him with crossword puzzles and his hobby buying antiques. But I feel like I could be doing so much more."

"Sounds like a great job to me. He could be awful or gross or something."

"I'm here!" Jo said, clicking in on her heels and taking her coat off with a flourish. She set it on another stool and then unwound her scarf. "Sorry I couldn't make the show—meeting." She made a face.

"Well, you aren't five, so you didn't miss much," Phoebe said with a grin. "Noelle was filling me in on working at the Harrington mansion. She says it's weird."

Jo pulled a chair over from one of the tables at the side and sat down, leaning forward, concern on her face. "Weird?"

Noelle glanced over at Lucas, who was sending beams of red light across the stage under the direction of one of the crewmembers. She rubbed her face. "I don't feel like looking after someone is the right job for me." She didn't even want to think about William and Alex and how they were making absolutely no sense, the two of them contradicting each other, making it more uncomfortable, or the unexpected chemistry she and Alex now had…

"You've barely been there any time," Jo said.

"I just always thought I'd end up at the bakery, you know?"

Phoebe frowned, her bottom lip protruding in a pout to show her concern, Jo nodding in understanding.

"I don't really know where I'm going anymore and I'm worried that I'm setting a terrible example for Lucas." She felt the lump in her throat as she said his name.

"You don't have to know where you're going all the time," Phoebe said, scooting closer to her in a show of support. "Look at me! You think I want to play the Snow Queen at Christmas and work in the children's theater all my life? I have big dreams of getting that great part, and I know that I'm living in the wrong place to get it. I don't know where I belong either. But I do know that, as you always say, the *stops along the way* are pretty great. Quit worrying so much."

"Give it a chance," Jo said tenderly.

"Maybe you're right." She mustered up her courage and looked both her friends in the eyes one at a time, her hands beginning to sweat. She knew they could read her and she was about to drop a bomb on them. "This is about more than the job," she said, her heart starting to hammer in her chest.

"Whaaaat," Phoebe whined dramatically. "You're killing me with that face. What is it?"

Noelle swallowed and took in a steadying breath. "He kissed me," she said quietly, throwing a quick glance over to Lucas. He was busy, listening to one of the crew as he pulled the velvet curtain on the side with the long cord that stretched to the ceiling.

Jo's eyes nearly popped out of her head and Phoebe fell over backwards, catching herself on the lighted makeup table.

"Twice."

"Oh my God!" Jo squealed, slapping a hand over her mouth. "How in the world did you manage that?"

"I have no idea." And truthfully, she didn't. It had all happened so fast. But as she looked at her friends' stunned faces, it became real. "And now I'm totally confused because the Alex that my father and Pop-pop described isn't the Alex that I've gotten to know. I'm not sure Alex has connected me to the bakery either." And by letting Alex into her personal life, she was also letting him into Lucas's, and that was bigger than just a few dates. Lucas really liked him. If and when they broke things off, Lucas might not forgive her.

"So what happens now?" Phoebe asked.

"Um…" She was still thinking, scrambling for some way for all of this to make sense. "I guess I take it one day at a time. Speaking of one day at a time, he wants to come to Wednesday Night Karaoke." She made a face.

"Oh my God!" Phoebe shrieked, silencing Lucas and the men. They all looked their way until she waved a dismissive hand.

"We don't have to do it this Wednesday," she said. Having a guy meet her friends wasn't something she would usually do unless things got serious. And their relationship wasn't significant enough yet. How would she ever explain it to her father? For that matter, she didn't know how to explain it to herself. She knew she was letting her heart guide her when she should be thinking with her head. How were her feelings for Alex honoring her gram? She already knew the answer: they weren't at all. But maybe she should stop overthinking things and just go with it, like her friends had said.

"You're telling me that I have a chance to see Alexander Harrington sing karaoke and you want me to wait? Are you kidding me? Happy hour starts at five. You all can meet me at the bar!"

❄ ❄ ❄

"Hi, Alex!" Lucas said, walking quickly over to him with a grin as they entered the house. The sun had gone down hours ago, the cloud-covered sky now an inky black. The chandeliers in the grand entranceway sent shimmers across the shiny floors.

Noelle hurried after Lucas, worried, by the swiftness of Alex's clip as he was walking by, that he had something to do. Lucas was a few paces ahead of her, going full speed, and she had to suppress the panic that her son actually liked this man. Why did she and Lucas have to connect with Alex like this? How could she ever have in their lives the man who took Gram's bakery? It would always come back to that. After agreeing to let him meet her friends, she'd been beating herself up about it the whole ride there.

"Hi, Lucas," he said, stopping and flashing those perfectly white teeth at him.

He turned to Noelle. "How was the play?"

"It was good." She didn't elaborate, as she risked mentioning that Phoebe was already planning karaoke.

"Did your mom show you my office?" he said to Lucas. "There's something new on the shelves." Alex raised his eyebrows in anticipation, for Lucas's benefit, making her feel sick to her stomach. She was uneasy at the way he could get her attention, and it was even worse how he could command her son's. And now he was going to look like the hero because he had money to throw around, buying all those books. She needed to face it: When the excitement wore off, where would they be? She couldn't compete with all this.

"I'm heading there now. Come with me."

"I'd like to check on William," she said, hoping Alex would take her suggestion that they do it another time.

"Oh, he can spare five minutes, I'm sure. Jim just told me he got him a glass of brandy. He's reading to him in his room."

Noelle pressed her lips together to keep from pleading. After all, Alex was the one paying her, so she shouldn't argue with him. She wanted to tell him to be careful with Lucas because he was a quiet boy already and he didn't need any disappointments drawing him further inward. And she knew that if she was feeling this way for him, she could only imagine what Lucas felt. She didn't even want to think about how it would feel when Alex moved to New York. She was already trying to put that idea out of her mind.

Alex tousled Lucas's hair and led him down the hallway, Noelle walking up beside them. When they entered his office, Lucas ran in, immediately noticing the additions to the shelves of old books. With a look back at Alex, he pulled one off the shelf and inspected the cover, excitement showing on his face. She knew that kind of excitement. She felt it when Alex did something nice for her too.

"I've seen this book!" he said, turning it over in his little hand, concentration taking over his features. "It was at the book fair at school." The book fair where he hadn't bought anything. The book fair that she'd had to ask him to browse for his Christmas list because she didn't have enough cash to send to school with him.

"Look up," Alex said, alight watching Lucas's reaction.

Noelle was still processing when she realized that Lucas had climbed the ladder and was pulling another book from the shelves. He grinned down at Alex before something caught his eye.

"What's that?" Lucas asked, pointing toward the telescope.

"Come here and I'll show you," Alex said, walking over.

Lucas climbed down the ladder and joined him. If Noelle squinted, their bodies looked like silhouettes as they inspected the telescope. She came closer.

"This was my great-grandfather's," Alex said. "It's difficult right now with all the winter clouds, but when the stars come out at night, you can see the constellations through it. You can even see the craters on the moon. It was the best of its kind in his day. You can get them a lot smaller now."

Deep down, buried where no one could ever see it, was the tiny wish that Lucas could have a father figure in his life who could do this very thing: tap into his interests, share his time with him, make Lucas feel special. He had her dad and Pop-pop, but there was something magical about having a father, someone to wake up to every morning, who could talk to him over breakfast and read stories with him at night before bedtime. She was doing her very best, and she didn't let that wish enter her mind often, but it was always there, lurking, troubling her.

"We should probably see William," she suggested. She'd been gone all afternoon and, while she'd been given the afternoon and evening off, she didn't want to leave him all by himself for so long. She also knew she was trying to get Lucas away from Alex before he could get too invested, but she was worried that she couldn't keep Lucas away forever if they lived and worked there. She thought again about her friends' faces and letting Alex into Lucas's life, and she was beginning to wonder if she'd made a mistake getting involved with Alex. She'd have to just take it one day at a time, like she'd said.

"All right," Alex said. "We can't see anything right now anyway. I'll show you the moon one night when the sky is clear."

Reluctantly, his focus still on the telescope, Lucas followed his mother out of the office and Alex sat down at his desk. Her mind whirring with thoughts, she hurried Lucas down the hallway.

"You finally get to meet William," she said. "I think you'll like him." She knocked on the door to William's suite to announce their presence before opening the door.

Lucas didn't respond, his attention on the book he was still holding. He must have realized she'd spoken because he looked up blankly to acknowledge her. Noelle smiled at him. Alex had made Lucas happy today, and she was thankful for that.

"Who do we have here? I see an outline of a child," William said, teetering over on his cane to meet them as they entered. Lucas's eyes were on the handle of William's cane—an ornate ball of silver and gold with stones set into the surface of it.

"This is my son, Lucas," she said, ushering him forward. "He's looking at the handle of your cane. I hadn't noticed it before. It's beautiful."

William lifted his cane up, catching it in the middle and tipping the end of it toward them so they could get a better view. "This handle was made sometime before eighteen ninety-nine—we aren't sure of the exact date. It's French. It's been passed down in our family for generations and I have a special cane-maker who added it to the top of this cane."

Lucas reached out and ran his finger over it, clearly captivated.

William squinted toward Lucas. "Are you holding something? What do you have there?"

"It's a book Alex got me."

William's eyebrows shot up, surprised. "Oh?"

"I like Alex. He's really nice," Lucas continued.

"Is he?" William's interest was unmistakable. "How is he nice?"

Lucas looked up at him. "He talks about things I like. He knows about dinosaurs."

"Ha! Does he?" William laughed despite himself.

"Did you teach him about dinosaurs?"

William sobered, leaning back on his cane. "No, I didn't, I'm afraid," he said, some sort of thought swimming around his face—regret? Sadness?

"I wonder how he knows so much, then."

"He's a very smart man. He went to all the best schools and he studied really hard. Do you like school?" He slowly led the way over to the sitting area.

"Yes," Lucas replied, not very convincingly.

William must have noticed Lucas's polite but not believable answer. He sat down and patted the sofa next to him. Lucas joined him, his little feet dangling above the floor. "If you could change school, how would you change it?"

Most kids would've said to add more play time or only do drawing all day, but Lucas said, "I'd have more exciting things."

"Like what?"

"Math is really easy for me. I already know how to do it. I want to learn the kind that the big kids do. And I want to do their projects. One of the tables down the hall had volcanoes that really erupted and models of the ocean floor—I want to do that."

Lucas had never told Noelle any of this.

William smiled knowingly. "I understand why you like Alex now; thank you for explaining it to me. I think he was probably a lot like you as a boy." He looked up toward Noelle to let her know he was speaking to her. "Alex stood apart from the others as a boy, and he still stands apart now. Even though he has his eye on business most of the time, he notices things, he takes in what's around him. For that, I'm grateful."

Lucas had started reading his book, lost in the pages. Noelle smiled at him and then turned her attention back to William.

"I wasn't good at showing how I felt about people. I'm still not great at it. But he is. I heard about your outing today. I pried it out of Jim," he said with a smile. "Alex doesn't let many people in, Noelle. And I've never seen him go to lengths like that for anyone."

She nodded, feeling more unsure of what to do next by the minute.

Chapter Thirteen

Noelle had driven Lucas to her mother's for school, wishing she could talk about Alex with someone. Her friends were too blinded by his money and good looks to think clearly. But she was finding it difficult to slow her feelings for him for other reasons. She'd fallen asleep last night thinking about how William had found similarities in Alex and Lucas, the idea of this thrilling her. She'd never thought in a million years she'd find someone as perfect as Alex was for Lucas. But in the light of morning, she could easily see the facts: she didn't need a karaoke date with Alex. She needed Gram's bakery. However, it was getting increasingly challenging to keep herself from falling for him.

After returning to the mansion, she decided to call Pop-pop. She needed to hear a friendly voice, and to run her feelings by someone close to the bakery. She wasn't ready yet to tell her parents about her feelings for Alex—she'd opened her mouth to say something twice when she'd dropped Lucas off, both times quieted by fear. But Pop-pop would lend a listening ear. Gram used to say she'd told him all her secrets and she knew he was The One because he'd always been there for her, listened to her.

"Do you think Alex Harrington is a bad guy?" she asked him with no warning, after a few minutes of chatting. She'd always confided in Gram before, so telling Pop-pop was new. She trusted Gram, and knew that if Gram could talk to him, then Noelle could too. She'd just never told him her inner troubles before like she had Gram.

"Why do you ask?"

Her hands shook as she mustered the courage to explain. "I like him," she said simply. "The more I get to know him, the more I like him and it's confusing me." It was all coming out and the pressure was lifting with every word she uttered. "He's kind to Lucas and…me. I really like being around him."

The silence buzzed in her ear, and just when she'd felt a release from getting it off her chest, the lack of response from Pop-pop seized her up again. Finally, he said, "Noelle, be careful."

She wanted to ask why, but she already knew why—she'd known all along; she just didn't want to admit it to herself. Disappointment sank deep into her stomach. Noelle had hoped that Pop-pop would hear her out, tell her that weirder things had happened, and make her feel okay about the feelings she was having. If anyone would see past the situation and think objectively, it was him—Gram had said so herself, and Noelle had seen him listen to Gram. They were like magic together. He always kept a level head, and Noelle could count on him for his honesty. "Okay," she said in surrender, putting her face in her hands.

"It's just—"

"I know," she cut him off. It all came back to his actions regarding the bakery. "I'm glad I called, Pop-pop. I just needed to hear your warning to use caution."

After she hung up with Pop-pop, Noelle poured a cup of coffee for herself and some tea for William before entering his room, trying to clear her head of the back and forth. She was fighting what she knew about Alex and she concluded that she needed to just face it: being with him wasn't possible, so she needed to get over it. Quietly, she set the cups down on the table in the sitting room.

"Good morning," William said, hobbling in on his cane.

"Good morning," she returned. "I wasn't sure if you were awake yet. I brought tea."

"Excellent." He smiled, putting her racing mind at ease. "Now you're making yourself useful," he teased. He'd warmed up to her and she was glad for that.

As he sat down, however, she noticed that he was still wearing the sweater he'd had on yesterday. Come to think of it, he was also wearing the same top, and trousers.

"What?" he said defensively, lowering himself down slowly. He could always sense her thoughts as if he were somehow in tune with her movements. She realized then that her silence had caused his question.

"I was just looking at your clothes," she said carefully.

"Can't a man wear what's comfortable?" He seemed to already know her concern, clearly overly sensitive about it, making her wonder.

"Of course you can. It's your house. You can wear whatever you want."

He ran his hand down his chest as if he were smoothing out wrinkles.

"Did you sleep in that outfit?" she asked.

He pursed his lips; the jovial look had now vanished.

"You know I'm here to help you. I'm getting paid to do it. If you need something, just tell me. I'm all yours." She got up and walked into the closet that was the size of her old apartment, thinking she was going to encounter the rest of his suitcases. She'd only put a few things in drawers, and she hadn't been in here. But as she stood, looking in, she was speechless. There were walls of shelving at least ten feet high with hanging pressed shirts, folded sweaters, slacks, dress suits—more clothes than a clothing store. There was no way he could see enough to get any of it down. She came back out.

"Is all that yours?"

"Yes," he said, knowing already where she'd gone. "I had it moved prior to my arrival, and I've just used the suitcase of clothes the last few days or so."

She'd thought she'd been so helpful unpacking for him and tidying up his room when really someone else had done all this for him. Why was she even here? The truth of the matter was that William had everything he needed—except a person to listen. He didn't have anyone to be with him, to make sure he was okay, and to talk to him. He had so much to say about his wife, about his life, and his thoughts regarding Alex, yet there was no one to hear the stories.

Noelle wanted to listen because she knew how important it was to have someone to talk to. Without Gram, over the last year, she'd struggled to find that perfect person to confide in, but she still had a wonderful network of people who cared about her. Whom did William have? The only family she knew that he had were Alex and Elizabeth. While getting William to open up to Alex would be a tough sell, she wondered if perhaps he'd actually enjoy talking to Elizabeth. But first, she had to get him dressed.

"Is there some reason that you have more clothes than Saks Fifth Avenue but you're choosing to wear the same outfit to bed?"

After a long pause, he looked down in defeat. "My back is hurting me, and I'm having trouble lifting this arm." He rubbed his right shoulder. "I couldn't get my sweater off."

It occurred to her that a man of his wealth and stature probably wasn't used to having to ask for help in this way, and perhaps that was why he'd been resistant to the idea. "That's all it is? Well, let me help you get it off."

He nodded. "When my eyesight first started to go, Elizabeth helped me. Now I just try to do it on my own, but it's getting harder," he worried aloud. "I miss her."

"I was just thinking about her," she said. "I liked the story you told me about the notes she'd leave on your pillow. Did you keep them?" They walked into the closet together as she guided him.

With a heavy sigh, he said, "I didn't. I feel terribly guilty about that."

"Don't feel guilty. Not everyone keeps those kinds of things. How about tan trousers and a button-down shirt?" she asked, tugging on a shirt to view the color.

"Sure. And I don't feel guilty just because I didn't keep them. I feel guilty because I thought enough to keep letters from someone else, but not from her, and it haunts me now."

"Someone else?" She turned around. He looked lost in his memories, so she walked with him back into the bedroom, the outfit hanging from her fingers. Once she had it all laid out on the bed, she had him hold out his left arm and she pulled his sleeve. When she'd gotten both arms out, she lifted it up over his head and lumped it on the bed.

William began to unbutton his shirt while she got the new one off the hanger. When he slipped it off, Noelle gasped before she could catch herself. He had an enormous scar running the length of his shoulder. His clouded eyes met hers, and she could tell he felt exposed.

"What happened?" she asked, her voice gentle, completely forgetting her other question.

He reached out and took the new shirt, slipping his left arm in. She helped him get his right arm through the sleeve and he buttoned it up. "I was hit by a car."

"Oh my gosh! When?"

"I was nineteen." He smiled an uncomfortable smile. "Coincidentally, it has a lot to do with the three letters I'd kept." His expression turned downward with the heaviness of his thoughts. "They're hidden away, but this will always remind me." He placed his hand on his shoulder.

She stretched his sweater over his head, working on his right arm. "How did it happen?"

"How about I tell you over tea?"

"Certainly," she said.

"Will you open the drawer of my nightstand? The letters are in there. I'd like you to read them to me. While we're reading, I'll tell you the story."

When William was dressed and silver pots of fresh coffee and tea were delivered on a matching tray with a single rose in a vase and two cups and saucers, Noelle sat down to hear William's story, with the letters in her lap.

William insisted on handing her coffee to her, the cup rattling in its saucer as he held it out. She added cream and sugar, stirring it with a delicate spoon.

He left his cup sitting and ran his hands along his thighs, pressing his lips together as if he were deciding where to begin his story. Then he looked up and said, "I used to pass this little café in town. It was a lovely spot with outdoor tables and a blue-and-green striped awning over the door. Every day I passed it and I never went in. I just wanted to see the girl who sat at the table outside with her croissant and coffee, reading her book. She had wavy dark hair that fell just above her shoulders, the sides pinned up in little clips. On cold days she sat inside but always right at the window, as if she were just waiting to get back out into the sunshine."

Noelle was mesmerized by the way William's face lit up when he spoke about this woman, and she couldn't wait to hear what he said next.

"I wanted to talk to her so badly, but I didn't know just how to do it, and I wanted to get it right because she was the most beautiful girl I'd ever seen, so I started buying a cup of tea and bringing my own book every day. I sat on the other side of the café and read."

"Did she notice you?" Noelle asked, already dying to know the answer.

His cheeks wrinkled with happiness as he thought of the answer. "If she did, she didn't let on. One day, I finally mustered up the courage and sat down at the table next to her. I started talking to her—about the weather, our coffee, her book, anything I could think of to have her eyes on me. I was nervous, and I remember keeping my hands in my lap to hide it. After a few minutes I said, 'I won't keep you. I have to leave anyway.'" He smiled, almost laughing. "Her face fell into the most adorable frown and she said, 'Oh. I thought you could stay. I'd like to keep talking… since I don't have anything else to do.' She said it in the sweetest teasing voice, the kind that made me think she did that a lot. Then she offered a little smile and my heart melted right there."

Noelle couldn't move a muscle, her mind abuzz, speculating how in the world this wonderful story could end with that nasty scar on his shoulder. She sipped her coffee, utterly enthralled. "Did you stay?"

"Of course I stayed!" He laughed again. "We talked about everything under the sun, but I have to admit that some of the time I was lost in my own thoughts, wondering how I'd gotten so lucky to have met her. I came back to meet her every single morning after that."

"What happened then?"

"It was a whirlwind. We took trips to the beach for the day, we rode horses through the countryside, we drank wine together in a family friend's vineyard. We shared secrets and opinions—and she was opinionated! But she was so careful with her words that I almost felt like I'd side with her in an argument even if my beliefs differed. I completely fell in love with her. But I had to leave her." He cleared his throat the way he did, emotion rising.

"Why did you have to leave her?"

He drew in a breath, the lines in his face showing years of emotion. "My father heard about us and he told me I was forbidden to see her anymore. She wasn't the pedigree he was looking for in a daughter-in-law."

"Pedigree?"

"Family lines, you see."

"You mean she didn't have money."

"Yes. I wasn't allowed to go back to that café."

Noelle needn't try to draw any conclusions because she already knew how that applied to her own situation; it was now very clear. Any affection Alex had shown her would never amount to anything because when it came down to it, she wasn't in his league. While it had loitered in the back of her mind, it was now emblazoned on her consciousness. She wondered if William was sharing this with her as a warning.

"Open the first letter," he said, tearing her away from her thoughts. "Would you read it to me?"

She refocused on the paper in the delicate pink envelope, tugging on it until it slid out and gently straightening it. She turned it over in her hand. The handwriting was an old-fashioned, curly script.

"There's no name on it," she noted.

"Yes. We couldn't risk putting names since my father wouldn't allow us to see each other. I caught her once quickly to tell her that if she wanted to get in touch with me she could leave a letter behind a loose brick on the property wall, where I would return the correspondence."

"What was her name?"

William looked at Noelle, climbing out of his memories. "I've never mentioned her name to anyone. While I don't mind sharing her story, I feel very strongly about respecting her privacy. I don't know if she'd told anyone about me. She's from this area so I'd hate to give her secret away to someone by accident…"

Noelle didn't know a soul in his age range that would have a story like this, but she respected his wishes. "Of course." She nodded. Then she looked down at the letter as he urged her to read it.

"*I feel that I can tell you anything, so I hope to share my deepest thoughts in these letters, so you will always know how you've touched me. I'm heartbroken. I've lost all hope without you. I go to the café and sit, staring at my book but unable to read the pages. The words just cloud within my tears. I yearn to have your company and I feel lost. I never felt alone before meeting you but now my heart aches with emptiness. I'm not telling you all this to make you feel awful. I just want you to know how much you mean to me.*"

William sniffled and Noelle looked up. "Wow," she said, folding the note and placing it back into the envelope. Noelle had never said anything like that to anyone, and she suddenly felt the weight of such a great love lost. What would this woman's life have been had she married William? Would he have run away to New York all the time like he had while married to Elizabeth? Or would he have stayed?

"You can see why I saved it," he said. "I'd never known another person who held me up as high as she did. From the moment I met her, she thought I walked on water, and when I was in her presence, she made me feel like I could." He rubbed his chest just above his heart, where the scar from his shoulder ended.

"So how did you get that scar?" she asked, his gesture jogging her memory. She'd been so caught up in the love these two had that she'd almost forgotten about the scar she'd just seen. It was as if their love could fill a room without either of them even there—the vastness of it like nothing she'd ever seen before. She'd had glimpses of it by watching Gram and Pop-pop together, but this really affected her. It resonated with her. Perhaps it was because she knew that it didn't have a happy ending. Like an explosion, it plumed, consuming everything around it, only to dissipate into nothing, leaving wreckage in its path.

"After her last letter, I'd secretly planned to meet her at the café. I had to see her. I was running late and I'd just arrived. She'd thought I'd stood her up. I saw her a few paces ahead of me, starting to leave, her back to me; she stepped into the road… The car was flying, literally flying, toward her. I called her name but she didn't hear me."

"Oh my God. What happened?"

"I ran—sprinted—toward her and reached her just in time, pushing her to the sidewalk, but the car hit me instead."

She gasped, clapping her hand over her mouth, the coffee cup in her lap tipping. She got herself together and steadied it.

"That was the last time I saw her at that café. My father knew where I'd been by the location of the accident and he refused all visitors. She'd followed the ambulance that she'd called to the hospital, and she'd stayed with me until my father arrived. Once he'd cut off visitation, she was gone. And while I was recuperating, he forbade me to see her again and if I did, he'd withhold my inheritance and I'd have nothing. I was young and scared. I didn't know how I'd manage the lifestyle I was used to without the money. It took me years to realize that money didn't matter." He sat up, moving as if his back were giving him trouble again. "You know, that café is gone now. It was bulldozed about twenty years ago to make room for an automotive shop. I saved one of the napkins that had the name printed on it. I keep a piece of it folded in my wallet. I don't know why."

"Maybe because it's a symbol of life—how it moves, how you were saved that day, how you saved someone else."

He smiled. "Maybe. I went on to love again, so my heart, too, was saved."

"So what happened to the woman?"

"I saw her once more after that, but I'll tell you about it another time if that's okay. I'm getting tired."

"It's clear by looking at you that reliving those memories has exhausted you," she said, wishing he'd share more, but understanding why he couldn't.

"It's not just the memories," he said. "I carry the guilt of loving my wife and wanting to be everything to her, while having that kind of first love unfinished in the back of my mind. You know, I didn't save those letters because I was emotionally unfaithful to Elizabeth. I saved them because that other woman made me feel alive, like I was a better person than I am, and every time I read them, I am reminded of who she thought I was. That is what exhausts me."

Chapter Fourteen

"Come on, Noelle!" Phoebe pleaded. Phoebe and Jo had met Noelle to do a little Christmas shopping since they had less than a month until Christmas—all three of them taking the day off. Noelle had wanted to pick up some things for Lucas, and with her new paycheck on the way, she was thrilled to finally be able to buy him things that were actually on his list. She put them on her charge card without a second thought.

"We'll never get this chance again," Phoebe continued, as she ducked through a tunnel in the enormous Christmas tree set in the center of the mall for shoppers to pass through. Its lights sparkled against the gray sky. Phoebe popped out of the other side, meeting Jo and Noelle, who'd walked around the tree. "When will we run into Alexander Harrington or, much less, hear him sing karaoke?" she pressed her friend, boring into Noelle with her stare. "I think he isn't really that hot, and you're just trying to hide it."

Jo laughed, peering into the window of a homeware shop, its display full of cotton snow, and red-and-silver packages surrounding a few choice pieces of furniture.

"I talked to Charlie," Phoebe said, her eyes round as if this one statement would tell them both everything she was thinking. Charlie was the owner of the karaoke bar, aptly named "Charlie's," and a great friend of Phoebe's. "He said if we could get Alexander Harrington to walk through his doors, drinks were on him for the first hour. That will save me at least fifty dollars."

"Good grief! How many drinks do you buy in an hour?" Jo said, coming up between them and throwing one arm around Phoebe's shoulder and the other around Noelle's, her small shopping bags dangling from each wrist.

"I'm trying to get my money's worth. It's not often that we get free drinks." She leaned in toward her friend. "Noelle, if you don't say you'll invite him, I'll never forgive you." Phoebe offered her best sad-puppy-dog face.

"Fine," Noelle said, trying to hide her grin.

"Are you going to get Alex anything for Christmas?" Jo asked.

"I probably should. I've always gotten my bosses presents in the past." But buying him a present would be difficult because they'd been so intimate with each other. Suddenly, she wanted to know what he liked to eat, how long he could read before he got tired, whether he matched his socks to his trousers or his shoes...

They stopped to watch a boys' choir singing "Carol of the Bells," their voices sailing into the cloud-filled sky, their hands wrapped around shiny brass bells that would ring in perfect time to their song. The whole time, Noelle thought about the Harrington family. It was just the two of them in such a big house with no other family and Elizabeth all by herself in that home. She just couldn't stand by and let their Christmas go on like it was.

"Do you know who I should get a present for?" she asked. "Come with me. I need your help."

❄ ❄ ❄

Jim met Noelle at the gates of the property just as she'd asked him to do, driving the family's black Mercedes. "Thank you for coming out here," she said, standing in front of her little car, a spruce tree tied to the top of it. It had taken her, Phoebe, and Jo to get the tree up there and she'd driven at a snail's pace all the way back to the mansion, praying they'd secured it well enough. Jim, who was outside his car as well, the engine still purring, eyed it with a puzzled look.

"It's for William's suite," she explained. "He doesn't have a tree."

"Miss Parker, we would've been more than happy to place a tree in his suite for him should he have requested it."

"Well, that's just it: he hasn't requested anything. He doesn't know I've bought him one. I want to surprise him." She reached into the back. "I've even got the biggest Christmas lights I could find so, hopefully, he'll be able to see the outline of the light a little bit. And the spruce smell is incredible." She tugged on a shopping bag, dragging it across her backseat. "I also got peppermint candles."

Jim raised an eyebrow.

"I'm going to sprinkle a little Christmas spirit over him. Now, I need you to distract him."

❄ ❄ ❄

"Noelle," William said, as he and Jim came down the hallway together toward her. "I'm so glad you're here. A dealer told me that there's an antiques auction online that's starting in twenty minutes, and I'll need your help to bid on a few things. There's a Queen Anne table I'm dying to get my hands on."

"No problem," she said, with a wink at Jim. "I wanted to show you something in your suite anyway." She took William's arm, her gesture dismissing Jim, and led William down the hallway.

"You're excited," he noticed, to her amusement.

"How can you tell?" She smiled at him, giddy with the idea of what he was about to encounter in his room.

"Your voice is unusually bubbly."

"I'm always this excited to give you your heart medicine," she teased. Then she laughed at his face, his lips set in a look of mock annoyance. "I have something to show you."

She opened the door to his suite and he immediately stopped and pointed to the corner. "What in the world is that?" he asked, heading that way, his cane rapping along in front of him.

"It's a Christmas tree."

He reached the tree and extended his hand, touching the lights. "I can see them," he said with a smile. "And if I can see the lights, they're probably enormous and gaudy."

She laughed. "Yes. They are."

He faced her. "Thank you for thinking of me, but why would you get a tree for my suite when I've told you that I don't need one?"

"Because you do need one. You need to celebrate Christmas. And that takes a little planning sometimes. Think about the best plan you've ever made for Christmas. Have you ever wanted to do something huge for someone just to show you care?"

He didn't answer, and she wondered if he hadn't ever done anything for anyone, but then he sat down on the sofa and beckoned her over, as he said, "I have a secret."

"Oh?" She sat down beside him.

"Remember those letters I'd had you start reading? I'd like you to get the purple envelope, please."

She got up and went into his bedroom, opened the drawer in the nightstand, and retrieved the purple envelope as instructed. When she returned, she found him twisted around, looking toward the tree. "That was the kindest gesture anyone has ever made for me," he said, as she sat down again.

"I just thought you needed a little Christmas spirit."

He smiled. "It did something to me because I feel like I need to share this secret with you, and I've never shared it with another soul in this house."

"Wow. I'm honored." She set the letter in her lap and focused on his hands, which were shaking again.

"I need you to keep this a secret," he said, his voice low. "But I know I can trust you. You have an honest, caring way about you that's undeniable."

"Of course."

"You asked me if I'd ever made a huge plan at Christmas…" He turned away from her and it seemed as though he was upset with himself. "I did something that I've regretted my entire adult life. That loose brick in the wall that surrounds the property… After she wrote me, and I left my response behind the brick, I knew she'd check again." He shook his head. "Even now I can't believe what I did."

"What?" The suspense was killing her.

"I didn't lose my mother's ring—the family diamond. I put it in the wall behind the loose brick. In a moment of blind love and weakness, I told the woman from the café that I would never love anyone as much as I loved her and if we couldn't be together, I wanted her to have the ring. It was Christmas and I wanted so badly to show her how I felt about her. It was the most reckless thing I've ever done."

"Oh my gosh." Elizabeth's hunch was right. Noelle felt the weight of this secret already because Alex had said if William had given it to someone else, he'd never forgive either of them.

"Yes. 'Oh my gosh,' indeed. She tried to refuse it, leaving it with a letter, but I responded and said that if she didn't take it, I'd leave it there behind that loose brick forever, so she'd better take care of it for me. I never told her it was in our family for generations. I didn't want to put that kind of pressure on her. I only told her it meant everything to me, just as she did."

"Does she still have it?"

"I have no idea."

"We could get it back from her!"

"It's hers. I gave it to her." He fluttered his fingers in the air. "Read the letter," he said.

With a steadying breath, Noelle opened the envelope and peered down at that looping handwriting.

"*My dearest, I cannot accept a gift of this magnitude. However, I do feel the love you share by giving me this ring. I will protect it as you wish as a symbol of my own devotion to the feelings I have for you, but please know that I am only the guardian of it and if you ever want it, I will return it to you. It is in safe hands until then.*"

"Why didn't you get it back when you met Elizabeth?" she asked.

He closed his eyes. "I hate to admit this, but I was afraid to see the woman again, to see the love again in her eyes, or worse, the judgment that I'd chosen my inheritance over love. She held me in such high regard that, either way, it would kill me. Even after I married Elizabeth, I couldn't bear to be here for fear that I might run into her, so I stayed away. Elizabeth begged me to leave New York and live here, but I thought if I worked myself to death that eventually she'd give in and leave this house behind. I loved my wife so much that I wanted to give her all of me, so in a very unhealthy way, by staying away from here, I was trying to give myself wholly to her."

Noelle slipped the note back into the envelope and took his shaking hand. The trembling was worse than she'd ever seen it. "In the end," she said carefully, "it was just a ring. It can't go with us when we're gone. But love can. You were very kind to show that woman the depth of your feelings. But now, you need to show Elizabeth. Remember those notes she left on your pillow? She missed you. She probably misses you now. You should see her."

He was quiet, obviously thinking. He closed his eyes again. "I'm exhausted. I think I'd like to rest now."

She nodded and then left him with his thoughts.

Chapter Fifteen

It might be nice to do a little karaoke to take my mind off things, Noelle thought as she climbed into Alex's car. To appease Phoebe, who'd blown up her phone all evening, she'd asked him if he wanted to go, and right away, he'd agreed. Phoebe had squealed like a schoolgirl when Noelle had told her he was coming. Then she made both Phoebe and Jo promise not to bring up the bakery tonight. It was neither the time nor the place, and she just wanted to enjoy herself.

"Will I meet your friend Phoebe?" he asked, glancing over with a grin as he pulled the car around the half-circle drive toward the road. "That should be entertaining. I can't wait."

Trying not to let herself break out into a rash of hives at the sight of his smile, she turned and looked out the window. She'd already decided that tonight would be about her and her friends, like it always was, and if he wanted to tag along, that was fine. It would give Phoebe something to talk about for the next five years at least.

The rest of the journey was quiet, the seat warmers keeping the chill off her as the car glided down the wet roads, a mist in the air, teasing them, dangling the opportunity for a white Christmas in front of them but not allowing them to have it until Mother Nature was good and ready.

They parked the car, Alex opening Noelle's door for her, helping her over a puddle and onto the curb outside Charlie's. She spotted Phoebe and Jo's cars in the lot, a prickle of anxiety crawling down her limbs as Alex took her hand and led her to the door.

When they entered, Phoebe waved from the bar, her eyes as round as saucers, but she seemed to be trying to hide the expression with an enormous, open-mouthed smile. She got up to meet them, tugging on Jo's sleeve and bumping her drink.

Noelle led Alex through the dark room, the karaoke stage illuminated with blue-and-white lights, a few tables of people holding cocktails and bottles of beer, the music pounding in their ears. "Hi," she said loudly over the music when she reached them. "This is Alex Harrington. Alex, this is Phoebe and that's Jo."

He shook their hands. "Nice to meet you both," he said, stepping toward them to ensure they could hear him.

They settled into their little spot at the bar. Charlie was madly wiping it as if he could somehow buff the finish into gold.

"Want a drink?" Phoebe asked as she stared at him, star-struck. "What do you like?"

"What do you suggest?" he asked, his brows pulled together as if he'd just asked a nuclear physicist her views on particle physics, his face serious and focused on her, clearly trying to be polite.

The corner of Phoebe's mouth twitched just slightly and she raised an eyebrow to Charlie, who was gawking at them while wiping a glass with a towel. He set it down, popped the top off a bottle of Budweiser, and slid it down the bar toward Alex. "We wouldn't want you to stand out," Phoebe said, with a smirk toward Noelle.

"I'll have the same," Noelle said quickly, feeling protective of Alex all of a sudden. He could've dismissed her and Lucas when he'd met them, but, no matter what was happening with the bakery, he'd been kind to them, and she wanted to make sure her friends were kind as well. He wasn't just some hot local celebrity with a lot of money; she was starting to believe he really was a decent person.

Charlie slid another bottle of Budweiser Noelle's way.

"Shall we find a table?" Alex asked, handing Noelle her beer.

She turned toward the now-crowded room; the only open spot was directly in front of a large table full of squealing girls, obviously there for a birthday party. The birthday girl was wearing a shirt covered in candies. Noelle thought back to the date Alex had planned at the arena, watching the ice skater, and insecurity swelled within her. She wanted to show him a good time, and this was a lot of fun for her. She just hoped he'd like it as much as she did.

They made their way over to the table, the mass of girls quieting just slightly to pose for photos. One of them had a camera with a large flash and a zoom lens. Noelle noticed Alex's interest immediately.

"Would you like me to snap a few photos of everyone?" he asked them, setting his beer on the table beside Noelle's.

The girls giggled, clearly having already had plenty to drink. The one with the camera handed it over to him.

"Why don't you lean your forearm on the table," he said to the birthday girl. "The rest of you, come around on either side." He leaned in and scooted a few of the newer drinks into the shot and slid one of the brightly colored presents into view. "That's great," he said, his eyes already behind the camera as he viewed the shot. "On three: one, two, three." He snapped the picture. "I'll just get a few other things for you." He took a couple of stills at attractive angles of martini glasses, the presents, a pink boa hanging from one of the chairs, the girls together in pairs, and the stage. Then he turned the camera around and showed them. Their reactions were similar to Noelle's when she'd seen the photo he'd taken in his office that day. The girls gasped, thrilled with his work.

Noelle liked watching his thoughtfulness. She enjoyed seeing him delight in taking the photos. There was nothing in it for him, and he certainly wasn't trying to win anyone over. He just saw an opportunity to do something nice and he did it. Exactly as he had with Lucas. She pulled her eyes from him, focusing on the tiny silver Christmas tree on stage, trying to calm the excitement in her chest.

"Are you a photographer?" one of the girls asked, swirling her drink with the little straw that had come with it.

"No." He handed the camera back to its owner.

"You should be!" the birthday girl said. "You're amazing at it!"

Clearly, they were just tipsy enough that they didn't seem intimidated by the fact that they were talking to Alexander Harrington. Noelle couldn't help but laugh.

"I got our names in early," Phoebe said, pointing to a large screen with the list of singers in order of performance.

Noelle was up next with… Her mouth hung open. "Phoebe, I always do Beyoncé!" She blinked to try to clear her vision just in case she wasn't reading it correctly. "Does that say 'Let's Get it On' by Marvin Gaye?"

Alex laughed, nearly choking on his beer. When he'd recovered, he said, with fondness in his expression, his gaze lingering on her, that adorable smile on his lips, "I think you should do it."

For an instant, she was paralyzed until she realized he meant that she should sing the song, not get it on. She tipped her beer up and drained it.

"*I'll* do it," he said, challenge in his eyes.

All three ladies stared at him, speechless.

He turned around and raised a finger to Charlie, who appeared at their table as if he'd been drawn over by some invisible magnetic pull.

"I'd like a shot of tequila and two more beers, please," Alex told him. "You two ladies okay for drinks?"

Phoebe and Jo, still silent, nodded, their drinks full in front of them.

"Great. Thank you so much. What do I owe you?"

"The first hour is on me," Charlie said.

"How kind of you." Alex reached into his back pocket and retrieved his wallet, pulling out a credit card. He held it up with two fingers. "After that, put the rest for this table on a tab and I'll pick up the total."

Charlie hurried away and, with lightning speed, returned with the shot and two beers. Alex downed the tequila in one swig, tapping the shot glass on the table as he set it down. "There's one catch," he said, turning to Noelle. "You've got to go up there with me."

It was already their turn.

He got up and held his hand out to Noelle. Reluctantly, she took it and they climbed the stage stairs. The white spotlight shone directly on them and, to her surprise, he ran back down the stairs, asking a group of people at the front if he could take an empty chair from one of the tables. He set it on the stage and offered it to Noelle as he took hold of the microphone. She sat down, her heart hammering.

The beat started and Alex zeroed in on the lyrics running across the screen. His voice poured through the microphone; he was a beat ahead and off key but he put everything into it, serenading Noelle as if he were Marvin Gaye himself. She threw her head back and laughed as he walked around her, dragging his finger along her shoulders. Phoebe stood up and whooped. Jo had her hands over her mouth, and Noelle could tell she was laughing. Noelle didn't notice his bad singing or the other people in that room. What she did notice was that he was letting her know that it was all okay, that he could do this world too, and while it made her relax a little, it clouded her judgment even more. When she was with him, he made her forget about everything else. She was trying to hold back her feelings, but in the short time they'd had together, she was already falling completely for Alex Harrington.

Chapter Sixteen

"Mom's crying," Heidi told Noelle on the phone as she walked out of her suite to get a cup of coffee. Her sister had called ridiculously early, before the sun had even risen.

Noelle had been out with her friends far longer than she'd planned, so Lucas had stayed at her parents' house. Her head was pounding when she'd woken up, her mouth dry, but she'd had one of the best nights of her life. Alex had been fantastic, and they'd all talked and sung songs until Charlie had literally turned the lights off on them. Gram had always given Noelle a cup of vanilla coffee to help her clear her head after nights like that and now she had a lot on her mind, so she hoped it would help.

"She's awake at this hour?"

"Yes. She's upset with Dad. I think we should go over there to be with her."

Noelle tiptoed down the hallway, worried about being on her phone in the echoing corridors. The house was so large she felt as if she was in public—it was like a really quiet shopping mall. "I know he's been upset with all that's been going on." She walked into the kitchen.

"I've never seen Mom like this, Noelle."

"Are you okay?" she heard a voice say from behind her, making her jump.

The phone still to her ear, she faced Alex. "You scared me."

He was up early, already wearing a casual sweater—gray with little flecks of colonial blue in it.

"Sorry," he said, so many thoughts behind those gorgeous eyes. "I couldn't fall back asleep this morning." He smiled just a little, and she wondered if he'd had as much fun as she'd had last night.

Heidi was still talking through the phone, confused and asking how she'd scared her, so Noelle stopped her for just a minute and looked back at Alex. "It's my sister," she said, holding out the phone and wiggling it in the air. "She says my mother needs us."

Alex had a folded newspaper in his hand. He set it on the counter and walked closer, looking down on her with concern. "Melinda's on vacation and I've let Jim off for the day… I can check on my grandfather and take care of his needs once he's up until you get back. How long do you think you'll be?"

"Oh, I wouldn't ever ask you to do that."

"Why not?" His face was kind as he waited for an answer. The lamp on the side table and the light above the restaurant-sized stove were on, giving his skin a warm tone.

"I wouldn't want to put you out."

"You won't. I don't mind at all."

"Oh my gosh!" came a squeal from her phone. *"Is that Alex Harrington?!"* Noelle put the phone under her arm and pressed it to her body to mute her sister, her cheeks burning. She really needed to keep her phone away from Alex. Why did everyone lose their mind around him? When she looked up, all she saw was *him*. The real man. Nothing else.

"Go," he said with a smirk, having obviously heard her sister. "It's really fine."

With relief, and a little bit against her better judgment, she put the phone to her ear. "I'm on my way," she said, and then hung up. With a promise to be lightning fast, she headed out of the kitchen to get herself ready.

❄ ❄ ❄

When Noelle arrived, the whole house was lit up for Christmas, in the dim light of morning, giving her a nostalgic feeling. She sat in her car under the gray sky to take it all in. The white lights on the railings of the front porch were glowing, the candles on in the windows, a wreath made from fresh spruce they'd gotten at the Christmas tree stand in town hanging on the door. Gram had taught them how to make wreaths, and they'd continued the tradition every year. Her mother always got up first thing in the morning and turned all the lights on. They stayed on until they all went to bed. Even though she was upset now, her mother had still turned them on.

Heidi waved from the living room window so Noelle got out of the car, and went inside. Her mother was sitting at the kitchen table with a box of tissues, but, for Lucas's benefit, she'd clearly been trying to hide the fact that she'd been crying. She brightened at the sight of Noelle. Noelle came in and hugged Lucas, who was up despite the early hour.

"I woke him up pacing around," her mother said.

Noelle nodded supportively. "Did you have fun last night?" she asked Lucas. Now that they were living in the area again, her mom had made it a plan to have movie night once a week with Lucas. Since he was staying over, last night had been movie night. When Noelle had called to check on him, her mother had told her they'd popped popcorn, eaten Christmas cookies, and drunk hot chocolate until their bellies hurt.

"Yeah. We watched *Toy Story* and it was lots of fun." He got up and took his cereal bowl to the sink.

"Lucas, if you're done with breakfast, and you aren't sleepy, your grandpa's got the model trains set up in the spare room upstairs if you'd like to go take a look?" her mother said. "We never got to them last night with the movie and everything."

He immediately ran out of the room, Muffy barking behind him. Noelle sat down beside her mom, Heidi on the other side.

"What's happened?" she asked, as she shrugged off her coat and hung it on her chair.

"He just blew up over nothing this morning, when we both woke up because it was so cold. It was the upstairs heating unit, but you'd think it was the end of the world," her mother sniffled, tears brimming in her eyes. "Luckily Lucas didn't hear. Gus has been on edge so much lately that I feel like I'm walking on eggshells around him, trying not to upset him. I'm so anxious because of it that I snapped and told him I couldn't do it anymore. He has to figure out how to handle all this."

Noelle shot a look over at Heidi, but she knew what her mother had meant by *all this*. Their father was having difficulty accepting the closure of the bakery—he didn't like to see his mother's hard work disappear any more than Noelle did and she was certain he worried about Pop-pop. Suddenly, the finality of the situation came crashing down. Noelle trusted her father, and she knew his instincts. Normally calm and collected in times of stress, if he was losing it, that meant that he thought there was no other way.

"I'm sorry, Mom," she said. "We'll figure it out." Noelle put her arms around her mother and gave her a squeeze.

"Losing the bakery is tearing us apart," her mother said, her voice breaking. "I just wish your father could be stronger, but he's too emotionally connected. I think the guilt of losing it is too much for him. If only he could see that it isn't his fault. We're all in this together."

"We'll get through it," Noelle said, but she wondered how. The reality of it all made her feel like she was drowning suddenly, like she'd been terrible for enjoying herself with Alex when, because of him, she was losing the most important thing her gram had ever built.

Noelle drove back to the mansion in complete silence. Lucas had fallen asleep on the backseat and she was glad for that. Her thoughts swung around in her head, making her stomach hurt. She didn't want to have to face Alex when she returned because she couldn't make small talk after seeing her mother like that, but she was too tired to jump into a long discussion. Her own tears welled up as she ached for Gram and the life they'd had before all this mess. Her fears over the bakery, her feelings for Alex, and her future were definitely getting the better of her.

Choking back her emotion, she parked the car and got out, helping Lucas across the icy driveway. She tipped her head back to see a hazy mist still dancing across the gray sky—and then a tiny break in the clouds. With a deep sigh, she went inside the Harrington mansion, Lucas running ahead as she hung back. She stood in that enormous expanse of an entryway and caught her breath. Then, with resolve, she stood up straight and headed out to find Alex. She'd decided. She'd just go into his office, let him know she had returned and was available for William, thank him for giving her time to see her mother, and quietly leave him alone. Then she'd deal with the conversation she'd been avoiding when she had a clear head. She was too emotional to say anything now. She needed to get her plan of how to save the bakery in order first.

Pulling her from her thoughts, she heard quiet talking in Alex's office and recognized Lucas's voice. She peered in. Alex was smiling, pointing out of that huge back window, and explaining about constellations and moon craters while Lucas was standing on a stack of books and looking through the large telescope.

Noelle hung back to watch them. There was a gentle, easy quality about the way the two of them were together. It was as if they just *got* each other.

"The moon is out this morning," Alex said quietly to Lucas. "So we might be able to see the craters on it." He caught sight of Noelle out of the corner of his eye and turned to face her across the great room. "Hi there," he said, as if looking at the moon with a six-year-old was a normal occurrence for him.

She walked across the room to meet them.

"Lucas came in just as I'd finished what I was doing, so I told him that maybe we could try out the telescope. We might catch a clearing in the cloud cover."

"That's thoughtful of you," she said, her head starting to throb.

"It's no problem," he said. "How about I walk you to your suite?"

"Yes, kiddo," she said with a grin. "We need to let Alex get some work done. Or at the very least let him get some breakfast."

Lucas walked over to her and she put her arm around him.

Her mind was racing as they walked down to the suite. Lucas was uncharacteristically chatty, asking Alex questions about the constellations. Alex had all the answers for him too, answers that Noelle couldn't provide because she'd never had an interest in a topic like that before. She had the urge to start studying just so she could talk to Lucas about it.

She'd always imagined her son sitting at the counter of the bakery while she gave him cookies and milk and helped him with homework.

But now she wondered if her dreams didn't coincide with his destiny. Lucas would be better off somewhere that could challenge him, and she didn't know how to do that. All her plans were unraveling right in front of her, unnerving her. The throbbing in her head that had started at her parents' had exploded into a full-blown headache, stretching across her eyes and into her temples.

When they got to their suite, Noelle walked Lucas to his room and asked if he'd work on his puzzle for a little bit while she had a quick talk with Alex. He agreed, and as she was leaving, he said, "I have fun with Alex."

She nodded, taking in the sight of his sleepy eyes and rosy cheeks. "I love you," she said.

Then, with a deep breath, she went out to talk to Alex. She couldn't wait until she had a plan. This needed to be dealt with sooner rather than later or she might explode.

Alex's back was to her. He was sitting on the sofa with his legs crossed and his arm stretched out along the back, and that relaxed manner made her wonder if she could change his mind about Hope and Sugar Bakery. It was time she took action. She couldn't just sit around anymore. They needed to face this, and she had to know once and for all if she had a chance to get her bakery back. She rounded the side of the sofa and sat down next to him.

"Are you all right?" he asked, noticing her change in demeanor immediately. "You look like something's bothering you."

Deep breath.

She didn't want to do this now, with her head pounding like it was, but she didn't know any better time to do it. "Something is wrong."

He turned his head just slightly, and he looked so adorable that she almost couldn't do it. But then she thought about Gram and how much work she'd put into the bakery and how Noelle's own life would have a gaping emptiness without it.

"You're closing my bakery."

"Your bakery?" Just like the first time she'd met him, the question came out like a statement.

"It's my family's—Hope and Sugar Bakery. My grandfather owns it and my dad runs it. He told me you've hiked the rent up and he can't compete with the new businesses in the area."

A spark of hope flickered in her chest as she watched him listen to her. His face was kind, understanding, and it was as though he was giving it a lot of thought. He pursed his lips and looked down at his hands as if deliberating about something. Maybe his affection toward her meant more to him than she thought it might, and he'd help. Certainly after the fun they'd had together, he'd at least entertain her ideas.

He looked into her eyes as if still deciding something and she could hardly keep her optimism from overtaking her. "It's a good business move to close it," he said instead, and Noelle's heart fell to the floor. "The property could do with an update, and a new tenant would breathe life into that street again."

Her chest felt like a cinderblock had been set on top of it. "It has life," she said defensively. "My grandfather promised my gram that he'd look after the bakery, and he never breaks a promise. He's doing the very best he can…"

"I don't doubt that, but sometimes things have to move forward even when we think it isn't the best move."

"*Think?*" she said, feeling the tears surfacing. "Even if we *think* it isn't the best move? I know it isn't the best move. It's the *worst* move. It's so bad that it's ruining our Christmas, but more than that, it's tearing my family apart and it will ruin my life." A tear escaped and she turned away from him. Everything came down to this for her. None of it mattered if he didn't support her in this because the bakery was who she was and without it, she was lost. She turned back around and stared at him, waiting for him to save the moment with something great, but he was silent.

She felt his hand on her shoulder and jerked away, standing up and going into the bathroom to get a tissue, more tears rising up. She was disappointed that he wouldn't at least try to help her figure something out. She realized then that she'd subconsciously avoided this very discussion because if he let her down, she couldn't continue feeling for him the way that she had.

Lucas's door was shut—he was probably reading, and she was glad for that because by the time she got there, she was crying. Alex could put on that Mr. Nice Guy act, but the truth of the matter was that he didn't care enough, because if he really cared for her, he'd want this for her as much as she did, and he'd said nothing. She grabbed a tissue and blew her nose, tossing it into the bin. Then she grabbed two more and headed back out.

"I think you should go," she said weakly.

"I'm sorry you're upset." He took a step toward her, but she backed away.

She swallowed, the lump in her throat aching. "I'd really appreciate it if we could keep our distance and remain professional from now on."

"If that's what you want." He looked hurt, but she wouldn't believe it. Why should he look upset? Perhaps he wasn't used to being told no.

"Yes. It's what I want."

Chapter Seventeen

Noelle was so thankful for her family. In the end, that was what mattered the most. Lucas was growing up feeling that his grandparents' home was as comfortable and familiar as his own, and he enjoyed spending time there. That was the kind of atmosphere she wanted for her son, and maybe they wouldn't have a big family, maybe this was it for her—just the two of them—but it was good. As she'd tended to William today, her mind had wandered to the rift between him and Alex, and she was so grateful that she had her family to count on.

She was the first to arrive at the restaurant after work. With Lucas choosing to make a gingerbread house at her parents' instead of coming with her, she sat alone, her knee bouncing under the table; she was full of nervous energy, despite the ridiculously early start at her parents' this morning. She'd left Alex with a sinking feeling and she couldn't bear all this alone—it had ramped her up all day. She needed to tell someone what had been going on—all of it. She'd spent the rest of the day thinking about Alex, how he made her feel, and how the universe seemed to be against their relationship.

She needed her support group. They'd been wonderful, coming out for her so much in the past few days, and she couldn't have gone through this without them. Hopefully, they'd have some words of wisdom tonight. Heidi would have the family interest in mind, keeping her level-headed; Jo would be practical and tell her exactly what she thought; and Phoebe would speak from her heart, hopefully assuring her it would all be okay.

She'd arrived early, and she knew exactly what drinks to order her two best friends and her sister. Jo liked a glass of white, house wine acceptable; Phoebe was always a dry martini; and Heidi liked a white Russian when she was out on the town. Noelle, feeling low despite the evening out, tried to lighten her mood with a cranberry Christmas cocktail. The waitress set the drinks down and lit the candle in the center of the table.

The restaurant's main lights were dimmed for the dinner hour, little lamps on the wall illuminating every table. The doorways and windows were dripping with fresh Christmas garlands and candles in glass jars flickered on the windowsills. Groups of people gathered at tables in their Christmas dresses and festivities, laughter and the buzz of conversation filling the air.

How had December turned out this way? Noelle didn't want to feel sorry for herself, but she couldn't believe that she was in this position. She had no idea what to do next.

Phoebe entered the dining room, waving madly, a big smile on her face and a brightly wrapped package under her arm. She plopped it on the table next to her martini. "Oh!" she said, lifting it to her lips before she'd even finished taking her coat off. "You are fabulous." She sat down and wriggled into a comfortable position, scooting her chair under the table. Then, she slid the package toward Noelle. "You sounded really upset on the phone, so I brought you something. I was going to wait until closer to Christmas, but it doesn't really matter, does it?"

With a grin, Noelle let the atmosphere and the good company soak into her bones. If she had to be going through something like this, at least she had her friends and family close by.

Jo and Heidi came in together and sat down. Jo dumped a handful of mints on the table. They were the little chocolate mints that could only be found in the shop next to Jo's apartment—Noelle's favorite.

"I thought you could use something sweet," she said, sitting down. Noelle had told them she'd talked to Alex about the bakery, and all three of them could guess that something had gone wrong, but she needed to tell them in person.

"What did Alex say about the bakery?"

Where should she begin? "It isn't just the bakery. It's a whole lot of things." Noelle started with Lucas. That was where her world began so she might as well open with that. She told them about the bond that Lucas had developed with Alex, the way they were together, that Lucas asked about Alex when he wasn't there. Then as they ordered, had a few more drinks, and eventually dinner, she told them everything. She told them about William, about Elizabeth and his mystery lady, and about how the family only allowed a certain type of person to date a Harrington; how she felt about Alex, the way he'd been so wonderful to her, and then what he'd said about the bakery.

"What a disaster," Phoebe said.

"You're supposed to be making me feel better."

"If you want to look on the bright side, you have experienced what most women only dream of—you've actually kissed Alexander Harrington," she returned, raising an eyebrow. "I'll bet it was a million-dollar kiss like everything else he has."

"Yes," Jo said. "Dish. How was the kissing?"

Noelle smiled at her friend. She knew they didn't have answers for her, so the least they could do was make her laugh. "Pretty amazing." Noelle sucked down the rest of her drink, trying to drown the multitude of feelings she was having, but it wasn't helping. "What am I supposed to do?"

"Beg him to reconsider. He's gorgeous and he likes you! That's pretty amazing," Phoebe said, her eyes like stars with the excitement of it all.

"I don't know, Pheebs," Jo said, shaking her head, concern on her face. "She can't let him believe he can do what he wants. He needs to think about someone other than himself."

The table hummed with indecisive chatter before Heidi said, "Don't try to develop a plan or anything right now. Just get through tomorrow and then the next day. We'll help you as you go. We'll think of something."

Phoebe drank the last of her martini. "Right, now, open your gift! It'll make you feel better."

Not any closer to a resolution, Noelle decided Phoebe was right. She should just enjoy the night out with people who loved her, people who were like her, people who had her back no matter what. She took the gift off the table and unwrapped the end, pulling the tape free.

"You're so slow!" Phoebe teased. "Just rip it open."

Noelle laughed and tore the paper. With a nostalgic smile, tears welling up, she held it out so the others could view it. "It's a tiny jukebox radio," she said.

"It's like the big one your gram always played at the bakery. This one plays Christmas music."

She adored Gram's old jukebox, and she'd been devastated thinking her father might sell it once the bakery closed. "I love it." She kissed Phoebe on the cheek. "Thank you all for coming and being supportive. I know I've been pulling you away from your family time. Please thank them for me."

"We're always here," her sister said. "And these are all just blips, remember? Just stops on the way to your destiny. That's what you always say."

"I'm not sure I believe that anymore. But I'll take your word for it."

"Can I say something?" Phoebe interrupted. "I don't know if the others will agree with me, but I'm just going to say it. I think you should give Alex a chance."

There was a collective gasp at the table and Jo caught the eye of the waitress, gesturing for another round.

"How can you tell her that, Phoebe?" Heidi said. "He has no regard for her wishes at all. What kind of guy is that? She doesn't want to be with someone who's only interested in his own gain."

"Because Noelle underestimates herself. Face him, Noelle. You don't have to know what to do, just face him. Keep facing him until he knows you so well that he wants nothing more than to help you. You are amazing, and he's seen a little of that. Let him see it all. Be yourself and follow his lead. Talk to him. See what happens."

❄ ❄ ❄

Even with her new jukebox playing music softly, Noelle wasn't sleeping well. She couldn't get a good night's rest in this big house. Every night she tossed and turned. No vanilla coffee like Gram used to offer or music or evening out seemed to help. She got up and checked on Lucas—he was sleeping soundly, so she decided to take a walk through the house, trying not to think about all that she, Phoebe, Jo, and Heidi had discussed tonight at dinner. Perhaps a walk would clear her mind.

She slid on her slippers and wrapped her bathrobe around her, running her fingers through her hair. Then she opened the door to her suite and headed out into the colossal expanse of the hallway. She passed a floral arrangement on a table that was easily four feet tall, with blooms in whites and greens—roses mostly, but with white oriental lilies mixed in. She leaned in and took a whiff—fresh, not silk. As she walked through the house, the rooms and hallways quiet, she was able to really take in its beauty. It was like some sort of storybook that had come to life. Everything was perfect. Anyone walking around would have no idea of the turmoil that filtered through this family.

No closer to sleep, Noelle walked down to the hallway that held Alex's family photographs and stopped to look at them. Now, knowing he'd taken them, they had a different feel, a more personal light. She looked at his grandmother's smile and realized that it was directed at Alex, and the love in her eyes was so apparent. His grandfather's face didn't just look serious; it looked stern, focused, as if he were setting an example for his grandson with his stature.

There was a creak and she turned, startled. William was in a pair of striped pajamas and moccasin slippers, holding his cane. "Can't sleep?" he asked.

"No. How come you're walking around by yourself? I would've come to help you. You can't sleep either?"

"Nope. Not good at sleep these days. Too much on my mind."

"I feel the same way."

She peered up at the photos.

"What in the world could be weighing on your young mind?"

"Just because I'm young doesn't mean I don't have big life choices to ponder. I'm planning my future, you know. That's a big deal." She offered a half smile, but she knew he couldn't see it so she allowed it to slip back to a neutral position. "Look at you: you had to deal with a major injury and a crush on a girl at only nineteen. Those are pretty big."

"You're right."

Seriousness washed over her as they sat down on the hallway bench. It creaked with their weight and she wondered if it had been one of the antiques William or Elizabeth had purchased. "Would you tell me about when you met the woman again? You'd said you'd seen her…"

William nodded.

"Tell me what happened?" She liked William, despite what Alex said, *and* maybe the story would help her get to sleep. William was a wonderful storyteller. She thought about the kind of grandparent he could've been and couldn't help but feel like he'd lost in that realm. She enjoyed hearing about this mystery lady.

"I saw her for the last time after I'd met my wife, when Elizabeth and I had just started dating," he said quietly. "We were out to dinner when I passed a woman, her smile and scent overwhelming my senses, jarring my memories of her. She stopped, recognizing me as well. We were obscured from the tables in the small hallway at the back of the restaurant—she was coming from the ladies' room and I was making a business call on the pay phone at the back. We both just stared at each other for what seemed like ages and mere seconds simultaneously.

"She offered a nervous smile and said, 'How are you?' but there were so many more questions behind those words. I told her I was fine, and she said she was there with someone. I remember nodding and telling her I was glad to see her. Then, something came over me—to this day, I don't know why I said it—I said, 'In a different world, I would kiss you right here, right now.' I couldn't believe that thought had actually come out of my mouth. It was so forward of me and not within my character—because I believe in treating a lady with respect—but I felt it in the depths of my soul. What surprised me was that she didn't flinch. She just smiled that gorgeous smile of hers and said, 'In a different world, I would let you.' Then she left. That was it."

"You never crossed paths after that?"

"No. But I knew that it was over because I'd read her last letter. I'll let you read it."

"That's so sad that you didn't ever see her again," she said.

"Well, the woman I was with that night was Elizabeth. She became my wife, bore my child, shared my life. So maybe things happen for a reason."

"Did you love your wife?" She wanted to ask point blank to put to rest any assumptions Alex might have about this man.

"I loved her so much. I still love her." He turned his head to attempt to view the photo of her, but his disappointment was clear when he couldn't make out the image. "The woman from the café is just an if-only. *If only things had been different.* But she isn't my life. That life wasn't meant for me. I have to believe that or I'll drive myself crazy."

They fell into an easy silence after that but Noelle's thoughts were on one sentence he'd said: *That life wasn't meant for me.* Was she chasing a life that wasn't hers? If having Gram's bakery wasn't the life she was meant for, she wouldn't know her purpose. A quiet desperation filled her, telling her that no matter what, she couldn't believe that to be the case.

"Come back to my suite with me. I'll let you read that letter," he said. "Maybe it will help us sleep."

They headed back down the hallways together, walking slowly. William was using her more than usual for support, and she wondered if the late hour was making his muscles tired. She led him into the suite and he sat down on the sofa in the sitting room while she retrieved the last letter. When she got back to him, William had lain back, his head tipped as if he were looking at the ceiling.

She opened the envelope and unfolded the letter.

"I want you to know that I am always here. On that street corner, in that shop, in your heart if you'll have me there. But I am no longer going to make myself available to you through letters hidden away, because it is time for me to move forward. You are the biggest surprise of my life so far, and if you and I aren't meant for one another, then I cannot wait to see what's ahead of me, because meeting you was already quite amazing. If there's something bigger and better than what you and I had, then I want to race toward it with my arms open instead of shrinking back. I will never forget the time we had and it will remain in my heart forever. This is my final letter but I wish you nothing less than the greatest love the world has to give. I hope it finds you."

Noelle felt the prick of tears at such a heartfelt note. She turned to see William's reaction but he'd fallen asleep. Even still, she thought she saw the tiniest hint of a smile on his lips, and she hoped that one day she could find someone who loved her as much as this woman had loved him and he, her.

Chapter Eighteen

The alarm went off and Noelle sat straight up in her bed. When she'd finally drifted off to sleep last night, she'd slept like a rock. Normally, she was up before her alarm, waking naturally at five o'clock. She only ever set her alarm as a precaution in case she accidentally slept in, which never happened. Until this morning. She padded out to find Lucas and get him ready for school, but his room was empty. She ventured into the sitting area and realized she was the only one in the suite. Where was he?

Quickly, she rushed out to find him. She grabbed her phone and texted her mom to tell her she'd take him to school. She knew just where to go. With swift strides, she made her way to the office and went in. But it was empty. She went into the main foyer—no one.

"Lucas?" she called out quietly, but enough for her voice to carry. She sharpened her hearing and came up empty. "Lucas?"

Jim came down the hallway. "Good morning," he said with a smile. "Nice to run into you. Everything okay?"

"Good morning. I'm looking for Lucas. He's late for school. Have you seen him, by any chance?"

"I believe he's outside with Alex," he said, pointing to the large window overlooking the grounds. "I saw them together earlier this morning."

"Oh." She'd have to talk to Lucas about leaving the suite without her. What if he'd interrupted Alex while he was working? Not to mention that she didn't want Lucas spending extra time with him. He wasn't someone who was going to be around long-term, and she knew how much Lucas liked him. She felt the need to protect Lucas's delicate heart.

"Use the side entrance on the East wing," Jim said. "Your boots are there and the snow is accumulating."

Noelle hurried to the door and let herself out. She hadn't planned to be outside, and she didn't have a coat, the air frosty, still dressed in her flannel pajamas. She crossed her arms for warmth. "Lucas?" she called as she faced a maze of hedges, all perfectly pruned and looking as though they'd been glazed in ice.

"Hi, Mom!" Lucas called from her left. She turned to find him walking up beside Alex. "I found Alex in his office this morning. He's been showing me how to use his cameras! We've been taking pictures together. Look at the photos I took!"

Alex approached her cautiously, she could tell, and truthfully, she didn't know how to act around him either. He was so likeable, and they'd been so close, but his actions regarding the bakery weren't demonstrating the feelings she thought she'd seen. He hung back and allowed Lucas to keep the camera as he ran up to meet her.

"Aren't they cool?" Lucas said, holding out the camera. "Here's the zoom lens and then there are all these little dials to change the perspective, like this one that shifts focus. See?" He could barely stretch his little fingers around the circular lens. "I took this one of the tree, and this one of the snowball I made. Alex and I had a tiny snowball fight." He looked over at Alex, and she saw that look on Lucas's face; it was the look he had when he was completely comfortable with someone, amused, and happy, all at the same time.

"Wow," she said, as she peered down at the photograph on the digital screen. It was really good. "I like that." Her love for Lucas welled up, seeing his excitement. He was so happy here.

There was a click, distracting her. Alex had snapped a photo of her and Lucas with another camera; he was looking at the small screen with a smile on his face. When he finally made eye contact, that cautious look returned.

"Let's go inside," she told Lucas. "I'm freezing and you need to go to school."

"I'll get us all some hot chocolate," Alex said.

"Lucas needs to get to school," Noelle said with a loaded look, as he caught up with them and opened the door for her. The heat from inside gave her a shiver.

Alex moved the cuff of his coat to view his watch. "He's already late. What's a few more minutes this close to the holiday?"

She knew well and good that he remembered what she'd said about the two of them staying away from each other. Clearly, he'd decided to do what he pleased instead, which made her prickle with annoyance. If he really cared for her, he'd respect her wishes. "You and Lucas can have hot chocolate—quickly. I'm going to let William know I'll be a little late because I have to take Lucas to school."

"Wait," Alex said, grabbing her arm gently, the affectionate movement of his thumb making her weaker than she should be. "I need to ask you something."

She pulled away from him mildly. "Ask it."

"I will," he said. "Over hot chocolate."

He was going to have his way no matter what. She followed him into the kitchen.

With a brief whisper to one of the staff, he pulled out a barstool each for Lucas and Noelle, then climbed up beside Noelle on his own seat. It wasn't long before all three of them were facing large white mugs with whipped cream, marshmallows, and a candy-cane swizzle stick.

"What did you want to ask me?" she asked, as Lucas used his candy cane to fish out the marshmallows. He lifted one ever so gently into the air before it plopped back into the whipped cream.

"I know you wanted to..." He looked at Lucas, considering his words. "...focus on your work, and I'd focus on mine," he said, clearly as code for going their separate ways like she'd suggested. "But I want to go see my grandmother before I leave for New York. I'd really like it if you would go with me."

The shock of his request had made it from the pit of her stomach to her face, she could tell, because that uncertainty showed on his for just an instant. He looked down at his hot chocolate, pursing his lips in disappointment. "I just really want to see her and I can't do it alone."

"Why don't you ask William?"

He ground his teeth, his jaw clenching in irritation. "I don't want to see her with him. I want to see her with someone I enjoy being around because I might need your strength when I face her in that condition."

"I don't know..." She wanted to be supportive but at the same time, it was a very personal thing he was asking her to do, and probably something he should be doing with family. Not to mention she'd put her foot down. How could he expect her to do something like visit his grandmother when he was literally ripping the bakery out from under her? The idea that he'd put her in this position was maddening.

"You must not remember our last conversation as well as I do."

"I do," he said, nodding in defeat.

A tiny part of her was screaming to tell him she'd go with him. Her heart ached for him, and she could hardly bear telling him no, but what did he expect? She locked eyes with him, refusing to answer.

With a deep breath, he must have comprehended her dilemma. He stood up and turned to Lucas. "I'm taking this with me to my office. I've got work to do, buddy." He held up the mug and winked at Lucas. As he left, his gaze lingered on Noelle just a little longer than she was comfortable.

❄ ❄ ❄

The whole way to school and back, she got more agitated, thinking about how Alex was putting her in a terrible position because she felt bad for not going with him, but to her family he was Enemy Number One.

"Alex asked me to go see Elizabeth," she said to William when she returned. "I told him he should go with you, not me."

"I wish he would," William said, emotion in his words.

"Have you tried to talk to him?"

"He won't talk to me." William stood up from his sofa, shuffling toward the window. He bumped into a side table, steadying himself with his cane, his agitation clear. He was obviously torn to pieces over his grandson's refusal to make amends with him, and Alex failed to notice. She felt awful for poor William.

"I'll try to talk to him," she said. "Let's get your medicine and then I'll see if I can change his mind."

Noelle hadn't wanted to be involved in all this but the truth was that Alex wouldn't listen to William—she knew that. And for some ridiculous reason he'd listen to her. So, when she left William's suite, she went down to his office to convince him to talk to his grandfather.

With resolve, she pushed open the closed office door and walked in, clicking her way across the room. Alex was on the phone, his head down, his hand poised over a notepad, but his eyes on her. She had her game face on.

"I'll have to call you back," he said. Then he hung up, set his pen down, and waited.

Alex was frustrating her more than she could stand, and she wanted to set things straight right here, right now. "So William didn't show you affection when you were a young boy. That was terrible. But now, he's an old man. An old, broken man. He misses your grandmother so much it brings tears to his eyes to even mention it, and you refuse to be the better person and take him with you to see her." *There. Take that.*

Alex stood up. "You don't know what you're talking about."

"How so? Because I've spent enough time with William to know that he loves his wife and he wants to see her, but, just like you, seeing the shell of a woman with whom he's spent his life, who doesn't recognize him, is heartbreaking. You're being awful, Alex."

Still composed, he walked around to the other side of his desk and looked down at her. "*I* am being awful?"

"Yes." She was standing her ground. He couldn't push her around like he had everyone else in his life.

"What if I said that my grandmother told me one night when she knew the Alzheimer's was getting the better of her and it might be her last lucid moment that she'd always feared my grandfather had been in love with someone else? He never loved my grandmother, Noelle. And she deserved that love. She was amazing."

"He loved her. He told me. He also told me about that other woman. That was before he'd met Elizabeth. We all have relationships that end. Why is he being held to this one? Let it go."

"My grandmother said she saw him talk to another woman in a restaurant once. She'd never told him that she'd seen him, but she had. She said that, from what she could hear, he made it pretty clear to this other woman that if things had been different, and he'd been allowed to see her, he would have. My grandmother was devastated. Her family had already consented to her marriage to my grandfather, and in those days, it was her duty, given her upbringing, to marry him. And she really did love him, so by that point she couldn't leave. She tried to be the best wife she could be, but in the back of her mind, she was always competing with that mystery lady she'd seen that day."

Noelle put her hand over her mouth, the stories coming together. "Elizabeth saw them," she whispered. William and the woman had both been there with other people but Elizabeth overhearing them changed the situation.

"Yeah. I'd rather not take the man who made her feel like that to see her. She was trying to be the perfect wife because she felt some need to do better than this woman who had his heart. I'll just go myself," he said, the tension in his face making him look tired.

Noelle felt the air leaking from her lungs at this revelation, and she realized that she really didn't know the whole story from every perspective, but she wondered if any of them did. "I shouldn't get involved," she said honestly, feeling terrible for making a snap judgment about Alex's feelings. He wasn't just being awful to William; he had a real reason to be upset. Here Alex was telling Noelle that his love for his grandmother and his need to protect her fragile feelings were the reason he wouldn't go with William to see her. That was a very sweet and caring gesture, and it made her want to put her arms around him, but she knew better.

The tension in his shoulders dissipated. “We don’t have to get into all this today,” he said. “I’ll figure it out.”

“I’m sorry,” she said, not knowing what else she could offer.

He nodded and then went back to his work, his disappointment clear. Without another word, she walked out of his office.

Chapter Nineteen

"I got my plane ticket!" Phoebe nearly shrieked through the phone. "OhmyGod, ohmyGod, ohmyGod… I'm actually going on the audition. I'm doing this."

"You did?" Noelle flopped down on the sofa in her suite and lay back, the phone at her ear. She'd finished work for the day, not seeing Alex again, and was glad to hear a friendly voice. "Phoebe, you've got this. It's in the bag. Act your you-know-what off when you get there. This is it. This is what you've been waiting for your whole life."

"I know." Her excitement trailed off. The line went quiet and Noelle checked her screen to make sure they were still connected. Finally, Phoebe said, "I told Paul."

Noelle chewed on the inside of her lip. She knew how difficult this was for Phoebe. Her friend rarely opened up to anyone and she'd let Paul in. She'd told him all her secrets, how alone she'd been growing up and how depression had consumed her mother, leaving her alone to raise herself most of the time. Phoebe didn't let those demons out to anyone. She channeled them into her acting instead, and, if she let herself, she could convince the hardest cynic with her tears.

Noelle had seen her do it during a stage play once. Her character was supposed to have lost a grandparent. Phoebe sat in the middle of that stage, her legs crumpled under her gauzy white dress, a single beam of light on her. Her lips quivered and then her eyes filled with tears. In complete silence—the auditorium frozen with emotion—the tears slid down her cheeks until she put her face in her hands and sobbed.

Noelle always wondered if she'd been thinking about her mother. Phoebe would tell her that when her mother wasn't depressed, she was amazing. She had a sense of humor that could send Phoebe doubling over into fits of laughter. She was caring and gentle, and Phoebe adored her. But when the depression overtook her, her mother slipped into her own darkness, refusing to see her daughter, pulling the curtains closed and staying in bed all day. If Phoebe tried to get her up, she'd yell at her, tell her to get out. For a child it was very confusing, but when Phoebe was old enough to understand the disease, she came to terms with it as best she could.

"What did he say?"

"He's worried. He said that I'm so talented that there's no way I wouldn't get it, and wishing for anything else would be a crime."

"That's sweet." Noelle rolled onto her side. "What will he do if you get it?"

"I think he wants to try to convince me to come back after I've shot all the episodes, but it's a TV show. It could have multiple seasons if I'm lucky. And it could be the start of something. I don't think I'd want to leave Los Angeles. I need to see where my life is heading, you know?"

She nodded even though Phoebe couldn't see her. She knew all too well. Alex wasn't budging on the bakery, and she knew that taking care of William wasn't what would fulfill her forever. There was nothing left for her here. The significance of this moment hit Noelle like a thunderbolt. Fate was stepping in and giving her a nudge. Just like Phoebe, if the opportunity arose for her to leave and find something else, she felt as though she should go because why would she stay? The idea of this turned over in her mind and she thought about her childhood pact with Phoebe.

"If you get the part, I might really move there with you," she said. "Just like I promised." Saying it terrified her and ripped a hole in her heart with the loss of the bakery, but she was out of options. Maybe she needed a fresh start.

"Oh, it would be amazing!" Phoebe's voice broke with excitement. "I wouldn't have wanted to ask you really, but I don't know if I could make it alone. Having you and Lucas there would mean the world to me."

"I know. And I'd really enjoy watching your dreams come true."

"I love you like you're my sister, you know that?"

She smiled. "Yeah. I do."

❄ ❄ ❄

Right as Noelle was heading to her parents' house to pick up Lucas, Heidi had called her for an emergency family meeting. Noelle was mentally tired already. She kept trying to figure out a way to make everything better, but she just couldn't. She was struggling.

She parked the car and braced herself for this meeting. She had to be strong for her mother and her father—they were going through a lot, and she needed to be there for them.

She went inside and said hello to Muffy, who followed her past the glowing fireplace, and into the kitchen, her tail wagging furiously. Her mother, father, and sister were all sitting at the table, but to her surprise, Pop-pop was there too.

"Where's Lucas?" she asked.

"Kelsey from next door has come over to play with him while we talk," her mother said. "He's upstairs. Have a seat." She pushed a plate of cookies toward Noelle but she ignored them, her curiosity getting the better of her.

"What's going on?" she asked, unbuttoning her coat. By the looks on their faces and the dramatic way they'd assembled, she feared the worst: Were her parents struggling so badly that something awful had happened? Surely they weren't splitting up…

Heidi was the first to speak. "I told Mom and Dad about you and Alex."

"What about us," she said slowly, replaying everything she'd told them at dinner the other night. "There's nothing to tell."

Her mother leaned forward with the same look she had when Noelle had hidden the phone under her bed as a girl so she could call Jo instead of sleeping and she'd denied having it. "Last time I checked, my daughter was relatively selective about who she made out with."

Noelle knew her face must be scarlet by the fire that she felt in her cheeks. "I did not make out with Alex Harrington. What did Heidi tell you?" She'd had a few drinks when she'd finally told them, but jeez, she knew she couldn't possibly have described their kiss in such a way as to make her mother believe that she'd had some raunchy make-out session. She knew she hadn't embellished the story at all.

"I didn't tell her you made out," Heidi said. "But I did tell her about the light in your eyes when you talked about him."

"I had to tell your father," her mother said.

Noelle didn't look at him. She couldn't. She felt like she'd betrayed everyone, and she didn't know what to do. "I'm sorry," she finally said, her eyes on the table.

"I told him," her mother said, "because I couldn't let the business get in the way of your happiness."

Noelle raised her head, confused. Then she looked over at her father to gauge his reaction. She remembered his face when she'd mentioned getting the job. Now he looked bewildered. She had known he wouldn't be happy about it.

Her father took a wobbly hold of his water glass before piping up. "I have something I need to confess to you," he said. All of a sudden, that panicky look took on a different perspective. He looked scared, not angry.

"What is it?" she asked.

"The raised rent wasn't the reason the bakery is closing—Alex did raise it slightly, but no more than anyone else would with inflation. He was fair. The bakery has been losing money for quite a while now. I made a few poor business decisions… I bought all new equipment in the kitchen and reduced the bakery items to try to cut costs to pay for it. I tried to go into the catering market—weddings and such—but without your gram, I wasn't getting the orders."

Her mind spun.

"I blamed Alex because it was easier not to feel the guilt myself. I blamed his hike in rent, but if I would have made the right choices, the rent wouldn't have been a problem. This was all my fault," her father said, looking toward Pop-pop, worry streaking his face. "I tried to help when Pop-pop told me he was floundering. I gave him the suggestions and I got it all wrong. I don't know how to run the bakery either and without your gram, we're sort of lost. I kept fighting the closure, so angry with myself for screwing it up. Pop-pop still needs the income, and now I've ruined it for him."

"You were just trying to help, son," Pop-pop said.

So this wasn't Alex's fault? He wasn't kicking them out at all; he'd just found another tenant when they couldn't afford to stay. This news rocked Noelle to the core, and what he'd said about the bakery began to filter through her mind, as she now saw it in a totally different light. Why hadn't Alex just told her all this when she'd spoken to him about it?

Noelle promised her family that she'd do her very best to see if she could change Alex's mind to give them more time, and she asked for complete control of the bakery. They all agreed. Ideas were swimming around in her head faster than she could process them, but Noelle warned everyone that she had to get Alex to allow them to stay first.

❄ ❄ ❄

After she'd spent the evening with Lucas doing puzzles and reading his new books, they talked about his day at school, and then he finally drifted off. Noelle had one last check on him to be sure he was asleep, and then she walked down to Alex's suite and knocked on the door.

As he stood in the doorway, sock feet, jeans, and a sweater, she had to swallow to keep her emotions at bay. Part of her wanted to throw her arms around him and tell him she was so sorry for blaming him, but the more rational side of her was cautious, confused, wondering why he hadn't told her the truth.

He opened the door wider to allow her to enter. Alex's suite was more masculine than hers, with brown leather furniture and a widescreen television, a modern element that looked a little out of place in the historic setting. The décor was sleek and unfussy, a lot like he was. "Is everything all right?" he asked.

"I hope so." She took a seat on the soft leather sofa and he sank down next her. "I want to talk to you about the bakery." She curled her legs underneath her, but she was jittery, too eager to sit still, so she straightened them back out. She twisted slightly toward him and tried to keep her knees from bouncing.

Noelle explained what her family had told her as quickly as she could because she wanted to get to the question she was about to ask. "Why didn't you tell me?" she said.

He deliberated before speaking but then with an inhale, his chest filling up with air, he said, "When you first came through the doors of this house, I knew exactly who you were. I'd seen you at Hope and Sugar Bakery with your father. I'd come to look at the state of the property and I was sitting in my car across the street. You were there with your dad and your grandfather, carrying in boxes. Your dad bent down to help you and the two of you laughed at something—it was clear to me how close you all were just by watching you. I've never known that kind of closeness except with my grandmother. I wanted to protect that relationship and I knew that in the end, you could be angry with me more easily than you could be with them. I wanted to take the brunt of it for them."

"But you can't go around lying to me to protect me! That isn't how I do things. I want you to be honest, and I'm not sure how honest you're used to being." After all, he didn't tell her, and no matter the reasoning, it made him seem like he could never be as truthful to her as she was with her own friends and family. At the very least, wouldn't he have wanted to make her feel better?

"That's fair," he said, rubbing the evening scruff on his cheeks. "I could sit here and tell you how I promise to be straightforward with you from now on, but I know that I've let you down. I don't know how to handle this sort of thing. I've never met anyone like you before. I want to protect you and make you happy at the same time and I don't always know how to do that."

"Practice right now. I need a little honesty from you. If I can figure out how to pay the rent, would you let me keep the bakery open?"

He looked thoughtful but also a little doubtful, making her pulse pound inside her ears. *Please say yes*, she repeated in her head.

"I have a surefire renter, a lucrative company, and they're planning to move in at the beginning of January..." He stared at her, the corners of his mouth turning upward just slightly. "You're going to need a rock-solid plan."

She squealed and threw her arms around him, elation taking over her body. Her excitement made him laugh, and he was clearly delighted he'd made her so happy. Then he unwound her arms from his neck, a serious look on his face. "Being honest," he said, "I don't know if you'll be able to pull it off. I'm just giving you the reality of it. That area is changing and it might not be the best location."

"It'll work," she said, certain that she was on the right track. If she felt it in her gut, she could trust it. "Let me think about it and I'll draw something up."

"Let's see what you can do by New Year's," he said. "You've got until December thirty-first. That's nearly a month. By then I'll be able to take a look at some initial numbers."

Chapter Twenty

"I'm liking this!" Jo said, entering the bakery and ducking behind the glass case to snag a cookie. She motioned to Heidi to see if she wanted a cookie, but she declined, suggesting coffee instead. They'd agreed to meet today for a weekend brainstorming lunch at the bakery, all of them chipping in for pizza. All except Phoebe, who was preparing for her audition.

Tossing the empty pizza boxes into the trash can, Noelle turned on the brand-new espresso machine that was part of the equipment her dad had bought, offering everyone coffee and cookies for dessert. Lucas sat with Pop-pop in the comfy chair by the bookcase, her mother and father both on the small sofa near the window. Noelle was at the counter, still thinking.

Snapping out of her thoughts, she said, "Pop-pop's got vanilla and caramel syrups. Who wants vanilla?"

Jo's hand shot up like it had in school. She always had the answers back then. Perhaps she'd have them today too.

After Noelle had made coffee for everyone, Lucas stayed in the chair to read his new book about the continents that Alex had gotten him, while the others gathered around the table. Noelle wrote the date at the top of her notepad and shuffled the few papers she'd printed off the computer in the back room.

"I have a very general idea," she said. All eyes were on her. When Pop-pop and her father had handed her full control of the bakery, she'd asked Heidi if she wanted a part in it, but her sister had said she had her hands full with work at the moment. She did say she would be more than happy to pitch in whenever Noelle wanted her there. They were all chatting, abuzz with excitement to hear what Noelle had in mind.

"The new espresso machine got me thinking," she said. "What if we transform the bakery into a coffee shop? People love them. The drinks would be our main focus, with the bakery items as an added bonus. We'd have to start small, but we'd focus on gourmet, specialty beverages—things like honey-cream lattes with local honey; we'd only include food pairings that would complement the coffees."

"Would you offer breakfast and lunch options? That could pull people in," Jo said. "Just thinking out loud…"

Noelle tried not to get discouraged as she looked at the financial spreadsheet she'd printed. "We're in the red right now. We have no funds to increase what we have in the inventory currently. We're going to have to start really basic, like I said, and make very calculated purchases. I suggest we create a tiered plan with forecasts and possible directions we could take the shop at each stage as our revenue increases, but yes, Jo, that would be a great direction eventually. And we're on a time crunch," she added. "Alex wants to see what we can do by New Year's. If we're making money, we'll get more time."

"What about the name, Noelle?" Pop-pop said. "Hope and Sugar was Gram's choice. Would you consider keeping it?"

Noelle remembered Gram's explanation of the name Hope and Sugar. "Absolutely. Hope and Sugar Coffee House sounds amazing."

"So where do you suggest starting, then?" Jo said.

"We've already got new machines. I say we research the five most popular coffees and get the ingredients for those; we continue with our bakery selections, but focus on pairings rather than cakes and pies. Perhaps biscotti and cookies should be our focus. We can offer small packages—a coffee and three cookies or latte and croissant—and maybe, if we can get going quickly enough, we could make Christmas bundles and sell them as gifts."

"What about bite-sized pastries?" Her mother spoke up. "I'm always overwhelmed at coffee shops because their pastries are huge. We could sell seventy-five-cent cake bites or things like that?"

"Could be good for the bundles. Maybe we could start with Gram's most popular double chocolate meringues. I'll bet we could make those smaller."

"Absolutely," her mother said.

"I also had the idea of doing deliveries," Noelle continued. "We could go into the new offices in the area and deliver coffees and pastries. Once we get up and running, we can try a small selection of sandwiches, like Jo suggested, and then move on to breakfast items. We'll start everything with a big re-opening and invite everyone we know."

Pop-pop's eyes were glassy, his hands folded in front of his lips hiding a smile. "Your gram would adore this—everyone coming together."

❄ ❄ ❄

By the time she left the bakery, it was evening. Noelle's notepad was full of scribbled plans, ideas, and possibilities to update both the interior and exterior of the coffee shop for the grand re-opening she planned to have. She had a to-do list a mile long: find a new coffee supplier, research exterior sign designs, new furniture layouts, advertising options...

Even though it was Saturday, and she'd had the day off, she and Lucas went straight to William to check on him. She actually missed him when she wasn't with him for the day.

"How was your meeting?" William asked, coming in from his bedroom, leaning heavily on his cane for support. Distracted momentarily, he leaned down toward Lucas. "Hi, young man," he said.

Lucas smiled but then said "Hi" and Noelle wondered if it was because Lucas knew William's eyesight was failing him.

"It was great!" Noelle said. "I was with my family creating a plan to save my gram's bakery."

"Oh?" He sat down into a chair and leaned his cane against the nearby side table.

"It turns out we're renting from Alex and things haven't been going well. But he said if we could come up with a plan, he might let me keep it going." She could hardly contain herself, her smile widening. "I've wanted to run Hope and Sugar Bakery my whole life and I can't wait to move forward with it."

William's face dropped pensively, his breathing speeding up. There was a hidden panic lurking in his features, but he kept pushing it back, his breathing not slowing.

Suddenly, Noelle realized that if all this went through, she wouldn't be able to care for William anymore. Caring for him had been just a stop on her way to where she belonged, but looking at him, she wondered if he didn't see it as just a stop. Perhaps he had been hoping she and Lucas would stay. She hadn't meant to seem insensitive and now she worried about who would look after him. She didn't know what to say.

Whenever things were uncomfortable and complicated, there was one thing that Gram knew would get her through it: baking. She watched William, thinking. Then she turned to Lucas. "William has never experienced Casa Grande."

Lucas's eyes got big and she could see the wheels turning in his own head.

"I think we should show him."

"When?" he asked excitedly.

"Tomorrow. We can make it for all the staff for Christmas."

William snapped out of his thoughts, turning an ear toward them. "What are you two planning over there?" he asked suspiciously.

Noelle giggled with Lucas. "You'll have to wait and see!"

Chapter Twenty-One

Alex walked in, eyeing the contents filling the enormous kitchen counter, his brows furrowing in that way of his and making it very difficult for Noelle to focus on anything but his face. She turned toward the line of crystal bowls and the rainbow of colors inside them, the smell of gingerbread saturating the air.

"What is all this?" he said with a grin.

The entire counter was full of candy: Skittles, lemon drops, Jolly Ranchers, peppermint twists, Runts, citrus slices, licorice, fruit sticks, candy canes, M&Ms, mini chocolate bars, gummy bears… "The ingredients for Casa Grande," she laughed.

"Casa what?"

"It's the name my sister and I gave to the gingerbread house that we used to make with my gram. It all started with an order from the old toy store downtown. They wanted a gingerbread house the size of a small playhouse. Gram had to bake bricks of gingerbread because an entire wall wouldn't fit in the oven. Then she literally built it, keeping each brick in place with icing. We helped her decorate the outside with candy. After that, we made slightly smaller versions of it every Christmas."

"And you're making it today?"

"Yes." She smiled excitedly. "The staff is very excited. I told them they could eat it when we're all done." Then, as she picked up a bowl and stirred the green icing, she said, "Why don't you help us?" She knew she was omitting the fact that William had been invited as well, but there was something electrifying about planning the changes to Hope and Sugar Coffee House, about renewing her purpose, that made Noelle feel like she could do anything—even make William and Alex talk to each other.

He picked up a tube of white icing and contemplated. "What time?"

"Three o'clock."

He hesitated and shook his head. "No good. I'm meeting with the moving company at three." He set the icing back down on the counter and the buzzer on the oven went off.

"Moving company?" Noelle asked, maintaining eye contact while she grabbed the potholders and opened the oven door, sliding one large, perfect piece of gingerbread out and replacing it with an uncooked one. She set the steaming piece on the cooling rack.

"I'm planning to have my things moved to New York before Christmas so I can spend the holiday there. That way I can be all moved in and settled by January."

She felt her mouth drop open and she had to work to snap it shut. What was all that talk about making her happy for if he planned to move? She remembered William mentioning it, and she knew it was a possibility in the future, but right now? It hit her like a ton of bricks. She wanted to say, "What about us? What about Lucas?" but she had no right. She didn't have any claim to him.

She set the potholders down and faced him. "Don't you want to be here for Christmas? What about going to see your grandmother? Don't you want to do that?"

He stared at her, clearly trying to keep his thoughts from her, but she could tell that he wanted to say something.

You know what? Noelle told herself, *I need to practice what I preach. I told* him *to be honest with* me… "What was the point in our date at the arena, going to karaoke, and asking me to visit your grandmother if you were just going to leave anyway?" She willed him to come up with some sort of explanation that would prove he cared about her, because right now it felt like she'd been the very last person he'd considered.

He stood slightly stunned, his lips parting ever so slightly, and his shoulders dropped. "I acted hastily. I'm sorry. I don't usually act on impulse but you make me feel like I can do anything. I didn't consider my move to New York when I asked you out. But if things progressed between us, perhaps I could visit more often or you could come to New York."

"I hate New York." She hadn't meant the words to be harsh, just true. She didn't like the idea of all that hustle and bustle. She hated rushing around just to climb to the top of some high-rise for a moment's peace. She didn't want to live in a place where every door looked the same and every home behind each door was miles away from a yard full of flowers, a walk down a country path, or a visit to a shop owned by someone she'd known her whole life. She preferred a more laid-back, relaxed atmosphere where people took time to get to know one another, where they shared things about themselves.

Alex had looked startled by her comment but then pensive. He nodded in understanding and took a step toward her. "I don't know how to do this," he admitted. "I've said it before. I'm not that great at it." He stared straight into her soul, his eyes so honest and vulnerable.

His confession caused her resolve to slip. "Then let me show you," she said. "We'll do the gingerbread house at four instead of three. Will that give you enough time?"

"Yes." Those eyes that had been so intent lightened and he smiled, causing an electric current through her chest.

"Great. Now hurry up!" she teased, trying to lighten the mood, turning him around and pushing him playfully toward the door, making him laugh. It gave her that flutter again and she had to remind herself that her heart was on the line. She'd better be careful.

❄ ❄ ❄

"Come with me," Lucas said, pulling Alex by his hand. "You're going to love this!" Lucas had been itching to get Alex out of his office and Noelle hadn't let him until four o'clock on the dot. The very second the hands changed on the clock, Lucas went sliding in his socks all the way to the office. The two of them walked toward her across the expanse the Harringtons called a kitchen, the white surfaces gleaming despite the cloud cover. Flurries were falling outside, giving the area by the kitchen table a cozy feel as the flakes fluttered past the large picture window beside it.

Alex was smiling, looking adoringly at Lucas.

The whole of the kitchen table was covered in decorations for the gingerbread house and the construction itself—Casa Grande—sat just behind the table in the corner. Noelle had worked for hours, making the chocolates and icing. The rest, she'd run out and taken from the bakery.

"Sit here." Lucas pointed to one of the chairs. "Beside me."

Alex took a seat as he glanced over at Noelle, and he looked so relaxed and content that she wanted to freeze the moment. "It's started to snow quite a bit," he said to her.

"I know. I love snow so much. We have fun when it snows, don't we, Lucas?"

"Yes!" Lucas was on his knees in the chair beside Alex, sitting extra close to his new friend. "We go to the park and sled down a gigantic hill. It tickles my tummy!"

Noelle was glad to see Lucas's excitement about sledding. It made her happy that she'd created memories that resonated with him. She decided then that he needed both types of experiences: the kind Alex could offer and the ones she could. "Maybe the snow will pile up and we can go out in it," she said.

"Would you come with us, Alex?" Lucas asked, leaning toward him, bouncing a little on his knees.

"I'd love to—if it's okay with your mom."

Their conversation came to a halt, Alex's smile fading to a questioning look. Noelle turned around to follow his gaze as William entered the room. The only sound was the tapping of his cane as he made his way to the table, his eyes squinting toward Alex and a wary look on his face—he knew it was him. She remembered then that she'd failed to warn either of them that they'd be decorating the gingerbread house together. It was probably best, given that they'd managed to avoid each other the entire time William had been there, and judging by the looks on their faces now, that she hadn't said anything.

"Was this some big ploy to get me in the same room as my grandson?" William snapped through pursed lips.

"It only occurred to me a couple of hours ago," Noelle said. She hadn't meant to cause an awkward situation. She'd only wanted to give the two of them a place where they could be together without worrying so much about the past. She turned to Lucas. "Tell them how much fun it is to make gingerbread houses. It's fun, isn't it?"

"It's so much fun," Lucas said. "But if you and Alex are having trouble being friends, you don't have to share the candy dishes. There are enough for both of you to have your own."

Both men smiled despite themselves.

"Thank you," Alex said seriously, for Lucas's benefit.

Lucas slid two bowls toward Alex. "These can be just for you." Alex reached in and grabbed a shiny red piece of hard candy. He tossed it up in the air and caught it in his mouth, making Lucas giggle. The harshness in William's look withered a bit.

Noelle shook her head, amused herself, and grabbed the large tube of icing. "I think we should get Alex to reinforce the roofline. He's tall enough and he probably has a steady hand. Plus, we need to get him away from the candy before he eats it all." She gestured for him to meet her at the gingerbread house and, with a laugh, he stood up and followed her over, grabbing one more piece of candy before he left the table. She pointed to the crack between the wall and the roof, where the two pieces of gingerbread met. "We'll want to pipe some icing in right there."

Alex squeezed and a blob of icing bubbled out, dripping down the gingerbread. "Oops," he said, making a face at Lucas.

"That's okay." Noelle wiped it off with her finger and cleaned her hand with a kitchen towel that she had nearby. "Alex just dribbled the icing," she told William. Then she turned back to the house. "Try again."

William looked toward them, and, even though she knew he couldn't see well, she was suddenly keenly aware of her movements with Alex: the way she smiled up at him, the proximity of her arm to his, the lack of personal space in general between them. She wondered what William must think.

Alex squeezed once more, and this time the icing shot out all over the roof in a big splat. Lucas giggled again.

"Oh, for heaven's sake. Did he not do it? It's a straight line, son," William said, standing up and tottering over. "Give it to me. I can't see and I'll bet I can do it." With a wobbly hand, he took the tube and tried to line it up, using his other finger to find the gap, unsteadily squeezing until a tiny dribble came out, filling the space just slightly before pumping out air because he didn't have enough pressure behind it. It made a splat of air and icing.

"See?" Alex said with a laugh. "You think you know it all, but it's hard to do, isn't it?"

"Let me show you," Noelle said, delighting in the ever-so-tiny bit of banter she was seeing. She took the tube from William, squeezed the end until the icing had filled the front of it, and pressed with all her might, trailing a perfect line of icing just under the roofline. Alex and Lucas both glanced at each other, Alex in awe, before looking back at her. She continued piping, drawing little arcs across the roof for shingles and lining the pieces with more icing. "You all can start sticking the candy on, if you'd like," she said.

Alex stood behind her. "May I try again? You make it look so easy that I just can't sit back and accept the fact that I couldn't do it." Gently, he put his hand on the icing tube. "Show me."

Wrapping her hand over his, Noelle showed him just how to work the icing from the bottom of the tube, and she drew their hands along the edge, creating a neat line, while William and Lucas pushed candy into the icing.

"I think I can do it now."

She let go and Alex piped one of the windows she'd drawn on prior.

"Perfect!" Lucas said, clapping his hands.

As they started placing more candy on the house, Noelle caught Alex pinching a piece of chocolate between his fingers, taking a small bite. She'd seen him get one a few minutes ago and now he was going for seconds. It made her smile. "Caught you!" she said, causing him to look over in surprise.

"Sorry," he said. "This chocolate might be the best I've tasted."

Interested, William reached over and felt around the table until he could get a piece, popping it into his mouth. With raised eyebrows and a frown of contemplation, he nodded his approval.

"My mom made it," Lucas said proudly. "It's my favorite too."

"You made it?" He put the whole piece in his mouth, chewed, and swallowed. "It's delicious."

"Thank you. It's a caramel truffle. It was my gram's recipe."

"We should make cookies for the neighbors!" Lucas suggested. "Like Grandma does."

Alex smiled at Lucas, noticeably pleased to see Lucas's delight in his mother's work. "It's quite a long way to the next neighbor," Alex said. He was sitting at the table, his chin in his hand, that gorgeous happiness on his face. He ate another chocolate.

"Have you ever met your neighbors?" Noelle asked.

"No." Then, upon seeing her reaction to his answer, he added, "How could I? They're at least a mile away."

"So?" she said in playful defiance. Alex picked up another of the chocolates but she snagged it from his fingers and popped it into her mouth.

Alex watched her eating it, amused by her audacity. "Have you met them, Grandfather?" he asked William.

William frowned and shook his head.

Noelle clasped her hands together, the gesture making one single clapping sound, a smile on her face. "Then we definitely need to make cookies for them." She tugged on Lucas's sleeve affectionately. "We should show these two guys how we do it! That is, unless they're scared to spread a little Christmas spirit..."

"Is that a challenge?" Alex teased.

"Absolutely."

"Challenge accepted, then."

They all turned to William.

"Will you help us, William?" Noelle asked.

With a shrug and a smile, he said, "Sure." He cleared his throat.

Noelle had the same excitement that she felt whenever she and Gram made Christmas cookies to stuff in the stockings on the mantel that they filled for kids in need. She also felt that same excitement when she was baking with her sister, when she and her mother filled the trays of cookies that her mom kept on the counter during the Christmas season.

"We'll need to get some ingredients," she said. "We've got a ton at the bakery. We'll go tomorrow after school. Alex, will you meet us there to help us choose what we'll need? It's clear that you have your favorites already but you might want to have a few taste-tests to decide what we should bake. Tell him why, Lucas."

"Because the best part about making cookies for the neighbors is that we get to eat all the broken ones."

Alex laughed.

Chapter Twenty-Two

Noelle, Jo, and Phoebe raced through the corridor, pushing past throngs of travelers, Jo simultaneously running and flipping her wrist over to keep them abreast of the time. Noelle's day had started with a trip to the airport to take Phoebe to her audition after she'd called before sunrise and said she was feeling too jittery to drive. They plowed on, underneath the enormous Christmas wreaths hanging from the terminal ceiling, Phoebe's bags trailing behind them.

"We're not going to make it!" Phoebe panted, her boarding pass in a wad in her hand.

Noelle and Jo had sat outside Phoebe's apartment for ages, waiting for her to come out so they could take her to the airport to catch her flight to Los Angeles. This was the big day. She had burst through the door in a panic, saying it took her ages to pack, her face full of fear. They'd all jumped into Jo's Mercedes and put that fancy engine to the test to see if it really was all it was said to be. Minutes ticked on as they paid for parking, found a spot, and raced into the airport to Departures.

"We'll make it," Jo said, her words desperate. She grabbed Phoebe's arm and pulled her down the hallway faster.

Out of nowhere, Phoebe stopped dead next to the twinkling Christmas tree outside one of the souvenir shops, and Noelle and Jo, who were both holding onto her, nearly fell over with the jolt of it.

"I'm scared."

"Well, if you stop now, you should be scared." Jo pushed her runaway lock of hair behind her ear to focus on Phoebe, her breathing still unsteady. She was shiny with perspiration from running in her coat. "The plane is going to leave. Why are we slowing down?"

"I'm scared to do the audition."

Noelle had seen that kind of fear on Phoebe's face before, when her mother had told her in one of her low moments that she'd decided to move away, leaving Phoebe completely on her own at eighteen. She understood now why Phoebe had been running late: she was deciding whether or not to go through with it.

Noelle looked at Jo, and Jo told her to handle it with her eyes. Noelle knew just how to get through to her friend. "Phoebe, you were born for this. What in the world is there to be scared about?" she asked, glad to have a moment to catch her breath but knowing they were running out of time. "Don't sabotage this out of fear. Sure, you could never go and be safe, but you may miss out on the very best life for *you* because you were trying not to get hurt. Get on that plane. You can text me once you land and I'll keep talking you into it."

"You're right." She started to run again and Noelle and Jo followed her, picking up speed once more. The rest of the time, they were silent, working together to get their friend to her flight.

They reached the gate and Phoebe thrust her boarding pass into the hand of the flight attendant, then took her bags from Jo and Noelle, telling them with her expression how thankful she was. Phoebe bit her lip as it started to quiver. Then, with a quick hug—out of lack of time and probably because she might not board otherwise—she headed toward the entry gate. "What is a Virginia girl doing flying out to LA for an acting part?" she called out.

"You're only a Virginia girl right now," Noelle called back. "After a few shows, you'll be an LA girl!"

With a decisive nod, Phoebe started down the passenger boarding bridge but she stopped and turned back to her friends, still looking unsure. "Noelle. I can't do this without you."

"Yes, you can."

She hesitated.

"You *can*! I'll text you, remember?"

The flight attendant urged her to board the plane. "Promise you'll come to LA with me if I get this!"

"We'll talk about it after you get the part."

"Promise!"

The flight attendant started to get more urgent.

"Okay! I promise!" Then she watched Phoebe disappear from sight.

With a huge sigh of relief, Jo flopped down into one of the chairs. "I didn't think we'd get her on the plane."

"I know. This is huge for her. I think she's worried that her dreams will come crashing down if someone tells her she isn't good enough. Without acting, she wouldn't know who she was. This is a turning point in her life, and it could go well or it could totally crush her."

"You understand her so well, Noelle."

Jo rubbed her shoulder, causing Noelle to be aware of the pinch in her own from dragging those heavy bags so far. "My back is killing me. What the heck did she have in her luggage?" Noelle said with a laugh.

"Why don't we go get a cup of coffee? It would do us some good."

❄ ❄ ❄

"What does your day look like?" Jo asked, holding a latte with a heart drawn in the foam. After leaving the airport, they'd found a great little shop to settle in and relax. They'd chosen the oversized sofa, both slumping back into it, holding their warm mugs and trying to stay awake from getting up so early.

"I'm doing a little organizing and calling around to get estimates for work at the bakery and then I'm making cookies with William and Alex Harrington."

Jo's eyebrow shot up in her famous what-the-heck look.

"And then Alex is going to help me and Lucas deliver them to his neighbors."

Jo laughed. "What?"

"Alex and his grandfather don't get along but I think that if they just spend time together, they could. They're both amazing people, you just have to scratch the surface to see it."

Jo offered a cautionary look. "I'm not sure that's part of the job description. You always care so much about people, Noelle, but I wonder if you'll find yourself in over your head. This is a powerful family, and if they don't like one another, there's probably some reason—some *big* reason."

"There's this mystery woman that apparently got between William and his wife and it caused a rift with Alex."

Jo set her coffee down, her eyes wide, interest on her face.

Noelle held her mug and sat up straighter, poised to tell her friend every detail she'd learned so far.

When she'd finished, Jo said, "How sad. I wonder where this woman is now. I wonder if she ever thinks about this forbidden love affair?"

"I don't know. But I do believe that things happen the way they were meant to happen. William loves his wife. But his first love affected all of them. It's as though something needs to be set right between William and Alex. I just don't know what."

❄ ❄ ❄

With William having his routine doctor visits, Noelle spent most of her day at the bakery, on her laptop, making spreadsheets for the new Hope and Sugar Coffee House. She'd organized exterior and interior changes, which were minimal, given her tight budget, and she'd come up with a simple menu and drink options.

The thought occurred to her that in the evenings, she might be able to get live music in there—perhaps set up an acoustic solo artist on Saturday nights. She'd have to start with local musicians—very small, maybe even a few who would play just for coffee at first. There was a tiny patio out back that just held the trash cans and empty freight boxes until they could be broken down. What if she could clean it up for the summer, squeeze a few tables with umbrellas out there, string patio lights above them? But she'd have to get some sales first to prove to Alex that her plan would work and keep the bakery going until then.

Noelle's mind was humming with ideas. She also thought about having a few taps with local beers, and she'd called three breweries to see if she could get a deal if she wrapped up the sales in some sort of advertising for the breweries. Her thought was to make this a whole-family location: cookies and milk for the kids, music and beverages for adults, and then in the daytime, it could be a quiet retreat for those looking to sit by the fire and enjoy light conversation. But right now, she had to focus on the re-opening. She wanted everything to go off without a hitch.

Noelle had cashed in her emergency savings, transferring them to her checking account, and bought paint and a few select décor items online that would update the interior quickly. She was going to sink all her money from caring for William into the taps for the beer, area rugs to hide the flooring for now, and an updated iPad sales station, the current cash register barely working enough to ring people up. The café tables were a bit dated, but she had a few ideas for those.

With plans moving along, and William still asleep when she'd called Jim to check on him, Noelle went to see if Alex would come to get the ingredients for the cookies.

❄ ❄ ❄

They'd had more flurries on and off, yet they hadn't had any real buildup of any kind, but now the snow was coming down. Noelle had been hoping it would so they could go sledding. Alex had texted that he'd be at the bakery shortly, and she was just starting to prioritize the changes she wanted to start soon on the interior when she noticed something new. Noelle walked over to the wall separating the dining area and the kitchen. She'd been so busy on her computer that she hadn't noticed the puckered wall, or the enormous water stain streaking it.

Noelle was still inspecting the wall when Alex walked through the door.

"What's wrong?" he asked, his smile quickly changing to concern as his eyes moved from her to the giant spot on the wall. "Oh no."

"Something's leaking, and from the looks of it, has been going strong all day. I only just noticed it."

Alex set his coat on the counter and walked around to the other side to get a better look. He tapped his foot, his pricey wingtips looking out of place on the old flooring. It sagged under the weight of his shoe. "This wood is damaged," he said. "It looks like the leak has been going on a while, it only just now surfaced. I'll have it repaired."

"But Christmas is only three weeks away," she said, feeling sick. "I'd planned to do the re-opening just before Christmas."

"I'll call right now." He took out his phone and started searching for a plumber.

Now they had to repair the leaky pipe, the drywall, replace the flooring, and paint. Along with all her other changes, it would drastically push the timings back. She looked down at her spreadsheet. "I'll have to do the painting myself. I was going to use a low-cost painting company that I found, but now we'll have to wait until the wall's fixed."

Alex had started talking to someone on his phone. Noelle stared at the wall while he told the person on the other end what he was seeing. When he finished, he hung up and said, "They're calling me back and I'll set an appointment then, but after describing the situation, they're estimating way more time than you'll have."

"I'll get it done, along with my family; we'll work into the night if we have to."

"I'd love to give you more time, Noelle, but I'm already committed to a solid renter in January..." He showed deliberation, clearly wanting to give her what she needed, but she didn't want handouts. She wouldn't take special favors because she knew too well that time was money and every extra day she took was money out of his pocket. She wouldn't be able to live with herself if she couldn't do this the right way.

"I'll get it done," she repeated, for emphasis. She wasn't going to get this close to saving the bakery only to walk away from it. "Enough about this for now. Just let me know when they'll be here to fix it. In the meantime, we have cookies to make!" She straightened her back to keep the ache in her chest from pulling her forward. "My dad ordered enough ingredients for another month of business," she explained, walking behind the counter. "We're making seven different kinds of cookies, so I might need help carrying it all to the car."

"It's no problem," he said with a smile, his eyes moving around the room. "When I was here last, I was focused on the structure of the building, and I didn't really get a chance to look around..." He peered into the glass case of cookies and muffins.

"Feel free to take a seat, get comfortable," she said, heading into the kitchen. "I'll just grab what we need for the cookies and start stacking it on the counter."

"Okay." He was already at the window, leaning over the huge peppermint cake that Heidi and Noelle had made together.

Noelle went into the kitchen and stopped, taking a look around at the empty cupboards, the looming changes becoming so real. It was clear that her father didn't expect a whole lot of traffic this season, the supplies he'd left out barely enough to cover an hour in the bakery's heyday, and he and Pop-pop must have been packing up. The shelves where their mugs and plates had been were now empty, with only a few sitting on the counter, the rest in boxes. Fear swept through her as she worried she wouldn't be able to make this work, but she shook it from her mind and focused on the cookies.

Noelle walked into the large pantry at the back, and, mentally listing the ingredients she'd need, she tried not to think about anything else or she'd break down into tears of worry. This was about what was meant for her, but it was also about Gram; Noelle couldn't let Gram down. Every time she thought about it, all she could see were Gram's pleading eyes that day in the hospital when she'd asked Pop-pop to keep the bakery open.

She rolled her head on her shoulders to alleviate the pinch and closed her eyes to visualize Gram's recipes. They'd be making ginger snaps, cheesecake truffles, coconut macaroons, chocolate-dipped shortbread, peanut butter and sugar cookies, and peppermint bark.

Noelle remembered having long conversations with Gram about the perfect complements when it came to cookie pairing. Gram had told her that her most popular assortment had always had exactly seven different types of cookies: just enough to love each type, not enough to tire of them. When asked how she got her data, Gram had simply said, "By the smiles on people's faces." The funny thing was that, while Gram had no formal way of knowing these things, she always got it right. Noelle pulled a box of sugar and two bags of flour off the shelf, wishing she could hear her soft, reassuring voice.

With her arms full, she went out to set what she had so far onto the counter. When she got back into the main room, Alex was squatting in front of the old jukebox. He noticed her entry and stood up. "That's amazing," he said, throwing his thumb into the air to gesture toward it. "It's an antique."

"Yes. It's one of my favorite things."

"It's not working. Have you had a look inside to see what's wrong with it?"

Noelle shook her head.

"Do you mind if I take a look?"

Panic pelted her insides. She didn't want him tampering with it. The last person to touch it was Gram. She'd chosen the order of the records; she'd decided which were the best. He took a step back, just as she realized she'd moved between him and the jukebox.

"Are you all right?" he asked, looking concerned.

"I'm sorry. It just has sentimental value." She forced herself to calm down but seeing Alex in Gram's shop, messing with things, gave her a sense of uneasiness that she couldn't shake. What if she made the wrong choices and lost the bakery? This was her last chance to save it. The elation she'd felt before had now turned to an immensity in her shoulders, and she felt the tears coming unexpectedly, the emotions rushing out like a runaway tide.

Obviously noticing her stress, Alex slid into her view, his hands on her arms, concern overwhelming his features. "I won't touch it," he said. He looked down at her as she blinked away her tears.

"I just feel that without Gram, without this bakery… How can I move forward? I can't even enjoy Christmas, and that's the most exciting time of the year for me. I can't allow myself to enjoy it when I have all this on my shoulders."

Gently, he added, "Sometimes, though, if you can pull yourself from the past, you'll be able to see a future that's even better than what you're missing."

Noelle stood there with him, stunned by his statement. It was the perfect thing to say. It was like something Gram would've said. "I love that saying," she admitted.

He smiled and rubbed her arms a little before letting go. "My grandmother told me that once. It was when she was going in and out mentally and I wasn't sure if it was babble or what, but it made me think of my parents and how much I miss them, and how I judged my grandfather for not being like the picture of a father that I had envisioned. It also made me wonder if she was hoping that my grandfather would pull himself from his past to see what was right there in front of him." With a gentle smile, he said, "I won't make that mistake. I won't ever live in the past."

She delighted in the honesty she saw in his eyes, the fluttery feeling returning.

"It's also why I decided to move to New York."

The words washed over her like an icy chill.

"I was holding on to the house because it made me feel close to my grandmother, and I was protective of it because I didn't feel like my grandfather deserved the home he'd refused to live in while I was growing up, a home my grandmother absolutely loved. But I know that if I can break free from what holds me here, I'll probably be better off because of it."

She'd only allowed herself that one moment of vulnerability and then he'd hit her with a big dose of reality, so many thoughts flooding her mind: Who was she kidding, thinking he'd stay? He had nothing to stay for. She'd need to prepare Lucas. His little heart would be broken once Alex was no longer in the house. And how was she going to juggle the new coffee shop plans with caring for William? Should she give up a job that paid well to take a wild chance that the bakery could be successful as a coffee house?

"You're worried," he stated. "I can tell."

She shook her head, but not to disagree; she didn't want to try to discuss it. There wasn't any point. Things were what they were. That was it.

"It's too heavy emotionally in here," he said. "Let's get out and bake some cookies."

Chapter Twenty-Three

Noelle held the phone away from her head to save her eardrum as Phoebe screamed through it from across the country, "I got the part!"

"Oh my gosh! That's so awesome, Pheebs! I can't believe it! Well, I can—you're very talented. But I can't believe it all worked out for you!" She ran a brush through her hair, pulling it up into a ponytail. It was a habit: every time she baked, she'd put her hair up. Gram had coached her to do it as part of the rules for the bakery and she'd carried it into her personal baking as well. "Clean hands, hair up, big smile," Gram would always say.

"I can't believe it either," Phoebe said, "I actually got the lead in a sitcom! It sounds so weird saying it out loud. This is potentially life-changing."

Noelle set the brush down, the phone wedged between her shoulder and ear, and pulled her apron from one of the drawers in the bedroom where she'd put her things. It had been Gram's apron, straight-seamed, pale blue, with little flowers on it. She slung it over her arm and walked into the sitting area to let Lucas know that she'd only be a minute more on her phone call. He was reading about dinosaurs in the book Alex gave him again.

"Did you meet any of the other actors? What kind of vibe did you get?"

"I met the producer and director as well as my co-star. They're all really great. I can't wait to get home and tell you everything!"

Noelle wanted to ask about Paul, but she thought better of it, worried she'd spoil the moment, and Phoebe was clearly very excited. "When are you coming back?"

"The day after tomorrow. The jet lag is gonna kill me, but there's no use in staying here all by myself when I just want to be home with you and Jo. I want to get together right away!"

"Okay," she laughed. "Call me as soon as you get back home."

"I will."

Noelle got off the phone and plopped down next to Lucas on the sofa, the apron draped between them. Lucas picked it up in his little hands. "It still smells like Gram," he said.

Noelle nodded, willing herself not to breathe in the scent for fear she'd get misty-eyed. It had been a year now and still it felt like yesterday when Noelle had wrapped her arms around her. "Ready to make some cookies?"

Lucas jumped up. "Yeah!"

"Awesome. Let's go!"

They met Alex in the kitchen. He was standing at the bar, reading the *New York Times* aloud with a cup of coffee in his hand while William sat beside him. They were being stoical, their laughter during the gingerbread-house-making now gone. But Alex read a little bit out to him and offered his opinion, William nodding in agreement. Were they actually getting along?

When Noelle and Lucas neared them, Alex folded his paper and set it aside. "We were just waiting for you guys," he said. Then he turned to Lucas. "Hi there. Are you ready to show me how to make some cookies?"

Lucas nodded excitedly.

Noelle slipped her apron over her head and tied it behind her back, walking over to William. "How about you?" she said. "Are you ready to bake some cookies?"

"I suppose so," he said, but she thought she caught the hint of a smile.

"We need Christmas music," Lucas said. He turned to Alex. "Do you have a radio in here?"

"I can do better than that." Alex pulled out his phone and hit a few buttons. Before he'd even slipped it back into his pocket, Nat King Cole came sailing out of speakers that were hidden in the crown molding. "Better?"

Lucas burst into a grin. "Yes. That's really good."

"Do you have a favorite Christmas song?" William asked, his features lifted as he listened to Alex and Lucas.

"'Rockin' Around the Christmas Tree.' Remember how we danced to that, Mom?"

Noelle couldn't help her smile at the memory and the fact that Lucas remembered. It was last year. They'd been gone all day, running errands: a doctor's appointment for Lucas because he'd had a sore throat and their weekly grocery run. They'd gotten home late—after Lucas's bedtime. By the time they'd unpacked the groceries, it was at least nine o'clock.

She was rushing, stressed out, upset at herself for keeping Lucas up to get it all done, the guilt of having to do it alone eating at her. Then Lucas said, "Mom, listen to that."

"Rockin' Around the Christmas Tree" was on the little radio in the kitchen. The smile on his face made her realize that none of her worries mattered because, to Lucas, it was all okay. She reached into the freezer, pulled out a popsicle for his sore throat, and gave it to him. With it in one hand, she grabbed his other, and started to spin him around, his socks causing him to slide all over the floor. As quiet as he usually was, he was so happy that night, letting loose with the delirium of illness and no sleep, and he'd laughed and laughed.

"Will you show me how?" Alex asked, typing on his phone again. Abruptly, the song changed to that familiar tune.

"How to dance? Easy. You have to take your shoes off," Lucas said with a giggle.

"Okay." Alex leaned against the barstool where he was standing and slipped his shoes off. Noelle grinned at his striped socks. "What?" He looked down at them and then eyed her playfully.

"Nothing," she said, straightening out her face.

"What's he done?" William said. "Don't leave me out. I need a play-by-play."

"He's wearing striped socks," Noelle said, trying to hide her affection for him. William took a seat and, with a dramatic flair, removed his own shoes while winking toward Noelle, making her outright laugh. "What socks did you pick out for me this morning?" he asked, wiggling his toes.

"Black," she said, unable to hide her amusement.

While Noelle began pulling bowls from the cabinets and preparing the ingredients for the various cookie recipes, Lucas had Alex by the hands, dragging him around in circles. Alex made a silly face before twirling Lucas and making him double over at the hilarity of it. William was laughing along with them, and, while Noelle's hands were busy, her mind was as well—*this* was more like it.

When the song ended, Noelle had most of what they would need set out. Lucas climbed up on the barstool next to William and Alex came up beside them. "There are three kinds of jobs in this business." Noelle repeated the words that Gram had used with kids, smirking at Lucas. Holding up a finger, Noelle said, "One: the scoopers." She held up a second finger. "Two: the pourers. And—" she held up the last finger. Lucas snickered. "—The squishers. Who should be our squisher, Lucas?"

"Well, there are four of us." He pursed his lips. "You are a great pourer, Mom. You be that. I can be a scooper. And then let's make William and Alex the squishers!" He burst into laughter, and Noelle tried to slow her racing heart. Lucas was having the time of his life, and she sent a silent wish into the air that they'd have many more days like this one.

"Oh no," William said, with a look of mock worry, his toes still wiggling in his socks as he sat on the barstool, leaning on the counter on his elbows. "I'm afraid to ask what a squisher is."

"I'll show you," Lucas said.

"Shall we make the ginger snaps first?" Noelle said, pulling those ingredients forward. She measured out the sugar, flour, molasses, cinnamon, ginger, and everything else that Gram usually put in the recipe. With the molasses, she couldn't wait to see William and Alex do this… "You'll need to wash your hands, gentlemen."

To her surprise, both men walked over together, Alex guiding William to the sink, and they turned on the water, lathering up side by side.

After they had dried their hands, Noelle ushered both men to the table and set the enormous bowl, full of gooey ingredients, in front of them. "You might want to push up your sleeves," she said, conspiring with Lucas as they complied.

"We need you to mix it up," Lucas said. "Put your hands in and squish it all around until it's all brown and sandy-looking."

"Alex can handle this job on his own," William teased.

"It's a big bowl, William," Noelle said. "We need four hands."

Both men sunk their hands into the mixture and began to squeeze their fingers, moving them around inside. Lucas was holding his tummy, giggling.

"What's so funny?" William asked, taking one hand out and trying to scratch his forehead without getting the dough on his face.

"You're all messy," he said, hiccupping with laughter.

"Oh, you think it's funny, do you?" Alex stood up, dropping batter on the table. He went over to the other side with his thickly covered hands held up like monster claws. Lucas scrambled from his seat and started to run, sliding on the shiny floors. He slipped and caught himself on one of the chairs, darting around it, laughing uncontrollably while Alex began to chase him through the kitchen.

"You're going to make a mess," Noelle said, but she was having the time of her life.

Alex stopped and turned toward her. "So it's okay for me to have to get my hands messy but no one or nothing else can get dirty? That's not fair." He started toward her and she offered her you-wouldn't-dare face. But he kept coming, a devious look in his eyes. She popped up and scooted a chair between them just as he dashed around it, sending her running across the room.

"Get your hands back in that bowl!" she demanded, ducking behind a display of poinsettias by the door. He swiped at her. She dipped down and ran off before he could catch her.

"And what will you do if I don't?"

"Everyone listens to Mom," Lucas said, before throwing his head onto his arms and laughing again.

"Oh, fine. I suppose I'll have to listen then." With an affectionate look at Noelle, he stopped chasing her and sat back down, but, before dropping his hands back into the bowl, he took one last swipe at her, making her squeal.

❄ ❄ ❄

With the last batch out of the oven, Noelle and William settled around the table boxing up the cookies, a large assortment on a platter in front of them. Against her wishes, Lucas had said he was getting tired and asked if Alex could read stories with him in their suite. She'd told him no, but Alex had promised that it wouldn't be a problem at all. She'd warned him that Lucas would need to brush his teeth as well, but Alex had pulled her aside and said, "Don't worry. I've got this."

She'd never had a man tell her that before. His face had been so sure, so honest, that she didn't have any choice but to believe him. And what she didn't want to admit to herself was that she totally did believe him. She knew Lucas was in good hands.

"You and Alex are something," William said, after Alex and Lucas had left. He put a piece of peppermint bark into one of the boxes. "I've never seen him like that before. It brought back so many memories."

"Of?"

"When I was with…" He bit his bottom lip, unable to finish for a second. "She had a personality a lot like yours—playful but responsible."

"The woman from the café?"

He nodded, closing the box of cookies with trembling fingers. "I can't believe it—I've spoken more about her since you've come to live here than I probably have my whole adult life. I don't know why the memories keep surfacing. Maybe it's because I'm back here where it all began." He lifted his head from the box. "I think it's also because of all the life I see in you. I saw that in her too. There's something untamed, that just was, with her. I can't put my finger on it, but when I see you and Alex together, I feel that same thing. Tell him not to move to New York. He'll listen to you."

"I'm not so sure he will," she said. Noelle was realizing more and more how this woman affected William. While he'd moved on, and found love again, it always came back to her, against his will. She had to wonder if she'd have the same fate: years later, torn apart by their very different lives, would she compare everyone she met to Alex?

Her heart ached just at the thought of Alex going to New York and she had to know that her life would get better if she had to live without him. "Tell me about Elizabeth," she said, before William could counter her difference of opinion regarding Alex's move.

William smiled a sad smile as if he'd read her inner thoughts. "She had a laugh like angels," he said. "She could make a perfect bouquet of flowers and insisted on doing it herself for every occasion. She had a heart for stray dogs, and, while she never had one here, she organized adoption parties with local shelters and found homes for hundreds of them. The news made her cry—real tears—so she wouldn't watch it." He broke into a huge grin. "At parties, she was completely oblivious to current events, and she told me she didn't care because the news was all about things that had already happened, things she couldn't change, so it didn't matter whether she knew what was going on or not. She said when it was her time to go—whether that be by war, an accident, or by natural causes—she didn't want to know when it would be, so the news was pointless. She held firm to that her entire life, and you know what? I think it made her so much happier."

"She sounds wonderful," Noelle said, feeling a lump form in her throat. All she could think about was how lucky William had been to find that kind of love twice. If she had to find it again, would she be so lucky?

Chapter Twenty-Four

After getting William going for the morning, Noelle, carrying two boxes of cookies from last night, each tied with a large red bow, knocked on Alex's office door. She was meeting her parents and Lucas at the bakery this afternoon once she'd gotten off work, so she had no time to waste and she wanted to talk to Alex. "I thought maybe you and I could take the cookies over to the neighbors," she said, after he looked up from his laptop.

"Do you know if they're home?" he asked.

"No, but that's part of the fun. If they aren't, we'll leave them a surprise on the front steps. Do you know their names? I wanted to personalize the boxes."

"I don't. I've never met them."

"You have neighbors on either side of you and you don't know who they are?"

"I've never had reason to meet them."

After she thought about it, he was probably right. Noelle doubted that he'd ever had to borrow an egg or a cup of sugar. He had a whole staff just to water his plants for him. And she was nearly certain he hadn't needed a dog sitter like her mother had for Muffy…

"What are you thinking about?" he asked as he stood up.

"That you need a dog." The sudden idea of this gave her a punch of happiness. She could just imagine Alex chasing after an enormous Labrador as it ran away from him with his favorite shoe.

"A dog? As in a live canine?" He took the boxes from her and tucked them under his arm, leading her out of his office.

She smiled, nodding. The look on his face made her laugh. "There's so much space for a dog to run on this property. And William told me how Elizabeth loved dogs but never had one. It's as if the house was meant to have a dog. It might be fun!" She knew she was only teasing him because soon he wouldn't be here anyway, but she couldn't help the tiny flicker of hope in the bottom of her chest that he'd decide to stay.

They paced together toward his suite, where Alex grabbed his coat. "I'm not sure my apartment in New York allows dogs," he said, as if reading her mind. "And I'd have to walk it in the city—not my thing." He slipped an arm into his sleeve.

"There's a way to solve that issue," she said.

He closed the door to the suite. "What? Get a dog walker?"

"No. Don't move to New York."

He didn't respond for a few steps as they started down the hallway. She looked over at him to see his face, hoping she could tell what he was thinking, but he wouldn't let his thoughts show. Then, out of nowhere, he stopped and faced her. "I didn't plan for any of this. I had no idea a month ago when I signed the extension on the lease for my apartment and hired a full-time staff to run my company in New York that I'd be delivering cookies to strangers because the only person who's come waltzing into my office with the biggest smile I've ever seen is also the first person who is able to pull me away from my work, because I can't keep my mind on it anyway now." He took in a breath, his jaw set as he shook his head. "But I can't just throw it all away, Noelle."

He was right, he shouldn't throw it all away, but at the same time, she deserved to have someone who would do anything to make it work, and clearly he wasn't the one to do that.

"There are jobs on the line here," he said, obviously finishing his thought. "I'm sure you could imagine what it would be like for them if I change course now. Many of the people I hired in New York would lose their jobs—at Christmas. Not to mention that, for what I do, it just makes sense to work in New York. That's why my grandfather lived there for so many years."

"He said it isn't all that you think it is." She didn't know if she should be sharing William's thought with Alex, but then again, maybe William and Alex should have this conversation and she could get things started.

"He's just being sentimental about the house. He doesn't mean that." Alex started walking again, thoughts clear on his face. Finally, his voice calmer, he said, "We won't solve this right now. Let's get these cookies to the neighbors."

They didn't talk about it anymore on their walk over. It was quite a way in the cold. They'd walked along the street instead of over the grounds, the snow beginning to accumulate. But the whole way there, she thought about Alex and that hurt little child that was still inside him. Of course William was sentimental about the house, and Alex probably was too, even if he wouldn't admit it. But it was a lot more than that.

❄ ❄ ❄

They'd met Mrs. Bruster, the nearest neighbor. She was lovely and thankful for the cookies. She'd asked them in to warm up, but Alex had declined politely, telling her he'd hate to impose and they'd just wanted to say hello. She'd been curious about him, and over the years had wondered about his family, and she was so glad to have met him. The entire time they spoke, Noelle was thinking, and by the time they got back to the mansion, she had a plan.

"Come with me," she said, taking Alex by the hand after they'd come in and taken off their coats. She lumped them on the railing.

His eyes trailing from the randomly placed pile of coats, Alex followed her. "Where are we going?"

"To fix something." Her feet were numb from walking in the cold as she marched down to William's suite.

"Is something broken? I can call—"

"This isn't something they can fix," she said. "Only you can mend this."

Alex stopped just as they reached William's door. "What are you doing?"

"I'm putting an end to your and William's issues once and for all." She knocked on his suite door and entered. "He's wonderful. So are you. You two need to see that."

"You're trying to change a lifetime, Noelle."

William stood at the door and regarded them curiously, stepping back to allow them to enter. Noelle went in first, turning to face them as Alex shut the door.

"Just because we can sit together without killing each other doesn't mean that everything will come together like some kind of Christmas miracle. You can't erase a lifetime of absence with a few days of cookie-baking."

"Right," she said, pointing to the sofa for both men to sit down. "But you can listen to one another, try to understand each other. I know both of you well enough to be sure you're capable of that." She turned to William. "Tell him why he shouldn't move to New York."

William sat, wide-eyed for a second, and she paused in her argument long enough to realize that she and Alex had burst in without any notice whatsoever. But she held her ground. "Tell him," she said, more gently.

With a moment to gain his composure, he turned to Alex. "You don't have to go chasing it," he said.

"Chasing what?"

"Wealth. Success. Whatever will get you away from here."

"You know as well as I do that I need to be in the center of real estate—big real estate—to know what's going on in the business, to see trends, to be at the forefront of decisions. You said it yourself, ninety-nine percent of this job is being there."

William's head dropped down, the lines on his face more evident with his frown.

Alex addressed Noelle. "That's what he told me on my thirteenth birthday when he wasn't going to be at my party. He spent it in New York." His voice was hurt rather than the usual irritation that she heard when he spoke to William.

"Because I was being stupid; just like you are now."

Alex's gaze snapped over to his grandfather, his hands on his knees, the blood rushing away from his knuckles, the anger returning in a flash.

"There's a little boy here who reminds me so much of you when you were that age. And I see how angry you've become with me. And I know that I've contributed to that anger. I'll bet he'd love to have you stay."

The mention of Lucas clearly affected Alex and for just a minute he looked as though he'd been blindsided. But once he'd gained composure again, he said, "Well, I'm not going to stay." Noelle had to wonder if this ridiculous move of his was more to spite his grandfather than out of necessity. It was as if his resolve to move had been built out of years of yearning to have his grandfather's love and now that William was here and needed him, Alex wanted him to feel hurt, just like he had as a boy.

"Alex, it's true that being in New York makes sense for what you do, but I've lived it. I've done it. And I left a gorgeous, wonderful wife and grandson here all alone," he said, his voice breaking. He cleared his throat. "With a little bit of forward thinking—which I know you're great at—you can do it from here as well."

Alex stood up, his expression so vulnerable that Noelle worried that he felt they were ganging up on him. "I'm going. That's it. You won't convince me otherwise." He turned away from them and left the suite, the door shutting loudly behind him. Noelle wanted to scream at him and tell him that she thought he was doing this to prove a point, more than just to get ahead, but the truth was that if he didn't care enough for any of them to stay, then there was no use in saying anything, so she let him go.

Chapter Twenty-Five

Noelle had thought about Alex the whole way to the bakery. After she'd pulled herself together with a cup of coffee and a little time in her suite, she'd gone back to see William. They'd decided to give Alex time to see if he'd change his mind. Her heart ached, and she'd spent all night wondering if he would. But for now, she pushed the thoughts away. She had a coffee shop to open.

Noelle and her family were working like little buzzing bees. Her mother had taken Lucas to school that morning while Noelle picked up the paint she'd purchased a few days ago online, which had been delivered to the home improvement store. The new sign she'd ordered was leaning against the bakery's front door when she'd gotten there, and she'd dragged it inside but hadn't had a chance to unpack it, her time consumed with calls to local television and radio stations regarding advertising.

With quick directions to her father, she'd asked him and Pop-pop to begin sanding the woodwork and shelves for painting. She'd wanted to take all the books down for them, but hadn't had time. She'd labored tirelessly to organize the repairs on the wall and flooring with the company Alex had emailed her. The calls and preparations had taken nearly all morning, and before she was really ready, she'd had to leave them to it so she could run over to the mansion, to check on William. Slightly late to give him his medication and help him get dressed, she raced down the hallway to his suite, skidding to a stop to get herself together before going in.

When she entered, he was sitting on the sofa, the fire going beside him, holding a glass of brandy. "I've been thinking," he said with no introductions. "I want to see Elizabeth. She shouldn't spend Christmas alone."

Noelle knew that it would be hard for him to see her, but she was so glad he had decided to. She guessed that it had been on his mind since he'd talked to Alex yesterday. It meant that he'd worked through his own sadness enough to realize that she needed him just like she had for all those years he was away, and even if she didn't fully recognize him, there was a part of her that might.

"Would you take me?" he asked.

"Of course."

"I have one more request."

"Anything."

"Use that charm you have on Alex to see if you can convince him to go with us. You ground him and make him a good man. But even if you can't get him to say yes, I want you there."

She knew what William was asking wasn't easy for her to accomplish, and it didn't seem like Alex was as apt to do things for her as William thought, given his decision to still move to New York, but she'd give it her best shot. Alex had said, himself, that he'd wanted to see his grandmother, and he'd even asked Noelle to go with him. She might be able to convince him to let William come along. "I'll see what I can do," she said, determined to make it happen.

❄ ❄ ❄

When she got back to the bakery, the first thing Noelle did was put the "Coming Soon" sign up in the window. Then, Pop-pop helped her hang the new Hope and Sugar Coffee House sign. She'd called Heidi yesterday and asked her to clear out the pastries before her dad and Pop-pop got there and to be thinking of the best selection of coffee syrups to have on hand. Heidi had said she'd box the cookies up and take them to their parents' house. They could all nibble on them while they tied up loose ends and she'd bag up the smaller ones to use with the combination packages. Then, she sent out the large stack of invitations that Heidi had addressed for her, sending a little prayer that each one would be met with excitement. She wanted this re-opening to be not only a great start for the coffee shop, but also, in a way, a celebration of Gram and all that she'd accomplished with the bakery.

After school, Lucas and Pop-pop had emptied the shelves, the books lying in haphazard piles on the floor under a tarp to protect them from the sanding dust. One of the books had slipped out from under it. Noelle reached down and slid the bookmark back into its spot to keep the place for whoever had last left it and blew the dust off the cover. She'd had a call from the plumber that he wouldn't be there until next week, and, while that was pushing things, she had to go with it. The problem was, the flooring guys couldn't start until the leak was fixed.

"It's looking good!" she said loudly to her father over the noise of the electric sander, trying to stay positive. She gave Lucas a squeeze, his smile doing little to calm her anxiety at seeing the bakery in shambles, the time literally racing away from her.

Her dad stopped, the squeal coming to a halt, and turned to her with a smile that pushed his safety goggles up just a little, making her edgier, his trust in her apparent. "This, I can do. Deciding which cakes to make is more your thing. I have high hopes for the coffee shop, Noelle. I know you can pull it off. Your gram would be so proud."

She smiled back, trying not to worry, as she leaned on the old jukebox, now draped with a sheet. Even given the difficulties, there was something intoxicating about making her own decisions and seeing her plans come to life that made Noelle feel like this was what she'd been born to do. She'd do everything she could to make it work.

"I'll be done with the shelves shortly," he said. "Then you and Pop-pop can start painting those while I sand the bottom of the counter."

"Sounds good!"

Noelle had chosen a buttercream color for the trim, the shelves, and the counter. She couldn't wait to get her hands on that beautiful counter to spruce it up. Pop-pop had made it from an antique dresser, the legs of it spindly like an old claw-foot tub. He'd replaced the middle drawers with lit-up glass-fronted units for display. With the larger pastry case beside it, the whole counter glowed with sugary goodness. The top was an enormous slab of granite—a pearly-gray swirling pattern that, in itself, looked good enough to eat. As a girl, Noelle had thought it looked like cake batter just before all the ingredients were stirred together. Right now, the wooden base of the counter was a dark-wood color, like the rest of the space, but it was time to lighten it up.

The small bistro tables would get a buttercream makeover as well, their worn tops covered in articles from a few coffee magazines she'd picked up, and sealed with glass. To complement the browns and creams, she'd planned to paint the chairs a bright turquoise. She'd also found petite glass vases to fill with coffee beans for each of the tables, which would accompany yellow-and-turquoise tea-light candles in their centers.

"How's this?" Pop-pop called from across the room. He was holding a huge framed blackboard against the wall. That wall had been exposed brick since the shop had originally opened and she was going to leave it just like that.

"Oh, that looks perfect," she said, envisioning the pastel chalk menu that would be scrawled across it soon. The darkness of that wall and the blackboard would look so lovely against the bright yellow she'd planned to paint the other three walls. She ran her fingers along the granite countertop. "Pop-pop, you know Gram's old dresser that's in your bedroom—the one that matches this?"

With a nail between his lips and the electric screwdriver in his hand, he looked over his shoulder, nodding.

"Do you think I could have it for the shop? Right now, the coffee machines are in the back, but it might be nice for people to see us making the coffee. We could paint it to match the counter and set it right here." She pointed to the open space on the other side of it.

With a buzz of the screwdriver, the blackboard was hung and Pop-pop came down from his ladder. "I'll do you one better," he said. "I've got another slab of that granite sitting in the shed. I've had it for years and didn't know what to do with it. I'll make it match for you."

"You will?" Her voice came out squealing with excitement. "What will you put your clothes in?"

"Who cares?" he said, with a big smile. "Gram would be so thrilled with this that I think she'd put her clothes in boxes if she had to." Then, with a sentimental look in his eyes, he said, "But may I ask one thing?"

"Anything."

"It's full of her stuff. Would you help me go through it?"

Noelle's skin prickled at the thought of filling her lungs with Gram's scent, running her hands across the blouses that she used to wear. But maybe it would bring a little of Gram to her when she needed her most. Noelle's emotion bubbling just below the surface, she agreed.

Chapter Twenty-Six

Phoebe's apartment was in a shabby building above a bar, downtown, only a few minutes' drive from Noelle's parents' home. The only entry door was glass, but the view in was completely obstructed by stickers for bands and local shops and merchants. Noelle hit the buzzer to alert Phoebe that she was there and then she heard the click and let herself in. The stairway was narrow, the steps creaking loudly with her weight, and the paint in the dark hallway had yellowed with age, years of coats painted over the cracked and peeling plaster. But when Phoebe opened the door, Noelle would always smile because it was the apartment itself that was worth the rent she paid for that ramshackle of a building.

The walls were exposed brick, thickly painted bright white, surrounding an enormous picture window that overlooked the city, the colors on the street below so vibrant that they made the window look like an enormous painting on that wall. The fireplace was also painted brick, and so grand that it reached the high ceiling. Above the mantel, Phoebe had hung a simple wreath, and silver candles were clustered at one end of it. She had a Christmas tree in the corner, all done up in greens and reds, complementing the reds on the street awnings below. Her furniture was simple: white slip-covered sofas and chairs with a stone table in the center. A candle was lit on it this evening, and Phoebe was bouncing with excitement on the sofa.

Jo came in from the kitchen with three glasses of wine and set them down. "I'm so glad you got here when you did," Jo said. "She's gonna explode if you make her wait any longer to tell her news."

Noelle plopped down beside Phoebe and took a glass of wine. "Sorry. I just got done with work. I had to check in on William before I came." She and William had talked for quite a while after she'd come back from the bakery for the evening. She hadn't even had a chance to ask Alex about seeing Elizabeth yet, and she'd been planning to speak to him, but just allowed William to talk instead.

"I'm having a really hard time," Phoebe said. "I keep wondering if I'm messing up a perfect life here. I've already found an apartment in LA." Then her face dropped considerably. "But..." She grabbed her wine and took a sip. "I talked to Paul and he won't go. I can't stop crying over him." Her bottom lip started to wobble.

"Oh, no." Noelle reached over and put her hand on Phoebe's arm.

"I can't blame him," Phoebe said, her voice quivering. "Everything he's worked for is here. And everything I need to move forward is there. But what if I'm meant to be here in Richmond with him? What if we could build a life together?" Without warning, she burst into tears. "He's so good," she said. "I've never met anyone who's been that good to me before."

Gently, Jo said, "If you don't go to LA, you'll always feel like you should've. And especially if things don't work out with Paul down the road. Wouldn't you feel awful, like you'd missed out on the one thing you've wanted your whole life?"

Phoebe nodded, more tears surfacing. Noelle couldn't imagine the decision that was on her friend's shoulders. Paul truly was a great guy. He might even be the perfect guy for Phoebe. She'd always struggled with relationships after her mother had left, her fear of abandonment keeping her from letting anyone in. And she'd let Paul in. But her big break was sitting right there, waiting for her to grab it with both hands and hold on for the ride.

"I know I have to say yes to LA," she said with a sniffle. "But it doesn't make this any easier."

❄ ❄ ❄

Noelle went to her parents' house to pick up Lucas, who'd asked to have dinner with them after helping in the coffee shop, Noelle's mother cooking his favorite spaghetti dish. But Noelle had something else to do as well. She was emotionally drained, worried for Phoebe, not sure what to tell her, and knowing it was going to be a bumpy road. She could've stayed there with her longer, but she needed to share the rest of her plans for the coffee shop with her father and Pop-pop so they could finalize the last few things for the re-opening. She shifted her arms to keep her notebook of ideas and her laptop steady as she opened the door. After she greeted Muffy, Noelle went inside.

"Hey, baby!" she said, giving Lucas a hug with her free arm. "Whatcha been doing?"

"We practiced reading the holiday play he's doing with his class and we've been talking a little about his vacation… He's been asking to go," her mother said. "He can't wait to get back to the mansion to see Alex." She offered Noelle a loaded look and Noelle's heart fell into her stomach. She was going to have a very difficult time telling Lucas that soon Alex wouldn't be there anymore. She was always so good at explaining things to him, but this was something that she just couldn't get her head around because she didn't understand Alex's decision to move at all. William was right there telling him he could do his job from the mansion, and she thought there was something between her and Alex, but he wouldn't budge. It was so confusing. Didn't he even want to try? It made her feel like she was nothing to him at all, just something to pass the time—she kept giving him chances and he kept making her feel that way. While she couldn't make Lucas understand how Alex had made her feel and the possible reasons he might be leaving, she'd decided to tell him that Alex simply had to move for his job.

"Sorry, baby," she said with a smile. "We'll have to wait just a little longer to see him. I need to talk to your grandpa for a second."

"He's in the kitchen with Pop-pop," her mother said. "Lucas and I were about to work on our puzzle anyway. This year's scene is Santa coming down the chimney."

"I remember doing that one," Noelle said, glad that Lucas would have a chance to work on the family puzzle. It sat out the whole holiday and any time one of the family got bored, they'd work on it, helping each other find the pieces until it was done. They'd leave it put together until New Year's, when it would be packed away for the next year. Noelle had always hated taking it apart, all that hard work being disassembled.

She left them to it and found her dad and Pop-pop waiting for her in the kitchen. With a thud, she set her computer and notebook on the table, both men looking at her expectantly. As she took in their faces, she thought about all Gram had built, how the bakery had been her dream-turned-reality, and the weight of its future fell heavily on Noelle's shoulders. She put her game face on and took in a deep breath.

"I've made some headway regarding the final changes," she said, sitting down. "But it's going to take everything we've got. We need to finish the transformation as soon as possible. And I'll be tied up with caring for William Harrington most of that time. I'm gonna need your help."

Gus and Pop-pop were focused, serious, ready to tackle this. Pop-pop nodded. "Tell us what you've got."

Chapter Twenty-Seven

"You wanted to see me?" Alex said, standing in her doorway, his voice hollow like he was holding back his emotions, the gray morning light filtering in on his face. The warmth that Noelle had once heard wasn't there anymore. Why? She longed to hear it, and the absence of it made her want to grab him and make him explain. Was his work really so important to him that he'd put it over everything else—over Christmas, over her, over Lucas?

She stared at him, trying to get him to look her directly in the eye, but when he did, his strength seemed to falter, so he looked away. She'd noticed staff members through her window this morning, taking boxes out of the house, and she wondered if those boxes were full of his things headed for New York.

"Your grandfather wants to see your grandmother," she said. "I'm taking him. I'd like you to come with us—William asked specifically."

His lips were in a straight line and she could see the tensing of his jaw as he fumbled for an answer.

"You'd said you wanted to go," she said softly.

"I hear you," he said to her surprise, his face surrendering his emotions. "I haven't said anything, but I've thought a lot about what you said about my grandfather. The past is the past, and I'm trying to see him for who he is now. I know he wants me to visit my grandmother with him… But I can't. I won't be here tonight."

"We don't have to go tonight. I was planning to go in a few days, perhaps." She opened the door wider to allow him to enter, but he stayed in the doorway.

"I'm leaving *for New York* tonight," he clarified.

She had to keep her mouth from dropping open. "Just like that? Were you even going to say goodbye?" A surge of anger and sadness exploded within her, and she couldn't help herself; the words just came tumbling out. "I have a little boy who adores you. I've never seen him talk to anyone like he talks to you. He was asking for you last night. I made up a flimsy excuse as to why we couldn't knock on your door. You were just going to leave and break his heart?" Noelle dared not express her own feelings about him, of how he didn't think enough of her to stay, even just until Christmas. She swallowed, trying to alleviate the lump that had formed. She felt lost all of a sudden, the moment becoming painfully real, and she knew in her heart this wasn't right. He shouldn't be leaving.

Scrambling to hear his soothing voice telling her it would all be okay, she looked up at him, but his eyes were distant again, his face unchanged, and she knew that he'd made up his mind. Unexpectedly, her tears surfaced. She looked away, blinking to keep them from spilling over and embarrassing her completely. It was clear that he didn't feel the same way.

"So this is goodbye then," he said evenly, and for just a moment, she saw something flash in his eyes, giving her hope despite his words, but then it was gone, taking her heart right along with it. "Tell Lucas I'll keep in touch. If… that's okay with you."

She nodded, unable to speak for fear that the tears would turn to sobs.

"Goodbye." He turned away and, without looking back, headed down the hallway.

She watched him go until he was out of view. Slowly, she shut the door, walked numbly to the sofa, and slumped down into it, unable to think, and then she allowed the tears to fall.

❄ ❄ ❄

Noelle found William in the grand living room. She hadn't spent any time there, the space so large that it swallowed them up. William was at the back, behind the formal furniture, at the oversized window that overlooked the rear grounds. He tipped his head just slightly as she walked in, letting her know he'd heard her enter, but he kept facing the window.

"You know, I can only see a blur of green and white, but I like the light on my face," he said, once she'd reached him. "So many times I sat with my back to this window, never bothering to pay attention to what was on the other side of it. And now that I understand a bit more about how to live my life, I can't see it. All I want to do is look out and view the yard." He turned to face her. "He's missing it, Noelle. Alex has got it all right here and he's missing it. I can finally see this life as it truly is and I'm too old to enjoy it, but he isn't."

"Who says you're too old?" she protested with conviction. She respected William. He was right: he'd figured out how to live; he knew what was important, and she didn't want him to think for a minute that he couldn't enjoy himself. She liked being with William, and she needed to get her mind off everything for a little while. "Come with me. Let's go Christmas shopping."

"I can't. I can't see where I'm going. I'll drag you down."

"Nope. You're going. Get your coat."

❄ ❄ ❄

"Do you hear that?" Noelle said with a smile, as she helped William out of the back of the car. He'd insisted on calling his driver so they wouldn't have to find a place to park. The driver had let them out of the black sedan just outside the mall.

"Hear what?" He tugged his coat together at the neck as an icy breeze blew.

Her smile widened. "Christmas. Listen. I hear Santa's bells and music and people talking—it's amazing. I just love it."

The car pulled away, leaving them on the step to the walkway beside one of the restaurants. It was full of people heading in for lunch. She helped him up onto the sidewalk.

"I hear the car driving away, which means that we're stuck here until you text my driver, and it's cold."

"Perfect! It's supposed to be cold at Christmas." She took his hand, walked him over to one of the benches and dragged his fingers in the tiny bit of snow that had settled with the flurries. "We even have snowflakes falling."

"So how am I going to help you pick anything out when I can't see it?"

She could tell that he felt helpless because of his failing eyesight. It occurred to her then that, given his upbringing and career, he'd always been in control. It must be awful to lose a little of that; perhaps that was why he'd been so edgy when she'd first met him. "Don't worry. You'll be able to help me." She linked her arm with his and started walking slowly toward the candle shop. "We're shopping for my mother first. She loves candles. You can help me pick out the scent." She took him inside, the smell of peppermint, caramel, spruce, and vanilla all mixing together in a delightful aroma that could only be found at this time of year.

Noelle picked up a large jar and took off the lid. "How's this one?"

William inhaled over it and then coughed, choking on the scent. "No," he said, shaking his head and coughing again.

"Not a fan of floral, then?" She giggled, grabbing another one. "This one better?"

He leaned in and sniffed. "That one's not bad."

"It's Pumpkin Pie." She set it to the side and opened a third. "Is this one better or worse?"

William put his hands on the jar and smelled it. "Oh, I like that one."

Noelle was glad to see him loosening up a little. "That's Salted Caramel. You're definitely a food-scent man. You'd love the smell of my grandmother's bakery. It always smelled like the most delicious cakes and pies. As a girl, my tummy would rumble the minute I got inside, just from the aromas."

He seemed lost in thought, and so far away all of a sudden.

"You okay?" she asked.

"Yes," he said, snapping out of it.

She was glad to see him pondering the wonders of the season. "Let's buy this one and then get a drink, shall we?"

❄ ❄ ❄

Lucas sat in the wide bathtub that evening, amidst a breadth of bubbles with suds in his hair. "So Alex isn't coming home anymore?" he asked, his little eyes sleepy but concerned.

Noelle had managed to get through picking him up from her parents' and dinner before he'd asked. He'd run into the mansion and she could tell he'd been searching for Alex. He'd even stopped at Alex's office and looked in. He hadn't said anything then, but Noelle knew the question would come. Finally, when she'd filled the tub for his bath, he asked about Alex. With a deep breath, she told him that Alex had gone to New York, trying to keep her voice even as if it was a totally normal thing for him to leave. She knew it was just her way of trying not to upset her son, but he wasn't stupid. He knew better.

"That's right," she said. "He said he'd keep in touch with you, though." The words felt acidic on her tongue as she said them because she knew it was probably a lie. How would he keep in touch? Send him emails?

Lucas made a fist and sunk his hand under the bubbles. "He won't be here for Christmas either?"

She shook her head, feeling just awful.

Lucas was quiet as the water made lapping sounds against the tub. Then, after he'd washed his arms, he set the washrag in a wad on the edge of the tub and looked up at her. "I'm gonna miss him, Mom."

"I know," was all she could manage. She was trying to remain strong for him, but she wanted to cry right there.

Chapter Twenty-Eight

Noelle went to Pop-pop's first thing in the morning. She needed to start early if she wanted to maximize her time at the bakery before she had to tend to William. The flooring repairmen were coming today to assess the damage, and they'd start as soon as the plumber had fixed the leak. It was early and the walkway to Pop-pop's front door was a sheet of ice, worrying her. She hoped he wouldn't try to walk on it himself. She let herself in with her key—both she and Heidi had a key—and called his name, knowing he was up.

Pop-pop woke every morning before sunrise and made a cup of coffee. Then, he sat and watched the travel programs on television. She'd asked him once if he ever wanted to go to any of the places he'd seen. He'd said, "If you watch the travel channel, you don't need to go," but she'd wondered if he really would like to see the world. She shut the door behind her and followed the roasted, chocolaty perfume of coffee to his favorite chair in the back room.

The living area was extraordinarily tidy, just like when Gram had been there. Their décor was simple, with just a sofa and two chairs, a coffee table and a small television on a stand in the corner, but the chairs both had quilts thrown over the backs and there were throw pillows waiting to make each spot comfy. A lamp in the corner of the room cast out a dreamy yellow light, making the room seem as though it were lit by candlelight. An early-morning glow filtered through two windows on either side of the room, illuminating the photo of Pop-pop and Gram that was on the wall opposite. Pop-pop was standing behind her, his arms around her, and Gram had an adoring look on her face as her eyes met the camera, making it look as though she could see Noelle standing there right now. Turning away before the emotions rose too high, Noelle smiled when she saw that the television was tuned to a show about Barbados.

"Morning!" he said, as chipper as ever. "Ready to clean out that dresser?"

"Yes," she said, so glad to see a friendly face.

He got up. "Let's get you suitably caffeinated first," he said with a wink. Then he led her past the small Christmas tree he'd put up in the corner, strands of colored bulbs shimmering in the dim light of early morning.

"It's been a year, Noelle," he said, pouring the steaming liquid into one of Gram's mugs. "A whole year, and I still haven't been able to go through her things." He handed her the sugar and then reached into the fridge to get the cream.

"Why do you have to?" she asked. "If her stuff reminds you of her and makes you happy, there's no need to disturb it."

He considered her perspective over a sip of coffee before topping off his cup.

"You were quite able to offer me the dresser, so I don't think you have some sort of unhealthy attachment or anything. You just miss her."

He smiled, holding his mug in his weathered hands. "I did find a few more things for you in the bedroom. I was saving them until I had a chance to give them to you." He scooted his mug closer, looking down into it. "You know, when I met her, she was quite shy, not really opening up to me, but I could tell there was so much there." He met her eyes. "I told her, 'Sophia, I am crazy about you and if you don't go out on a date with me, it will kill me. You don't want that on your conscience, do you?' She'd smiled that gorgeous smile of hers and, even though I could see the reluctance in her eyes, she agreed. A few years later, she said, 'You are the reason that it never worked out with anyone else. You are the greatest man I've ever met.'" When Pop-pop swam out of his memory, his eyes were glassy as they landed on Noelle's mug.

"You *are* the greatest man," she said, giving him a hug.

"Grab that box over in the corner and follow me. I've emptied it out—it had old magazines in it," he said, as they made their way down the short hallway to the bedroom.

When they entered, Noelle felt the prick of emotion once more. Pop-pop had made the bed. It was perfectly organized, every pillow in place. Gram had always badgered him to make the bed. "He's the last out of it," she'd said, only half serious, her love for Pop-pop evident, "but I have to go back in and make it." One time, he'd said that no one made it as beautifully as she did and she'd rolled her eyes humorously at him.

Noelle set the box on the bed as Pop-pop opened the first drawer. It was full of Gram's sweaters—dainty cardigans. Noelle closed her eyes, remembering how Gram would throw them around her shoulders like a shawl when she was chilly. Carefully, Noelle set her mug on the surface of the dresser and lifted a perfectly folded pile of sweaters out, noting that it had been Gram who'd folded them.

"Where should I put them?" she said, the importance of making the coffee shop work swelling in her stomach. Gram had told Noelle once that she'd started the bakery with all the money she and Pop-pop had. She'd wanted to have a café-style location where people could enjoy themselves, meet up, and have a treat. They'd gotten married in a simple ceremony in the park, and she'd worn a thin little dress that she'd made herself. They had no money to start their life together, but they were deliriously happy.

"Put them over on the chair," Pop-pop said, pulling her from her memories. She set them down and then emptied the rest of the drawer.

The second drawer had an eclectic grouping of things: books, Gram's glasses case, more clothes—all neatly arranged. Pop-pop instructed her to put the things in the empty box, piling the clothes along with her sweaters on the chair. At the back of the drawer was an insubstantial paper box about the size of a shoebox. She looked at Pop-pop but he shook his head with a baffled frown.

Carefully, she opened it. It was full of old memories: postcards from friends, stamps, a letter from a little boy she'd sponsored overseas, a few bookmarks that Noelle remembered making in school… She grabbed her coffee and sipped on it as she thumbed through the rest of the contents, happy that Gram had kept all this. Pop-pop sat quietly beside her on the bed.

"Why don't you keep this box. She'd have liked you to have it, I'm sure."

"Thank you." She felt like she'd just gotten a little Christmas present from Gram.

They continued sorting until the dresser was empty, and Noelle picked up the box of Gram's things, so glad she'd come today to get them. She held them in her arms as if she were giving Gram a big squeeze. Just as she was leaving, Pop-pop told her he'd get started right away on the dresser for her.

"Oh!" he said, stopping her at the door. "Let me get those few things that I'd found for you. It's not much—just a couple more teacups and another piece of her costume jewelry. I know you'd taken those when we divvied some of her things." She followed him into the kitchen.

Pop-pop gingerly set two teacups into her box. One had a delicate pink floral design, and Noelle remembered Gram using it. She smiled at the memory. Then he opened a drawer and dug around inside it, removing a small velvet ring box with no insignia. "You know how she loved that jewelry of hers," he said, shaking his head, his emotion showing. "I found this at the back of one of the kitchen drawers. Not sure how it got separated from her other jewelry."

Noelle set her things down on the kitchen table and took the small box from Pop-pop, opening it gently. She peered down at an enormous square white stone surrounded by more white stones—diamonds? On either side of the silver surface of the band were leaves that looked as though they'd been hand designed. There was something very familiar about it, yet she knew she'd never seen it before. Then her mind went back to William's story. It couldn't be... Her lungs felt like all the air had been pushed out of them, and her fingers started to tremble slightly. She worked to keep them still as she pulled the ring from the box and inspected the band. Engraved in the band were the letters HHA. She looked up at Pop-pop's unbothered face, swallowing to try to keep herself from being nauseous, but it didn't work.

"You don't know where she got this?" she managed, praying that she'd found it in some old antique shop or something.

"Nope. I've never seen her wear it. I wonder how in the world it got pushed way back in the kitchen drawer." He shook his head with a chuckle as he picked up the box and handed it to her. "Oh well," he said. "It's yours now. Maybe *you'll* wear it."

She willed the color into her face, knowing for certain that it must have drained completely out, her heart hammering in her chest, her pulse banging the inside of her head. She was feeling sweaty and lightheaded. So many questions were scrambling for answers: Was Gram the woman from the café? Was this really the ring? But it had to be; it looked exactly like the ring William had described. Did Pop-pop know? Alex had said he'd never forgive William if he'd given away the ring, and they were just starting to make headway. She couldn't possibly keep it. It needed to be back with the family. Should she give it to William? Or Alex? Or should she pretend that it never happened? She knew she couldn't. She managed a smile for Pop-pop and headed out to the car with what she knew was the Harrington ring in her hand.

❄ ❄ ❄

Noelle spent the rest of the day at the bakery not speaking to anyone apart from answering their questions. She'd said she had a really bad headache, and they all told her not to let the stress get to her, but she was really thinking about the gazillion-dollar ring in the glove box of her car.

Noelle's dad had done all he could for the day. He had a bad back, and she knew she couldn't push him, but the bakery was still in complete disarray. He'd struggled to get the baseboards sanded, having had to bend down for so long. Pop-pop certainly couldn't do it at his age, and with Noelle's job, she didn't have the time. She'd spent the entire day cleaning equipment and discarding old inventory, as well as clearing out the trash that had accumulated on the back patio. She had to leave for the day, but she'd planned to go back that night. She'd arranged for her mother to watch Lucas for her, feeling awful because she was already having to watch him so much, but knowing that in her current state, she just needed to be alone to think things through.

With all the sanding left, and the plumber still to come, she couldn't paint the walls, so all she'd done in the main room were the bookshelves, and she still had a third of those to go. Phoebe, Jo, and Heidi were all working but promised to help her tomorrow. Her mother had been there some of the time, and she was with Lucas the rest of the day once he got home from school.

As Noelle pulled into the drive at the mansion, she rubbed her sore shoulder and tried not to think about what she was going to do with the precious cargo in the glove box. She had to get a quick shower, her body covered with dust and dirt, and then tend to William. With nervous energy zinging through her, she opened the glove box and pulled out the ring, taking it from its container and slipping it onto her finger. Was she just being crazy? She tilted the diamond to see if it shone. Was this just some sort of insane coincidence? Perhaps the diamond wasn't real at all but some piece of jewelry Gram had found in one of those eclectic shops she liked to visit and the initials happened to be the same. Remembering the story of the names scrawled in William's bedroom, she looked around and then, closing her eyes, pressed the diamond to the window of her car, dragging it down the side a few inches.

She didn't want to open her eyes for fear of what she might see. The ring sat on her finger, a perfect fit, the heaviness of the stone weakening her resolve to see, once and for all, if it was real. With the car engine off, a chill ran through her, the reality setting in before she'd even looked. Then, she opened her eyes and gasped as she stared at the etched surface of the glass, her vision blurring with the realization that the diamond was real.

"Hey!" She heard Alex, his face appearing at the window, causing her to jump out of her skin. She threw her palm over the diamond, hiding both hands in her lap.

"I thought you'd gone."

"I got to the airport and felt awful the way I'd left things. I took a few meetings via phone and changed my flight so I could have a minute to talk."

He opened her door and she got out, feeling like her knees were going to buckle at any minute. She jammed the hand with the ring into her coat pocket and leaned against the car for support.

He looked down at her. "I'm sorry about the way I left things. I don't want you to think for a minute that I am leaving you specifically. But it's something I have to do."

Could his leaving for New York be just like Phoebe's situation? Was he taking that chance to see how successful he could be? Why was it happening now when her and Lucas's hearts were on the line? She looked into his eyes, letting his sincerity seep down to her bones, the flutter returning and making her momentarily forget about the ring on her finger for that moment.

"Are you okay?" he asked, his brows furrowing. "You look really rattled. I didn't mean to startle you. I just wanted to see you before I left. My flight's tonight." He reached out and put his hands on her arms, trailing down them, grasping for her hands, but impulse took over and she jerked away from him, the ring still on her finger. She frantically tried to get it off with her thumb, but her hand had become hot in her pocket and it was stuck.

He stepped back, nodding subtly as if she'd just pulled away because she didn't want him to touch her. "I'm sorry," she said quickly, trying to fix the damage. "I didn't mean to do that. I just..."

"It's okay," he said. "I just wanted to see you."

"I'm glad," she said with a smile, keeping her distance.

"Call me if you want to talk. I'm always just a phone call away."

She nodded.

"I'll walk you in," he said, peering into the car. "Is that box coming with you?"

"Yes," she said, her face flushing with heat at the sight of the open ring box on the seat. She willed him not to recognize it.

He reached into the car and pulled the box out. Then he leaned back in and grabbed the ring box. "This too?" he said, not a bit of recognition on his face.

She could hardly breathe. "Yes," she said, in almost a whisper.

He snapped it shut and set it into the box of Gram's things. Then, he put his hand on her back and led her to the front door, the snow beginning to fall all around them.

Chapter Twenty-Nine

"What do you think William would like?" Noelle asked Lucas, as they sat on the bench at the mall, drinking hot chocolates next to the giant Christmas tree. She was so glad to have the ring in a drawer in her suite, hidden from both the Harringtons and her conscience. Lucas's feet didn't reach the ground, his little shoes swinging above the pavement.

"I don't know," he said, scratching a spot on his neck where the wool scarf that Noelle's mother had wrapped him in was bothering him. "I'd say a good book, but he can't read, can he?" He pondered this for a second as he held his hot chocolate. "I can't imagine not being able to read."

"We could do audiobooks," she said. "I wonder if he'd like that."

"Oh, that's a good idea."

"But we need something for under the tree. Something we can wrap." She stood up and Lucas hopped off the bench to stand beside her. "Let's see what we can find."

They started toward a row of shops when Lucas turned excitedly to his mother. "I know! Why don't we text Alex and ask him what to get him? He'd know for sure because he's his grandson."

She didn't want to be in contact with Alex for a variety of reasons: one, she feared he'd hear the guilt over having that ring in her voice, and two, she missed him and wanted him to come home, which would do nothing but cause him to feel awful for leaving. She also didn't want Lucas getting any more involved than he was with Alex Harrington. Especially if he might eventually find out that it was her grandmother who'd ruined Elizabeth's life. Carefully, she said, "I don't know if he would."

"Why not? I know what Grandpa Gus likes. He likes new tools and stuff for the grill so he can have his summer cookouts. He likes that fancy barbecue sauce and he likes that really smelly lotion for his hands. Alex would probably know what his grandfather likes."

"But William and Alex don't talk like you and Grandpa Gus do."

"May I text him? Just to see?"

With a sinking feeling, Noelle wondered if Lucas really wanted a chance to connect with Alex again, and she just didn't feel like she should contact him. It wouldn't change anything for Lucas. He wasn't coming back.

"Please?" he asked.

But then again, he'd taken to Lucas. He'd be kind to him if Lucas called. "Okay," she said with a sigh, and pulled out her phone. After all, none of this was Lucas's fault. "Here you go." She handed it to him and took his hot chocolate so he could text.

With a slight pep in his step, Lucas pulled up Alex's contact information and began texting, his little fingers flying on the keyboard. "I'm just telling him it's Lucas and saying hi first," he said, not looking up from the phone.

His fingers stilled after he'd finished, and he waited for Alex to answer. Noelle prayed for those three little dots to show, alerting her that he was checking the message. *Please, Alex,* she chanted in her head. *Please don't let him down.* The screen started to go dark and Lucas tapped it to keep the text open, both of them waiting, Noelle holding her breath.

"He might be at work," she said, trying to soften the blow in case Alex didn't reply, worried he wouldn't answer. "He just got to New York. I'm sure he's really busy. Maybe he's not near his phone," she added.

Then the three dots appeared and a new wave of fear swept over her. *Say something to him*, she thought. *Don't leave him hanging.*

Finally, a text: *Hi, Lucas! I'm glad you texted. Can I text you back tonight? I'm in a meeting right now.*

Lucas typed, *Okay*, and Noelle could see the disappointment on his face, but she was glad that Alex had responded. That was good enough for her. And it was sweet that he was texting him back during his meeting.

Another text floated up: *Seven o'clock tonight, just before your bedtime stories, okay? I promise.*

Lucas typed back, *I can't wait.*

After that, Lucas handed the phone back to his mother and the two of them walked quietly past the shops, looking in but not saying anything, and she wondered if they both missed Alex so much it felt like their hearts would explode. Or was that just her?

❄ ❄ ❄

They'd ended up getting William a new scarf and one of the candles he'd liked when Noelle and William had gone shopping together, and she'd found an audiobook about antique furniture. She thought maybe he'd like that. What she hadn't expected to buy was a tripod for a camera. It had caught her eye, and something inside her wanted to buy it for Alex. It made no sense at all because she had no reason to buy him a thing. He'd pretty much abandoned whatever had started between them, and any future they might have even as friends was up in the air, given the ring that sat like a boulder in her bureau drawer. Besides that, she didn't even know if it would fit his camera, even though the clerk had said it would complement any standard camera. Alex could certainly buy his own camera accessories, but she'd put it on her credit card and then asked the store to gift-wrap it.

Lucas had been so helpful as she'd dragged him from shopping to caring for William and then to the bakery, where she'd gotten a good start painting the trim while Jim was looking after William during her free hours. She'd kept herself busy all day, trying not to focus on the discussion she had ahead of her: she'd decided that at some point, she had to tell William about the ring, and she worried that in Alex's eyes, that knowledge of the whereabouts of the ring would put her and William on the same side of his invisible wall between them. But she knew, after hearing William's story, that she couldn't keep it. It had never been meant for Gram; it should be Elizabeth's.

Lucas was more excited today than he'd been recently, and she cringed inside, thinking it was because he knew he was going to talk to Alex tonight. She recognized that feeling easily; she'd had it too, whenever Alex would enter a room.

So when Lucas nearly bounced into the living room of their suite after his bath, she let the worry go. Lucas deserved to enjoy this moment, and perhaps a few texts would be enough for him. Although, in the back of her mind, she knew Lucas deserved more than that.

At seven o'clock on the dot, Lucas was holding Noelle's phone in both hands, peering down at the screen. At 7:01, he asked, "He said seven, right?"

"Give him a minute. He might have gotten caught up with something." She felt jittery, worried Alex would let Lucas down. Did he realize how much this text meant to her son? She peered over at the phone: 7:03.

Then, a text came through and relief washed over her. Lucas opened it: *Sorry I'm late, buddy. Are you still up?*

Lucas's fingers moved madly over the screen as he typed, *Yes. I'm up. What are you doing?*

Why don't we do a video chat so you can see?

Lucas looked up at Noelle, his eyes wide with excitement. He typed *Yes* as she scooted next to him on the sofa.

The phone lit up with a video call, Lucas answering immediately. Noelle couldn't help the thrill that danced around inside her when she saw that smile on the screen.

"Hi there," Alex said.

Lucas waved.

"Let me show you something." Alex turned his phone around and gave them a view of the entire city of New York, the skyscrapers' lights like stars in the inky blackness.

Lucas gasped.

"Cool, isn't it?" Alex said. "It's the view from my office. I'm still working but I wanted to stop to give you a call. So, tell me. What did you do today?"

"Oh!" Lucas said with a little bounce on the sofa, wobbling the phone. Noelle helped him steady it. "We got you a present!"

"Lucas!" Noelle hadn't expected him to tell Alex. She didn't even know if she was going to give it to him.

"Mom picked it out."

It was difficult to tell on the small phone screen but Alex seemed happy. "Well, I got you and your mom each something too."

"Tell us what mine is!"

He laughed. "I suppose I could, since you can't unwrap it anyway. I found a summer camp—it's only a week long. They specialize in science experiments, and you get to take home a load of stuff including books."

Lucas's face was more excited than Noelle had ever seen it as he turned to her, bouncing in his spot on the sofa.

"Oh, that's an awfully grand gesture." She was certain a camp like that was probably expensive. "I couldn't let you buy something like that for him."

Lucas's smile dropped.

"Perhaps I could try to pay for it, but it just seems too much for Alex to offer," she told Lucas, but Alex could hear. She leaned in to the camera on the phone so Alex could see her, repeating, "I can't let you buy a gift like that."

"Of course you can," he said.

"No. Absolutely not." She was standing her ground on this. If Lucas loved that camp, and it was one of the best experiences of his life, he'd in turn love Alex for giving him that gift, and when time crept in between them, and Alex's texts and calls dwindled, it would break Lucas's heart. Best she made a memory like that come from her, even if it drained her wallet. But his gesture had given her a tiny fizzle of hope that Alex missed them. He was thinking about them, buying them presents.

"Noelle, at least consider it," Alex said.

"Sure. I will. I'd love to talk to you about it," she said, with a sudden ulterior motive. "If you come back for Christmas," she heard herself say. She knew why she'd said it: ring or no ring, family crisis or not, *she* missed *him* terribly. She just wanted to feel those eyes on her, to see that smile directed at her.

Alex looked at her through the screen, not saying anything.

"Yeah!" Lucas piped up. "How else will we give you your gift?"

"We'll see," he said, his face unreadable.

Lucas frowned. "Oh no. 'We'll see' always means no when Mom says it."

"Maybe he'll surprise us," Noelle said, looking straight at Alex.

Chapter Thirty

"I can't believe Alex isn't coming home for Christmas," Phoebe said, as she sat the wrong way on one of the shop chairs, her arms folded on the back of it. She'd come to help Noelle with converting the bakery, and, after removing every piece of furniture in the main room for the flooring to be replaced, they'd taken a much-needed break.

Noelle knew that Phoebe was also helping all day because she was trying to avoid having to think about the major life decisions she had to make, and Noelle understood. Phoebe had said that she and Paul had talked for hours and, in the end, he didn't see how things could work for them right now, but it didn't make it any easier and whenever she tried to talk it out with Noelle, she cried, so they hadn't brought up the subject a whole lot.

Whenever Phoebe was quiet about something, she was working through it, and this was probably the biggest decision of her life. Noelle let her think. They'd toiled all day, and it seemed they weren't any closer to being ready. She was losing time, and they were running out of hours to get everything done. What had she been thinking? There was no way she'd get the place remodeled and stocked before New Year's, let alone the re-opening.

Noelle plopped cross-legged on the gritty floor. "What's bothering me is that Alex would do something like buy Lucas a week at camp, as if it were nothing at all, but not bother to show us his affection by coming home for Christmas. Anyone can buy us things…"

"You need to talk to him, Noelle. He might understand if you could explain it to him? The more I think about it, the more I wonder if he probably thought he was just doing something nice, and he doesn't see the significance of coming home."

"I asked him to spend Christmas with us and I didn't get an answer." She shook her head. "I have no idea why, but something inside me tells me that he needs to be here. I have this overwhelming feeling that what he's doing is all wrong." She didn't even want to mention the connection between Gram and William, or the ring, until she'd spoken to William, and she was still trying to figure out how to do that. She knew it would have to be soon because it was weighing on her.

Phoebe offered a tender smile. "You don't think it's just you wishing for something more, do you?"

Noelle rubbed her tired eyes, groaning in surrender. "I don't know."

"It's not the end of the world if you want something great for yourself, you know? You work really hard to get everything you have. Who says you can't work for this?"

"I shouldn't have to work for it," she said, her voice matter-of-fact. But was Phoebe right? Was that pull Noelle felt to have Alex come home really just wishful thinking? The thought entered her mind that Alex hadn't made any effort to communicate with her; he'd only corresponded with Lucas. Maybe Alex hadn't fallen for her at all. Maybe he had a soft spot for Lucas—it was easy to do. "You know what?" she said, the sting of her thoughts causing her to prickle. "I think I should tell him not to bother. He probably won't come anyway."

❄ ❄ ❄

"I've been wondering something," Noelle said to William, as she toyed with the ring box in her pocket nervously. Today was the day to tell him. Strategies for how to begin the discussion with William had filtered into her thoughts all day and she'd run through different ways to bring it up, but just now she'd jumped right into it instead, her nerves getting the better of her. Plus, she just didn't want to put it off anymore. "You seemed to really be affected by your first love. You said you even kept things—a napkin? She impacted you, it's clear. Do you ever wonder what could've been with her?" They were sitting in the large living room in the main house. He'd had her pull up a chair near the windows so he could try to see the snow. He'd said that he could see the transformation of color to white and it was calming. She'd need him to be calm for this, but before she told him, she wanted some answers.

"All the time," he said, his gaze remaining on the window. "Many nights I felt guilty wondering. It wasn't fair to Elizabeth, but you have to know, I loved my wife. I loved her more than the first woman I met."

"But could you have loved the woman more if you'd given her a chance? Could she have been the love of your life?"

"I don't know," he said simply.

"Why didn't you go after her? Why did you let your family dictate your actions?"

He pursed his lips in thought, something dawning on him. "This isn't about me and her, is it?"

It caught her off guard. "What?"

He took in a deep breath, stillness between them. "This is about you and Alex. You want him to try harder, to come back to you."

"That's not what I meant..." she said a little too quickly, but the fire under her skin probably gave her away.

"What if I said this: When it came to me and the other woman, *she* didn't push it either; she didn't try to get me to change my mind. Probably because, without really knowing what I'd done, I'd hurt her. Terribly. I didn't realize what that might have been like for her until it was much too late. I think you're a similar person to her. Alex is a tough nut to crack. And I think he runs from things that scare him. I'll bet you scare the life out of him because he's terrified he might fail you. And he's never failed at anything in his life."

"I'm not going to chase after him," she said, the cold air in that big room making her shiver. She felt cold both inside and out.

William nodded. "I know you're not," he said, with a knowing smile.

"If she'd chased you, what would you have done? Would you really have left all this behind?" She wanted him to say yes, to give her hope that something wonderful could happen.

"You are so much like her," he said, causing a chill to shoot up her spine. "Why don't you give it a shot with Alex and see?"

"I'm like her?" She held the ring box in her palm inside her pocket.

"So much."

With her free hand, she took his and held it. "My gram and I are a lot alike," she said. "Her name was Sophia." She turned his hand over and placed the ring box in it, closing his fingers around it.

His chest heaving with his breath, he opened the box and ran his finger along the diamond, complete shock consuming his face. Noelle waited, unsure of what to do next, her own breath barely able to fill her lungs, her hands shaking uncontrollably. Without warning, a single tear rolled down William's face. "I did wonder sometimes," he whispered. He put his hand on Noelle's face, the tears falling freely now. "Did she have a good life?" he asked, barely able to get the question out through his tears.

"Yes." Noelle's eyes were clouded with emotion as well as they both placed their hands on the ring. She squeezed his fingers tenderly. "She married my Pop-pop and they were wonderful together. They danced in the kitchen, they took me to the beach where they made their own recipes for cocktails and sat in the sand drinking them until the sun went down… I could go on and on. She had the life I only wish I could have."

He pulled away from her, leaving the ring in her hands, covered his face, and sobbed, but his tears sounded like relief, like complete happiness that she'd been okay. And that was the greatest show of love that Noelle had ever seen.

❄ ❄ ❄

Noelle and Lucas stood in the office the next morning, looking out the wall-sized window at the snow. It was really coming down. Noelle had spent most of the night wondering how they were going to tell Alex about the ring. William had been so emotional that she hadn't gotten into it with him, so it left her with a million scenarios that swirled around in her head all night. She knew they were going to have to tell him, and it was probably William's place, but the fact that she knew made her glad Alex was in New York so she wouldn't have to face him until she had a solid plan in mind for what she wanted to say—if anything.

"Can we go sledding once it piles up?" Lucas asked. "I wonder if it's snowing in New York?"

"I don't know," she said, already dreading the possibility of having to contact Alex for Lucas. "Maybe."

"Let's text him and find out. I want to see if it is!" Lucas was animated, smiling, nearly jumping up and down.

Steadying herself to keep worry from eating her alive, she handed Lucas her phone. She didn't want to alarm him by not allowing him to contact Alex. She just hoped that she wouldn't have to talk to him. Lucas knew how to use her phone perfectly so he wouldn't need her at all. He'd practiced texting his grandparents and he'd gotten really good at it. Noelle looked back out the window. The snow had started to cover the Christmas greenery on the balconies and exterior brick walls, the garland bending slightly under its weight. Her heart felt just as heavy.

"He isn't texting back," Lucas said. Only then did she realize Lucas wasn't bouncing anymore. "Maybe he's busy," he said, disappointment in his eyes.

"You know what?" she said, trying to keep her voice from breaking under the immensity of it all. "It's only two weeks until Christmas! We should start celebrating. We need a big cup of hot chocolate and a few nibbles of Casa Grande. There's still some left after the staff got ahold of it." She winked at him, completely hiding her trepidation.

"Okay," he said, handing her the phone. She checked once more before clicking it off, but there'd been no response.

"Let's have a little fun," she said with a smile.

Chapter Thirty-One

Noelle fell back onto Phoebe's bed, a pillow toppling down off the pile of them, landing on her chest. She hugged it. She'd needed a friendly face, so after she'd taken Lucas over to her parents' early for school she went straight to Phoebe's. "I don't have a plan," she admitted. "For the first time in my life, I don't have a plan. Everything's going wrong."

"And you came to *me* for a plan?" Phoebe said dramatically. "Was Jo busy or something?"

Noelle laughed despite herself. "I don't expect you to have a plan," she said. "I came to you to make me feel better, and you are. You're so good at it, Phoebe. I wish for one second I could see the world like you do. You just take things as they come without a care in the world."

"My spontaneity got me a big fat breakup with my boyfriend," she said, shaking her head, her face dropping. She was folding laundry from a basket, and putting the items into her closet.

"Everyone has difficult decisions, whether we're planners or not," Noelle said, "but I just wish I could throw caution to the wind and change my life. Do you realize you're about to change your life, Phoebe? It may never be the same again. Sometimes I wish I could do that."

Phoebe stopped and looked at her friend, the heavy pink sweater Noelle had gotten her for her birthday last year dangling from her fingertips. "Then do it."

Noelle rolled over on the bed and sat up, crossing her legs and putting the pillow in her lap for an armrest. "Do what?"

"Be impulsive!" Phoebe plopped down on the bed beside her. "Come with me to LA like you always said you would. You'd have an apartment, I'm certain you could get a job, Lucas would have a new school with a new start, you could help me keep my mind off Paul so I don't fall apart… Maybe bring a little of our world to the west coast. I'm imagining a busy coffee shop with a big sign that says East Coast Coffee and Bakery."

"I just bought a new sign," she said, that being her only argument.

"So? You aren't a planner in this scenario, remember. We'll get a new sign with my first paycheck."

"What about the coffee shop? Gram would've wanted it to succeed here in Richmond." With that question, Noelle told herself that she wasn't considering this ridiculous idea; she was merely making conversation.

"It will succeed. Just in a different location. I'll even help you move that gigantic jukebox." Phoebe pushed her red hair behind her shoulder, a nonchalant look on her face as if it were no big deal at all, but Noelle knew that she was *really* asking. This breakup with Paul was hitting her harder than she let on and Noelle knew that she would love nothing more than to have her support, because Phoebe always said that without Noelle, she'd go crazy. "Your stuff is probably still packed in that trailer, and if it isn't, you can have it all packed in a day. Come with me. There's nothing holding you here."

Noelle picked at a loose string on the pillow in her lap, trying to figure out why she wasn't saying anything to Phoebe, and she knew it was because she was actually contemplating the pros and cons of this ludicrous idea. Phoebe wasn't entirely right. She did have one thing holding her here: her family. She'd miss her mom and dad, Heidi, and Pop-pop. Her mother had been the force that had held it all together, watching Lucas for her when she was working, and her dad had never let her go a day without a helping hand. Pop-pop would want to see the success of the coffee shop. Then there was Jo…

"You're thinking too much," Phoebe said. "I can tell. Don't worry about the people you're leaving—I know you are. I left Paul, for God's sake. They'll all still be here. You can invite them to visit anytime you want. You know I love to give Gus a hard time," she said with a smile. "Don't think it through. Just do it."

Noelle had thought through every decision she'd ever made, and she was no better off than if she hadn't planned a thing. But could she move across the country?

❄ ❄ ❄

"If and only if the coffee shop doesn't make money by the New Year's deadline, I've come up with a list. Here are the pros," Noelle told Jo, as they sat across from each other, two plates of pasta in front of them. She'd been making a mental list ever since she'd left Phoebe's. At first, the idea of moving seemed ridiculous, but now, Noelle wondered if it could be just what she needed. When Noelle had said she wanted to meet Jo for lunch, her friend had come right away, like she always did. "I already have an apartment with Phoebe; I'd be able to expose Lucas to another location, which I love to do; and I could leave the Harrington mansion behind."

Jo twirled her fork on her plate and lifted a bite of pasta. She'd ordered something with white wine sauce. "That last one is a pro? Or a con?"

"Definitely a pro. Lucas is way too attached to Alex and he's going to get his heart broken. I'm a nervous wreck about it. Alex has already made his decision. He's gone, Jo. He's moved to New York. There's nothing I can do about it." She took a drink of her ice water, her mouth feeling abnormally dry. She'd said it as if it were easy to leave, and she knew it would be harder than that, but if Alex wasn't coming back, William would be the only person keeping her there, and she could easily stay in touch with him. She'd considered how much she'd miss him, though.

"Fair enough. So what are the cons, then?"

"I'll miss everyone so much—I'll be a very long flight away. I'll have to find a new job. I sank every penny I own into the bakery so I might not have the money that I'd need to make a move like this."

Jo nodded in understanding. "What about Lucas? How would he deal with moving?"

"I'm going to ask him, but I think he would be fine with it, although he might have a tough time being away from my mom and dad. He's always up for an adventure, though."

"I think this one is really up to you, Noelle. I don't see anything wrong with making a new start. People do it all the time. You just have to decide if it's what you want." She smiled and picked up her wine, holding it by the stem. "I'm proud of you for even considering it. You're finally thinking about you instead of everyone else."

❄ ❄ ❄

By the time Lucas was heading to bed, Noelle's temples were throbbing. She'd contemplated the move with Phoebe to Los Angeles all afternoon, going back and forth between thinking it was the stupidest idea she'd ever heard of and feeling completely hopeful that it might be something great. She wanted to talk it out with Lucas just to get a feel for his thoughts, but she was worried that this might not be the time to ask him because he'd been a little bit blue this evening. Alex hadn't texted back.

The snow had been coming down and it was accumulating rapidly. To lift his spirits, she'd suggested to Lucas that they could go sledding. He'd been happy about it but still preoccupied; he'd checked her phone twice since they'd gotten home from school and Alex still hadn't responded. This situation made the idea of moving even more enticing.

After his bath and stories, she lay down with him, both of them looking upward at the glass chandelier above the bed, and she decided to bring up moving. "It's cold," she said.

"Mm hm." He didn't turn to look at her.

"Wouldn't it be nice to be somewhere warm right now?"

He finally turned. "Like the beach."

"Somewhere with palm trees and sandy sidewalks."

"Yeah." He straightened back out and peered up at the ceiling again.

"Phoebe wants us to take an adventure with her, but I wasn't sure if you'd want to go."

Sleepily, Lucas rolled over onto his side and propped his little head on his hand. "What kind of adventure?"

"She wants us to move with her to Los Angeles, California. We'd live with her. It's warm all year round there. And we could go to the beach after school. I was thinking I might even be able to open a coffee shop there."

"Maybe it could be an ice cream shop," he said with a little smile. Then his face crumpled with his thought, his brows pulling together and his tiny lips pursed. "Do you think that's where we belong? Or is it just another stop?"

Unsure how to answer, she said, "I guess we won't know until we get there. What do you think? Would you like to go? We won't go if you don't want to."

"I think it sounds fun."

She couldn't help but smile. The warm breezes and sunshine might do her some good. She needed to get out of this rut she was in and figure out what she was meant to do. It felt completely unfamiliar and a little uncomfortable, but maybe that was what she needed. Perhaps by getting out of her comfort zone, she'd find what was meant for her.

"So that's a yes, then?"

"I was hoping this was where we belonged."

She didn't want to admit that she did too. "It is nice here, isn't it?'

"Yeah, but not as much without Alex, so I'm okay if we move again."

Her heart broke for him. She'd known this would happen. And she felt like it was all her fault. She'd allowed Alex into their lives and she shouldn't have. She was too caught up in her own feelings and now this was the price she had to pay for it.

"I'm okay with it too," she said.

Chapter Thirty-Two

Noelle had been mulling over the idea of moving for the last couple of days. She worried about leaving Gram's shop behind. She could take all Gram's things with her—all the pieces of Gram that she loved: the recipes, her favorite dishes, the jukebox, the books… But she felt like it just wouldn't be the same. She tried to convince herself that the building was just a place and she'd have the memories and all Gram's things with her, so it would be fine, but she still felt a little uneasy.

She parked at the end of the street down from the bakery and walked her usual path, as she went to meet Pop-pop. It was the first time she'd seen him since she'd been to his house and she felt a little uneasy with the knowledge she was holding about Gram's connection to the Harringtons. He was waiting for her at one of the tables in the main room. It had been pushed to the edge near the others that still had the chairs turned upside down on top of them. He was smiling, looking around at her hard work, but all she saw was a lot more ahead of her, with not much time to do it.

"I've been considering something," she said, setting down her coat and pulling a chair over to sit next to him, "but I wouldn't dare do it without your consent." She had more than the bakery to talk about with him, but she figured she'd start with the easier topic first. She wasn't ready to tell him what she knew about that costume jewelry he thought he'd found.

"What is it?" he asked, looking concerned. "You seem really intense."

"I'm struggling, Pop-pop." She slumped in her chair, as the daylight streamed through the window in the form of a white hazy mass, the cloud cover preventing the golden glow they usually got in the afternoons. "I don't know who I'm supposed to be anymore. I feel like there are versions of me now, yet when I try them on for size, none of them feel like they fit." She shifted uncomfortably in her chair, ready to ask the big question while Pop-pop looked on lovingly, as supportive as ever. "Phoebe wants me to go out to LA with her."

His eyebrows lifted with interest.

"She wants me to move there."

"Do you want to?" he asked.

"I don't know." She shook her head. "But if I did, I'd want to open the coffee shop there because no matter where I am, I wouldn't feel whole without what Gram started."

He agreed, thoughts behind his eyes.

"Would I have your blessing to move the coffee shop?"

He sat quietly for a bit, clearly thinking it over. Then, with a small smile, he said, "Noelle, you have your whole life ahead of you and where you make that life isn't nearly as important as whom you make it with. So if Phoebe is the person you want to spend that life with, then you have my blessing."

That was just like Pop-pop. He knew that, while she loved Phoebe, the rest of her heart was here with Jo, with her family, even with William. So, while giving his blessing, he'd also told her what he thought, and she loved him for that.

"You said you had different versions of yourself—we all do. But there's one version of us that's the perfect version. You need to find that."

"Do you think you and Gram were the perfect versions of yourselves?"

Pop-pop broke into the biggest smile and then he said quietly, as if there were others in the room with them, "When I met your gram, she was a different version of herself."

Noelle didn't take her eyes off him.

"I've never told a soul about this, but she was in love when I met her. She was in love with someone else. And she was broken—he'd ruined her spirit, crushed it. Now, being the optimistic guy that I am, I decided not to be intimidated by this. Instead, I showed her what love was like with me, and it didn't take her long to realize that she'd been heading the wrong way, and her real path in life was right there in front of her. Later on, she told me all about that lost love of hers, and years after, we shared a good chuckle over the idea of what she might have become. But it was funny only because, after being together for decades, the thought that she could've been anything other than who she was, was ludicrous to both of us."

"I know that story," she said, the burden lifted from her chest.

Pop-pop tilted his head to the side in surprise. "You do?"

"William told me."

"Ah. Yes." He didn't have to say anything else for her to understand that he knew Gram had been in love with William.

"He fell in love again too, and he shared charming things about his wife with me."

Pop-pop grinned, not a trace of animosity in his face. "Glad to hear it," he said.

"It doesn't bother you to talk about it?"

He frowned and shook his head. "Why would it? Gram and I had our storybook ending, didn't we?"

He was right, and the exhilaration she felt from his answer lifted her spirits. "Yes," she said, feeling happier than she had in days. "Yes, you did."

❄ ❄ ❄

Noelle's phone rang just after she and Lucas had gotten ready for bed. They'd brushed their teeth and washed their faces side by side in the bathroom at the two sinks that were nestled beautifully in a slab of marble. She picked the phone up quickly before Lucas saw who it was. If he knew that Alex was calling, he might get excited, and she wasn't sure, after not hearing from him, what Alex would say. She needed to talk to him anyway and tell him what she was considering.

She walked out of the bathroom in her pajamas and answered it.

"I need to talk to you," he said.

"I need to talk to you, too." She was still hurt by his silence when Lucas had texted him, but she didn't let that show in her tone.

"Who is it, Mom?" Lucas called from the bathroom, peeking his head out.

She smiled, shaking her head kindly and shooing him back into the bathroom. She checked in on him and he was combing his hair after his bath, running the comb under the stream of water first like she did, even though his hair was soaking wet, making her smile.

"I've been thinking," Alex said. "A lot. I can't stop thinking…"

She waited, walking back into the living room and sitting on the edge of the sofa, noticing how cold it was this evening without a fire going.

"I want to see you."

A silence fell between them as she tried to figure out what he'd meant by that statement. Confusion swam around inside her, and without any answers herself as to his motives, she asked, "Why?"

"I left because I was terrified," he began. Before she could process what he was getting at, he continued. "I was terrified that I would let you and Lucas down, like my father and grandfather let me down. I don't have any practice being good to a family; I'm not sure I know what to do."

It was exactly as William had thought.

Lucas came out and climbed onto the sofa beside her, making her heart race more than it had already. She thought about how Alex had run at the first sign of difficulty and William's story about how the family hadn't accepted someone who wasn't wealthy—it all made her unsure of where to go from here. She filtered through the times when William and Alex were together and how broken their relationship was, and her possible plans for LA.

"This isn't all about you, you know?" she said quietly, glad Lucas had gotten restless and hopped back off the sofa. He was tinkering with the fireplace boxes. "I can't just drop everything and come to New York because you want to see me. I'm not someone who will simply pop in and out of your life when you have the whim."

"I know." He was quiet. Then he asked, "What can I do to show you that I'm serious?"

"How about texting Lucas back, for starters."

Lucas's head snapped up. The line buzzed in her ear. Alex didn't say a thing. She knew she'd gotten him. "Hang up," he said suddenly.

"What?"

"Hang up."

Her cheeks burned with worry, but she knew she hadn't done anything wrong. Did he really want her to go? He wouldn't have said it if he hadn't meant it. Her breath shallow, she ended the call. Just after, a text floated onto her screen: *Lucas? It's Alex. Are you there?*

Hesitant, Noelle handed the phone to her son. Lucas looked at the screen, his face erupting into an enormous smile.

Lucas texted back.

Another text came through from Alex: *I'm so sorry that I missed your text. I was a little busy. You see, I was traveling and my phone was off while I was on the plane. Then I spent all my time working to get things done for Christmas. I won't miss another text, I promise.*

Noelle read over his shoulder, trying not to think about how wonderful Alex was with Lucas. She felt bad for snapping at him a little like she had. After all, he'd only missed the one text. Lucas responded that it was okay.

Alex replied: *I miss you and your mom.*

Lucas was elated by that comment. "He misses us!" he said, waving the phone in the air.

Noelle asked if she could text back and Lucas handed it to her. She typed: *This is Noelle. If you really miss us, then come back for Christmas. Stop running.* She hit send and then got distracted by an odd noise at the door. It went on for a bit, getting louder and more unusual with every sound. Alarmed, she got up and opened the door, gasping as she saw what was there.

Tapping around in front of her was a tiny yellow Labrador puppy with the biggest red bow around its neck, the tails of the ribbon trailing behind it as it ran back and forth across the shiny floors. Lucas lifted it into his arms, cuddling it while Noelle looked both ways in the hallway, trying to figure out what was going on. Then, out of nowhere, Alex stepped into view, holding his phone, his eyes locked with hers. "I'm one step ahead of you," he said with a crooked smile, making her heart beat like a snare drum.

"Alex!" Lucas said, running over with the puppy as it squirmed in his arms.

Alex scooped him up along with the puppy and gave him a squeeze. "This is Henry. He's moving in," he said with a look over to Noelle, and she recalled their conversation about how he should have a dog. He'd remembered. "I named him after my sixth great-grandfather—since he built this house, and it's where I met you."

She loved the name he'd chosen, but what she loved more was how much he'd thought about it, and how he'd picked something to let her know that he cared. For someone who'd claimed he didn't know how to do this kind of thing, he was certainly good at it. She couldn't wipe the smile off her face.

❄ ❄ ❄

Alex stayed and helped put Lucas to bed, Henry sleeping soundly in a crate in Lucas's room. Alex had texted Jim, who had jumped at the chance to take care of the puppy, promising to come get him once Lucas had fallen asleep so he could take him out during the night the first few weeks. After Jim had left, Alex got the fire going and he sat down next to Noelle. She could see the exhaustion on his face.

"This is a surprise," she said, her plans becoming unclear again.

"I know." He put his arm around her and trailed his finger along her shoulder. "I've never had another person affect me like you have." She took in his honesty, the way he looked at her, the complete adoration he had for her in that moment. She thought about Pop-pop's advice, mentally trying on this version of herself—the one where she and Alex had their happy ending; it felt so good. But this version hadn't been what was meant for Gram, and she was just like her gram.

"So much has happened," she said, feeling overwhelmed by it all. "I, uh…" Her idea about moving to LA seemed a bit more difficult now, but she had to keep a clear head about it. "I've been thinking about moving to California."

"What?" He sat up and twisted toward her.

"With my friend Phoebe…"

She couldn't finish her sentence, the lump in her throat making words nearly impossible, her emotions surprising her. Phoebe had left the person she thought might be the perfect guy, to do this for herself. And now, Noelle was facing the same fate. If she stayed here, she may encounter the possibility of a failing coffee shop, no direction workwise, and no real plans for the future.

"Do you want to go?" he asked. His face had dropped, his smile gone, his eyes wide as he hung on her answer.

"I think it's something I could do. I deserve a shot at making a living the way I want to make one."

"Keep the bakery open," he said almost frantically. "I'll let you stay."

She shook her head, stopping him. "I want to be successful on my own, not because you're funding it like some sort of extravagant hobby."

He leaned forward, his elbows on his knees, his hands pressed together against his lips as he considered what she'd said.

"I need to be successful myself," she repeated, still feeling like she was going to cry and worried she was making the wrong decision, but how could letting him pay for her coffee shop be what was meant for her?

He sat up, took her face in his hands and kissed her forehead. "Okay," he said, his disappointment clear. Then he shook his head. With a deep breath, he said, "We can talk about all this later. I came home because you asked. Will you spend Christmas with me? I want to show you the best Christmas you and Lucas have ever had. I have some surprises up my sleeve."

"There's more than the puppy?"

"Yes. Much more than the puppy. And will you at least give the coffee shop a chance here? Let's see if you can make Christmas magic there because if anyone can, it's you."

She smiled despite her emotions. "Okay."

Chapter Thirty-Three

With Lucas home from school for the holidays, Noelle hadn't planned to take him to her mother's, but she did one last time. He'd wanted to show her Henry, and he just knew that Muffy would be overjoyed to have a new friend. Noelle had agreed because she had something to do. She met Alex in the kitchen with William. There was no way she could leave the two of them the way they were right now if she went to LA. She had to feel like she'd made some kind of difference in their lives, like there was some reason that she'd had this stop on the way to where she belonged.

"What's going on?" Alex asked, his eyes on William.

"You both want to see Elizabeth; you've both told me so. Today's the day. Get your coats. We're going to see her."

When Alex didn't respond right away, she added, "In my house, Christmas was always about family. The two of you can put aside your differences for the holiday and see someone you both love."

❄ ❄ ❄

They'd all sat together in the back of the car as the driver maneuvered them through the snow to see Elizabeth. Noelle had never been on a quieter ride; neither Alex nor William said a word the entire way.

It gave Noelle time to think about how much her life had changed this holiday, and she prayed she would make the right decision for her and Lucas. If she stayed now, and one day, when all the fairy-tale moments with Alex were over and they'd gone their separate ways, she'd be working a job she wouldn't have chosen and giving Lucas just a mundane childhood, she'd never forgive herself. Moving across the country was an opportunity she'd never get again because she wouldn't go unless she had a reason, and her friendship with Phoebe was a great reason, even if she did feel a little uncomfortable about leaving the people she loved.

When they arrived at the assisted living home, Alex was the first from the car. He helped Noelle out and then steadied William as he got up. Noelle took in the tall, hospital-like structure, the automatic doors that swished open, allowing two nurses to exit past them. As they entered the main entryway, their shoes clacking along the polished floors, Noelle offered an uncertain look at the woman working the front desk; her smile was welcoming, but it didn't change Noelle's opinion of the place. It was a fine facility, but it certainly wasn't like home.

"We're here to see Elizabeth Harrington," Alex said, his face stoic, as he put a hand on Noelle's back while greeting the woman behind the gleaming front desk. She was still smiling, perched on a stool that gave her a view between a plastic leaflet-holder and a vase of flowers.

"Yes, sir," she nodded. "May I just have your identification, please?"

Alex handed over his driver's license.

"She's in the Pembroke wing, suite seven forty-three. Would you like me to give you directions?" The woman returned Alex's card.

"No, I remember." He produced a smile, but Noelle knew that it wasn't his natural look of happiness. "Thank you." Then, without warning, Alex took Noelle's hand, intertwining his fingers with hers. For an instant she could see that scared little boy he must have been all those years ago. She gave his fingers a tender squeeze.

"William, are you okay?" Noelle said, turning to check on him. His hand was trembling on his cane, his eyes teary. He nodded, clearly trying to get himself together. "You can do this," she whispered to him. "Do it for her."

He cleared his throat and took a step forward.

The three of them walked side by side, like a united front, to Elizabeth's suite, where a nurse was leaving. She greeted them warmly. "Ah, visitors. Mrs. Harrington is doing very well today. She'll be glad you came by." Then she left them outside the door.

William leaned against the doorframe, hanging his head, as if he needed the support before going in. Alex reached around him gently and opened the door. They entered into a small living area, the furniture sturdy and basic, but the side tables had more flowers like the ones on the front desk. The overhead lighting was off, lamps illuminating the space around them and the daylight from the wide windows filling the rest of the room as it reflected off the newly fallen snow.

A woman was on the sofa furthest from them, and Noelle recognized her from the photo in the Harrington mansion. She'd been under a quilt but was standing up to fold it, her eyes on William. She had gray hair pulled away from her face by a clip at the back, and she was wearing little diamond earrings. Her expression was kind and soft, and Noelle could understand how William had found both her and Gram attractive—they had similar attributes. Elizabeth draped the blanket on the arm of the sofa and came over, facing him first.

"I get so cold," she said to him, without a hello.

He cleared his throat, emotion getting the better of him. "You always did."

She smiled at that, searching his face. "Where have you been?" she asked in nearly a whisper, as if he'd been out shopping or something.

"At the house." William wiped a tear from his eye, barely able to keep himself steady with one hand on his cane. He smiled warmly at her. "You always wanted me to live there. I know why you liked it so much. And Jim sends his love."

She smiled at him absently, but then her focus narrowed as if there was some spark of recognition.

Noelle took a second to pull her eyes away from Elizabeth to focus on Alex. Tears brimmed in his eyes as he rapidly blinked them away. "Hi, Grandmother," he managed. "It's me, Alex." He swallowed hard.

Elizabeth turned toward him, that searching look returning. "Have you come for Christmas?" she asked, her face crumpling in confusion. "I didn't have time to get anything."

"You didn't need to get me anything," he said, taking a step toward her. "You'd be very happy," he said with a smile. "I got us a dog."

Her face lit up with that news. "We have a dog?"

"Yes. His name is Henry. I wasn't allowed to bring him, but I'd like to have you visit so you can see him. Would you like that?"

"Very much." Then Elizabeth's eyes landed on Noelle, and her mouth dropped open, the confusion returning for a moment. "Sophia," she said, looking at her as if she were an old friend.

William gasped.

Noelle knew she resembled Gram by looking at Gram's old photos, but she never thought for a second Elizabeth would confuse her for her grandmother. Her skin went cold and her breathing turned shallow. What if she said something to tell Alex about Gram? What if Alex put two and two together? Noelle hadn't had a chance to talk to him about it yet, and even if she had, she wasn't sure it was her place to say anything. She hadn't discussed it with William.

"It's been a long time, but I remember your name—Sophia."

The corners of Elizabeth's mouth were turned up cautiously; she didn't look distressed in any way.

Noelle opened her mouth to say something but Elizabeth cut her off. "Sophia, take care of William. I'm in here and I can't, but I know he loves you."

"What?" Alex said quietly, trying to make sense of her babble.

Noelle turned to William. His jaw was slack, his eyes round, as he attempted to see her face. She also knew that William was only finding out now that Elizabeth knew Gram's name.

"Who is Sophia?" William asked, her gram's name rolling off his tongue easily, probably because he couldn't believe she could know.

"She was your first love." Shaking her head, slightly agitated, she said to Noelle, "You look like her. I'm sorry. I thought…" Elizabeth was perplexed, blinking, looking at the floor.

Noelle's face felt like it was being pricked with a million needles, the heat spreading down to her neck, but she kept herself together so as not to worry Elizabeth. Alex's eyes were moving between William and Noelle, and she knew she'd need to provide an explanation for what she was about to say, but the important thing right now was to keep Elizabeth calm. "I do look like her," Noelle said carefully. Her grandmother and Alex's grandfather… would Alex be okay with that? She looked over at Alex again, but this time, it was clear that he'd caught on as well, his face expressionless as it always was when he was processing.

"I can't take care of him," Elizabeth said, her voice suddenly breaking with emotion. She was fidgeting and welling up herself. "I just…" She shook her head, still confused. "I don't think I was…" She sat down as if to get herself together. "I wasn't everything he needed."

Noelle sat down beside her, William and Alex following her over to the sofa. "You know, Elizabeth, my grandmother told me once that, on the ride of life, we make a lot of stops to get to where we belong. Sophia was just one of those stops for William. He belongs with you. He loves you."

She looked up at Noelle. "Oh," she said, simply, relaxing and becoming still, leaning back comfortably on the sofa. "Now you tell me."

They all laughed, tears in their eyes.

Noelle took William's hand and drew him nearer until he was standing in front of Elizabeth. "This is William," she said. "Do you remember him?"

Elizabeth tipped her head to see him, and smiled. "I think so," she said. "I think so." She nodded as if convincing herself.

"He loves you very much."

This made her smile.

"And this is Alex." Noelle stood, taking his hand and pulling him close for support.

"And *he* loves *you* very much," Elizabeth said, startling Noelle.

"He does?" Noelle chuckled and turned to Alex, but his face was now serious yet adoring, and all her worry about William and her gram dissolved away the moment she saw the way Alex looked at her. In that moment, she could see his face on every Christmas morning, watching Lucas in his school plays, having dinner with her over glasses of wine, holding her in the early light of morning.

"Yes, he does, Sophia," Elizabeth said, before pulling the quilt off the arm of the sofa and covering up. "Thank you for coming," she said. "William, will you sit with me now? I'm tired."

William lowered himself down beside her and put his arm around her. She covered them both with the quilt and laid her head on his shoulder. William closed his eyes and cuddled her, wrapping both arms around her.

"Mm," she said with a smile. "I always loved it when you did that."

❄ ❄ ❄

After they'd gotten home, Noelle, Alex, and William had spent some time in the grand living room talking. Noelle had gone and gotten the box that she'd filled at Pop-pop's and she had it in her lap. She didn't mention the ring; she'd decided to let William tell Alex about it—and she knew he would in his own time; she'd leave it up to him because, in the end, it was still Elizabeth's and, as Gram had said, she was only protecting it for him.

"The thing is," William said, "I thought by not explaining Sophia, I was protecting Elizabeth. If I'd known she'd seen us in the restaurant that day, if she had confronted me, I'd have told her everything. I never knew." He had his forearms on his knees, clearly affected by this revelation.

"I believe you," Alex said, putting his hand on William's shoulder. "When I saw you with Grandmother today, I could tell how much you love her. Staying away so you wouldn't run into Sophia seems ridiculous now."

"You're right," William agreed. "I couldn't have changed whom I fell in love with, but I could've changed how I handled it." He clasped a hand around Alex's wrist as if to drive home that point.

Alex looked over at Noelle, and by the expression on his face, it was clear that he understood his grandfather's message. "If Sophia was anything like Noelle, I could see how you fell in love with her, Grandfather," he said, not taking his eyes off Noelle.

Remembering William's story about the café, Noelle pulled a pink napkin with gold lettering that read "Early Bird Café" from the box Pop-pop had given her. Then, she turned it around for William to view, knowing he might not be able to make it out. "Gram kept a napkin from a café—I wonder if it was the same one as yours?"

William placed a shaky hand over his mouth. After he'd gotten over his shock a little, he reached into his back pocket and pulled out his wallet, opening it up. From it, he retrieved a tiny square of something the exact color of the napkin that Noelle was holding. "Sophia was the very first person who taught me about the kind of man I wanted to be. I kept it to remind me of that." Carefully, he unfolded it, revealing that it was a perfect match to hers. "Does it look like this one?"

Unable to catch her breath, Noelle said, "Yes, it does." It was an exact match, which meant that Gram had found that napkin just as special.

With a huge smile on his face, William laughed, the complete surprise of it nearly too much to bear. A look of awe overtook his features as he strained to see her, his determination showing. Then he leaned out a little to try to view Alex, who had his arm around Noelle now, fiddling with the seam in her sweater. "And here we are today," William said, "two generations later." His smile dropped to a look of warning. "You know, the love I had for Sophia was fleeting, but I hope, this time, the outcome will be different." He turned back to Noelle. "Thank you for making us go today," he said.

Alex smiled, and, for the first time in a long time, agreed with his grandfather.

❄ ❄ ❄

After Noelle had brought Lucas and Henry back to the mansion, the snow piled up so high that the roads weren't clear enough to drive. Noelle had promised Lucas they'd go sledding the next day, but she wasn't sure how she'd get him to the big hill that they liked to go down. So, when they met Alex in the informal dining area for dinner, she decided to ask if he knew of any great spots.

"I actually do know of a great place," he said, as Lucas climbed up beside him, smiling at him. "It's on the other side of the woods on the edge of the property. But we can go around to get to it. It just might take some creativity in all this snow… Let me think about it tonight and I'll have something prepared for us tomorrow afternoon." He ruffled Lucas's hair. Noelle couldn't hide her excitement that Alex was planning to join them.

Noelle was glad for the diversion after visiting Elizabeth. Her mind was swimming with conflicting thoughts. Never before had she been so up in the air about what to do.

"It's the night of the first really big snow," Lucas said, sipping from his dinosaur cup. "That means it's camp-out night."

Noelle had completely forgotten. Every year, on the first big snow, she and Lucas took all the blankets and pillows in the house and piled them up in front of the TV in the living room, popped popcorn, and watched movies and read books as late as they could before falling asleep in the middle of it all. "It's already late," she said. "We've used up valuable TV time. How about tomorrow night? Can we do it then?"

"Okay!" Lucas turned to Alex. "Will you come too?" he asked. "Mom always told me I could invite a friend but I never had anyone to call until now."

Alex gave him a loving look. "I hope you're not sleeping outside during this camp-out," he said with a chuckle.

"No!" Lucas giggled. "It's in the living room. Will you come?"

"Absolutely," he said, not bothering to ask Noelle, probably because he didn't want her to find a reason why he shouldn't. The thing was, she didn't want to find a reason. She wanted him there just as much as Lucas did. But the last thing she needed was to have him sleeping next to her in her living room because if she let him, there was no way she'd be able to sleep.

"Yay!" Lucas got so excited he nearly knocked his dinosaur cup over. He caught it with his little hands and laughed.

Chapter Thirty-Four

William had asked Noelle to come to see him early that morning.

"I'm going to have to tell Alex the story about the ring at some point," he said, without any prior discussion as she poured milk into his cup of tea for him. "I know the fact that Elizabeth didn't have it has always bothered him, and things were going so well after seeing her, I didn't want to bring anything up that would put a damper on things."

She took in a steadying breath, knowing that he was right to tell Alex. Certainly, he wouldn't get so upset at this point—the ring had been returned. But then he'd know that she'd held this secret about it, kept if from him. She also couldn't get out of her head the idea that he'd said he'd never forgive William if he gave it to someone other than his wife. Would he still feel that way?

"It's your decision and I think it's the right one. I just worry that Alex will hate me for keeping it from him when I knew about the ring."

"You don't give yourself enough credit," he said.

She stirred his tea with a silver spoon, the handle embossed with some sort of crest. His remark surprised her. "How so?"

"You're thinking of giving up. That's the real reason why you're considering moving across the country. You're assuming that Alex will be upset about the ring, you're assuming you can't get that coffee shop in order before New Year's, and you're assuming that things with you and Alex are too good to be true. But you haven't given it everything you've got yet."

His assertion yanked all her insecurities to the front of her mind, all the things she'd refused to ask herself because she didn't have the answers.

"Talk to Alex. You have an incredible way of making him calm and relaxed—I've never witnessed anything like it. Be honest with him. He'll understand about the ring; he has the business sense you need and you have the dream and vision for the coffee shop. Together, you two could make this work. And for God's sake, you two should be together."

"I don't know..."

He looked directly at her and for an instant, his gaze was so intense she thought he'd regained his vision. "Yes, you do know," he said. "That feeling you get when you look at him, I know that feeling. It doesn't come that often. I was lucky enough to have it twice. How many times have you had it?"

She chewed on her bottom lip, not wanting to admit that she'd only had this feeling once and it was with Alex.

❄ ❄ ❄

Noelle wouldn't have all the answers now, so she'd decided to put the questions out of her mind and enjoy the snow. She and Lucas had bundled up to meet Alex. When they arrived at the front door, Noelle's eyes nearly popped out of her head as she looked at the large tractor in front of them. Clattering loudly at the end of a long clearing of snow sat an enormous plow. Carefully, she helped Lucas down the steps as she squinted to see Alex in the driver's seat, his head down, working on his phone, waiting for them. With a jerk, the front plow raised above the cab and he waved.

"Do you know how to drive this thing?" Noelle asked when they reached the open door on the other side. Alex looked out of place in the seat, one of his hands on the gearshift and the other on the steering wheel.

"Nope. Never driven it in my life."

Lucas giggled as he wriggled into the center of the bench seat, Noelle climbing in after him. "Then how are you going to drive it?"

Alex smiled a crooked grin at Lucas. "Trial and error. But if we want to go sledding, it's the only vehicle I have to get us across the grounds in all this snow." The tractor gave a lurch as he put it into gear, throwing Lucas forward. He caught himself on the dash just as Alex threw a protective arm in front of him.

Noelle peeked behind her seat—in the back of the cab was a bright yellow plastic snow sled. It was long and thin like a boat, with a rope handle. Lucas had noticed it too.

"I think I might need some help," Alex said, eyeing him. "Why don't you sit on my lap and you can drive? Then I can focus on hitting the gas and shifting this thing."

Lucas looked at him in delighted disbelief. "I don't know how to drive!" He laughed.

Alex reached around him and scooped Lucas up by grabbing under his arms, sliding him onto his lap. "Well," he said with a chuckle, "you're going to learn right now."

Lucas looked over at Noelle, his eyes wide, his smile so big she felt like her heart would burst as he sat on Alex's lap, his tiny hands on the steering wheel. These were the kinds of experiences she knew he'd been missing without a father in his life, and suddenly, she didn't want to live without them.

The tractor heaved once more, causing Lucas to throw his head back and laugh as Noelle caught herself and gripped the edge of the seat. "Hold on!" Alex said, throwing an amused glance over at Noelle. He shifted, the engine groaning as the wheels rolled through the thick snow. Lucas was still laughing, his head swiveling between the front and Alex.

"Don't look at me," Alex teased. "Watch where you're going!" Lucas turned back to the front and yanked the wheel as they swerved in a long arc around one of the Christmas trees on the lawn.

Alex pointed to the back corner of the property. "Head that way," he said. They bumped along through the snow, Lucas now intently watching in front of him, the steering wheel vibrating in his hands so badly that Alex had to grab the bottom of it occasionally to keep it steady.

When they arrived at the back edge of the property, Alex slowed them down until they came to a stop.

"You could work this better than you said you could," Noelle said, unable to hide her smile. Lucas was still on his lap and the two of them seemed so comfortable that anyone else looking on would think they'd known each other for years.

"I had the groundsmen show me how," he said. "They thought I was crazy, I could tell." He turned off the engine and lifted Lucas back onto the seat. "But I had to take drastic measures because we couldn't miss this great sledding opportunity!" He winked at Lucas. "Let's get the sled out of the back and see what it can do!"

Alex dragged the sled behind them as they clomped through the snow. It had piled up so high it was nearly at the top of Noelle's boots and she worried for Lucas. "Is the snow getting into your boots?" she asked.

"A little," he said, unworried.

"It'll make your feet cold. We won't be able to stay out very long if your feet are wet."

Alex handed Noelle the sled and lifted Lucas up onto his shoulders. Lucas squealed nervously and grabbed onto Alex's head, covering his eyes.

"I can't see," Alex laughed.

Lucas, too nervous to let go, kept his hands planted where they were.

Alex reached out in front of him as if he were checking for obstacles. Noelle slipped the rope of the sled onto her wrist and took his hands. "I'll guide you," she giggled.

With the sled bouncing along lightly at their feet, she led him through the snow until they reached a hilly area where they stopped walking, the snow-covered landscape spreading out in front of them in every direction. Lucas gasped when he saw it, his hands finally dropping.

"That's bigger than the hill we usually go down!" he said animatedly, his booted feet swinging by Alex's chest.

Alex lifted Lucas and set him down in the snow. "Ready to try it?"

"Yes!" Lucas said. "Would you go down with me?"

"Of course," Alex said. "But to be fair, I'll have to go down with your mom too, so she doesn't feel left out." He offered a sideways grin toward Noelle, a confident look on his face, and she took in a deep breath, the butterflies wreaking havoc in her belly.

Alex climbed onto the flimsy sled, barely able to fit his broad frame into it. He left a small spot open at the front and Lucas got in.

"Ready?" he said, inching them toward the tipping point where they'd go sailing through the snow.

It had started to flurry again, the flakes settling on Lucas's navy blue stocking cap as he nodded excitedly, squeezing his eyes shut and grasping Alex's knees for something to hold onto.

"Here we go!" Alex pushed off, sending them sailing down the hill at tremendous speed, Lucas's giggles floating up into the air and trailing behind them, like runaway balloons, all the way down the hill. His laugh was so genuine and lovely to hear that Noelle put her hands over her mouth to stifle her excitement. It made her heart full to witness Lucas and Alex having so much fun. It didn't threaten her anymore, because she realized that Lucas wasn't choosing Alex's interests over hers. They each offered something different that, together, gave him the very best experiences.

"That was fun, Mom!" Lucas said, winded, as he walked up the hill. His nose and cheeks were bright pink against his white teeth as he beamed. "Your turn!"

Alex got the sled back into position and sat at the end of it, patting the empty spot at the front.

"You can't take us down as fast as you did with Lucas," Noelle said.

"She screams on the baby rides at the amusement park," Lucas said, with a conspiratorial look at Alex, before throwing himself back into fits of giggles.

"You're in good hands," Alex said, with a laugh, beckoning her to come over.

"Not too fast," she repeated.

"Of course I won't go too fast." Alex gave her a look of mock seriousness, causing Lucas to double over.

"I'm serious." She sat down, Alex's long legs on either side of her, the two of them barely able to fit. They'd probably weigh the sled down enough to keep the speed to a minimum.

Just as he had with Lucas, he pushed them off with all his might, propelling them like a rocket down the hill. Noelle squealed, feeling as though she'd left her stomach at the top of the hill, her face burning from the icy wind, her limbs feeling loose and tingly from the sensation as if she were falling from a great height. And then, Alex's arms were around her, holding her, his face right next to hers. "I've got you," he whispered, making her forget all about the hill as they sailed to the bottom.

When they came to a stop, her heart was pounding and she couldn't decipher whether it was the ride or his words that had caused it. She could hear Lucas cheering from the top of the hill, but Alex's arms were still around her. They stayed there for just a second. She didn't notice the cold or the snow falling; she just felt warm, perfect, and she didn't want that feeling to ever go away.

Alex finally let go and got off the sled, offering a hand to Noelle. She took it and he helped her up, their faces so close that she could reach up and kiss him, but with Lucas looking on, she didn't make eye contact. By the way his breath came out, she could tell he was amused by it, his warm laughter like a whisper to her heart.

"Ready to go again, Lucas?" he called up, and she finally looked at him. When she did, she couldn't believe how familiar he looked after such a short time, and she didn't think she'd ever get tired of that face.

❄ ❄ ❄

When they'd first left the mansion to drive the tractor, Noelle had noticed Alex madly typing on his phone. He'd put it away when she and Lucas got up into the cab, so she'd figured it was work or something and she'd let it go, forgetting about it completely.

Until they'd gotten back to her and Lucas's suite.

The furniture and floors had been completely covered in blankets—big, soft, feather blankets—and there were pillows everywhere. In the corner of the room was a popcorn machine that was furiously popping buttery popcorn, the entire glass case full of it. Beside it was a table with paper cups, and more bowls of chocolate bars than she could count. The widescreen television was on, and there was a stack of movies on the coffee table—or at least, she thought it was the coffee table; it was peeking out from under more blankets. In the back of the room, there was an enormous tent, the front tied back to reveal more pillows. Henry was in his crate in the corner, waiting for them, looking out with big eyes.

Noelle turned to Alex for an explanation.

"You said a camp-out, right? Something like this?" He looked over the room.

"We've never had a camp-out like this before!" Lucas said, running and diving into a pile of pillows. When he surfaced, he said, "Is all that chocolate for us?"

"Yes, but after dinner," Alex said, tossing another pillow into his pile playfully. "We're having hot dogs and hamburgers. How does that sound?"

"Yeah!" Lucas was jumping from pile to pile. Then he came to a screeching halt, plopping down by the fireplace.

Noelle took a few steps over to see what he'd found.

"He told me that he'd finished reading the last of the books I bought him at his grandmother's house," Alex said, leaning over her shoulder. "I got him a few more."

"A few?" Noelle said, turning to look at him. He'd bought Lucas an entire basket of books—so many that it would take him at least a month to get through them all. "You're going to spoil him."

With a smile, he leaned in and kissed her cheek, then whispered, "It's Christmas. Let me spoil the people I care about if I want to." His words sent a shiver down her arm, and she had to refocus to keep her mind on his words rather than his lips. "I figure that no matter what happens in our lives, we should always have Christmas to show our love for each other."

"That might be the most perfect thing you could have said."

He tipped his head toward the other side of the room, where there was a silver bucket of ice containing a bottle of champagne, two flutes, and a plate of chocolate-covered strawberries. "Appetizer," he said, flashing those pearly whites and clearly knowing he'd done well.

There was a knock at the door and one of the staff rolled in a silver tray full of hot dogs, hamburgers, French fries, pickles, ketchup, mustard, relish—all the fixings for a great camp-out meal.

"Lucas," he called. "Come show me the best way to eat a hot dog."

❄ ❄ ❄

Lucas had alternated between playing with Henry and watching the movie, and was now asleep in the tent, the movie he'd chosen still going, but Noelle wasn't paying attention to it. She'd curled up with Alex on the sofa, under a blanket, his arms around her while Henry, exhausted from all the fun, snoozed in his crate.

"You were very thoughtful tonight," she said, enjoying the feeling of being next to him. "Thank you."

"You're welcome. I just wanted to do something nice, but I feel like it wasn't enough."

"Not enough?" She sat up and looked at him. "I'd hate to see what too much looks like to you."

He smiled warmly at her. "I meant it wasn't enough to show how much you and Lucas mean to me, how much I missed you once I got to New York, how much I wanted to be back here with you." He looked her directly in the eyes. "You told me not to run," he said. "You're running from us just like I did. Stay with me. Live here."

"I'm not running from anything. I'm trying to make a life for myself and Lucas that's worth living and I can't do that if I haven't found what I was put on earth to do."

"What do you think you were put here to do, then?"

"I think I need to run Gram's bakery." She rubbed her face, the frustration over the possibility of not being able to make it work eating at her. The truth was, even if she went to LA, she was out of money, and she didn't have enough, even if she saved, to start right away, so she'd be on the same path as she was when she'd lost her job.

Alex pursed his lips, considering this, the skin between his eyes wrinkling in that adorable way. He got up and poured them each a glass of champagne, handing one to Noelle. "What would you need to make the bakery work?"

She took in a deep breath and let it out. "Time. The rest will come."

"What if I take over with William so you can devote more time to getting it re-opened? It's only a short while and you're paid in full for this month, anyway."

"I could never do that to you or William. You have your work. I'd feel awful abandoning William and adding more to your plate."

"I'd feel awful taking the coffee shop from you without giving you ample opportunity to make it work. Consider it my Christmas gift to you." He looked at her almost carefully, as if something else were on his mind.

"What?" she asked, his expression piquing her curiosity.

"Do you… need money for the shop?"

Immediately she shook her head. "No. I don't want anyone giving me handouts. I can do this, and if I can't, then it wasn't meant to be. I've never taken money from anyone and I won't start now."

"Okay," he said quickly, looking down at his glass. She could tell he'd gotten the point. "Time it is, then. I'll give you as much time as you need. If you want me to watch Lucas, I will—just let me know. And I'll take care of my grandfather until Christmas so you can get the coffee shop up and running—it's only a little over a week. Will you try to make it work?"

"Yes." She smiled, wrapping her arms around his neck and hugging him.

He pulled back, his grin fading. "And what if your plan fails? Then what?"

"We'll cross that bridge when we get to it."

Chapter Thirty-Five

Noelle had spent all morning talking to the plumbers regarding the leak in the wall of the coffee shop. They'd turned off the water for now, and, even going as quickly as they could, it would be a stretch to get the pipes fixed and the wall patched in time for the re-opening in two days, they'd said. The small area of wood floors that had buckled with the water saturation would have to be completely replaced. The flooring repairmen were in the process of searching for matching wood so they didn't have to change the entire floor, to save time, although it was looking like it would require a complete overhaul. They'd said it would be a few days and then they'd just have to put a final finish on the floors. As the owner of the property, Alex had said he'd have it all taken care of, but it still took time to get these things done. With the wall and floors still to do, she had no idea how she'd be able to open on time, but she pressed on, hoping for a miracle.

Phoebe and Heidi had spent all day painting the other walls and woodwork, and Jo had come in several evenings after her own long days at work to finish odds and ends. Pop-pop and her parents pitched in where they could, and Lucas was in charge of making sure everyone had what they needed. One of the glass tops Noelle had ordered especially for the tables had come broken and the company was sending her a replacement. She hoped it would get here today, but she had nothing ready just yet for the tables anyway, so it wouldn't matter. She also had to run out to buy more baking and coffee supplies if she wanted to be prepared.

"The table top's just been delivered!" Jo said excitedly, as she wobbled the large box into the dining area. "Moment of truth!" She slid a box cutter under the tape, securing the box, and pulled out the heavy glass, Gus rushing in to help her. "It's in perfect shape!" Jo and her father set it on one of the tables on top of the magazine articles about coffee Noelle had found. She'd planned to découpage them on but with the time crunch, she decided to just lay them under the glass.

Noelle stopped to take in the progress, trying not to get anxious about the state of the place. She'd decided that all wasn't lost. She'd get everything she possibly could do done, and as soon as the painting was finished and the floors completed, she was going to reset the dining area and they'd be in business. She could wait on the varnish for the floors. Right now, she just wanted to open the doors on time. With only the plumbing wall to paint and no finish on the floors, she would be ready. She might not sleep, but she could do it. As they completed the day's tasks, wrapping up and coming to a stopping point, there was a knock at the door. Noelle opened it to find a florist standing in the doorway. "I have a delivery for Noelle Parker."

"That's me," she said, looking over her shoulder at her friends and family, none of them offering any answers as to what this was all about.

The deliveryman handed her a Christmas card and then began filling each of her tables with fresh greenery and berries with little candles in the center. As she pulled the card from its envelope, she noticed that he had started hanging beautiful swags of the greenery on her windows and over her doors outside. She read the card: *To show you how much you mean to me, I'm sending the first of my Christmas letters to you. You'll have to wait to see what comes next.*

Noelle flipped the card over in her hand—no signature. "Who is all this from?" she asked the deliveryman. He was arranging a large vase of red roses by the new checkout area, Pop-pop having brought the finished dresser this morning. It had taken six grown men to carry it in—all friends of his who'd said they'd help when they heard about Noelle taking over for him.

"It's a secret," he said.

"Do you think it's Alex?" Heidi asked, taking the card from her sister and peering down at it. Jo raised her eyebrows, looking over at Phoebe with a grin. Heidi handed the card back to Noelle.

Noelle held the card to her heart, unable to keep from smiling, knowing it was.

❄ ❄ ❄

Alex had denied that he'd done anything when she'd asked him after getting home late last night. She'd been so happy to find him still up, expecting everyone to have gone to bed at that hour. Even Lucas had stayed at her parents' last night, as she gave it everything she had to pull off the re-opening. She'd gone to bed without an admission from Alex.

But this morning, when she'd arrived at the coffee shop, Heidi was shaking her head in disbelief. "Did you order all these?" she asked, pointing to the entire wall of coffee syrups that had been delivered before Noelle had arrived.

And the floors were done.

"No. We don't have money for that many," she'd said, looking at the new floors, the tables already in place, the flower arrangements displayed on each one. But she hadn't said anything more because she'd noticed another card.

The card said: *Okay, so it's me, Alex. I wanted to get you a few Christmas presents, and here's another. I hope you can make a lot of coffees with these. And I had the crew patch the wall and finish the floors last night. They painted this morning, so be careful, it's still wet.*

"What's this box?" Heidi had asked, tugging on the top to open it. It was enormous, sitting on the floor by the register.

When they'd gotten it open they both peered inside, and Noelle gasped. Carefully, she'd reached in and pulled out the most gorgeous mug. It was thick white porcelain with hand-painted flowers in vibrant shades of pink and yellow and blue. She'd pulled out another to look at it—the box was full of them, each one unique.

"There's another note," Noelle had said, spotting a card in the box. She'd read it aloud. "*I thought you'd like these. But they aren't the big gift. I have one more for you. Can't wait to hear what you thought about it all. See you tonight!*"

Nothing else out of the ordinary had happened, but *the big gift* had been floating around in Noelle's mind the whole time as she'd finished painting and setting up the place. They had worked all day, and she and Heidi had settled down in the chairs for a trial cup of their hazelnut latte.

As she sipped her coffee, she looked around at all her hard work. The black surface of the large chalkboard was covered in curly pastel writing, listing all the beverage and pastry offerings, the specials outlined in little flowers. The dark-brick wall was a warm contrast under the champagne-colored lighting from the small lamps she'd installed on every table, each one with its own little white shade, illuminating the festive table decorations that Alex had sent over. The Christmas tree was lit in white lights next to the fire, sparkling onto all the worn books neatly replaced on the newly painted buttercream shelves, a bowl of complimentary pastel bookmarks with the coffee shop's logo on the side table. The counter Pop-pop had made from Gram's antique dresser was just perfect, with its spindly legs and pearly-gray swirling granite shining under the candles, little piles of napkins, and a decorative easel with a black-and-white photo of Gram icing a spice cake.

The re-opening was tomorrow. They'd baked, made baskets full of cookies, and they'd gotten all the dishes placed and ready for the crowds.

"This is good!" Heidi said, her fingers threaded through the handle of her cup, wrapping around it for warmth. "Gram's macaroons would go well with it, I think."

Before Noelle could answer, there was a knock. Both women looked at each other. Noelle got up to answer it, finding a man at the door, holding a toolbox. "Good evening," he said.

"Hello," she returned, looking over her shoulder at Heidi to see if there was any recognition on her face. None. She turned back to the man.

"My name is John Perkins. I'm an antiques specialist. I've been hired to fix your jukebox."

A wave of heat washed over her. Put on the spot right then, she wasn't sure if she wanted anyone to touch Gram's jukebox.

"Don't worry," he smiled gently at her. "I know how much these things mean to people, and Alex has briefed me very well. I won't disturb a thing while I'm working. I'll leave all the settings the way they were and I can even keep the records in it while I work. May I have a look?"

She opened the door wider and let him in. He had a kind face, and she knew that Alex wouldn't have hired someone unless he was trustworthy. She sat back down, her eyes on him as he quietly and meticulously opened the front of the machine. His hands were careful while he checked things over. Then, after a little tinkering, he replaced a few very small pieces.

"Would you like to do the honors?" he said, addressing Noelle.

With anticipation in her smile, she stood up and clicked the button. The first record slid forward, the metal arm grabbing it and spinning it. Then, suddenly, "We Wish You a Merry Christmas" sailed out through the speakers. Like clips in a movie, Noelle could see Gram wiping the counter, her hips swaying to it; twirling around in front of the jukebox; laughing as she sat in the chair where Heidi now sat. As she looked around at all the new paint and décor, it was as if Gram were right there with them. All those memories swimming in her head, she blinked to keep the tears at bay, Heidi doing the same from behind her coffee cup as she sat in the chair by the fire with her feet folded under her. Without any warning, Noelle threw her arms around John and hugged him.

"Thank you," she said.

He laughed, clearly startled. "Merry Christmas," he returned.

Chapter Thirty-Six

The high ceiling in the old stone house was full of silver helium balloons, their strings made of white ribbon streamers, dangling above the heads of all Noelle's friends and family. Hope and Sugar Coffee House was packed with familiar faces this morning, who'd come to celebrate what Gram had started and the transition to Noelle's new coffee shop.

Noelle had organized a slideshow of black-and-white photos, set to music, of Gram and Pop-pop in the early years of the bakery: Gram rolling dough, her hands covered in flour, Pop-pop putting the angel on top of an early Christmas tree, Noelle's father as a child as he chased a spinning top on the floor—so many moments. The slideshow had ended with photos of the shop now, all the hard work that had been done, and then they'd all had a celebratory cake and the coffee bar had been opened for free drinks.

Lucas was playing checkers at one of the tables with Pop-pop and her parents, Francis Evans from the bookshop was there, Noelle's neighbors she'd known growing up, Phoebe, Heidi and her husband, Jo and hers, Gram's younger sister who'd come up from Georgia on the train, and a ton of regulars from the bakery had been invited. Even William and Alex were coming by that evening after Alex flew in—he'd had a last-minute meeting with some investors in Chicago.

Gram's jukebox played "Rockin' Around the Christmas Tree" as the fire that Pop-pop had made in the fireplace before opening this morning cracked and sizzled, warming the small area by the bookshelves. All the side tables had Alex's flower arrangements of greenery and berries he'd had delivered. Mr. Santori had dressed as Santa Claus and was seated in one of the chairs by the fire. The whole place smelled of minty pine and the rich aroma of coffee, the warm buttery scent of cookies filtering in occasionally as everyone chattered excitedly, oohing and aahing over their coffee and cake. The window boxes full of berries and holly outside were white, the snow falling again, stark against the warm yellow light of inside. Noelle looked around at all those familiar faces, still in shock that they'd actually gotten it done.

"The place looks absolutely adorable," her mother said, putting her arm around Noelle and squeezing her tightly. "You are amazing."

Noelle smiled at her mother. "I couldn't have done it without all of you."

"Ready?" Heidi asked, her face full of anticipation as she held the shop's window sign in her hand. It was hanging from a hook in the window, with "Closed" in a swirling purple font on one side and "Open" on the other. With dramatic flair, she turned it over so the word "Open" was now facing the outside of the shop. They both stood behind the counter, peering through the new glass-paned door they'd had to install once the flooring was finished. Heidi had taken a few days off to help Noelle at the counter, and then she'd go back to her regular job, but Noelle had planned to ask her to run it with her if it was successful. And now, a week before Christmas, they were going to see.

Noelle had placed a few small ads in the local papers, she'd called three of the area radio stations to put out announcements, and she'd set up social media pages, putting out ads on those. Beyond the preparations for the re-opening party, she and Heidi had packaged all kinds of delectable goodies and their coffee selections were plentiful but still within budget.

"I wonder if the snow will keep people from going out?" Heidi worried aloud, as they both got the last of the macaroons ready in the kitchen, placing each one in a single cellophane bag with curly red-and-white striped ribbon while Pop-pop sat behind the counter until they returned.

"I'd think it would make them want a warm spot to sit and a good cup of coffee. And passers-by will see the amazing crowd we've assembled and want to stop in and check it out."

As they came back out front, the opening party winding to a close, their friends offering hugs and warm wishes, a woman walked by, turning to look in, and both Noelle and Heidi did a little spring forward, but the woman kept going, out of sight, and Noelle found herself still looking up the street through the window.

"That was definite interest," Heidi said, raising her eyebrows and nodding happily.

❄ ❄ ❄

They'd had three people stop in to the coffee shop so far today.

Three.

"I just sold one of your favorite cookies," Noelle said, with a smile, to Lucas. "The gingerbread one with the red icing." She didn't make eye contact with Pop-pop, for fear that she'd see worry on his face at the small number of patrons, and she wanted to keep a positive atmosphere for the opening guests that remained, but she wondered if they'd all noticed that they'd been the only ones there for the most part.

"I knew you should've made those!" Lucas was beaming as he slid one of the checkers pieces across a square. "King me!" he said to Pop-pop. They'd started up another game since she hadn't needed any extra hands behind the counter in a while.

Noelle busied herself at the cookie display, trying not to think about the less-than-stellar opening they'd had so far. The crowd of friends and family warmed her, forcing her to take it all in and enjoy all the wonderful support she had. She didn't want to think about sales right now.

Finally, after a lot of her friends had left, the bells on the door still for ages, no one coming in, someone walked through the door. "Hello," she said, looking around. "Are you open?" She pulled her wallet out and peered up at the chalkboard.

"Yes." Noelle smiled, standing up straight behind the counter. "For a few more hours. What can I get you?"

As the woman ordered, two more people came in, taking their places in line as if nothing were out of the ordinary. Noelle sent an excited glance over to Heidi.

She took their orders and they sat down at the tables. One woman read her book while the other two talked over the top of one of Alex's flower arrangements. Noelle watched in awe, delighted to see strangers sitting there, filling the space.

A few minutes later, the bells on the door jingled again and two more women walked through. "Have you just opened?" one of them asked.

"Yes," she said, trying to keep herself from giggling uncontrollably. In the last few minutes, she'd had more people come in than she'd had all day! She filled their orders as they settled in by the fire. They'd brought their cross stitch. They were all doing the ordinary things that people do when having a cup of coffee, but she saw something else when she looked at them: just like the name that Gram had chosen so many years ago, she saw hope, and the sweetness of that was intoxicating. Hope and Sugar.

The situation kept playing out in her head as she wiped down tables and served more people—could this actually work? Someone mentioned she was glad that there was a coffee shop on this end of town now. The steady stream of people with their Christmas packages and gift bags from shopping had been thrilling to see, but the slow day ahead of this surge was still a little worrying. The more she thought about it, however, the more she knew that this was where she belonged—business or no business. She wanted to see all these faces every day; she wanted to have dinner with her family and play with Muffy. She wanted to sing karaoke with Jo and drink cocktails on girls' night. But most of all, she wanted to see Alex. She missed him, and she couldn't wait to see him.

She grabbed her phone and texted Phoebe: *I can't go to LA*, she said. *I know I'll be staying for a guy, but I just realized something: I feel about Alex the way you feel about acting. I need to take the risk to see if it could be something spectacular.* She hit send and set her phone back on the counter.

Before she knew it, the place was packed and she felt like Gram had given her this moment, full of laughter and chatting, people drinking her coffees and eating cookies made from Gram's recipes. Noelle stood there, mesmerized by it. She couldn't base the coffee shop's success on an hour, when the rest of the time, business had been nearly nonexistent, but it sure was nice to see how things could be.

Another group of people came in the door and Noelle took their orders.

The door swung open again, and, this time, Alex came bursting through it, trailing snow behind him as he walked toward the counter, a huge smile on his face. He commanded attention, clearly not coming in to just say hello.

"May I have everyone's attention?" he called with purpose, silencing the room.

Noelle questioned him with her eyes, but he kept going.

"I found myself running through the airport to get to this woman right here. She has completely changed my life. And she might leave. But I want her to stay because I can't see my life without her and her little boy."

One of the cross-stitch ladies let out a loud "Aw," throwing her hand to her heart. Heidi gasped from the doorway of the kitchen, and Pop-pop and her parents were staring at Alex wide-eyed. Lucas ran up to him and threw his arms around him, Alex giving him a cuddle.

"And she makes a darned good cup of coffee, am I right?"

A few people were nodding and smiling. Lucas ran back over to Pop-pop excitedly, nearly bouncing all the way.

Alex turned to Noelle as she came around the counter. "Noelle, will you stay?"

"Yes," she said. Before she could even catch her breath, his arms were around her, lifting her up, the ribbons from the balloons dancing on top of them. The crowd clapped, and she caught a glimpse of Pop-pop, who'd broken out into an enormous smile. She slid down into Alex's arms and he looked at her.

"I missed you," he said, the corners of his mouth turning upward. "I can't let you go to LA. I'm in love with you and I want you to stay."

She smiled up at him. "I already texted Phoebe and told her I couldn't go. There was this guy I'd rather see..."

Alex looked as though he'd explode with excitement. He put his hands on her face, stepped nearer to her and kissed her, the crowd erupting into chatter and applause.

When they finally pulled away from each other, Noelle's phone lit up over on the counter. With a big smile, she turned it toward Alex. Phoebe had texted, *Go get him, sista!*

When everything had calmed down a bit, she said to Alex, "I'm not sure the coffee shop is doing all that well. We've had a busy hour but the rest of the time it's been dead."

"You don't have to worry," he said. "It's doing great! I'll bet on your route here, you come up Thompson Street and park at the end, don't you?"

She nodded.

"Well, there were two downed electrical poles from all the snow, and they'd closed off a bunch of streets. No one could get here. Half the town was blocked. It took the crews until now to repair it. I know this because it affected the power at a number of my buildings. There'd been a detour, and it bypassed Hope and Sugar Coffee House, so the only people who could find it were the ones coming up from the opposite direction. I think you'll be fine from here on out." Then he took his first look around. "It's amazing in here."

"I couldn't have pulled it off without your gifts. You did a lot for me," she said. "I can't possibly repay you for all you've done."

He looked into her eyes. "You already have. I'm not going to New York. I can't stand to be away from you. The office there will stay open, but I'll run it from home. You've ruined my work ethic," he teased, with a smile that gave away his fondness for her. "You've given me a future that I never knew could exist, and I'm going to spend every day showing you how much that means to me." He raised his eyebrows suggestively. "Starting with Christmas."

Chapter Thirty-Seven

Alex had been gone all week, getting the office in New York up and running so he could come back for good. He'd returned very late Christmas Eve and Noelle couldn't wait to see him. She and Lucas had stayed awake for his arrival. Alex had told them that it was difficult for Santa to get in and out of such a large house, and they should camp out in the grand living room. When they'd gotten there, Alex had a giant blow-up bouncy castle for Lucas inside the room. He'd also set up two camping air mattresses with tons of pillows and bedding for them, with strict instructions to stay there for the night.

When they'd finished jumping, the bouncy castle had been dismantled and removed, leaving the large room nearly empty. So Noelle and Lucas had pushed their mattresses over to the enormous windows and she and Lucas had watched the stars until they'd both fallen asleep.

Noelle woke up this morning to the sound of quiet holiday music coming from the radio, and, with a giggle, she looked down at the pajamas she was wearing. They'd been laid out on her bed when she'd gotten home from working at the coffee shop. Lucas had the same pair—red with little reindeer and holly all over them. She couldn't believe that Alex had gotten them without even knowing their family custom. Gram had started it with her father, and then Noelle's mother had carried on the tradition. Now it would continue with her and Lucas.

But that wasn't what had made her laugh this morning. What had made her giggle was the memory of Alex wearing the same pair when he'd come in to tell them they should sleep in the living room. He'd been holding a plate of cookies and a glass of milk to leave for Santa, looking adorable. Then he'd given Noelle a Christmas kiss and told her to get her rest for a big Christmas Day tomorrow.

Noelle noticed Lucas wasn't on his mattress. Stretching and running her fingers through her hair, she stood up and made her way to her suite to find him. When she got there and opened the door, she blinked her eyes to clear them and make sure that what she was seeing was correct, or if she was still asleep and dreaming. The entire room was full of red roses—hundreds of them. They were in silver vases, filling the end tables and the floor along the walls, on stands, shelves, the mantel—everywhere. She grabbed a small note on a side table, barely visible under all the roses. It read, *Merry Christmas! Go to your room.*

Lucas, who'd come out of his room, took Noelle by the hand. "Come into my bedroom," he said breathlessly.

They went down the hall together and the scene was similar in Lucas's room: there were giant dinosaurs, the walls had been covered with replicas of the solar system, there were books literally everywhere—so many she knew she wasn't seeing every single one. Covering the floor were puzzles, brainteasers, science kits, and even a huge volcano in the corner.

"Alex must have left some really good cookies for Santa," she said, still looking around, the note in her pocket. Then she forced herself to focus on Lucas. "I got a note that said we need to go into my room. Should we see what's there?"

Lucas nodded, shock all over his face.

When she saw it, Noelle could hardly keep the tears from clouding her eyes. On the dresser, leaning against the wall, was an enormous canvas in black and white with the image of her and Lucas's faces in the snow. The grays and whites were so vivid, the little flakes falling all around them, making them appear to be in some kind of winter wonderland. She turned to Lucas, but he hadn't seen it yet. He was reading another note. "Go to the tree in the living room," he said, running past her. She followed, and by the tree that she hadn't noticed with all the flowers in her view, there were more toys and science experiment kits, a real laboratory coat in Lucas's size with his name embroidered on the pocket—he already had it on by the time she'd gotten there.

Tied to the tree, she noticed another note. It read: *Open the door.* She walked over to it and turned the knob.

On the other side, Alex was in a tuxedo, his hair perfectly combed, holding another sign that said: *Look up.*

She tore her eyes away from him and tipped her head out the door to view the twenty-foot-tall dome in the ceiling of the hallway. A single cranberry-colored ribbon dangled all the way down to just above where she was standing and she couldn't believe she hadn't seen it before now. She walked over to it, recognizing something immediately, causing her to gasp, her heart slamming around in her chest.

Tied to it was William's diamond ring.

"William told me," Alex said. "I asked him if I could have it. He said that he couldn't think of anyone better to wear it than you."

Lucas had come over and was standing beside her, looking up at it.

"I want to ask if you'd consider wearing it as a token of my love for you. William and I talked for quite a while. I wanted to hear his side—why he gave it to your grandmother—because you always believe in him, and I trust your heart. All I could think about while he was telling me was that your grandmother and my grandfather had a love that was so big it spanned generations, and now it finally gets to have its day—with us." He stood up and untied the ring, holding it in his fingers. It shone brightly in the light of Christmas morning. Gently, he took her hand, and slid the ring onto her finger.

It occurred to her how incredible it was that it didn't have to be sized at all, as if it were meant for her finger. It was a perfect fit.

Just like the two of them.

Epilogue

Alex had worked diligently to secure flights in secret to get Phoebe to the Harrington mansion without any of the press finding out. She'd become quite the celebrity, her show topping the charts and now in its third season. Jo had arrived this morning and was puttering around the kitchen with Noelle, pouring them both a glass of wine as Christmas music played, the festive mood filling the mansion. Noelle had been so busy at the coffee shop that she'd hired a small staff, and both she and Heidi could be off today.

To make matters more exciting, one of the old warehouse buildings near the coffee shop had been converted into apartments, and it was full of young professionals who loved to set up their laptops in Hope and Sugar and binge on her honey-cream lattes while they worked. Word had gotten around and Hope and Sugar had become quite the hotspot.

"Thank you so much for having me with your family," Elizabeth said, from the chair by the Christmas tree. She was smiling, happy. For the last three years, Alex had gone to get her, so she could spend Christmas Day with all of them. Sometimes she remembered things, and she'd tear up or take William's hand. Other times, she seemed as though she were with a roomful of strangers. But either way, she was happy and she got to spend Christmas with her family. That was all Alex cared about. He gave her a cup of hot chocolate, made only lukewarm because sometimes she'd tip it a little, and her favorite quilt. She sipped her hot chocolate and looked on as the rest of them assembled.

"Helloooo," Noelle's mother said, coming into the kitchen with Pop-pop and Gus. Muffy tore through the room, finding Henry immediately, the two of them wrestling, unstoppable, on the floor. They would play together until they were exhausted, delighting Elizabeth, then they'd flop down beside her chair and sleep.

Jim helped Noelle's mother take off her coat, and the two men removed theirs. "Where's that gorgeous husband of yours, Noelle?" she asked.

"He and William are just getting Lucas ready." Noelle and Alex had gotten married last year under the stars in a glass dome of a greenhouse at the botanical gardens. She'd wanted to be surrounded by flowers just like she had been their first Christmas together. They'd had Elizabeth come to visit in the days leading up to the wedding, and before Noelle got married, she insisted that she and Elizabeth write their names together with the Harrington diamond on the window in William's suite. She'd slipped it onto Elizabeth's finger and told her what to do. Elizabeth had seemed happy that night, peering down at the ring all evening—they'd let her wear it. Before William helped her into bed, she'd slipped the Harrington diamond off her finger and said, "I think this is yours now," as she handed it to Noelle. They never knew if she was remembering or if it had been a lucky guess that it had been Noelle's.

Every night, William looked at Elizabeth's name beside Noelle's on the window before he turned in. He told them that he'd always wished her name could've been there in its place, and now it was, just like all her wonderful memories. Elizabeth continued to make memories with them, visiting every holiday and a few days in between.

Noelle handed her mother a glass of wine and then offered her father and Pop-pop one. Jo kissed Noelle's mother on the cheek before pulling back and laughing as she pointed to the corner of the room.

"Oh my gawd," she said dramatically. "Casa Grande?"

Noelle smiled. "Every year."

"I made it!" Phoebe sang as she came clacking in on heels that were so tall Noelle wondered how she could balance. She'd long given up her Snow Queen get-up for a more stylish ensemble. Noelle couldn't even keep up with the designers Phoebe had met. But like she always did, she thrust a bottle into Noelle's arms as she threw a kiss on both her and Jo's cheeks.

Noelle peered down at the selection. "Screw cap?" she said with a laugh.

"The fizzy kind!" Phoebe did jazz hands by her face while wearing an excited smile. "You can spill some on Alex later." Then she winked at her and they all cracked up.

Everyone took their wine and went to the grand living room where they met William, Lucas, and Alex. Noelle's mother held Muffy, and Lucas stood next to Henry. Jim had helped Lucas train him as a puppy and now Lucas was the only one Henry would listen to. Noelle handed the men each a glass of wine. They were all three wearing sweaters and jeans, Lucas's hair parted on the side and combed over meticulously, making Noelle smile. Gently, Noelle helped Elizabeth to find a spot among the group.

"Family tradition!" Alex said, setting up the tripod Noelle had bought him their first Christmas together and facing toward the stunning Christmas tree that had been erected in the center of the room—this one had a silver and light blue color scheme, long streamers of ribbon bursting from the top and cascading to the shiny marble below.

They all gathered together as Alex set the timer on the camera and jogged over to take his place next to Noelle.

With an air of Christmas merriment, they held up their wine with one hand, their other arm around the person beside them, and called out, "Cheers!"

The photo snapped and Alex took a look at it on the digital screen. "Perfect," he said, turning it around to Noelle as she came up beside him. With his arm around her, she saw everyone together and happy, and she knew without a shadow of a doubt that all those stops along the way had led to this: the place where she belonged.

Acknowledgments

I'd like to thank my husband, Justin. He has listened to my rambling about storylines and deadlines and my incessant clicking of keys at all hours. I could not have made it without his support and encouragement. He has been there every single step of the way.

A giant thank-you to Oliver Rhodes for his unwavering support. I'm so grateful for his guidance and listening ear throughout this process.

The Bookouture team is an amazing group of people and I thank my lucky stars every day to be one of their authors.

Natasha Harding, editor extraordinaire—I am so blessed to have her in my corner. She is such a delight and my organizational hero.

My gratitude goes out to my friends and family who have cheered me on and read my books in record time just to support me. Alaina DeHaven, I am so thankful for her editing eye—she is always up to the task of checking things over for me in a pinch. I am thankful for her time and effort. To Patty Larson and Tia Field, I thank them both for reading my random texts about whatever's going on in my writing world and chatting away with me about it all.

To the reviewers and bloggers who promote and support me and my stories, I am so very appreciative.

A Letter from Jenny Hale

Hi there!

Thank you so much for reading *We'll Always Have Christmas*. I hope you felt so warm and cozy after reading that you made a mad dash for the mistletoe and fuzzy Christmas socks!

If this was your first holiday book of mine, there are plenty more where that came from! Have a look at my other titles to carry the Christmas spirit throughout the entire season: *Christmas Wishes and Mistletoe Kisses, It Started with Christmas, A Christmas to Remember, Christmas at Silver Falls, Christmas at Fireside Cabins*, and *A Lighthouse Christmas*.

Until next time,
Jenny xo

About the Author

Jenny Hale is a *USA Today* bestselling author of romantic fiction. Her novels *Coming Home for Christmas* and *Christmas Wishes and Mistletoe Kisses* have been adapted for television on the Hallmark Channel. Her stories are chock-full of feel-good romance and overflowing with warm settings, great friends, and family. Grab a cup of coffee, settle in, and enjoy the fun!

You can learn more at:
ItsJennyHale.com
X @JHaleAuthor
Facebook.com/JennyHaleAuthor
Instagram @JHaleAuthor
Pinterest.com/JHaleAuthor
TikTok @JHaleAuthor